The Vagrant

PETER NEWMAN

The Vagrant

HARPER
Voyager

HarperCollins*Publishers*
1 London Bridge Street
London SE1 9GF

www.harpercollins.co.uk

Published by Harper*Voyager* 2015
An imprint of HarperCollins*Publishers* 2015
1

A catalogue record for this book
is available from the British Library

HB ISBN: 9780007593071
TPB ISBN: 9780007593088

This novel is entirely a work of fiction.
The names, characters and incidents portrayed in it are
the work of the author's imagination. Any resemblance to
actual persons, living or dead, events or localities is
entirely coincidental.

Typeset in Sabon LT Std by Palimpsest Book Production Limited,
Falkirk, Stirlingshire

Printed and bound in Great Britain by
Clays Ltd, St Ives plc

MIX
Paper from
responsible sources
FSC **FSC C007454**
www.fsc.org

FSC™ is a non-profit international organisation established to promote
the responsible management of the world's forests. Products carrying the
FSC label are independently certified to assure consumers that they come
from forests that are managed to meet the social, economic and
ecological needs of present and future generations,
and other controlled sources.

Find out more about HarperCollins and the environment at
www.harpercollins.co.uk/green

To Em,
for lighting the way

CHAPTER ONE

Starlight gives way to bolder neon. Signs muscle in on all sides, brightly welcoming each arrival to New Horizon.

The Vagrant does not notice; his gaze fixes on the ground ahead.

People litter the streets like living waste, their eyes as hollow as their laughter. Voices beg and hands grasp, needy, aggressive.

The Vagrant does not notice and walks on, clasping his coat tightly at the neck.

Excited shouts draw a crowd ahead. A mixture of half-bloods and pimps, dealers and spectators gather in force. Platforms rise up in the street, unsteady on legs of salvaged metal. Wire cages sit on top. Within, shivering forms squat, waiting to be sold. For some of the assembled, the flesh auction provides new slaves, for others, fresh meat.

Unnoticed in the commotion, the Vagrant travels on.

The centre of New Horizon is dominated by a vast scrap yard dubbed 'The Iron Mountain', a legacy from the war. At its heart is the gutted corpse of a fallen sky-ship; its cargo of tanks and fighters has spilled out in the crash, forming a skirt of scattered metal at the mountain's base.

Always opportunistic, the inhabitants of New Horizon have tunnelled out its insides to create living spaces and shops, selling on the sky-ship's treasures. Scavenged lamps hang, colouring the shadows.

One tunnel is illuminated by a glowing hoop, off-white and erratic. In the pale light, the low ceiling is the colour of curdled milk.

Awkwardly, the Vagrant enters, bending his legs and bowing his head, his back held straight.

Corrugated shelves line the walls, packed with bottles, tins and tubes. The owner of the rusting cave hunches on the floor, cleaning a syringe with a ragged cloth. He appraises the Vagrant with a bloodshot eye.

'A new customer?'

The Vagrant nods.

Syringe and cloth are swiftly tucked away and yellowing fingers rub together. 'Ah, welcome, welcome. I am Doctor Zero. I take it you've heard of me?'

The Vagrant nods.

'Of course you have, that's why you're here. Well, what can I get you? You look tired. I have the finest selection of uppers this side of the Breach, or perhaps something to escape with?' His eyes twinkle, sleazy, seductive.

One hand still on his collar, the Vagrant's amber eyes roam the shelves. They alight on a small jar, its label faded to a uniform grey.

'Ah, a discerning customer,' says Doctor Zero, impressed.

'Rare to have somebody who knows what they're looking for. Most of the rabble I get through here can't tell the difference between stardust and sawdust.' He picks up the jar, flicking something sticky from the lid. 'I assume whoever sent you appreciates the scarcity of good medicine . . . and the cost.'

In answer, the Vagrant kneels and places two platinum coins on the ground, sliding them across the floor towards the Doctor.

'I hope you aren't trying to trick me,' the Doctor replies, picking them up and tapping each one in turn with his finger. The coins vibrate and a brief two-note duet fills the cramped space. For a moment neither speak, both moved to other memories by the sound.

Doctor Zero holds them to the light, the clean discs incongruous with his sallow skin. 'My apologies,' he says, handing the jar over quickly, hoping no change will be asked for. 'And if you have any other needs, don't hesitate to come back.'

Doctor Zero watches the Vagrant go, his fingers twisting together, untwisting and twisting again. He picks up the syringe and, after a moment's deliberation, pricks his finger on it, wincing at the little stab of pain. A bead of blood appears on the end of his finger. He waits until it has grown to the size of a small pea and then whispers his message.

The Vagrant makes his way towards the city gates, famous for always being open. The Demagogue, demonic caretaker of the city, claims this is because New Horizon admits anyone, a lie to conceal their dysfunction. The great engines that control the gates are silent, critical parts stolen or broken long ago.

Beggars' cries mix with heavy drumming and the taste of sweat. A girl, aged prematurely by life, pulls at the Vagrant's arm. 'Ey, you come from Zero's? You wanna share?' She runs a hand over her curve-less frame. 'You give me high, I give you ride. Big high, big ride.' The Vagrant stops, looking at her hand until she withdraws it. He walks on, the girl's stream of curses following after.

A large, hound-like animal sits on its haunches, square in the middle of the road. Tainted by infernal influence, it is larger than its ancestors, fearsome, ferocious, a Dogspawn. No Handler is in sight and the usually easy-going wastrels of New Horizon give it a wide berth.

The Vagrant does the same.

It watches him with mismatched eyes. One canine, black in the poor light, unreadable, but the other human one: it flickers in recognition. Somewhere outside the city a Handler watches, viewing the wanderer through their swapped orbs.

For a time, both are still and the crowd follows the lead of the fading stars above, retreating, one by one into the darkness.

The Dogspawn pants heavily, its foul breath adding to the thick cocktail of smoke and rot that passes for New Horizon's air.

The Vagrant does not run. There is no point. Over the years, desperate prey has tried many things to hide its scent from these half-breeds: perfume, mud, excrement, even the blood of another member of the Dogspawn's pack.

All fail.

The hunters do not track the body's scent. The Vagrant knows this: it is why the rest of the pack and their Handlers lie dead.

With a growl, the Dogspawn stands up, refuse clinging to blood-crusted legs. It pads forward with difficulty, dragging itself through the muck.

The Vagrant watches, unmoving.

Eight metres from him, the Dogspawn leaps. It is a weak gesture, a mere suggestion of its usual power.

The Vagrant steps back, leaving it to sprawl exhausted at his feet. Its flanks heave, gasping and ragged. Blackish blood dribbles from its rear. Soon, it will die. The growls soften, become a whine which gives way to a fading, wheezy pant.

The Vagrant steps around the body but the Dogspawn is not quite dead. It snaps at him with the last of its strength, too slow to catch his ankle, but the long teeth snare his coat.

The Vagrant pulls at it, once, twice, the Dogspawn glaring at him through half-closed eyes. Its jaws stay locked onto the worn material in a last act of defiance. The Vagrant continues to pull: harder and more urgently until fabric tears on teeth. He pulls free but there is a cost, his coat is opened by the struggle.

The Dogspawn's eyes open one final time, widening at what is revealed.

In the crook of his arm, a baby sleeps, oblivious; chubby cheeks are dusted with fever spots. A sword hangs at the Vagrant's side, a single eye glaring from the crosspiece. It returns the Dogspawn's dying stare, peering beyond to find the tether of essence that will lead to its tainted Handler.

Swiftly, the Vagrant walks towards the great gates of New Horizon, pulling his coat about him once more.

The rust-bruised gates loom high, thick chains frozen along their length. To their right is a watchtower, ruined, its broken roof hanging from defunct cables.

The Vagrant passes under its shadow and over the city's boundary, walking purposefully into the gloom beyond.

Chunks of rock jut out across the barren landscape, a row of giant's teeth. Repeated bombardments and exposure to poisonous demonic energies have taken their toll on the environment. Craters pepper the ground like pockmarks. There are no trees, no colour and little life to be seen. The Blasted Lands are named without irony.

From nearby a cry rings out, quickly muffled. It is enough. The Vagrant turns and moves toward the sound.

Behind a jagged slab of stone sits the Handler cradling his head. His dark animal eye has necrosed in his skull, making nerve endings scream. The Handler does not know he is found.

The Vagrant crouches, carefully lays the baby in the dust. He stands slowly, his blade singing as it tastes the air.

Now the Handler realizes. He scrabbles backwards, promises babbling from his lips until the Vagrant's shadow covers him.

Abruptly there is silence.

Stick-like people and bloated flies gather in the twilight, both drawn to the still warm corpse of the Dogspawn. By morning they have picked the bones clean. By afternoon half of the people have died, their stomachs unable to accept the rich meat. By evening their skeletons are bartered over by Necrotraders.

In New Horizon nothing is wasted.

CHAPTER TWO

On the outskirts of New Horizon a caravan has formed, preparing to leave with the dawn. The Vagrant joins it, blending with the ragged collection of traders and travellers, lost and forgotten.

Axles creak and pack beasts grunt and people shuffle. As New Horizon recedes like a fading nightmare, tongues loosen and conversation hums uncertainly.

The yellow half of the sun is the first to rise that day, crowning the sky gold. The merchants, ruled by superstition, take this as a good sign, one even going so far as to share his drink with a neighbour in thanksgiving. For most though, the colour only alters the palette of hopelessness.

Soon the horizon takes on a reddish tint, heralding the second sunrise of the day.

Once, a single star warmed the world. None remember that time, though all agree that it must have been better then.

People thought that when the sun tore it would bring about

the end of the world but the two star fragments did not explode as predicted, nor did they blaze down from the heavens, raining fire and destruction. Instead they continue their slow orbit of the sky and each other, like drunken dance partners, struggling on long past the death of the music.

The Vagrant approaches one of the largest waggons, drawing the driver's attention away from his roll-up. A word squeezes out around the stub: 'Yeah?'

The Vagrant looks to the rear of the waggon and back to the driver. Another precious coin changes hands and the Vagrant is allowed inside.

Beyond the curtain the back of the waggon is full of boxes, scratched plastic and battered metal. No space is wasted, even the smells squeeze to fit between the crates. A few are covered with threadbare cloth, but they are the exceptions; the majority brazenly expose their wares.

The Vagrant is uninterested. He glances over his shoulder, pulling the fabric between him and the world outside.

In the cramped square of privacy he removes his coat and sword, squatting awkwardly with the baby he has smuggled inside. The infant sleeps unnaturally, immunized from the rough handling it has received in recent days by worsening fever.

Using his sleeve, the Vagrant mops its brow, blowing cool air onto the pink-red face. The baby wrinkles its nose, head turning sluggishly. As it begins to stir, the Vagrant takes out the precious jar, unscrewing the lid and scooping out lilac jelly with his fingers. He puts his finger into its mouth and waits. Toothless gums nibble and the baby starts to suck. Twice more, the Vagrant offers medicine on his finger. The baby takes it all down greedily.

For a time both doze, lulled by the waggon's creaking, rocking movements.

Without warning, a whisper comes from the recesses of the waggon.

'Help me.'

The Vagrant stiffens, turning towards a large metal cage. Grubby fingers pull back the covering cloth, exposing a child's face, not a half-breed born to tainted humans, but not quite free-born, not pure, either. His features are sharp, his body small and thin, forged by a lifetime's survival on scraps and wits. He misses nothing, mouth gaping open at the scene before him.

'That sword,' gasps the boy. 'You're a Seraph Knight. I thought you were all dead this side of the Breach.' He speaks in tones of hushed excitement and something foreign creeps into his eyes, the possibility of an alternative to death and pain.

'I'm Jem,' the boy blurts, whispering, urgent, afraid that stopping will give the Vagrant cause to leave, 'my mother trades between here and Verdigris, but, something went wrong last night, a group of men came, held her down, and then others came, angry, took me away, said she owed them money. I wanted to fight but then they'd have hurt me worse so I stayed small, like a bug. They pushed me in this cage and put me onto the caravan. I have to get back to New Horizon. I have to find her, make sure she's alright.'

The Vagrant says nothing.

'I'm sure she'd be grateful, she has money. Not lots but enough and' the boy falters, unsure of how to play things, 'she's pretty too, real pretty.'

Jem is one of the last born before the lean times, old

11

enough to remember the stories, to have been fed on them from a young age. To him the Seraph Knights are heroes from a time when childhood was more than the few moments between consciousness and disappointment. But he is also a child of the present, and knows how to bargain hard when necessary. He recites the words in a sing-song whisper:

'I invoke the rite of mercy. Save me, protect me, deliver me.'

The Vagrant closes his eyes.

Eight Years Ago

Ten thousand Seraph Knights march to fight in what will become known as the Battle of the Red Wave. Most strong men and women of the region walk with them, becoming squires and servants and soldiers.

Mechanized beasts carry the majority of the army, for the knights four-legged walkers with armadillo backs or metal snakes on tracks, for the soldiers waggons and tanks.

At their head is one of The Seven, borne across the sky in her floating palace. Sky-ships trail after, like ducklings following their mother.

The ground trembles at their passing.

For more than a thousand years, the crack in the ground known as the Breach has been watched by Seraph Knights in the name of the Empire of the Winged Eye. It was prophesied that the Breach would one day open, spilling terror. But as the centuries passed and that day did not come mankind lowered its guard. It is hard to be vigilant for a lifetime, harder still for generations. Even The Seven, ageless, flawless, overseers of the Empire, have become distracted, their visits to the southern region oft neglected. The first invaders to float up from the depths of the Breach find the knights unsuspecting. Hungry to exist, to claw some purchase in the world, the demons attack quickly and a sleepy thousand-year watch ends with screams and blood.

One man escapes, a squire who fled as the fighting began. He carries news of the catastrophe north, across the sea, all the way to the Shining City, capital of the Empire and sanctum of The Seven.

On bended knee, he gives his report, a stuttering, babbling confusion punctuated with apologies. He is forced to repeat it many times, moving up the chain of command, until he is taken to the Knight Commander, the Empire's supreme military authority who, within minutes of hearing the tale, brings the matter, and the young man directly to The Seven for guidance.

After two days of silence The Seven decide to punish the squire for incompetence. Once this is done, The Seven fall to pondering what action should be taken. Thirteen months after the first invaders arrive, the decision is made for the armies of the Winged Eye to ride out in force. Gamma of The Seven leads them, leaving her sanctum, her brothers and sisters and their devoted, for the first time in living memory.

They travel slowly across the Empire, parading, glorious. The young and strong of each region are collected, swelling numbers and pride. New recruits come eagerly, for all wish to become part of history.

When finally the army arrives at the Breach, the enemy are waiting. From the ravine walls of them rise, hissing, into the air like great clouds of blood. They are composed of indistinguishable things, unidentifiable save by their teeth, smiling knives side by side, a thousand thousand hungry mouths.

As the army of the Winged Eye forms up, the Breach vomits strange multi-legged things at them, a river of screeching scabs, scuttling towards the living.

The soldiers answer with cannon and lightning, and the knights draw their singing swords.

On the ground nameless monsters are blown apart or pierced or shot. They crumble to sludge, bodies unable to hold integrity so far from their native soil. In the sky, dark shapes flit between the turrets of the floating palace, plucking men from the battlements. Occasionally a turret pins one with fire, lighting its blue veins from the inside as it plunges to earth, a flaming rag of skin.

Then, from the Breach something powerful emerges. In time it will be known as Usurper, or Ammag, or Green Sun but it does not yet have form, appearing as a green shade, an unborn malevolence. Where it passes, husks fall, bearing little resemblance to the brave men and women they were moments before.

A ripple of fear passes through the army, the possibility of defeat rising in their minds.

Gamma of The Seven watches the battle with eyes that mirror the sky. Seeing the true threat reveal itself, she signals her attendants. They open the doors for her as she stretches, shattering the thin stone that encases her, like a bird emerging full grown from its egg.

On wings of silver and fire she descends upon the enemy. Her sword is her battle cry and its call turns the infernal foes to ash. At her approach, the formless thing pauses, retreating back towards the safety of the Breach. It is not ready to face her, not yet. Arrow-like Gamma pursues it and no creature from the Breach dares oppose her, the enemy falls away like leaves before a breeze, until she lands on the dark-shifting surface of her foe, plunging her sword deep into its formlessness.

Silent since it cannot scream its pain ripples outward in strands of boiling essence. It tries to flee and Gamma follows, her blade pouring hate into the wound, sowing seeds of itself within the enemy. They float within, dormant, waiting to bloom.

It is forced to turn from the yawning void and, reluctantly, face her.

They fight.

It is said that she fought well. It is said that she died well. The Knight Commander will not have it otherwise. Whatever else is said however, Gamma of The Seven fell that day.

The order to retreat comes soon after. Barely two thousand survive the first retreat.

There is no second retreat.

CHAPTER THREE

By mid-afternoon the broken suns have swapped places, dappling the mountains in gold and the sky in blood. The caravan continues its slow and lonely way north.

Inside one of the waggons a cage door hangs open. Stretching happily outside it is a young boy. He is watching the man who saved him, eyes expectant. It is evident he wants the man to come with him, perhaps even hopes he might become part of their lives; a companion to his mother, a father to him.

The man has offered none of these things however, sitting quietly while the baby sucks down the last of the medicine.

'So, I guess this is goodbye then?' the boy says eventually.

The Vagrant nods.

Disappointed, he leaves the man and the baby alone in the waggon. It is quiet without the boy's constant chatter.

The Vagrant stares at the coins in his hand, each with the power to buy and sell life. Only five remain now. They have been spent on necessities such as food and medicine as well as indulgences, acts of charity that do little to pay off the debt of conscience.

The last few coins have bought a boy's freedom, a goat and a modicum of privacy for the journey. Of the three, only the goat can be classed as a necessity. Not many creatures survive the Blasted Lands without change. After the arrival of the infernals most died or were altered by the tainted energy that flowed from the Breach. Over time the survivors have by its infection bred far from their original forms until only a shadow of their former shape remains.

Although the goat is scrawny, bad tempered and stubborn, she is otherwise untainted and a reliable source of anemic grey milk.

Gradually the caravan slows, circling itself like a cat preparing a bed. With a groaning of wheels and bones, the waggons and their beasts of burden come to rest. People eat their rations sparingly, jealously eyeing their neighbour's fare.

With renewed energy, the baby wakes and starts to cry. The fever is finally loosening its grip, allowing hunger to return in full force.

The Vagrant gets up quickly, gathering his things. He picks up the baby, covering it with his coat once more. Tucked in the dark warm space, it calms a little but continues to grumble as the Vagrant climbs out of the waggon.

When he approaches the goat, she eyes him with open suspicion. She tries to back away but is held in place by the wire tethering her to the waggon. Unlike many of the humans held in bondage to the caravan, the goat remains defiant. The Vagrant works quickly however, and soon the goat has capitulated to his wishes, chewing apathetically while he collects the precious liquid in an old tin cup.

A man approaches, fashionably starved, eyes alive with desperation. 'Hey pal,' he begins, mouth twitching. 'Doin' alright?'

The Vagrant inclines his head slowly.

'What you got there? That a baby you carryin'?'

Sounds of the caravan can be clearly heard as the two men look at each other; people cooking on makeshift fires, bolts being tightened, bent spokes knocked back into line again, blades being sharpened.

'C'mon, man, I weren't the only one that heard it. And I ain't the only one that'll take an interest. So let's talk.' He scratches the sores on his chin as he makes his pitch. 'I been watchin' you, got me some ideas 'bout what you're up to. You got an untainted there, right? You reckon you're smart, smuggling it out like you have. Gonna trade somewhere up north I'm bettin', make a nice bit on the side. Is it a boy or a girl? The Uncivil's offering a lot on baby girls, you could make a killing if you get that far. I've got a contact up that way, handles independent sales with the Fleshtraders, no questions asked? So, how about it? We could be partners, you got the goods, an' I got the contacts. We split the profits and keep it all nice and cosy, just between us. What do you say?'

The Vagrant's eyes narrow a fraction.

'Course if you don't like it, I could speak to some friends of mine an' we could take the little nipper off your hands, free of charge. Your choice.'

With deliberation the Vagrant puts the cup of milk on the ground, the baby next to it.

'Oh, that's a beauty all right. I really hope it's a girl, yes I do.'

The Vagrant stands up and takes a step forward. He is taller than the man by several inches.

'So, what do you say?'

At his side, beneath his coat, the silvered wings that curl about the sword's hilt twitch and the blade hums ever so softly. The man's blood is more than tainted; it is thick with the infernal.

'Well?'

The Vagrant's right hand flexes, a pained frown crosses his face. He reaches down, into his coat, pulling a coin from his pocket and offering it to the man. He puts a finger to his lips.

'Is that what I think it is?' The coin has already vanished. 'Not what I was hopin' for, but alright, you got yourself a deal. I ain't seen a thing.'

Back in the waggon, the Vagrant feeds the baby through a piece of rubber tubing. He listens to the sounds of the wheels turning outside and the voices of the people, whispering, gossiping.

Many miles south of New Horizon, the Fallen Palace languishes. After the battle of the Red Wave, it limped through the sky, fleeing the Breach and the monsters birthing endlessly from its rocky womb.

The Palace did not escape, pecked from the sky by the pursuing swarm until it kissed the earth one last time, cutting a new valley into the landscape and diverting one of the great southern rivers. Now the Fallen Palace is forever surrounded by fetid marshland.

Turrets and walls lean several degrees to the right, appearing drunk in the daylight, a sickly slant. Weaving towards them, unnoticed by poor souls wandering the sloping streets, flits a messenger, wings buzzing like tiny motors.

No glass remains in the Fallen Palace. Windows were shattered in the crash, covering the floors in a layer of cheap crystal. Now every shard has gone, from the longest sliver to the tiniest piece, all taken.

Many openings gape, from holes in the cracked pavements, from doorways, from windows, but they do not distract the messenger. It moves directly to a tower, where brassy walls fight a doomed battle against encroaching green lichen.

At the top of the tower is an arched window and in that window is a Man-shape. At the fly's approach, the Man-shape's face splits like a clam, yawning open: the fly lands on an overlong tongue, its work concluded, its frantic wings still.

The Man-shape closes its mouth, tasting the words hidden in the blood, hidden in the fly. It digests both and walks swiftly into the tower's darkness, untroubled by the tilt of the floor. Emerging into its master's chamber, it pauses, waiting to be acknowledged.

In the gloom, a great bulk stirs. The movement is accompanied by several excretions, as violent as they are small. The Man-shape eyes the bindings on its master's shell, even the newest ones are starting to fray. It mentally notes that they will need to hasten the next order.

Fully awake now, the Usurper moves, animating the body that once belonged to Gamma, distorting her features, beckoning for the Man-shape to come closer. The gesture is laboured, hardly fitting for the greatest of infernals and the Man-shape is glad that neither the Uncivil nor the First is here to witness it.

The Man-shape obeys, crossing the distance between them

eagerly, pressing its forehead against its master's, soft features appearing ethereal next to the ridged, splitting monstrosity.

Heads close, like lovers, the two touch tongues, and thoughts rush between them in a torrent.

'I have a finger in the skull of a Zero, who tells of singing coins and a silent man who hides his treasures.'

'He who culled the pack?'

'It must be, master.'

'He who tore our Kin?'

'It must be, master.'

'He who bears the Malice?'

'It can be no other, master.'

'I want him.'

'But your skin seeps, master, you must rest.'

'Rest will come again when the Malice is ours.'

'When will you leave, master?'

'At once. The Malice taunts me from the shadows and I thirst for action.'

'And what of the next display?'

'What of the next display?'

'It approaches, master.'

'So soon?'

'Yes, master. It comes and your majesty must be seen, the chains must be redrawn.'

'So be it. But the Malice will be retaken, send out the word.'

'Who is chosen to go in your stead, master?'

'The Knights of Jade and Ash.'

'I will send them.'

'The Hammer that Walks.'

'I will send her.'

They pull apart and the Man-shape retreats, plagued by thoughts that are not its own; echoes of the master's desires dominate as it moves down the tower steps. They have won many victories in this new world, claimed much of the land, but it fights them at every step, picking at their essence, peeling at their protections. Even just a few miles from the Breach, the sky presses down on them, hostile. The Man-shape feels the master's frustration and something else, an unwanted gift, a murmuring of fear.

For once it is glad of its separateness; for once its own simplicity is soothing. Still, the knowledge remains, now stuck fast: the Usurper is weakening. The Man-shape does not know how long this can be hidden from the Uncivil's agents or the First's nomads.

It glances at its own body. The skin remains smooth and unbroken, a testament to its control. The Man-shape's usual calm creeps over it once more. It turns back to the business of finding the Malice and the man who hides it from them, stepping out into the slick street.

It opens its mouth, tasting the air as the flies scrabble from its gullet, each sucking a droplet of the master's wishes before swarming into the darkening sky.

CHAPTER FOUR

Clanking and dilapidated, the caravan arrives at its first scheduled stop: the fields of Kendall's Folly. Though faded, the squares of green stand out vividly from the barren dust surrounding them.

In places, machines function, pumping greying water through metal pipes that arch twenty feet above the vegetation. Where they don't, slaves wander the fields with fat plastic pouches strapped to their backs, like pregnant women trapped in reverse.

Pairs of guards walk the perimeter, punctuating the barbed fence encircling the fields with hard looks and loaded guns. An Unborn hangs from a chain over the centre of the fields, quivering unseen within its coiled shell. On the outside it appears lumpy, off-white, a thing stolen from the depths of the sea. Suspending the chalky mass is a challenge but fertile land this far south is precious and the Unborn's infernal presence keeps away the hungry bugs and beasts of the Blasted Lands.

A mixed group comes out to greet the caravan, traders, travellers and pimps keen to get the best goods and latest gossip. Feral smiles are swapped first, a last approximation of enthusiasm. The Vagrant chooses this moment to leave, slipping from the back of the waggon and taking his goat with him.

For once, the eyes of the caravan do not follow him, too wrapped up in their present greed to remember the enigmatic man and his precious cargo.

Without a backwards glance he moves away from the noisy gathering, disappearing behind an assortment of battered metal fins that serve as windbreaks for those too poor or too weak to have fully enclosed shelters. A small heel kicks against his stomach. The Vagrant grunts and walks on.

Others have also retreated from sight of the crowd. A man is hunched down, nursing something soft in his gnarled fingers. Two more men have followed the first and approach from behind, secretly, hungrily. The man has sneaked away some precious fruit. They reach him just as he tears it open, a waft of sweetness gracing the air, kick him and pull him backwards, grabbing for their share of the food. He struggles and six hands dance, pulping the watery flesh of the fruit, ruining it.

The Vagrant watches, motionless. Again, beneath his coat, he is kicked by a tiny foot. Before him the fight continues. Hands have separated now and, feet take their turn, smashing into the ribs of the first man like eager lovers, keen to kiss and kiss, one after the other.

The man stops struggling.

The victors share the pathetic remnants of sticky flesh,

most of it licked from fingers, before slinking, dissatisfied towards the collection of rundown buildings forming the Folly's main dwelling space.

The Vagrant walks on, his gaze on the hard-packed dust at his feet. A third kick makes him suck a breath through his teeth. He glances about – only the goat watches him. Ignoring its malevolent stare, the Vagrant opens his coat to peer inside. The baby is awake. Their eyes meet and a few seconds pass. The Vagrant closes his coat and walks on.

Behind him the beaten man moans piteously.

The next kick is more vigorous. Pulling back his coat once again, the Vagrant frowns down at the baby. It stops kicking and looks up at him. He raises his eyebrows at it and the baby smiles. The cycle repeats several times, the baby smiling a little more with each repetition.

The Vagrant stops walking and sighs. He touches a finger to the baby's lips and closes his coat firmly. Then he turns round and walks back to the injured man on the floor. The goat objects to the change in direction as it takes them further from the fields.

She pulls against the Vagrant.

The Vagrant pulls back.

The goat knows she cannot win but tries again anyway. The miniature rebellion is rewarded with an even sharper tug on her leash. The goat concedes, this time.

Please, no more!' begs the man, covering his face with his arms. 'You took it all already.' Freshly broken teeth make him lisp.

The Vagrant waits, ignoring the enthusiastic beat being played across his chest and stomach.

Timidly, the bruised limbs retreat to reveal a matching

collage of red and purple on his face. 'Are you a new eye for the Overseer? I'm sorry.' With the lisp he sounds childish despite his age. He struggles for breath before continuing, 'I just took a moment, please don't say anything. It was just a moment. I'll go back now . . . I'll go . . .' lifting himself several inches before crumpling back in pain.

The Vagrant loops the tether twice around his wrist and offers the man his hand.

The man eyes it as one might a bomb or a snake. There is hesitation, then he grasps it, fingers trembling in the Vagrant's grip. Between the man's injuries and the Vagrant's burdens it is an awkward manoeuvre but eventually the man is upright and leaning heavily on the goat, who is pragmatic about her newest indignity.

'Thank you, stranger . . . I need . . . patching up before I'm much use to . . . anyone. Would you help me over to Lil's? It's just . . . over there.' He points to a crumbling building, blasted out from a single stone monolith. Incomplete lights display their half-memory of the structure's original name.

The Vagrant nods and begins their journey towards it.

After only a few steps the man gasps, 'Have to stop . . . a moment, catch . . . my breath.'

They wait, silence playing with their nerves.

Catching his breath eventually, the man speaks. 'I think I'd be a goner if you hadn't showed when you did. Look, I haven't had . . . much cause to talk . . . for a while. I know I don't look like much but . . . there was a time, before things . . . well, before, when I was known to be something of a talker, if you know what I mean.' He coughs, wiping blood and spittle on the back of his hand. 'Anyway, back when names meant a damn, people called me Ventris. What's your name, stranger?'

The Vagrant hauls open the badly fitting door, buckled metal scraping against stone to briefly obscure the inside of the building by a curtain of dust. One by one the group enters, a bizarre procession of Vagrant, injured and goat.

Within the room is a plastic tent, age turning the once-white fabric a mottled cream, a small island of clean. There is evidence that many battles against the encroaching filth have taken place. Beyond the small scrubbed circle are tables and benches lining the periphery of the room, separated by pillars of chipped stone. Between the tent and the entrance stands a woman and in her hands sits a gun. It too is remarkably clean . . .

'That's far enough.' The woman's voice still clings to a little youth. It left her face long ago.

The Vagrant steps aside, allowing the wounded man to struggle into view. Even the short journey has paled him, his cheeks ghostly under the bruises.

'Go easy, Lil,' the man wheezes. 'He's just . . . helping an old man.'

'Ventris, is that you under there? Suns, you're a mess!' Shooting the men an imperious look she does not wait for an answer. 'Well don't just stand there bleeding in my doorway. Get yourselves over here, and shut the door. I don't want anyone else thinking it's okay to wander in any time of day!'

Her orders are met without protest and a minute later Ventris is laid inside the tent and the Vagrant sits by the wall. They have been warned to touch nothing.

The tent only gives the illusion of privacy and voices drift through, secrets carried on the backs of whispers.

'So what happened this time?'

'I got careless.'

'You've always been careless, it's a wonder you survived this long. Tell me something I don't know.'

'Two of the workers attacked me, caught me by surprise. Bastards left me out for the worms.'

'Hold still. I think they've cracked a rib. Which ones? No, let me guess, one of the bunch that came from the north, Kell or one of his . . . I thought so. Now what aren't you telling me? Come on, Ventris, don't make me do something you'd regret.'

'I stashed a little pasha, sneaked it out. Guess I didn't sneak it well enough.'

There is the sound of an ear being flicked and a grunt of discomfort.

'You bloody fool! You're lucky it was Kell that saw you and not one of the Overseer's crew or I'd need more than a few threads to put you back together.'

'I wasn't that careless, none of them saw.' Another flick is heard. 'Ow, easy, Lil!'

'And if they notice something was taken, what then? I've a good mind to unstitch this and roll you outside for the scavs.'

'You're a good friend, Lil. Not many like you left.'

'Don't push your luck. This is the last time, you hear me? Any more stupidity and I'll shoot you myself and take what's left for trade.'

Unnoticed, the goat picks up a glove from the table and starts to chew.

'So,' she continues, voice not low enough, 'who's the guy that dragged your sorry carcass to my door?'

'Damned if I know. He's not one for conversation. Hasn't said a word to me, just popped up out of nowhere and brought me here. Maybe he's one of the half-breeds? I've heard stories that some of the unlucky ones don't get regular tongues.'

'He doesn't look like a half-breed to me.' There is the clink of something metallic being placed on a tray. 'I don't know what he does look like and that worries me. Don't think there's much room for a trader who can't shout. He's no slave either.'

'Well he's got some means.'

'Not that you'd know by his clothes.'

The man's chuckle is cut off by a hiss. 'Damned ribs!'

'And did you notice the way he moved? He's trying to hide something. I don't know if he's deformed or armed but I know that man's trouble.'

'Not like you to care what's under a man's coat, Lil.'

'I've seen under your coat enough times, Ventris. Nothing much to care about there!'

For a while there are only the quiet rustlings of needle against skin. Shadows pass the murky windows and flies buzz industrious at the door. Now an irregular snoring issues from inside the tent, and soon a woman and her gun follow.

'Okay, stranger, what's your angle?'

The Vagrant looks up, amber eyes tired.

'Let's be clear. Ventris hasn't got anything to give you, besides stories and advice and they're worth less than the air behind them. So if you're waiting for a reward you might as well leave.'

The Vagrant waves the idea away.

'So who are you and what do you want?' Her gaze is relentless, the gun's barrel unwavering. 'Well, you don't look dumb to me. You don't look shy either, so how about you stop playing games and give me some answers?'

The Vagrant takes a breath. His jaw works, but the air from his lips is empty. He looks away, eyes pressed shut. There is silence. The woman closes the space between them, laying a hand on his shoulder.

'I'm sorry, I didn't . . .' she begins but is cut off as she finally gets a response, a soft cry coming from his armpit. 'What the . . .?'

His shoulders drop a fraction as he lets his arm fall. She opens the coat and the baby gurgles happily, its feet now free to wriggle. With a jerk she throws the gun to the floor.

Chewing and snoring and gurgling blend in the stillness. The woman lifts the baby to her face, caught between grief and some thought now lost.

CHAPTER FIVE

A few days pass in unlikely peace. The world outside is cruel, but within the bubble of Lil's place an illusion of sanity holds sway.

Sunslight points through cracks in the doorframe, painting the dust red. Tiny fingers reach for sparkling dirt. They might as well reach for the stars themselves.

The Vagrant sweeps the floor methodically. His shoulders hang low, robbed of their usual tension.

Slowly, the goat chews, a mangled fabric finger hanging from her mouth. Her black eyes never leave the glove's twin, sat helpless on the table.

This quiet industry is underscored by a woman's voice. Lil is not normally one for talking but has been unable to stop since her new guests took up residence. She shares her observations about the workers at Kendall's Folly, which ones to watch out for, which to avoid, and the few who will last. She talks about her role as surgeon, how the workers often get injured. Those that can pay for treatment do so with food or supplies, those that can't are turned away. Lil is clear that she isn't in the habit of charity.

She pauses but the Vagrant doesn't take the bait, his broom's rhythm is unbroken.

Eventually she talks about her own story, how her grandfather raised her, taught her to survive. How he gave her a trade to make a living, and a gun to protect it. She remembers why she never talks about him, tears thought long gone returning to her cheeks. She retreats quickly to the back of the tent, her grandfather's voice alive in her thoughts: 'Tears are no good to you, Lil, tears will get you killed.'

As the light fails, Ventris gathers his scars and limps to the door.

'Thanks again, stranger,' he says, smile more space than teeth. His eyes flicker briefly to the baby, asleep in the Vagrant's arms. The smile grows a fraction.

After the old man has gone, the Vagrant stares at the door. Tension creeps back into his shoulders.

Faeces and sweet decay vie for dominance in the Overseer's domain, each smell determined to maintain a separate identity. Once the dwelling would have borne the name of office but now the walls breathe, as half-bred as their new master.

Vestigial wings sprout from the Overseer's back, small nubs mocking her bulbous body. Their only use is to indicate her mood to those that serve. Tonight they hum pleasantly.

'I am told you have something for me. I am told it will please me.'

34

The man opposite nods obediently. He is nearing the end of his productivity. Soon she will take him from the fields and lay him down for her children.

'Will it please me enough to compensate for what you stole?'

This time, the nod is fuelled by fear and accompanied by a meaningless apology.

'You workers are all the same, thinking only of yourselves. You think that a single fruit will go unnoticed. What you do not understand is that I have quotas to fill. The Fallen Palace has needs, New Horizon has needs, Verdigris has needs, everybody does. Even the First's nomads come to me on occasion. Every detail is accounted for, every action weighed by cost and value. I am going to reassign your value. I do hope it is greater than the loss you have incurred me. Now you may speak.'

The old man tells his story. As he finishes the hum of pleasure grows louder.

'You will return there and watch my prize until I am ready to take it. Once it is in my hands, I will consider your debt repaid. I might even consider a change in your status.'

He bows deeply, biting back the pain of the movement.

'Yes,' she continues. 'I think you have a place serving those dearest to me.'

He thanks her and hobbles out.

When his scent has faded she pricks one of her human fingers on a wiry leg hair. The flies pause in their feasting, drawn to the familiar ritual. The Overseer whispers into the liquid gem and waits.

More mundane means are used to summon the people in her employ and a common coin is enough to motivate. They are used to nothing, so the pittance she lays before them gains a dreamlike quality. As one, they leave, united in hunger and expectation.

As soon as they have gone, a fly settles on her finger, drinking deep the news that will make her fortune.

The Overseer sits back as the messenger speeds on its way. Her skirt of limbs twitches in anticipation; with the Usurper's favour comes the promise of completion.

She does not hear the soft whisper from beyond her doorway nor does she see the fly fork downwards from the air, landing twice, the message flecking the floor.

Casually, the door yawns open, drawing her attention.

The Vagrant enters, sword first, humming softly.

Between them the winged insects buzz their distress, they throw themselves against furniture, against each other, unable to escape the blood that vibrates within them.

The sound builds, shaking the Overseer's skull. She rises, stretching her body out to its full size, shadow sprawling behind, nightmarish.

In answer, the Vagrant raises his blade. At its hilt, silvered wings unfurl.

An eye opens.

Two storm-heads of sound build: infernal wings and dying insects vying with steel-bound song.

The Overseer sizes up her adversary, copied many times by her compound eyes. Each image is still and waiting. She falters under the glare of the sword; it hates her in ways she cannot fathom, stirring feelings of fear, of shame. Normally she would crush a man without thought but instinct tells her to be cautious.

Subtly the sound changes.

With no preamble or announcement, the Overseer moves first, reaching into a drawer.

In four steps the Vagrant has crossed the room, his blade stretching out for her across the desk. His mouth opens with the stroke, a mournful note blending with the sword's voice, igniting the air lightning blue.

Squealing, the half-breed leaps back, avoiding humming metal, shrivelling wherever flames touch her monstrous body. In her human hand she now holds a gun, ugly and battered and ready to kill.

The Vagrant freezes. There is little cover in the cramped room and less time to think. He spins to the left, blade pointed downwards, silver wings reaching to protect his face.

Six times, the gun shouts angrily, spitting its hot metal phlegm. Four are lost to the air, one is foiled by the sword, ringing out in fury but the last finds its mark, slamming the Vagrant against a moist wall.

Frantically the gun clicks, its voice momentarily spent. The Overseer begins to reload, many of the bullets spill hastily on the floor, rolling among the dead flies.

By the time she has raised the smoking weapon again the Vagrant has stood and drawn breath. He rushes forward, she squeezes the trigger. The barrel flashes but this time does not shout, yielding to the Vagrant's song. There is a wet smack as the Overseer's hand strikes the floor, leaving a stump waving in the air, pink and crazy.

Pain lances all thought from the half-breed and she latches her many limbs to the desk, its metal legs screeching as they're ripped from the ground. With a grunt she hurls it down on her enemy.

He answers with a long cry as he blocks, sadness

counterpointing the wrathful resonance of the sword. The desk crashes to the floor, once, twice. Neither half touches the Vagrant.

There is a flurry of movement, a mix of arms and sword, of man and half-breed, of bestial grunts and sharp song. When it is over, the Overseer lies prostrate and limbless, a grotesque pear-shape.

He plunges the sword deep into her. Fire burns blue, devouring the corpse greedily, until only charred chunks remain.

An eye closes.

The Vagrant hurries along the path. It is dark and starless. From their shelters people hear him stumble. They do not yet understand what has happened but they sense that change is coming and they tremble.

Neon letters sputter into view. They hang above a doorway where stronger lights blaze, telling a story of violence within.

Outside a man lingers, uncertain. He turns towards the Vagrant, squinting.

'Stranger, is that you? It's me, Ventris. Looks like you got here just in time. A whole bunch of guys showed up just now and barged their way into Lil's. I heard an explosion, suns knows what that was! Then gunfire and now, well, just the occasional groan. You better get in there, see what's happened, though you'd best prepare for the worst.'

'Liar!' sings the sword without words as it cuts loose from its sheath, splitting the old man's chin and nose. The Vagrant looks away as the body falls. He shakes his head, pressing onwards.

The door curls on the floor, battered into a cartoon smile. Flames dance on tables, smoking, and clouds of dust fill the air, blanketing the bodies of the dead and dying. Some have been burnt, others shot. He moves about them, his quiet sword giving mercy where needed.

The Vagrant proceeds into the tent, stepping over another corpse at the entrance.

The goat is over in the corner, Lil's body by her side, a gun just beyond her motionless fingers. The gun no longer shines, but smokes from use. From beneath her arm a tiny foot kicks angrily. He turns the woman's body over, revealing the blood-stained baby. His eyes widen in alarm.

The baby smiles.

It only wears the woman's blood. It has not been hurt.

The Vagrant sways, his face pale. His legs begin to tremble.

With a groan, the woman spits something thick onto the floor. 'Where the hell were you, you son of a bitch? I thought you'd run out on us.'

The Vagrant shakes his head, opens his mouth uselessly.

'Listen,' she says, pressing her hand against a spreading patch of red at her side, 'I'll be dead by the time you get your story out. So shut your mouth and save me. Everything you need is here. First thing you do is find my box of tricks. It's metal and oval and it'll be in the tent, you can't miss it.'

But the Vagrant does not close his mouth, nor does he move.

Eight Years Ago

Gamma of The Seven lies broken on the edge of the Breach. By her cracked beauty floats the thing that will become the Usurper, hungry for its prize. Above, Gamma's Palace lists drunkenly, plumes of fire racing each other skyward from rents in the walls and towers. Shapes flicker about the ailing fortress, relentless, swarming and diving and biting and clawing, delivering death through thousands of tiny indignities.

As it begins its casual fall, other shapes rise from the Breach. They too are formless, nameless, all seeking Gamma's remains.

Beyond mortal perception, the infernals fight, vicious clouds of dream that swirl through one another, blending, breaking and diminishing.

One removes itself from the fighting, descending upon the fallen men and women furthest from the Breach. It chooses with care: those that died from shock or single wounds, whose bodies are more or less whole. Into each it gifts a portion of itself, protecting its precious essence within a dead

41

shell. Reanimating what should not be, in stark defiance of the reality in which it finds itself. By fragmenting its essence it is weaker and safer, smaller but more numerous.

A man stands impossibly and the First is born. It gathers its brothers and sisters quickly and sets out to explore. Soon the First has vanished from the field, an uncomfortable addition to the new world.

Behind it, the fighting between the infernals continues until, with elemental force, one infernal drives back the others, winning the contest and stamping its majesty upon them, indelible. Above Gamma's body the claimants separate, blown outward from their new master, a smoke ring of losers. They retreat with ethereal hisses, seeking bodies easier to inhabit.

For the lesser beings this is simple, the ground is rich in corpses, but for the greater ones, Gamma was their only chance for a whole birth. Lacking the invention of the First and cowed by the Usurper's power, they panic. Many squeeze into bodies that cannot hope to hold them. Chests split and burst and essence spills, sliding into a soup of animal energy, bubbling with regret and rage. This pool of essence is raw and unfocused, an unnatural force. Lacking a will of its own, the tainted river surges forth, carried along by the multitude, following the other infernals blindly.

Seeing the fate of its peers, the last of the great shapes moves quickly, the world already clawing at its edges. Unable to find a suitable shell, it weaves a cloak of corpses about itself. Skulls, feet and ribs marry uneasily. Within the necrotic ball, the Uncivil is birthed.

New desires appear, flooding the Uncivil's senses: the wish to see, to experience, to grow. For now they are held in check by a greater power, resulting in a frustration that is almost too much to bear. Despite this, the Uncivil holds on to the idea of independence, of difference. It feels important to choose an identity now, to have something to hold onto when orders come from their new master.

Inspiration is close at hand. The bodies that make up her cloak each housed a unique being and it is easy for the Uncivil to sniff at their fading essence to gather ideas. A gender is chosen. It is not much but it is a starting point, a secret victory to build on.

She turns, awaiting her new master's pleasure.

Free to take its prize, the victor descends upon Gamma's body. Wind screams backwards, drawing the infernal essence into the once great shell. It twitches, animates and Ammag, Green Sun, the Usurper, takes its first physical steps. Compared to the First it is inelegant and brutish, lurching as Gamma's body buckles and warps, trying to accommodate the new host. But nothing of this world, even one of The Seven, can fully contain the Usurper. With irritation, it portions a fragment of itself into another body, a temporary home, the greenness slipping easily through the absence of eyes. This form does not animate, it is too weak, a box for safekeeping, nothing more.

Now stable, the Usurper turns its attention deep within. Buried in the heart of its essence, a wound festers, as alive as the weapon that caused it. The Usurper reaches down, looking for Gamma's sword, to smash the blade and end the dream of its undoing.

But the sword is gone.

The Usurper searches among the corpses, scattering them, and finds nothing. With increasing anger it lifts its gaze higher, over the carnage, over bodies mutating as infernal hosts settle in, until at last its attention is drawn by a glinting metal speck.

Distantly, beyond the feasting and the slaughter, a snake of metal flees the field, heading northward.

At the sight of the thieves the Usurper's anger surges but fear flickers beneath it. It is too soon for another conflict. Defeating Gamma and fighting off the other challengers for her body has been costly.

Unwilling to face the sword again, the Usurper dispatches its horde. The Uncivil is the first to respond, her eagerness to taste the new world dressed as loyalty. Others follow, the Fellrunners, the Earmaker's Three, Hangnail, all bound to their new master by defeat. Drawing the lesser infernals around them, a misshapen horde with lopsided wings and uneven legs, they spread across the land, a living fire.

CHAPTER SIX

'I swear if you don't do something right now, I'll put a bullet in your empty head!'

The woman raves, anger keeping back the urge to sleep. She has fought off many men, surviving against the odds, but now death comes for her again, stealthily. Not long now and she will bleed to death, each beat of her heart pumps precious blood from the hole in her side. Salvation is so close she could cry. She doesn't, instead using the last of her strength to reach out to the Vagrant.

He looks at her and through her, unfocused on the now.

Gasping, she pulls off her monitor ring. The pulsing light fades as it leaves her finger. A moment later it sails through the air, narrowly missing the Vagrant's ear, as do the curses that follow.

Small eyes glance between the two. Sensing a problem, the baby joins its strength to the ruckus, easily matching the woman's despair.

The Vagrant blinks, wipes perspiration from his forehead

and looks anew at the scene before him. At his attention, the baby wriggles, shameless and gory.

'Welcome back!' snaps Lil. 'Now here's what you have to do if you don't want me to kill you . . .'

She winces at his slowness, wonders if speech is the only thing he lacks as he plods, donkey-like under the lash of her voice, gathering the tools to save her life. She directs him to what she would call 'the good stuff', medical supplies that have been transformed into relics since the Overseer's arrival.

All business, she stabs herself with a needle, eyes popping open with artificial alertness.

'Okay, stranger, the first thing we've got to do is clean out the wound. Those amateurs were using cheap-assed shrapnel guns, which is about the only reason I'm still talking. There's a hand scanner and a pair of tweezers you can use. Don't waste the battery, we don't have any spares.'

His hands fumble about the job, hesitant, and Lil's patience rapidly vanishes. 'Just stop, please! Scav's teeth, I've got more chance of saving myself! Just pick up that mirror and hold it like I tell you, okay?'

The Vagrant nods, lips pressed together.

'All you have to do is keep it steady.'

Chemicals silence the pain in her side and she works quickly, no time left for squeamishness. Jagged bits of metal clink as they're dropped into the dish, shy at first, they allow themselves to come free with growing eagerness. She takes a handful of Skyn, slathering grey jelly all over the wound. Instantly it adheres, staunching the blood and darkening in approximation of Lil's muddy skin.

'There, that wasn't so bad,' she says, as much to herself as anyone else. 'Nothing I can't do with enough drugs and medtech. These corpses used to work for the Overseer, so we'd better not hang around. I don't know what's going on but I'm damn sure it's your fault.'

She jabs a finger at the Vagrant, who leans against the tent pole. He peers at her. Slowly his eyes close.

'Hey, are you . . .?'

Before she can finish, the Vagrant slides down the pole and topples over.

'. . . Oh, that's just great!'

The wound is small and clean. She assumes he has passed out through shock rather than blood loss.

Lil has seen a lot of bodies in her life, each with a story to tell, most depressingly similar.

On this body a few things catch her eye. The man bears the blade of a Seraph Knight, which immediately marks him out as a fugitive, yet his hands are callused as much through labour as combat. She turns them over to find smooth skin, the little hairs recently burned away. She notes his tongue is still intact.

Carefully, she removes the bullet. It has gone deep and released its payload but there are no spider web signs of skin degeneration. Amazed, she probes further until she sees the Burrowmaw's inert tail, tucked under his rib. Snagging it on a tiny hook, Lil works it out with slow, steady pressure, till finally the mouth sac comes loose. The little creature smokes in her hand; something has cooked it from the inside.

It joins the shrapnel in the dish.

The suns rise together, dividing the sky like a god's standard. Lil and the Vagrant step cautiously into the daylight. Ventris remains where he fell, face down in the dust opposite Lil's door. His boots have not.

Sounds of fighting are heard from the fields. News of the Overseer's death has spread quickly and people are keen to take advantage of the spoils before a replacement arrives. The goat wishes to join them, spitting out fabric fingertips in anticipation of greater prizes. Again the Vagrant holds firm to her leash but the goat senses weakness and pulls, rewarded with feet sliding in the dust.

The Vagrant regains his balance, grits his teeth but Lil puts a hand on his arm.

'She's got a point, we all need to eat. If we're going to have a chance out there we'll need supplies and goods to trade. There's a fortune to be had in the fields.'

He glances to her hand and back to her face.

'What? You got a problem with me touching your arm? A few hours ago I had my hands inside your guts; it doesn't get more personal than that.'

The Vagrant shakes his head, places his hand over hers. She pulls free quickly, drawing her gun as she runs towards the shouting.

'Look sharp, stranger, we got about three hours before the stims wear off!'

They run towards the field's perimeter, watched by those that have chosen to hide, the innumerable weak.

'Looks like we're not the first!' shouts Lil, voice full of excitement and chemicals. She points to the fence where it bends low, forming half of a barbed smile. The gap is spanned by a living bridge; guards who could not stem the greed-tide are spitted together, forming a carpet. Many boot-prints mark their writhing backs.

The Vagrant turns away.

He cuts a new path through the fence with his sword, impassive. The wire springs apart, making loose spirals by their feet. They watch as two opposing armies form clumps of fighting in the chaos; on one side guards, on the other workers. Neither has a uniform, both are desperate. Only the dead appear united, their faction already the largest. The battle is scrappy, motivated by greed not bravery. The brave have already fallen, piles of them still protecting their more cautious peers.

There is space between the clumps of fighters. With uncharacteristic energy, the goat finds an unspoiled patch and begins to gorge. Lil and the Vagrant fill sacks with precious fruit, loading them onto the goat. Rough movements and battle sounds wake the baby who voices its distress.

The Vagrant works faster.

Pendulous between the pipes that arch above the fields swings the Unborn, lulled in its slumber by the song of the dying. About its shell the air quivers but does not tear.

Emerging from the grasses at speed three men approach the laden goat, armed with sharp metal and hate. The lead man only just stops in time. A pistol presses into the skin of his forehead.

'I'll give you people one chance to back off,' Lil says, 'then I start shooting.'

Quick looks are exchanged, between themselves, at the woman, at her gun. A decision is reached and the men are gone.

The Vagrant nods, the hint of a hint of a smile on his face.

'There ain't nothing to smile about here you idiot!' Lil shouts. 'We'd better be gone before they're back in force.'

Carefully they pick their way across the fields. Bodies lie all around, racing for death. They cry for help, for mercy, for their mothers. The baby just cries.

Eyes locked on the horizon, the Vagrant walks onwards. The goat fights him along the way, sometimes winning a bite of the yellowing grasses, sometimes bowing to the leash. Progress is slow, the ground is boggy and full of debris but, grudgingly, the far edge of the field comes into view.

People have gathered in front of the gate, clustered like a flock around a man who moves with the swagger of power. His muscles are drug fed and firm, his rifle steady in his hands. Blue cables run from the gun to his backpack, fizzing with potential.

'Hold there!' he shouts in a voice rough with living.

Lil's pistol stares back at the rifle, neither blinks. 'Looks like you're moving up in the world, Kell.'

'Well damn, is that you, Lil? I'd heard you got blown up with your house!'

'Nope, still here.'

Kell laughs, the sound echoed eerily by his companions. 'For now maybe. Seems you been taking what's mine.'

'Listen, this doesn't have to turn ugly, just let us go and we'll be no more bother to you.'

'Maybe,' replies the man, rubbing his stubble with a nail-less finger. 'Or maybe you could entertain us a little first, then we let you go.'

'How about I entertain a hole through your head?'

Tension ripples through the group and weapons twitch in hands.

The Vagrant steps forward, he holds a sack open, displaying its contents, offering.

The Vagrant

'Well now,' says Kell. 'Looks like your partner here is feeling a little less confrontational.'

Lil scowls at the Vagrant. 'It's the best deal you're gonna get from us, Kell. We go free and you get goods to trade without risking any more of your men in the field. Deal?'

He makes a show of consideration. 'Deal!'

Handing the sack over, the Vagrant walks down the narrow path between Kell's followers, his shoulders brushing those on either side. The goat follows, for once obedient. Lil comes last, she and Kell turn slowly as they pass, neither willing to look away.

Under his coat, the baby kicks and whimpers.

Everything stops, focusing on the foreign sound.

The Vagrant closes his eyes.

Hands grab at his arms and shoulders, the baby's cries get louder.

'Well, well,' Kell crows. 'Looks like we've got a new deal on. You give us—'

The first bullet punches the rifle from his hands, the second goes through his knee. Kell screams reflexively as he falls forward.

Lil's pistol nestles in behind his ear. 'Here's the new deal: Let us go, right now, or I put a new piercing in your brain.'

'Argh! You'll die for this you bitch!'

'Not before you. Tell them to let us go.'

Kell spits on the floor, bites back another wave of pain. 'Let the bastards go. You hear me, let them go!'

The colony of grimy fingers retreats, and the Vagrant moves forward, reaching the gate.

Lil watches, the time is coming when she'll have to run for it. There are too many people and too few bullets for

51

her to succeed. She grits her teeth, allowing no time for tears or second thoughts, preparing to take her chance.

She turns, pointing the pistol at those immediately in front of her. They flinch away and she jumps for the gap, focusing on the goat's lank tail, still in sight. Her flight is brief, arrested by a chunk of stone that strikes her temple, stunning her. A fist catches her between the shoulders, and Lil falls into the pale grass.

Too late, the Vagrant sees. His hands itch for the sword but they are full already. His foot lifts, wanting to rush to her side, but he cannot put the baby down here, dares not take it back into danger. Head low, he carries on.

A crowd gathers around Lil, boots stamping down.

The tension in the air grows, drawing tighter with each kick. Kell's people step back. Between them, Lil's body lies face down in the dirt, a sliver of blood runs from her temple.

Alone, her death would be but a whisper. She is not alone. Many have fallen, each adding weight to a cry that passes beyond mortal ears and into another place, where it demands response.

With a shriek, the air splits above the fields, and something that should not be manifests within its shell. The pipe arches groan with the added weight, until the Unborn's chain snaps, unleashing its cargo upon the wretches below.

Just once, the Vagrant turns back.

The Unborn's burst shell rocks back and forth, spurting liquid from many cracks.

Long grasses undulate, a sea of pale yellow, allowing glimpses of the new horror birthing in the field. Where it finds people it consumes them, not the careful possession of its elders but a wild, destructive instinct.

Above it, the air ripples and folds, fighting to close once more.

Most in the fields have been taken by surprise but those further out pause in their petty struggles. Weapons are trained on the new threat, men and women briefly united in their desire to survive. Precious bullets are spent.

Voices fade away, the grass whispers.

Nobody emerges from the field.

In its sheath, the sword begins to hum softly. The Vagrant rests two fingers on the hilt but the noise does not quieten. He walks away, leaving Kendall's Folly to its fate.

CHAPTER SEVEN

Gravel crunches rhythmically underfoot. The suns rush across the sky, manic compared to the broken mountains that inch past. Under their uneven shadows, the Vagrant walks. Their progress is steady.

The baby will not stop crying. It screams beneath his coat, inconsolable. Neither the warm dark under his arm nor the stimulus of the landscape bring consolation.

There is little sustenance in the Blasted Lands, and so sacks of fruit and food are magnets for the lean denizens slipping between the rocks. New breeds appear regularly, half-breeds, quarter-breeds and blends unrecognizable. People have given up naming them. Most are lumped together as food, threat or nuisance.

Eventually steps slow, the group's previous exertions demand their due: the resting of tired limbs and heavy hearts. The Vagrant squeezes pasha juice into the baby's down-turned mouth. Even the sweet liquid fails to draw a smile, though the smacking of lips and swallowing is more palatable than the wailing.

As the hours tick by the Vagrant and the baby cling to each other, sometimes stealing snatches of oblivion. While the baby dozes, the Vagrant's amber eyes twitch.

Something ventures forward from the twilight, hunting. It scampers lightly, alert for danger. Scurry, pause, scurry, pause. Eyes dangle from its head, bouncing with each advance on sinewy threads. Its flickering tongue tastes the air before it storms the last few feet, scaled legs whirling with effort. Blisteringly fast, it seeks a way into the sack, racing up the coarse fabric, an opportunistic thief.

Overhead a shadow moves. Preceded by a spike of white hair, it descends, opening until it blocks the creature's path; a moving, living cave.

Feet frantically spin in the opposite direction but the creature cannot stop, momentum delivering it straight into the cavernous mouth.

As the suns rise, the goat chews.

A rising wind flicks at their eyes, throwing grit and flecks of moist matter. The Vagrant moves on, arm raised against the clouds of dust that blow past.

Distantly, shapes are visible, seeming to grow out of the ground.

At first the shapes are simply shelter. The Vagrant crouches behind a structure, leaning into boned fabric that gives but takes his weight. Breathing becomes less laboured and he looks around, running his fingers along the edge of the thing he sits by. Coarse plastic is stretched around a frame that juts out of the ground at a forty-degree angle. The external bars are two inches thick, made for burdens. His hand pauses as it reaches the frame's end; the metal there is flat, edged.

Something has cut through it.

The Vagrant frowns, investigates further. Objects lie just beneath the surface, so badly broken they seem foreign. He tightens his grip on the baby, digging one handed.

Half buried in dirt and tipped on their sides, the waggons from the caravan are not immediately recognizable.

Neither are the bodies.

A face emerges, brushed into view. Sores stand proud on desiccated skin. Something has stolen the moisture, the eyes and more from the corpse. Further excavation allows it to be worked free. Tattered clothes hang loose on shrivelled bones, ridiculous, clown-like. The Vagrant slides his hand between the layers and new smells rise up. Muscles work in his jaw but he does not stop, exploring nooks and secrets.

When his hand seeks air again, it brings out a prize. Small, silver, shining: a coin. The Vagrant stares at it, emotions threatening at the edges of his face. Amber eyes look back from the coin's flawless surface, accusing. Under that stare his compsure breaks, swept away by grief and guilt.

Disturbed, the baby stirs in his arms, wriggling until a more comfortable position is found. Sleepy hands find the Vagrant's thumb and establish a firm grip.

The Vagrant looks from coin to baby and back again.

Nodding grimly he puts it away.

When the winds falter after hours of pounding, and racing clouds slow and settle, the caravan's inglorious end is revealed. The scene appears ancient, aged by the elements.

The waggon's roof moves, rising at the centre, a plastic pyramid. Dirt rolls off as it sweeps upward, folding, falling aside to reveal its treasures. From the hole, the Vagrant pulls himself into the afternoon, squinting against the light. He walks around the wreckage, baby tucked under his arm. It sucks on his sleeve, watching his fingers as they tick off the bodies, one by one.

There should be more bodies than fingers but there are not.

Beneath the Vagrant's boot, things crunch. He steps to the side, finding more uneven ground; it flattens under his weight with a long wheeze.

The baby giggles.

Crouching, the Vagrant finds a blob of black rubber as big as his fist, trailing tubes, a backup lung now redundant. Standing, he drops it back in the dirt and it wheezes again.

The baby laughs louder, reaching for the sound.

He goes to move on but urgent tugging at his collar demands attention. He looks down at the baby, raising his eyebrows; in miniature, his gesture is mirrored. The Vagrant's eyebrows stretch a little higher, again he is matched. For a time both hold their position. There is no obvious winner in this contest, no clear rules.

Both parties break with dignity intact.

However the baby is dissatisfied. Straining against his arm, it points at the discarded respirator. Victorious or otherwise, it wants a prize.

Dutifully, the Vagrant delivers the lung to its new owner.

The Vagrant searches for abandoned treasure. From the wreckage he finds a crate full of decorated fabric. Some he cuts for the baby; a new wrap of shimmering girls and imaginary lakes. Some he cuts into a long strip, which he folds thick and lays across the goat's back. For himself, the Vagrant makes a scarf, covering his face with softness.

Further hunting procures food containers, a cracked scope and a navpack. He holds the projector high to help ailing solar cells. Sunslight seeps through and in return they stutter out an image, low-res and incomplete, mapping the land that was. A ribbon of blue light marks the caravan's route. Verdigris, the next place never visited, is close by. Further north are mountains and beyond them swirl meaningless logos; broken cities reshaped and remade by the Uncivil.

Lifting the scope to his eye, the Vagrant searches the horizon, turning slowly. In the distance he sees a figure watching, stone still, shaped like a person.

Soon they leave the caravan, striking out towards the mountains. A fast pace is kept and the nameless figure is left behind.

The Vagrant does not relax.

Sometimes they march to false wheezing and laughter, sometimes to muffled snoring but they do not stop until it is dark.

Their arrival has been noticed. From a crack in the ground rises a head, curious, leathery. The local peers at their camp but does not like what it sees, returning to the earth.

At first light the Vagrant looks through the scope again. Two figures stand distantly behind, unmoving. To the south east is a third figure, apart from the first pair, yet like them.

Frowning, he lowers the scope. Small hands tug at his collar and he looks down. The baby raises its eyebrows but this time the Vagrant's brow does not lift. He grabs the goat's leash and pulls it sharply, taking them away from their pursuers.

In his arms the baby freezes, shocked. Possibilities cross the tiny face. With renewed force, it tries again; eyes grow wide, stretching towards its forehead.

Glancing down, the Vagrant's mouth twitches but his attention soon flickers north, then south, scowling both ways. Dust rises at their feet, stirred by the returning wind.

Again his collar is tugged. His sharp look down is met by surprise; little features collapse inward, forming thunder. With all its might, the baby glowers.

Stolen from tension, two smiles bloom.

They press on. Dirty clouds belch over them, shrinking the world. The Vagrant stares into the obscuring mass, eyes watering. Often he glances over his shoulder, the view frustrating in every direction.

Ahead, a fence-like arrangement of bones stands tall, as if propped up like a proudly cleaned plate. The ribcage is several metres high, made massive by its infernal patron, now abandoned. The Vagrant attaches fabric to them, forming a colourful shelter. With each gust threaded women dance manically.

They wait for the winds to ease, eating, resting, and milking.

When calm comes again, the Vagrant jumps up, swinging the scope from left to right. He finds the three, still separate, closer now. A fourth and fifth emerge from the dust to the south west.

He rips the shelter down, splitting lakes, and prepares to run.

The dust retreats with them, offering a first glimpse of Verdigris. Four of its towers have fallen but three remain defiant, high discs glinting on their tops; golden ears warmed by the second sunset.

Between the travellers and the towers stands a sixth figure, too low now for the light to reach it.

The Vagrant slows, a muscle flexes in his jaw. Trapped.

Slow and inevitable, the hunters draw in.

The Vagrant looks back often and each time they are closer. He has yet to see them move. Five pursue, driving them towards one ahead, waiting, blocking the way to Verdigris and safety. In the sky, faster than either group, the suns have almost set.

Despite the failing light, details emerge on the figure ahead. A knight of sorts, risen from the ranks of the Seraph, an infernal mirror of what was. Behind its armour unseen growths reach for freedom, distorting metal, disturbing its cloak. Smoke wafts from its helm, marking cracks and joins.

With irrefutable firmness the goat stops, refusing to go further. The Vagrant does not argue, crouching slowly, laying the baby amidst the dirt. A wheeze is heard, followed by laughter. He does not react, his face unreadable as he stands again, facing the knight.

Only thirty metres separate them, the Vagrant crosses them quickly. At his side, the sword trembles with anticipation. He draws. The motion catches a final ray, lining its edge in gold.

In answer, the knight raises a bloated weapon, twisted steel and living jade, discordant, suffering.

Behind him, not close but not so distant, echoes come. Five moans join the first, then, from the north east, a tortured cry, longer than the others, closing.

Amidst the cacophony, the baby's whimpering goes unheard.

Sword high, the Vagrant attacks. As he nears the enemy his downward arc slows, struggling through air thick with wailing, welcoming the heavy parry.

The return attack is powerful, deathly.

The Vagrant does not wait for it, stepping, spinning and striking again. A hump of armour falls away. The Vagrant sees skin exposed, clinging like wet rag to shrivelled bone.

The knight stops swinging for its nimble opponent, groaning defensively, holding him at bay. It knows it cannot defeat him. It does not need to.

Inexorably its troop draws in.

The Vagrant feints left, goes right, makes an opening, doesn't take it, keeps moving, turning faster than his enemy, behind it now, cuts low, a triumphant note blasting bone and backs of knees.

It sways, moaning, descending as the Vagrant sprints back, scooping baby and leash in one hand.

He looks up; misshapen swords loom over them, too close.

They run. This time the goat is happy to oblige.

Ahead, Verdigris rises hopeful. Against its silhouette hulks another shape, charging, trying to cut off their escape. A seventh knight, like the others but greater, more purposeful. The threat spurs them to greater speeds.

Blade first, the lumbering figure reaches for them.

They feel the breath of its dirge but pass by safely, momentum unbroken.

The knight ploughs on past them, unable to stop. It tries to turn as it decelerates, unable to match its more nimble prey and is forced to watch as they near the city's sanctuary, well beyond sword-reach now. Frustrated, it returns the keening thing to its sheath and pulls forth a stubby lance.

Something flies past the Vagrant's shoulder, sizzling into the gates, munching stone. He turns, sword held protectively before him, backing the remaining distance. Seconds after the first, more shots arrive. He cuts them from the air, burning fragments showering around him. One ignites the corner of his coat, another catches the goat's tail.

Flame sprouts, the goat protests but they keep running, trailing smoke as they vanish into Verdigris' embrace . . .

CHAPTER EIGHT

The Knights of Jade and Ash form up around their fallen comrade. At their commander's nod four of them collect the torso, a fifth gathers the feet. Though rare, it is not the first time their shells have shattered. A remaking is called for.

But something is wrong. The body is too light, too brittle. Innards are dried out, failing in their role as infernal glue. The armoured torso collapses flat in mailed hands, powder spills on the floor.

They investigate the abandoned sword. It too has changed; jade has faded, gone still. With a boot, the commander prods and cracks yawn along its edge, falling away from each other a thousand times.

Instinctively, the knights step away.

From the city's archway comes a new sound, bones ratchet against each other, three jaws not quite in time, an approximation of laughter.

The knights approach the gates, alert to the newcomer lurking within.

Peter Newman

Not quite neutral, Verdigris is a city with two masters, torn a little more with every spin of the world. By day it belongs to the Uncivil, by night to the Usurper. In the grey between, things are often broken.

Normally the commander would wait for night to complete its fall; its instincts cry out to wait but there is no denying the Usurper's order. It steps through into the long archway. In formation the unit drops back, following. The commander's hands lower, weaponless palms forward. It waits.

From the shadows scuttles Patchwork, sometimes Duke, Southern Face of the Uncivil. Amorphous within its robes, it appears to glide, a moving puddle, tiny legs busy under the surface, until it is less than a foot away. With one long indrawn breath, it rises, thin body extending from multi-coloured fabric, matching the commander's height. A squat face slides beneath the robes, climbing the body till it finds the hood, pushing out rudely, tongue first.

The commander's helm swings forward harder than necessary. Contact is violent, essences touch, each pressing the other, testing, setting the tone for what follows.

66

Eight Years Ago

Two young men wait anxiously for the return of their heroes. Their youth makes them stand out – the other young and fit members of their village had been snapped up by the army when it passed through the first time.

To their utter dismay, they missed it. Missed Gamma's palace floating by, missed the armies of the Winged Eye and their Seraph Knights.

More than this, they missed their chance to be heroes.

All because their parents were too afraid and tucked them away, out of sight, tricking them into a cellar and locking it firmly until the army had passed. A deliberate act to keep them from joining up.

Selfish. Understandable. Wise.

But parents cannot protect their children forever and the young men are determined. They resolve not to leave their post until the Empire's forces return. Then, they will invoke the rite of mercy and the knights will be forced to take them in.

To stave off boredom, the men discuss what life will be

like, sharing well worn stories about the knights and rumours about how squires are trained.

And then, finally, they see movement from the south and stories give way to reality.

A metal snake winds its way through the countryside from the direction of the Breach. It is borne along on fat caterpillar tracks, wrapped around diamond capped sprockets. Twin stacks protrude from each segment of the machine, a dozen smoking plumes.

The villagers rush out to greet it waving homespun flags; a hundred homages to the Winged Eye. They are proud to salute their returning champions. The cheers die in their throats as the metal snake draws nearer. Cracks mar its silver skin and one of the stacks has split, belching hot black fumes at any that get too close.

A young knight stationed at the snake's head orders the crowd to part. He wears no helm, uniform brown stubble visible from crown to chin.

Stunned, the people comply, flags hanging limply at their sides. Nobody needs to ask, they know the battle has been lost. They do not know, however, that these knights are fleeing the enemy, that soon the infernal flood will wash over these fields in pursuit of their prize, wiping away the village and its culture. In years to come their descendants will forget the teachings of the Winged Eye, The Seven and their Seraph Knights, only remembering that it failed them when they needed it most.

The road ahead is clear, save for two young men, who stand boldly, too naïve to yet know fear.

From his seat in the snake's open mouth, the knight roars: 'Get out of the bloody way!'

The young men do not move. They glance at each other then up at the knight, chanting as one:

'We invoke the rite of mercy. Save us, protect us, deliver us.'

After a quick curse to the sky, the knight invites them in.

A few miles past the village, the metal snake belches black smoke and dies. The flanks hiss as they cool; a last impression of living.

The Knight Commander calls his last follower and the fresh recruits. The day's travel has taken its toll, he knows he has reached the limits of his strength, inside he is crumbling, broken.

'There is only one order,' he tells the three of them, 'return the cargo to the Shining City whatever the cost. Failure is unacceptable, everything else permissible. That is all.' The three digest the news. Even together they barely add up to one man. 'From now on, Sir Attica is in charge, you take your instructions from him.'

With effort the younger knight marshals his face to calm. 'What about you, Commander?'

'I'm not in the mood for running today, Attica, but I am in the mood to shoot something. Carry me up to the turret and you can be on your way.'

The youths have grown up with hard labour and make short work of moving the older man, armour and all, into the raised diamond on the snake's back.

Attica straps his superior into place. Plastic loops take the strain where muscles cannot. Words fumble out. 'Commander, I'm not sure I can do this.'

The Knight Commander injects courage into his man, mixing personal gravitas, legendary status and lies. Attica leaves straighter than he came, determined. Alone once more, the Knight Commander loads a comms-rocket for launch, and records a full account of the tragedy. His voice stays even when describing the scale and nature of the invaders, and the fate of the brave knights and soldiers that went to fight them. It only cracks when he speaks of Gamma's fall. He plays back the report three times, then waits for the rocket's pre-launch checks to cycle through.

The freshly made squires carry supplies, Attica a long lacquered box. Far behind them, fingers of smoke start to rise, a giant's hand raised hazily skyward. It grows from the village, the smell of smoke reaching the group, turning them.

Packs fall, forgotten, and two youths run back towards the village. Attica calls to them.

'But it's our home, we have to help them!' protests one.

The other keeps running. He ascends the hill they have just skirted, sparse strands of grass lolling over its top, a comb-over of yellow-green. The bitter view stops him dead. The other two catch up and stand by his side.

As they watch, a dark stain spreads from the edges of the village. A living seep, a pseudopod, it probes forward, tasting the land, searching. A ragged multitude of teeth and claws mark its growing boundary.

'We have to move on.' Shocked ears fail to hear. 'Come,' Attica repeats.

A beat later the three run.

No more words are exchanged.

CHAPTER NINE

The Vagrant runs along Verdigris' main street. Boots and hooves click on hard stone, the sounds distinct, punctuated by the goat's shrieks and a strong smell of smoke. The Vagrant darts down an alley and stills, eyes darting from the flames eating his coat to those that dance on the goat's tail, careless of the other less pressing dangers that surround them. The sword comes down once, twice, and strands of tail float to the ground, burning bright.

Without his usual care the Vagrant puts down the baby and the sword, rolling on the floor until the fire is out.

He gets up, picking up the baby in one hand and clamping the goat's mouth shut with the other. Both give him reproachful looks.

He waits for himself and them to calm before continuing, putting away the sword and pulling out the scope to check behind them, lenses piercing the night.

No one follows.

* * *

Engines hum softly in the gloom, waiting. Like the rest of the city, they hold their breath, poised for Darktime, when the Usurper's forces will command the city. When it comes, lights stutter to life, haphazard in their arrangement, illuminating unfairly. The signal brings people from their homes. Shops reopen, curtains of chain slide back out of sight, doors grind sideways, groaning. Signs lift, are turned by grimy hands and dropped with a bang. A hundred banners to the Uncivil wink, vanish and convert to the Usurper.

Soon, voices call out; exaggerations and lies masquerade as hope. Others join them with offers and bargains. Unbeatable prices for the belongings of the beaten.

People spill like vomit onto the streets, congealing into crowds.

The Vagrant weaves through, oblivious, till the leash pulls tight, yanking his arm backwards. The goat strains to look back at the charred thing on its rear, still smoking.

The Vagrant stops, and in Verdigris' marketplace stopping invites attention.

'Trouble with your beast I see? Yes, getting old now isn't she? Old and tired, I know how she feels!' The patter is only punctuated by laughs that come thick and fast and fake. 'Funny things these, only get more stubborn with age, not less, like my children!' More laughter. 'But forgive me, where are my manners, I am Ezze. And you are?'

The Vagrant blinks. Ezze's hand snakes around his shoulder, guiding him through sweaty bodies towards a set of wide open doors.

'And a truly noble name it is! I am pleased to make your acquaintance, from this moment on you should consider Ezze your friend. Verdigris is a grand city, full of wonders but many of them are shy, not like the women! Ah, come now, don't be like that, it is just Ezze's joke. A gift to you. Enjoy, it's the only thing you get for free tonight, that I promise! Now step this way my serious friend, I know a place where we can solve all of your problems.'

The shop is cramped, broken tech and old skinsuits compete with encroaching filth in the limited space. Jammed between twin cog stacks is a half-breed, shoulders bare, purple tinted. In his hands is a needle, potent and smoking. On his face a paid-for smile.

'Welcome to my shop,' says Ezze. 'Be at home here. You'll like Bruise—' a scrawny arm indicates the smoker. 'He's like you, not one for the words. Ugly too, eh? Well you cannot all be beautiful like Ezze!' He laughs into the silence. 'Not one for jokes, I see that. Now tell me, what do you think of this?' From the chaos a cylinder appears, scarred metal, topped with tubing, like wild hair. 'It may not look it but this beauty is fresh from Wonderland, the very finest Deadtech. She'll produce milk just as well as your beast but without the complaints.'

The Vagrant shakes his head.

'You are thinking Ezze is mad but he is not! Let me explain how it works. We simply extract the required organs of your beast and place them in the tube. The miraculous device will sustain them and stimulate them to produce milk whenever you need it. You look like one who travels; imagine how it would be to have drinks on tap, even in the middle of the Blasted Lands? Truly we live in an age of wonders!'

The Vagrant says nothing.

'You are worried about the cost. Let Ezze massage away your fear. The price will be fair and you can even part-exchange the rest of your beast to make the deal still sweeter. You see what Ezze did there? Ah yes, not one for the jokes. Are you ready to deal?'

Turning, the Vagrant begins to walk from the shop.

'Wait, wait! There are other things, many things, to interest you here. You do not want to miss out!'

Outside the street is choked with bodies sliding past each other, touching. Skin thieves weave through them, stock-sampling, tiny claws seeking, tireless. But something unusual stirs the crowd, drives them from Verdigris' southern gate. Amongst the anxious faces, glinting helms are glimpsed. Six predators spreading fear.

Vagrant and goat step back together.

A hand waits for each, sliding onto their necks. 'Friend, you have made the right decision! This time, Ezze will let you do the talking. Say what you need and Ezze will deliver or deliver you to it, whatever it is. What do you need, friend?'

The Vagrant reaches for the door, pulls.

'What are you doing?' Ezze's head appears between him and the outside, alert to strangeness, bobbing as it searches. 'There's trouble out there, Ezze sees it. That is not for us. We're in the business of living, yes? Don't close the door; you'll draw them to us. You best stay here and we make deals. Ezze finds a nice place for you, a safe one. You live a good long life. Understand?'

Nodding, the Vagrant pulls some fruit from a sack, throws it over.

Ezze smiles, rubbing his nose over taut flesh. 'The pasha is fine! You have more? Of course you do, you are a wise, rich man. This way, this way and don't worry, you are in safe hands now.'

The Vagrant

The Vagrant squeezes between piles of junk and lost treasures. The back room to the shop is small, shrunk further by the invasion of things, mysterious under cloth. A bed lines one wall, a jigsaw of rubber and foam, scavenged, forced into shape by wiry netting.

'Welcome to my inner sanctum!' Ezze proclaims with a flourish. 'You will be safe here tonight. Now, share with me your dreams and I will make them true for a very fair price!' Automatic laughter follows as the man pats the Vagrant's arm. He stiffens. 'So tense, my friend, maybe you want something to bring a smile back to that face of yours, eh? I have a friend, he has a girl, just tainted enough, hey!' A finger waggles for emphasis. 'You want Ezze to let you meet? For a little extra I let you use the room. What do you say?'

He shakes his head quickly.

'What is this? You have not even let Ezze tell you about her, she is good girl, diligent, yes? Ezze will paint her with words and you will not resist!' The Vagrant leans forward, it does not stop the words. 'She is pert, very healthy, no rashes, no growths, Ezze only brings his friends goods he can trust. Ah, her hips are . . . are . . . Is there a problem, friend, you look unhappy? Ah Ezze sees now,' fingers tap loudly against the shopkeeper's forehead, 'so obvious, Ezze is being blind man, many apologies. Forget the girl, she is too plain for you. I have another friend, he has a cousin, handsome boy, firm biceps, a tattoo, very tasteful, goes from the tip of his—'

The Vagrant catches the descending hand before it can point. He shakes his head, slowly this time, holding Ezze's gaze.

'Of course, of course, you are a serious man with a very firm grip and you like it that way! I see it all now. But give

Ezze something! What do you want? I work miracles for you, but first you say what markets you love.'

He releases Ezze, takes out the navpack, shining its flickering light between their feet.

'Is sad, yes? Looking at picture of what's gone.'

The Vagrant points to the image of the mountains, flicks his finger northwards.

'Ah, you wish to travel, to Wonderland? My friend it is an amazing place but trust Ezze when he says, it is not for you. Better that you stay here, make a life. Or travel south, so much easier to go back. The Usurper welcomes all to his cities but the north gate is watched, closed to the likes of you.' Ezze's frame shakes with a theatrical sigh. 'But Ezze sees your heart is set. It will take a miracle and lots of wealth but it can happen. You stay here out of sight and Ezze will go, see what can be done for you, my travel-hungry friend.'

With practised ease, Ezze slips out into the shop. 'Bruise, watch for customers. Remember, they cannot leave until they buy. And you, beast—' he picks up a heavy piece of striped plastic sheeting '—your hairiness must be hidden!' He throws the plastic over the goat's head. 'And if you shit on my floor, Ezze eats goat's eyes tonight, ha!'

Bruise watches his master leave, smile settling to a sneer.

In the shopkeeper's absence, other noises take their turn. Erratically, tech ticks and legs scuttle just behind the walls. Though dimmed the street continues to bustle outside.

Small hands press on the inside of the Vagrant's coat. He puts the baby on the bed, begins to search the room, lifting covers and lids. Mismatched earrings sit with nipple rings and nose studs, too clean to be innocent. Toes peek beneath a cloth in a corner, motionless. Frowning, the Vagrant pulls it away revealing a woman of foam, headless, her hips squished flat. He drops the cover back, searching no further.

A fresh smell fills the room, pungent, violent.

The baby giggles.

The Vagrant sighs, folds the soiled cloth and hides it, a secret memento. Bare legs wave excitedly, dancing to a beat unheard.

Hours pass. The baby drinks, wriggles, sleeps.

Footsteps herald the shopkeeper's return. The Vagrant's coat sweeps down, swallowing the baby once more.

'Now it is all clear! Ezze has heard rumours, strange things.' A hand waves towards the Vagrant. 'Ezze has many friends and they tell him that the Usurper's knights came here when they should not, entering the city before Darktime. Can you imagine such a thing? They are searching for a man. Some say he has killed one of them. Impossible, yes, but they are here. Ezze hears a challenge has been made between these knights and the Uncivil's Duke. The one who gets this man first, wins. Both sides, they are hungry for victory, they will give a great reward to whoever helps them win. You understand, yes?'

The Vagrant's hand drifts slowly towards the sword's hilt.

'All of Verdigris is looking for this man. If he wishes to escape he will need to be clever, to have powerful friends and great wealth. Ezze can be that friend, he has found people that can help but they are scared. Ezze is scared. But everything has a price; freedom, courage, it can all be bought if you have the right goods.'

Getting up, the Vagrant uncovers the goat, detaches a sack.

'Ah yes, Ezze is interested. What else do you have?'

The Vagrant's eyes narrow.

'Before, a sack of pasha would be enough. But now? Now everything is changed. Now they are looking for you, all of them. Terrible things would happen if we are caught and then what would happen to the thirteen children, the three sisters, the sick brother who coughs blood, the hungry wives, and the lovers who keep Ezze going?'

Sacks are lined up between them, leaving the goat skinny, unburdened.

'For this, Ezze can disguise you, get you to the gates a safe way, even bribe the guards. But you will need a distraction. It will cost. You understand, miracles are never cheap, eh?'

The Vagrant holds out a coin. It sits in his palm, too bright for the dingy room.

Ezze peers at the shining disk. 'But what is this, another mystery? Ezze is speechless! There is a good price for these on the market now, so rare.' Happy sweat lines the shopkeeper's lip. 'This is good, very good. Ezze accepts your offer.' The coin is taken, kissed and tucked away, soft luminescence hidden within folded sleeves. 'You still stare at Ezze, why? Ah you want change. Of course Ezze would normally give something back to balance such a valuable gift but it is not so simple. The coin is valuable, yes? Yes, this is not to be argued with but most have been seized, and to sell this one on will make questions. Ezze does not enjoy questions of this kind. When your distraction is bought and discretion for sale is bought, not much left for poor Ezze. So with much sadness I can give you no change.'

The Vagrant sighs.

'Do not be that way, deal is done.' Ezze's hands smack together. 'Now we must get to work, friend, if you are to escape Verdigris with all your fingers!'

The Vagrant

The shopkeeper rummages, commentary unceasing. A pile of objects begins to grow at their feet.

'Ezze sees problem. You are too strange, easy to spot. But fear not, friend, here are the answers!' A pair of horns is held up, painted plastic given the appearance of bone. 'For your beast,' Ezze explains. 'Make her look like a tainted male, yes? Ezze give her hump too, and fake double tail, even you will not know her! There used to be demand for costume, some customers like the taint, sexy, you know what I mean? Of course you do! But now market is full of real thing, so hard to shift costume.' The shopkeeper examines the Vagrant, shaking his head, pursing his lips. 'You are more tricky, for you Ezze needs to make purchase.' A bundle of grimy cloth is offered. 'Put this on while Ezze is out, and hide your things in a separate bag, we hide it in the hump, yes? They are looking for man with weapons so we give them something else to look at.'

Ezze leaves. Quiet follows.

The Vagrant begins to dress the goat, pulling it into the back room. Horns, tail and hump are attached, the latter's hollow space stuffed with the Vagrant's coat. The sword is too big for the hump. The Vagrant lashes it to a bundle of poles, crooked and rusty, wraps them in old sacking, hangs them by flaccid bags already slung across the goat's back. The goat does not care, her nose dives into a sack, comes away with stolen fruit.

He turns to his own outfit. Stale plastic drops over his head, a giant's poncho. He ties it loosely at the waist, slips the baby inside. It coughs delicately but does not wake. He waits.

Puffing is heard at the doors. 'Good news, friend! Ezze

finds perfect thing at Necrotraders.' The shopkeeper emerges, unfurling something long, suckered and dead. 'Impressive, no? Come closer, smell it.'

The Vagrant covers his nose, steps back.

'Yes! You see, friend? We disguise you not just as tainted, but as sick. We fix tentacle to you, pad your clothes more, add a little juice, make them think you have leak. Nobody goes near you, no searching, no troubles.'

CHAPTER TEN

The Knights of Jade and Ash return to the gate, hands empty.

Under the arch lurks the commander. It is still, redrawing its boundaries, shaking off the sense of Patchwork and the echo of the Uncivil. New thoughts swirl within, taken from the blending of their essences. Patchwork is afraid of their coming, that they will find something, a secret. It did not expect them.

The group forms a circle, leaning together, visor to visor, essences touching, thoughts running as one.

'Did you find the Malice?'

'No. No. No. No. No. This feels wrong.'

'Did you find its trail?'

'No. No. No. No. No. There is a hole where the seventh should be.'

'Patchwork will commune with the adversary.'

'They will fight us?'

'They will seek what is ours. We must hunt.'

81

'Yes. Yes. Yes. Yes. We are diminished. Will the Malice take us too?'

'We hunt.'

They separate, forming behind the commander, one a step behind the others.

People part for them, pressing against the walls, staring. The commander senses something is wrong. It observes the humans recoiling but not running, their lack of fear disturbs.

A building looms, original walls hidden under repair plates hidden under yellowing skin. The Usurper's banner hangs proud. Unlike the rest of Verdigris, it is forever loyal.

They push through unguarded doors, pass dozing half-breeds, moving deeper. They enter a hall, filled with living matter and walls that pulse, skin-cushioned, veined. A figure nestles within. It jerks up to meet them, features hidden within its robes. The commander remembers it was larger once.

It flinches from contact but the commander gives no choice, drawing out its fragmented essence.

'Why . . . you . . . here?'

'The master's will.'

'. . . Why?'

'Where are the others?'

'I . . .'

'Where are our allies?'

'They . . .'

'What have they done to you?'

The memories are scattered, muddled, enough. The commander's fists clench, powdering the empty shell beneath its fingers. This is the secret Patchwork hides. The Usurper's agency in Verdigris is broken. It has been for some time, allowing the Uncivil's hold on the city to grow strong. Her cults are swelling with new recruits, her Necrotech fills the markets. She already rules Wonderland and Slake, and Veridgris is hers in all but name. If the coup is successful, word will reach the other infernals and they will doubt the Usurper's majesty, flocking instead to the Uncivil's banner or contest the master themselves. The commander's thoughts fill with concern, with questions. How has the Uncivil become so powerful? How was this not seen? How did the master not know?

The group shuffles along Verdigris' main street. It is clearing, people instinctively seeking shelter before the Darktime ends. A desperate few conclude business, snatching bargains.

As the group passes, people take notice. They see a slave master and his three wretches, heavy with death's stench. First, they see the boy drool and moan, one eye open, the other pus-sealed. Second, they see the tainted man, his tentacle seeping, dead. They know he will soon follow. The third is a pitiful creature twisted by mutation, horns and tails sprouting from all available spaces, a second form grows from its back, mercifully covered from view. It moves slowly, every step a labour.

Hurriedly, the onlookers turn away.

Machines power down, their lights no longer needed. Verdigris stills. It is not the Uncivil's domain, not yet, but change can be felt, the air pregnant with Starktime.

The group moves on, now alone. None speaks save the boy, who wails as if under torture.

Old buildings lean together, making tired arches. In places they collapse, closing streets, forcing new ways to be forged.

Homes become throughways, windows become doors. In turn the piles of rubble accommodate life. Handlings scuttle between the cracks, competing for space with rats, ubiquitous, tainted.

Here, the group stops. The boy shrieks again, a fat blob of mucus splatters on the ground.

'What is with all the noise, boy?'

The pus-lined eye opens, winks. 'You told me I am dying, father, so I make dying noises.'

'Ey! Ezze say look sick, and why did Ezze say this?'

'To trick everyone?' The father's hand clips his ear. 'Ow!'

'Yes! To make them not look. Noise makes them interested, makes them remember us. If they look hard they see you are not sick boy, not diseased, just thick in head!' Ezze clips the boy's ear a second time.

'Ow! Why you hit me again? You always hit me. It's not fair!'

'Be grateful you have ears left to hit. Your aunt was stupid, yes?'

'Yes.'

'And Ezze is wondering, where is aunt of little Ez now?'

'She's been taken away.'

'Exactly! She is taken to breeding pits of Slake, and will not be seen again.' Ezze turns to the Vagrant. 'Actually this is something of a mercy, but,' Ezze continues, attention back on the pouting boy, 'she is stupid, she is worse than dead. So Ezze hit all the stupid out of you and you thank Ezze for it, yes?'

'Yes. Thank you, father.'

'Is better, now go wipe off your pus and make sure to get it back in the jar for next time.'

'Yes, father.'

'I'll meet you at home.'

'Yes, father.' The boy leaves them.

'Ah, he is good boy but stupid, so stupid. More like his aunt than his mother, but Ezze think you not interested in that story. Now we are here and deal is done.'

The Vagrant looks from left to right; his eyes rove empty streets and buildings.

'You are wondering where they are, yes? Of course you are. Have faith, my friend, they will come. So, Ezze will be leaving you now.'

The Vagrant's mouth opens, protesting.

'All endings in Verdigris are fast, yes? But Ezze must go. Please, keep the tentacle. Perhaps it reminds you of our friendship!' The shopkeeper starts walking quickly. 'May all your lovers be sweet and may their paths never cross, ha!'

The Vagrant shares a look with the goat as the suns rise. Starktime has come. Distantly, sounds are heard. Doors close, signs reverse, doors open, the first steps of Verdigris' daily dance.

Figures emerge from a ruined building, their clothes grey with hard living, uniform. Size marks them out. A man and a woman tower over the rest. Half-breed teenagers, covered in muscle and greening scars, the common Usurperkin markers tracing their lineage back to the Usurper. Patches of spiked hair decorate their skulls, black flags on a pitted map. Another man, normal sized, holds a gun, ugly and mismatched. It points at the Vagrant's head. The last is a tiny woman, barely four feet in height, ratbred teeth too much for her mouth to contain.

A wave of the gun signals the Vagrant to follow. Reluctantly, he does. Giant hands take the leash from him and the group return to the darkness. For a moment the goat resists, then the leash snaps tight and she flies after them, a furry, hate-filled balloon.

Underground, a chain of hands is formed, leading the Vagrant down, deep, through lightless buildings, then steps, then tunnels, the ratbred finding their way in the dark. More than once, big heads brush rock; curses fall till they are hissed quiet.

The Vagrant is taken down further, where cold becomes chilling. Objects are hefted, then replaced, a trail of obstacles left for any would-be followers. A torch shines yellow, recycled sunlight perched on the top of a gun. It pokes at the Vagrant's eyes, making him squint.

'What you make of him?' murmurs the male Userperkin, unimpressed.

The other half-breed shrugs. 'Good for spare parts, maybe.'

'Spare parts?' says a third voice, the one that belongs to the gun. 'This here's the real deal, at least he'd better be. We certainly paid enough to get him.' The light and the voice come closer still. 'I see what you mean, but we'll get our money's worth, one way or another.'

The Vagrant's squint becomes a scowl. Beneath the robe, his fists clench.

'Check him,' commands the voice behind the gun.

One of the giant half-breeds restrains him while the ratbred sniffs him over, bony hands probing beneath the robe. He pushes her away, hard, and she stumbles back against the rock. From beneath the robe comes a soft complaint. The Vagrant turns, placing his body between the gun and the baby.

'Try that again, pal, and I'll put a bullet in you. If you're lucky it won't hit the little one.'

The Vagrant's eyes widen, despite the glare.

'Yeah, you heard me. We know about the baby you're carrying. What, you think you can hide one of those squealers in a man's house and him not notice?' The gunman snorts. 'So hand it over, as well as any other weapons, and then we can all make like friends.'

He shakes his head. Again his eyes seek the sword but it remains bound with the goat, useless.

'In case you're simple or something, that's not a request.'

They rip the robe from him, using it to wrap the tentacle. The ratbred moves to take the baby but he pushes her away again.

'Oh for the love of . . . Maxi, make our friend cooperate.'

A thick arm circles the Vagrant's neck and squeezes. He pulls at it, kicking and twisting till air is thin and strength runs out. Afterwards, the baby is slipped from flaccid arms. It begins to scream. The Vagrant's eyes twitch but he doesn't move. They search him, this time there is no resistance.

The half-breed slings him over her shoulder as they make the last few turns. 'Thought you were gonna shoot him.'

'Shut up, Maxi!'

As soon as they enter the room the way behind them is sealed, stone grinding on stone, moved by pulleys and many hands. Intricate carvings line the walls, their lights broken, their gems stolen, an echo of an echo of what was. In their place are essence lamps, an innovation of the Uncivil, turning souls into fuel. Their flames burn green, held by cups, inverted; bright but cold, the unnatural sheen falls on many faces, all expectant.

The Vagrant is dropped, wheezing, on the ground.

A woman moves forward, her face inked in angry swirls, an arm missing. The others part for her. 'Hello there,' she says, speaking quietly under the baby's screaming. 'I hope they weren't too rough with you.' She tilts her head, examining him carefully. 'I'm sorry if they were. These times make monsters of us all. I'm told that you can't speak but that you hear well enough.'

The Vagrant's eyes open fully. He stares at her for a moment, then looks to the baby.

She waves a man forward who takes the baby from the ratbred. The Vagrant examines him. He is dressed pale like the others, his eyes as green as the flames in the room. The man hesitates, looks down, whispers. The baby's cries settle to an insistent complaint.

'Now, it is time for us to have a talk, you and I. But first let me make some introductions. The people here call me Tough Call, or Tough for short. If we get on I might even tell you my real name one day but given the look on your face I won't get my hopes up. Around here, names are important; they're about all any of us have left. I'll tell you how I got mine, so you know the kind of person you're dealing with.

'My parents used to run with the top dogs in Verdigris. And believe me they were strong. They always told me stay true to yourself no matter what the cost, anything less and you were already dead.' Tough Call sighs. 'So when Verdigris got taken over by the Usurper and the Uncivil, and my good folks were turned into suits for demons that took up residence in our home, I found their advice mighty hard to follow. But follow it I did. Along the way found me some good people who felt the same.

'We did a lot of fighting in those days, lot of dying too. Lost me an arm. Well, that's not quite true. I know exactly where it is, I keep it in a cabinet out the back. It's still moving, even now. Cut the damn thing off myself. It was that or give my body over to the taint and, no offence to the rest of you here, but I'd already given enough.'

The goat yawns.

'So that's me.' Tough Call points to the gunman. 'That there's Honest Joe. His name isn't really Joe and he's not really honest but the name's kind of stuck. He's a survivor though and proof that intelligence can make a man attractive.'

'Hey!' shouts Joe over the laughter.

'Tina's the little lady that helped you find your way in the dark and the twins are Max and Maxi, full grown, first generation, half-breed loyalists. They're usually pretty calm, so long as you're respectful and never get them mixed up.' Tough Call gestures to the others. 'There's a lot of folk here you haven't met yet but I want to make it clear: these here are people, determined people, they all got their own names and stories. They're all decent; turns out the taint don't always turn the mind, just makes it work a little harder.

'I'm hoping you'll help us because you really are some good-hearted knight right out of the past but if knowing us and our struggle's not enough then let's be clear on this too: you help us and we'll help you out of Verdigris like you want. You don't, and we take everything you've got and claim that fresh reward that's been placed on your head. Clear?'

The Vagrant nods.

'Good.' Tough Call smiles and puts a hand on his shoulder.

'So that's us. Now let's talk about where you come in. Word on the street is that the balance of power in Verdigris is changing, things are swinging against the Usurper and we don't want that to happen.'

The Vagrant glances over to the giant Usurperkin twins and back to her.

'No, Max and Maxi's inheritance has nothing to do with it. This is about survival. It'd be just as bad if the Uncivil's hold was broken. As things stand we can't hope to win a war but we can survive theirs, underground, in the cracks. We've been doing it for years. It's not glamorous but it's better than being dead. Fact is we need them focused on each other so they're not focused on us.'

The Vagrant's face is impassive.

'In the ruins at the centre of town is a cache of weapons, top of the line kit that got here just before the occupation. It was supposed to be sent south to support the war effort but by the time it arrived here the war was already over. We could use that firepower to strengthen our position and strike against the Uncivil's agents. Only problem is we can't get to them without drawing the wrong sort of attention.' She lets her hand slip from his shoulder. 'We need you to cause a distraction so we can move in and take the weapons. It just so happens that Patchwork's recruiter is holding a rally in town today. He's a nasty piece of work, literally.' A few of the crowd murmur in agreement. 'You're going to kill him and as many of his traitorous recruits as you can. Better they be dead than fight in the Uncivil's new army. We'll bring you up right by the place so nobody'll know you're there till it's too late. You go in, hit them hard and fast and then get the hell out of Verdigris. We'll arrange for the north gate to be open for you and help you get through. After that, you're on your own.'

With a frown, the Vagrant points at the baby burbling in the arms of the green-eyed man.

'I'll have Harm bring the baby and your things to the north gate. Succeed, and they'll be waiting for you.'

The green-eyed man keeps his attention on the baby, whispering sadness, guilt, shame.

'Do we have a deal?' Tough Call asks.

The Vagrant closes his eyes, nods.

'Good. Joe, give our man back his sword.'

A bundle of rods is taken from the goat's back, untethered and allowed to spill on the floor. Among them lies the sword, restless. Joe does not pick it up. The Vagrant steps past, collects it, leaves it sheathed.

'Looks like we have a busy day ahead,' says Tough Call. 'Good luck, all being well we won't see each other again.' She nods, ending the meeting, and turns back to her people.

The Vagrant watches the baby until they guide him from the room, reluctant.

CHAPTER ELEVEN

The square is full of people and flies baking together. It is Starktime and the suns are high overhead, giving each spectator two shadows, overlapping, imperfect, forever trying to align.

On a block of rusted iron stands what was a man. Like many of the Uncivil's creatures he is robed, the horror of his re-creation hidden. He has brought many over, pleasing Patchwork, his Duke and master. In return he is augmented, part infernal, part man. His arm is still recognizably human; it protrudes from the robes, unremarkable down to the wrist, handless, crowned instead with an old woman's head. Though the face's skin is black and shrunken, the people know the features well. Once, the head belonged to their leader.

The crowd are no longer disturbed by this sight, just relieved he does not display his other arm.

Tendons flex and old jaws move like an obscene glove puppet.

People listen, some held by fear, others by twisted hope.

Only one moves, sliding between the motionless figures, drawing closer to the speaker. His hand grasps his sword's hilt, eager to respond.

The sixth Knight of Jade and Ash returns, joining the others in darkness. Its head touches theirs and the commander's and essences weave in a metal circle.

'Report.'

'Nothing. Nothing. Patchwork has returned to the city with fresh purpose. Nothing. The Malice has resurfaced. Are we weakening?'

'Where?'

'Do we fight? Do we fight? Do we fight? Can we fight? In Verdigris' centre, it stalks Patchwork's mouthpiece. Will we go the way of the seventh?'

'No, let the Malice fall among our enemies, let the pawns of the adversary blunt its edge. Then we will fight, and win. For now we watch.'

The commander goes to break the circle but stops, troubled.

'What was that?'

'Nothing. Nothing. Nothing. We bleed from the hole made of the seventh. The Malice will end us. The Malice will end us.'

'Enough. We watch.'

Ending contact, the commander leaves. The knights form up behind.

Robes sit smoking on a rusty block. Inside them, meat sizzles.

The Vagrant sheathes the sword, striking out north across the square.

His spectators have no protocol for what they have witnessed and instincts take over. Bodies rush to and fro, bashing together, grunting, crying out. None of the crowd go near the Vagrant, peeling away from him, parting.

Tina peeks from a nearby doorway, pink eyes wide. She beckons to him, leading the way through rooms, numerous, empty of people. Beds and belongings vie for space, their little stories mingle in the mess, rendered meaningless, trampled under trespassing feet. They reach a boiler, stretching from ceiling to floor. Tina dives behind it and into tunnels below. The Vagrant follows, lines of rust painting his coat as he squeezes past.

Hand in hand they weave through the darkness, the Vagrant stumbling enough for both of them.

They emerge at the north end of Verdigris by a quiet street. Tina refuses to leave the tunnel's refuge. 'No further,' she says, lisping the words around curved teeth. 'You go on alone.'

He shakes his head but she is already retreating, trying to slip bony fingers free.

The Vagrant grips her hand tight and steps out, forcing her to follow. She protests, shielding her face with her free hand.

A passer-by at the end of the street turns, sees the pair, hides their concern and looks away with polished nonchalance.

Tina makes a decision and takes the lead again, showing him the nearby gate that waits as promised, open, unguarded.

Vagrant and ratbred step through the gate, entering the Uncivil's territory. Mountains loom to the left and right, battered and strong, like weary combatants. Ahead, the way is clear.

Tina's nose twitches in surprise.

The Vagrant's eyes narrow. He looks along the wall both ways. Between mounds of junk strewn the length of Verdigris' boundary, small things dart, otherwise it is quiet. No goats mutter. No babies cry.

'Shit,' says Tina, twisting free.

The Vagrant turns to find her running, head down, aiming back the way they came. His lips move, a silent curse, and then he re-enters the city, giving chase.

They fly across the street, Tina intent on the nearby tunnel entrance, the Vagrant drawing closer. He catches up as she dives for the window, her small body sailing easily through broken plasti-glass.

He grabs her mid-flight, fingers and thumb overlapping round her ankle, pulling her down, onto the jagged frame. He lets go and momentum drags synthetic teeth from her thigh to her toes. She hits the ground awkwardly, squealing childlike but not stopping, vanishing into the dark innards of the building.

Leaning on the wall, the Vagrant pauses, catching his breath. Ten breaths pass, becoming slower. He draws the sword, humming softly as it tastes air, then touches its tip to the newly stained window. Tainted blood flashes, burns away with a hiss.

He climbs inside, entering the tunnel, leaving daylight behind. The sword tugs at his hand, guiding him down and right; another flash, another hiss and he moves forward, drawn through the darkness, drop by drop.

Spread out across the northern quarter, the Knights of Jade and Ash wait, swords held high, softly moaning.

Only the commander moves, turning slowly, alert for trouble. Somehow the bearer of the Malice has eluded them and they are left directionless and exposed. If their enemies find them here in Starktime, war will follow.

Suns lower, starting their downward arc.

Then their swords flinch from a distant sound. The Malice has resurfaced. Brazen, the commander marches through the streets, intent on the trail, gathering knights as it goes.

From a side street, a strange voice calls out: 'Hold!'

The commander pauses as robed figures move between them and their trail. Something about them is wrong. Broken essence hangs from the humans, woven to them in bags of dead flesh. What madness has the Uncivil wrought? What are these non-things?

'You are in violation of the treaty,' says a Half-alive man. 'This is the Uncivil's domain. Return to your lair until Darktime immediately! Do it now and all we will demand is compensation. Disobey and Patchwork will have you ended!'

The knights await their commander. The master's orders are clear but surely war must be avoided? This twisted non-thing speaks truth, they are in the wrong, they should go back. But the commander does not retreat.

'I give you one last warning.'

The commander knows they should pull back, wishes it even, but the Malice is too close. The first wound burns and memories surface, of greatness, of coherence, lost.

The Uncivil's creature is talking still; words float by the commander. It does not hear them, raising its lance.

The knights understand, closing around the non-things, who begin to wail.

In panic the Uncivil's Half-alive men shrug off their robes, revealing bodies ravaged by extreme surgery, grafted dead limbs reanimated, original parts reworked, joints altered, muscles rewired, augmentations gifted by the Uncivil in exchange for service.

The commander squeezes the lance, spraying them all with liquid fire.

The Half-alive howl with pain, violently waving limbs that burn, trying to put them out, trying to fight their way towards the commander. Before they can reach their target, the knights step forward, tightening the circle, hacking at the flailing appendages. When the knights step back, gouts of fire pour from the commander's lance. Between each burst the knights close again, cutting away another layer of the enemy like skin from an onion. All the while their swords lament, twisting through bodies that burn, silenced.

When the last of the Uncivil's Half-alive men have fallen the knights move about the corpses ensuring every part of them is truly lifeless.

Then the knights pause, shocked into contemplation until the Malice whispers again from the north, agitating, setting them into motion.

Soon Patchwork will discover the carnage and war will follow. Despite its instincts, the commander doesn't mind.

Within Verdigris' underground, two men travel. One has green eyes and carries a grumbling baby; the other has a gun and pulls a goat behind him.

'Joe?' says the first, quiet.

'Yeah?'

'Something's wrong.'

'Yeah, it's a sign of our times.' Joe snorts. 'Or are you talking about something in particular?'

'We should be at the north passage by now.'

'Nah, I'm just being extra careful, we're taking a different route.'

The green-eyed man frowns and the baby chuckles like an old man, distracting, drawing his attention down. 'You like that don't you, little one.'

'Harm, you know it can't understand a word you're saying? It's a baby.'

The green-eyed man stops. 'You're not going to the north passage.'

Joe looks over his shoulder, biting back angry words. 'I told you, we're just going a different route, it's a bit out of the way but safer.'

'You did, but that was a lie.'

There is a moment, awkward, tense. Joe fingers the handle of his gun. 'Is that going to be a problem, Harm-less?'

'That depends,' Harm replies softly. 'Where are we going?'

'We're going to go and make a fortune!' Teeth glint in the torchlight. 'We're off to market. It's all worked out.'

'Really?'

'Yep, I've got a contact waiting, old friend of mine. He's going to sell the brat on for us, make us all rich. He's even throwing in a few extras for "the beast".' Joe tugs at the leash for emphasis. 'Which is why I haven't turned it loose yet, bloody thing keeps trying to go the wrong way.'

Harm whispers words that fall like feathers, light, just beyond hearing. The baby stretches, reaching for the source of the sound.

'What was that?'

'Nothing, but why take me?'

'To be honest,' Joe replies. 'Tough Call told me to take you, that's why.'

'She won't like this.'

'Yeah, which is why we aren't going to tell her.'

'I'm not sure I like this.'

'It's a bit late to grow a conscience now. There was that lad you scammed, what was his name, Ness? Nate? What did happen to him anyway, nobody's seen him in ages?'

Harm looks away, swallowing, the soft light of his eyes eclipsed. The baby struggles, frustrated by its lack of freedom.

'I'm pretty sure Tough Call wouldn't like to know about that or some of the other services you've been offering on the quiet . . .'

'Okay,' comes the reply, broken.

'Okay?'

'I'll help you. I'll say nothing.'

'That's smart. And don't worry, there's plenty of money to go round. You'll get your share, and money is the best antidote to guilt I know.'

They walk on until their lights reveal a sagging ceiling, cutting the passage in half. Joe wraps the leash around his wrist, pulling the goat's head low as he stoops to continue.

On impulse, Harm throws his torch at Joe's head and runs. Behind him he hears a clunk and a curse. The baby squirms in his arms, unimpressed.

Harm risks a backwards glance.

Joe swings the gun round for a clear shot but his other hand still holds the leash, linking him to the goat. The goat has no interest in turning; she pulls hard, arresting Joe's turn. He tries to hold his balance, tries to pull his captive with him. The goat pulls a second time and the small man falls, cursing again as he hits the ground, legs bent behind him.

The gun fires, loud and impotent.

The goat bolts.

Joe and the baby scream.

Harm runs.

Green eyes glow softly, twin moons too weak to penetrate the dark. He fights to hold the baby, unable to stop its noise in his haste while, unseen, uneven walls beat at his arms and shoulders, bouncing him from one side of the passage to the other. Distantly he hears struggling and swearing, and the sound of pursuit.

The chase is slow, both men struggling to find their way, both desperate to be faster.

Harm reaches a familiar door. He puts the baby down fast, and wrestles to open it. Little hands and feet rage against Harm's stomach as he lifts the unwilling bundle. Pale light issues from the doorway, glistening on the baby's back. He looks down, sees blood on the floor, the door, smearing its lower quarter. His hands begin to shake. The baby's cries stutter, transforming, becoming laughter, juddering.

His comrades wait in the chamber, tense, clustering around something, voices low and frantic. His arrival startles them but panicked looks turn swiftly accusatory, freezing him.

'What's happened?' he asks, throat dry.

They move aside, allowing him to see Tina. The ratbred looks pale, injured, angry. Fresh bandages cover her leg, red-stained from the inside.

'What happened to you?'

Tears of pain roll down her cheeks. 'Him! When he saw his baby wasn't there, he tried to kill me. I only just escaped.'

He avoids the glare of pink eyes. 'You didn't escape.'

'He was faster but I lost him once we got underground.'

Harm readjusts his grip on the baby, waits for Tina's thoughts to form.

'You think he's still coming? You think he followed me?'

He nods sadly.

'Oh shit!'

'I just hope Tough Call returns before he does.'

'Wait!' says Tina, small face crinkling with discomfort. 'Where were you and where's Joe?'

'Joe betrayed us.'

Amazement seizes the ratbred's features, contempt follows. 'Crap! I've known Joe years, I trust him. I don't trust you.' Mutters of agreement come from the assembled armed rebels. Harm has always been on the outside, Joe is known to all. 'What have you done to Joe?'

Hard faces and weapons converge, demanding answers. Harm sways under the pressure. 'I . . .'

'Ssh!' interrupts Tina, tensing with effort. 'Something's coming.'

The rebels take up positions covering the door. In the darkness of the tunnel there is a distant flash of fire, of amber, and a hiss, inhuman.

CHAPTER TWELVE

Essence lamps flicker, green-tinting the chamber. Rebel faces stare into the tunnel, trying to understand what comes. A couple flank the doorway while others form a line, barbed poles and repurposed tools held forth, aggressive.

Harm stands among them, unarmed save for a bundle of squirming irritation.

Humming, ominous, the point of a sword penetrates the room. The Vagrant follows.

As the lamps sketch him, Tina screams, dragging her injured leg towards the far wall. 'Don't let him touch me!'

'He's not here for you,' Harm murmurs, but none attend to the words.

'Get out of here,' says one of the rebels to the intruder, his pole indicating the exit. 'And we'll not hurt you.'

The Vagrant shakes his head, eyes intent on the baby. He takes a step forward.

The rebels exchange hurried looks. Poles quiver, uncertain. There are no weak rebels, Verdigris does not permit such to survive, but the strongest of the group have left, aiding their leader, seeking precious artillery. Courage has gone with them.

The Vagrant takes another step, raising the sword. A low note resonates from the motion, sending forth a ripple of sound. Teeth set on edge, essence lamps stutter; their unnatural flames dance away, bent by the sound, then cough straight again. The rebels retreat, leaving only space between Harm and the advancing Vagrant.

'Here,' says the green-eyed man, holding out the baby. 'I'm sorry.' There are more words, explanations, but they die in his throat when he meets the Vagrant's eyes.

The Vagrant reaches for the baby with his free hand.

The baby reaches for the Vagrant.

Fingers nearly touch.

A click sounds sharp from the doorway. 'Nah, I don't think so.' Joe spits. 'I'll be taking that baby.'

'It's over, Joe,' Harm replies softly.

The gunman rubs at the new swelling on his temple. 'Shut up!'

The Vagrant starts to turn.

'Don't move!' Joe shouts. 'And keep that sword where I can see it. If the bloody thing so much as waves I'll put you down.' He glares at Harm. 'And as for you, you freak, I'm going to put a hole right between those weird eyes of yours, you two-faced, double crossing c—'

The sword comes down in a swift cut. Air sings, Harm jumps back, Tina hides her face, rebels tense.

'What?' Joe says, incredulous, his hair lifting as the sound wave passes. 'You think I'm joking? I'll . . .'

With a chorus of gasps, the essence lamps go out.

'. . . kill you?'

Cries of alarm mingle with muffled footsteps.

Harm stands, shock-still, waiting for the first gunshot. The baby wails, its cry distinct in the dark. He curls his body round the baby as the second shot grazes his shoulder, pushing him down on his side, hard. The third bullet passes overhead. Cold stone slaps one cheek, a tiny fist the other.

One of the rebels rekindles a lamp, making sense of the soundscape.

People cower in corners, bodies scrunched small.

The Vagrant rises from his crouched advance, moving to strike.

Joe's surprise curves into a smile. More than a sword length separates them. He fires as the Vagrant swings.

Blade and bullet meet, sparks flare and the shot ricochets harmlessly upwards.

Still too far away, the Vagrant stands, sword stretched high, body exposed.

Joe levels the pistol but his smile falters at a sound behind him. Before he can understand its nature, an unknown force collides, charging hard against his legs, knocking him forwards. At speed, the goat emerges from the tunnel.

The Vagrant's eyebrows shoot up. The sword comes down, Joe follows a moment after. There are no sparks, no fire and this blood does not burn. It stains the blade, running along its edge, forming drops, falling.

The Vagrant nods to the goat but she doesn't respond, running past, head twitching left and right, searching for an exit. The Vagrant frowns, looks the way the goat has come, peering into the dark.

Faintly, something moves.

The sword's attention fixes on the motion, thrumming a warning against the Vagrant's hand. Its sound is caught by the approaching menace, sent back, distorted, a strangled cry of metal.

The Vagrant sighs, his shoulders droop, then he forces in a deep breath and straightens.

'The Usurper's knights are here!' Tina screeches. 'Shut the door, shut it now!'

Stunned rebels begin to move, unsure of which enemy to face first. Some watch the intruder in the room, others move to the door.

Harm pushes onto his knees. 'There's another way out of here.'

The Vagrant crosses to the green-eyed man, towering over him.

'I could show you.' Again, Harm offers the baby.

Sheathing his sword, the Vagrant takes the baby and holds it. His eyes close. Little fingers worm into his hair, turning circles.

Harm waits while rebels struggle with the door. It closes, a brief denial of what comes.

Reluctantly, amber eyes open. Harm swallows, meets them. 'We have to go.'

The Vagrant nods, retrieves the goat.

Tina has hobbled to the shadows of the opposite wall. At her touch one deepens, opens. Rebels race for the new door, friendships forgotten in the rush to live. The ratbred is knocked aside, crushed against the wall. Fatigue buckles knees, frustration drives her down. She draws a breath, 'Help me, please.'

The Vagrant walks past without looking down.
'Please!'
Harm closes the way behind them. The door pushes her back into the chamber, muffling the baby's cries on the other side.
Hands shaking, Tina reaches for the wall, pulls, begins to stand.
Behind her the essence lamps grow brighter.
Her injured leg fails and she clings to the wall until fingernails fracture.
Behind her the door shakes with impact, rippling like rusted water, boiling, moaning.

Sweaty faces shine in shielded lamps. Box-laden, men and women labour through tunnels. Maxi leads them, hair spikes combing the ceiling. At the rear of the group, Tough Call stands, watching for pursuit.
Max waits with her, huge hands cradling a cylinder, an acquired treasure. Fine engravings run its length, unnoticed through thick calluses. 'You think they're coming, boss?'
The kick is affectionate but firm. 'Keep your voice down! And yes, they're coming.'
'You see them?'
Tough Call hunches forward, peering into the pistol scope. 'Not yet.'
A droplet of sweat rolls down the back of Max's skull. Slow at first, it gathers speed down his thick neck, racing on to meet its fellows budding in the curve of his back. 'But . . . if you can't see them . . . how do you know they're coming?'
She kicks him again, firmer this time.

Robed figures enter her sights. They walk in single file, a queue of killers, patient. From the hidden recesses of their ranks she hears bones grinding together, an alien laughter.

Max forgets to whisper. 'Was that Patchwork?'

'Bring down the tunnel.'

'That was Patchwork wasn't it?'

'Max, bring down the tunnel.'

He looks over at her. 'You sure, boss?'

She doesn't look back, one eye closed, the other pressed against the scope. 'You want to be a glove puppet for the Uncivil?'

'No, boss.'

'You want to be turned into pick and mix for the half-lifers?'

'No, boss.'

'Then stop asking stupid questions.'

'Sorry, boss.'

She holsters the pistol, puts her hand on his shoulder. 'And Max?'

'Yes, boss?'

'Before you fire, give me a five count.'

'Sure,' he says but Tough Call is already running.

A low rumble shakes the underground room. Dust shrugs downwards, settling on the Knights of Jade and Ash, who wait, ever patient.

From the commander's hand, a ratbred dangles, bare feet lightly brushing the floor. She stares, eyes wide and vacant, temples pulsing in time with the living metal at her throat.

The commander releases her. It has been difficult,

connecting with essence so dry. Stubborn like cement, it slows thought, yet the commander has left the necessary mark in her mind. Around it, cracks have started.

Muscles fail on the ratbred's face and her right cheek succumbs to gravity, mouth turning down on one side, a confused squiggle. But behind the empty eyes she knows what is sought. With effort, she approaches the wall, injured leg dragging behind.

The knights watch, expressionless.

Memories move slowly, hands spasm in momentary rebellion, then they move among the stones.

The hidden door opens once more.

She sniffs, thick air invading her nose, making her sneeze. She sniffs again, sifting scents till she finds it, faint, hooking her nostrils, compelling her forward into the tunnel.

Like shadows, the knights follow.

In his arms, the baby nestles, content. The Vagrant blinks against the dust, pulling his collar across his mouth.

Ahead the earth roars again and chunks of stone fall from the ceiling, shattering around the feet of the fleeing people. Their essence lamps quiver but stay lit.

The Vagrant does not slow, staying close to their reluctant guide.

Forced to keep pace with him, the goat flicks her ears, irritated.

Other branches present themselves but Harm does not take them, still following the rebels, moving towards the source of the noise. He glances back at the Vagrant, eyes dipping guiltily to the hidden bundle. Ahead the rebels are conversing in tense whispers. They cannot go back, can they go forward? What should be done? Anxiety becomes inertia and they slow to a crawl as footsteps come pounding through the dark, numerous and giant. They ready their weapons.

Then a rebel cheers. A familiar voice answers: Maxi. Verdigris' resistance reunites, clasping arms, swapping well-worn names.

Tough Call moves among them, firing questions. She does not like the answers. Her last question is asked angrily. A forest of fingers points towards the Vagrant.

Harm speaks as she marches towards them. 'It's not his fault, it was Joe. He—'

'Looks like we have a problem,' she says loudly, pushing aside the green-eyed man. 'I've brought down two of the entryways to hold off Patchwork. With luck we've buried the bastard but more likely we've slowed them down. We were coming back this way to get somewhere defensible but now I'm told we've got trouble in the southern passages too?'

'The Usurper's knights are right behind us,' Harm says quietly, as if pronouncing a sentence.

'Wait a minute,' Tough Call says, looking round. 'Where are the others?'

None of the rebels answer.

'Did the knights get them?'

The rebels look uncomfortable. 'We're not sure,' says one eventually.

'Right.' Tough Call runs a hand through her hair. 'Everybody, crack open those boxes, looks like we'll be testing these weapons sooner than we thought.' She gives her attention to the Vagrant. 'My hands are tied here. There's going to be a fight and it'll be hard as hell. I don't know if I owe you or if there's bad blood between us and right now I don't care. We could use your help, now more than ever.'

The Vagrant shakes his head.

'I get the feeling that's non-negotiable.'

'It's this way,' Harm says, beckoning.

Tough Call puts a hand on her hip. 'You going too?'

'Yes.'

There is no time for argument. None is made.

'Good luck getting out of here. We don't use the other tunnels much and there's a chance they won't have survived the quakes we made.'

Nodding, the Vagrant starts to leave but Tough Call grabs his arm. 'Word is, those knights are only here cos of you. If you could draw some of them off, it'd give my people a better chance of survival.'

Shrugging sharply, the Vagrant breaks away, leaving the rebels behind. He goes Harm's way, weaving through passages long forgotten, crumbling. Away from the rebels and the fighting, silence presses in. Only footsteps and ragged breaths challenge its dominion.

Tiny fingers rise from inside his coat, probing upwards. They find stubble and pause, thoughtful. Not satisfied with his chin, the fingers stretch higher, questing. At full extension they find a nose and grip hard, scissoring, clamping nostrils shut.

The Vagrant coughs.

Harm's voice is gentle. 'It bothers you, leaving them behind.'

Nobody responds.

The baby squeezes harder. Torchlight glimmers at the corners of the Vagrant's eyes.

From far away comes the cry of fresh destruction. Harm and the Vagrant tense and the goat bleats unhappily. Walls rumble and rocks drop from above.

Gradually, things settle. The passage remains.

The group move on.

'I think that was more of Tough Call's heavy artillery.'

The Vagrant nods slowly, little fingers still clamped to his face.

'She must be desperate, trapped between the Usurper's knights and Patchwork's forces.' Harm glances at the other man, his face solemn. 'It'll be a slaughter.'

The Vagrant bows his head, keeps walking.

'I know we didn't do right by you but that's on me and Joe, nobody else.'

Their footsteps echo, rhythm unbroken, heading north.

With unknown purpose the baby's hand begins to twist, and twist. The Vagrant stops, his sigh nasal. Gently, he liberates his nose, guiding the hand back into his coat, then he draws the sword, tapping it lightly against stone. It sings, one note, long and round. When it stills he taps it again, and again, charging the air as minutes pass.

In time it is heard. Six off-key replies disturb, followed by another, deeper. The sword's silvered wings twitch in anticipation.

Harm smiles, soft. 'Thank you.'

At speed, they depart. Every few steps, every new turn, the Vagrant declares their presence. Now the replies are constant, gaining.

Without need to discuss, fast walking becomes jogging, then running.

Rubble springs up at the edge of their light. Fresh dust

floats, decorating the collapse. Harm examines the damage, hope of escape fading. 'We could go back, try another route?'

The Vagrant nods, sheathing the sword, and they rush the way they came, towards the hunters, coming to a side passage, narrow, unused.

Harm plunges in, strands of web break on his face, masking, tickling his mouth. He stumbles, the torchlight jerking, catching glimpses of skittering, shy things. In places the roof has fallen, forming mounds that trip, raising the floor.

An arm bursts from the Vagrant's coat, grasping. He tilts his head back, foiling fingers that scrape past his nose, snaring his bottom lip; the baby chuckles.

They run, breath coming harder. Legs slow, no longer light.

The passage opens up, becomes vast, its edges unseen.

The Vagrant stops, shoulders drooping. Harm collapses against the wall, letting ancient stone take his weight, lungs working like bellows. With an air of finality, the goat sits.

Harm moves the torch slowly, revealing the remains of the old city, a monument to what was. Buildings have become pillars, curves beautiful beneath flakes of rust; they stop the sky from falling. Just above head height, pipes run. They are dead now, purposeless. In the centre of the square is a statue, features lost to time. One arm is missing, the other extends, palm upwards holding a pitted orb. Hills of rock and debris intrude upon ancient streets.

They begin to explore. Cracks in the walls are numerous, big enough to promise escape. Other passageways present themselves, three still useable. The Vagrant points at the highest and Harm starts to climb.

The goat does not move.

The Vagrant frowns and tugs at the leash.

The goat does not move.

The Vagrant closes his eyes, swaying slightly. He takes a breath, exhales, opens his eyes, and pulls.

Much to its displeasure, the goat is standing.

With deliberation, the Vagrant follows Harm up the rubble slope. The goat bounds ahead of him, mockingly agile. The green-eyed man is waiting inside the new corridor, pointing at a gap in the stone wall. 'You see that?' A shaft of light cuts across the passage, winking sporadically. 'There's an essence lamp on the other side.' Harm peers into the hole. 'It looks like a cellar, still in use.' Using the back of the torch he begins to batter at the hole, making it crack and widen. The Vagrant joins in, kicking at the wall.

A sound stops them. Not the keening of a tortured blade but the clank of armour.

'They're close!' Harm says, voice fearful. He redoubles his efforts to break through.

The Vagrant looks back down the passage, then down to the baby. It giggles, reaching for his face again. He lifts it closer, lips pressing against its cheek, then holds it out towards the green-eyed man.

'What are you doing?' Harm asks, as the baby is put into his arms.

The Vagrant wraps the goat's leash around Harm's wrist and points at the hole, urgent.

Harm looks into the Vagrant's eyes. Words squeeze through a throat, suddenly tight. 'I understand. I'll wait for you, beyond the north gate.' He feels the Vagrant's fingers gripping his elbow, fingers hard against the bone. 'I understand.'

While Harm struggles through the hole, the Vagrant drags his feet back towards the cavern. He looks back, once, twice, and is gone.

CHAPTER THIRTEEN

From high in the cavern, the Vagrant sees them coming. Tina emerges first, slack limbed, followed by the Knights of Jade and Ash. He waits at the passageway's edge, hidden, his laboured breathing held slow and quiet.

At the commander's signal they spread out, searching for him, sensing his closeness. Without lamps, only their essence is visible, luminescence seeping green through visors, joints, and cracks in their living armour.

The ratbred looks up, pink eyes finding him in the dark. Her foot points in his direction but she does not let it move, refusing to go closer. Within her broken mind impulses war, fear rises, matching in strength the compulsion to obey. Taut muscles quiver, threaten to cramp.

In ignorance one of the knights walks the way Tina stares.

Seizing his chance, the Vagrant accelerates down the hill of rubble, scattering chunks of stone. The sword's wings unfurl, its unblinking eye fixed on the target. A low hum sounds as it splits the air, like a bomb from the heavens, descending.

But the Vagrant is tired, his edge dulled and the knight raises its own blade to fend him off, turning the mortal wound brutal. The knight falls back to the safety of its companions. Though the sword wants to strike again there is no time to finish the injured infernal; other knights already approach, like sharks drawn to blood. The Vagrant struggles in the dark, climbing towards his perch, to the exit he must bar.

This time, the knights are faster. Two scramble ahead, blocking his escape; another three advance together, blades reaching for his heels.

He is forced to face them, to catch the heavy blows with the sword, two handed, body jarring with each impact. They drive him up the slope, strike by strike, towards the pair on higher ground.

The Vagrant does not fight to win but to delay. Grudgingly, he gives way, pushing against every attack. Sweat coats his face, dampening the dirt that inks his scowl.

At the base of the rubble, the commander waits. It is nearly time to engage, to break the Malice, but something is wrong. Something is coming. Another's essence intrudes on the chamber, muted, dangerously close. The commander steps back from the fighting, prepares itself.

Lights wink from a lower passage and a river of robes rushes forth, numerous, violent. There is no mistaking the Half-alive cult of the Uncivil, or their leader. Patchwork has come, drawn by the sounds of the Malice and the chance to revenge itself against the Usurper's knights. The commander turns to face them, raising the stubby lance, but something snakes out from the shadows, dead flesh coiling around the commander's bracer, pulling the weapon wide.

Tina vanishes in the initial charge, final thoughts smashed beneath hammering feet. The half-lifers break about the commander, spilling either side, grabbing for arms and legs.

The commander begins to lean, a knee buckles. More bodies join the fray. The commander cannot move its arms, cannot aim its weapon. It fires anyway and flames belch outward.

Flesh, necrotic or otherwise, burns.

Further up the hill, the Vagrant is safe from the flames. He parries another wave of attacks, the sword-song losing resonance. The knights press their advantage, unaware of the shadow unfolding behind them. The Vagrant's mouth drops open and the sword glares at the new arrival. The knights pause, jade light pales, they feel the wrongness too late.

A shroud of teeth ripples through the air, wrapping itself around a knight. Within the black cloth, bones grind on metal, essence boils and Patchwork claims another victory for the Uncivil.

Four knights remain. Two between the Vagrant and Patchwork, two between the Vagrant and the way out. They are slow to react to the change of fortune, weapons twisting in their hands, grief stricken.

The Vagrant too is slow, arms drooping, heavy despite the sword's enthusiasm. Already to his right Patchwork begins to rise, ratcheting erect, wide-thin body becoming tall-thin, the curtain of robes lifting to reveal the ruined shell of its victim.

The Vagrant spins from the sight to the pair at his back and charges, swinging the sword wide, a desperate note. The first knight parries, its sword groaning with effort. The Vagrant pushes past and blades stroke each other, blue sparks dancing downward.

He stumbles on, head bowed, into the path of the second knight. It stands ready, sword poised. The Vagrant tries to raise his guard but muscles falter. The sword's eye bulges with anger as it dips, blade tip brushing the floor.

Defenceless, he steps forward.

The attack does not come.

With clenched teeth, the Vagrant raises his head, staring into the fathomless dark of the knight's helm. For a moment, neither move.

The knight sees no fear in his eyes, cannot read his essence, cannot think of anything save the sword that glares, promising death. All too easily, it remembers what the Malice did to its companion . . .

It wavers, uncertain, when the Vagrant steps forward again.

Another step brings them close, like lovers. The Vagrant doesn't turn from the knight, doesn't blink, he continues to push forward.

The knight steps aside.

The Vagrant keeps walking.

Behind him, Patchwork gives chase, dodging between the other knights.

From below, the commander watches, its armour scorched but intact. Corpses smoke, welded to their killer, a mass of smudged limbs. It pulls against them until an arm and a weapon come free. The lance is damaged, coughing tears of fire. More half-lifers threaten but the commander attends only to the scene above, raising his weapon at his enemy's enemy.

Patchwork glides after the Vagrant, coiling and launching after its prey, faces eager. Airborne, it closes the distance quickly but from behind comes a roar, faster.

It is the sound of the commander's lance misfiring, exploding.

Air ignites and rock falls, removing the Vagrant from sight and slamming into Patchwork, half burying the Uncivil's Duke. Exposed bones flap impotently, laughing no longer.

The commander looks at the hand that held the lance. The fingers of its gauntlet have been woven together in the lance's explosion, fused in a lump, unrecognizable.

New assailants approach the commander, half-lifers climbing over their dead brethren, keen to finish their hated foe.

The commander reaches for its sword.

Eight Years Ago

The Usurper has defeated Gamma of The Seven, has stood against, and surpassed, its infernal peers, becoming a monarch among monsters, yet this does not seem like victory. A remnant of Gamma lives on in her sword, a thing of malice, dreaming of its death, stirring wounds deep within.

The Usurper is growing accustomed to Gamma's body, adjusting to the feelings of being contained and defined. As it moves further from the Breach, the world's reality asserts itself, ever stronger, rejecting. The Usurper treats it like any other enemy, fighting, pushing back. Each time its forces kill or corrupt, the Usurper inches forward. Each time the Breach convulses and fresh clouds of essence belch into the world, it is like wind in the Usurper's sails. Even so, the invasion will be long and both sides are already injured.

The sound of a challenge draws the Usurper's attention. The head of the infernal horde is breaking around a metal snake, like a river around a stone. A lonely cannon spits defiance as the Usurper's lieutenants smother the ailing vehicle.

Something escapes however, a silver arrow streaking skyward, leaving bright fire in its wake. The vessel is too small to hold a body, too small even for a sword.

The Usurper wonders as to the arrow's purpose. In moments the clouds have hidden it from view.

Something about the lone warrior in the metal snake draws it in. Gamma's wings no longer allow flight, scything air as the Usurper moves forward in long, ponderous leaps. Sensing their master's interest, the horde abandons the attack, leaving a metal snake's shredded shell – on top sits the Knight Commander, head tilted like a merry king, fingers still gripping the triggers of the ruined cannon.

The Usurper studies the warrior like a favoured book, tracing the contours of strength and loyalty etched in the old knight's bones. It comes closer, raising the body it carries as an offering.

In response the Knight Commander draws his sword, cutting the air with song.

The Usurper waits.

The Knight Commander bares his teeth and sweat runs into his eyes. Muscles tremble, fight, fail and his sword slides downward with a sigh, wistful.

Slowly, the Usurper lifts the body towards the old knight, like a mother bringing a babe to breast.

'No!' exclaims the man, struggling, his seat unwilling to let him go.

From within the eyeless body, something stirs, issuing forth from red holes to pour into the Knight Commander's mouth.

He dies instantly but not soon enough.

The Usurper steps back.

It is not enough for the Usurper to simply take another

empty body, this man must be made to kneel, just as one day, the world will conform to the Usurper's design.

All through the Knight Commander's corpse changes occur. The sliver of the Usurper's essence absorbs the remnants of the man, blending with it, becoming something new, greater than before, and less. Unlike its infernal parent, this blended being has a claw-hold in reality, tenuous but enough. Enough to move freely, to hunt.

Straps tear from their housings and a new thing rises: the commander. The once proud Seraph Knight is no more. The commander's sword is lifted in salute and the blade shrieks in protest, cries stretching out as metal distorts, twisting, protesting, succumbing. Smoke issues from the rents in the commander's armour, hissing softly until the essence turns crystal, fossilizing, dull and green.

The commander asks no questions. It does not remember its previous lives but purpose burns within it, an urgency defying words, a memory of malice that must be quenched, of peace that must be found.

The Usurper approves of what has been wrought. It begins to search the battlefield for more of the Seraph Knights, hoping that some might yet live. Corpses do not interest it. To occupy a vacant space is insufficient. The Usurper wants more, to dominate, to re-envision. Of the ten thousand knights that came, less than a dozen survive. But one of them has already fled and two are quick witted enough to take their own lives. The Usurper gathers the others and returns to the Breach, blending the fragments of their souls with raw, alien essence, shaping twisted versions of what was: the Knights of Jade and Ash.

CHAPTER FOURTEEN

The Vagrant places one foot after another, slowly, never stopping.

Muffled through stone, he hears a sound, like the death cry of a giant. From its scabbard, the sword thrums in agitation.

He keeps walking, slowly, never stopping.

Passageway becomes cellar, becomes steps, becomes house, becomes street.

He heads north, slowly, never stopping.

The gate remains open and he goes through.

The suns are low in the sky and he squints against them.

He is alone, abandoned, betrayed.

He stops, shakes his head.

From behind a rubbish pile a voice calls, imperious and infantile.

The Vagrant smiles.

*   *   *

Under a lonely gold sun, a small group travels. Night is close; the red sun has already swung beneath the horizon, making way for eager stars.

Harm speaks, too low to discern, soothing the creature in his arms. Exhausted, the Vagrant walks alongside, pulled in jerks by a tyrannical goat making the most of fortune's reversal.

Verdigris fades easily from sight and memory, and the four walk in the last of the light, beyond the Usurper's reach, northward, towards Wonderland and Slake, jewels in the crown Uncivil.

Mountains line up either side of the valley, standing watch. Their stone faces are pockmarked with caves, a mix of homes, tunnels and traps for the unwary. In their shadow, travellers rest. Two are awake, alert with hunger. Two sleep.

Harm stares at the man and baby, sees the tiny hand making a bed in the larger one, snuggling under a thumb made blanket. He drinks in the sight, barely blinking.

In turn he is watched by the goat.

Both watchers appear guilty. Ignored in the chaos of recent times, the goat has her leash in her mouth and chews towards freedom. She does not care about the angst lines on the green-eyed man's face.

The sky begins to yawn lighter.

A small foot twitches.

The baby is awake.

The baby is hungry.

To the baby this is unacceptable.

Pink lips open and a small chest rises, doubling in size.

'Ssh,' says Harm, shuffling forward on his knees, until he is leaning over them.

Urge to yell forgotten, the baby stares up at him.

'It's alright,' he says softly, reaching down.

The baby's expression says otherwise.

With the utmost care, Harm takes the Vagrant's hand, turning it, releasing the baby from its grip.

Amber eyes snap open, the Vagrant jerks up, catching Harm's wrist in steely fingers, his hand reaching for the sword, muscles preparing for violence.

The baby holds its breath.

The goat drops the leash from its teeth, assuming an expression of nonchalance.

Harm's voice is strained. 'I'm sorry. I'm sorry! I didn't mean to shock you. Please, can you let go? You're hurting me.'

The Vagrant's gaze travels down from Harm's face, along the man's twisted arm to his own fingers. His eyebrows lift in surprise. He lets go.

Both men look away.

Small eyes flick between them. The baby is still hungry. It does not intend to suffer alone.

'Sorry to wake you,' Harm says softly.

The Vagrant holds up a hand and makes a dismissive gesture.

A loud cry from the baby stirs the other three into action and milk travels quickly from goat to tin to hungry mouth.

For a time there is peace and a golden sun lifts itself over the shoulders of the mountains.

'I know you're tired but we should go.'

The Vagrant nods, handing the baby over to Harm and picking up the leash. He does not notice the tooth marks.

Travelling north, they look back often. The Blasted Lands stare back, dusty and worn. They see no pursuers.

129

Harm's voice prods the silence gently, appeasing the baby, making one-way conversation. Shadows recline and split as the second sun rises. The redness catches in dark smudges under the Vagrant's eyes, like angry bruises.

'Can I ask you something?'

The Vagrant nods.

'We need supplies and shelter, do you have a plan?' Harm glances over, rubbing his wrist. 'I know a place we can go but we'll need something to trade. All I have are the clothes on my back. That is, if you want me to stay with you?'

The Vagrant stops walking, his face creasing in thought.

'I'd understand if you don't trust me. But if you'll have me, I'll come with you.' He reaches out a hand, the movement pulls back his sleeve, revealing red stripes recently made. The Vagrant tenses as he steps closer. 'I haven't always done the right thing. I have the feeling you understand what that's like.' Harm's fingertips brush against the Vagrant's arm, daring only the briefest touch. His voice is soft, barely a whisper. 'You don't have to be alone.'

A sorrow-woven smile touches the Vagrant's lips. He nods once, firmly, and walks on faster than before.

'Thank you.' Harm pauses, unwilling to break the moment. 'Do you have a plan?'

The Vagrant points north.

'And a way to get food?'

Slipping his free hand into a pocket, the Vagrant produces a coin, pure and silver.

Harm's fingers twitch, drawn to the singing metal. 'That's good but it's a long way from here to the next settlement.'

The Vagrant frowns but keeps walking.

'As I said, I know a place we could go. It's not much of

a detour and we could get everything we need. What do you think?' The Vagrant nods, though the frown remains in place. 'Then please, follow me.'

They walk for a while in a silence Harm finds unbearable. 'Can I ask you something?'

The Vagrant nods.

'Are you able to talk?'

The Vagrant looks up at the sky as if seeking inspiration, none comes. He shakes his head.

'I'm sorry, I hope I didn't embarrass you.' After a pause, he speaks again, papering over the awkwardness. 'They call me Harm. Everyone ended up being given a name when they joined the rebels. It wasn't official or anything, we called each other all kinds of things, but for me, Harm was what stuck. I hated it at first. The name seemed too scary for a man my size. It felt like a joke. Joe used to call me Harmless. Bastard. But I'd been called worse before, so I got used to it. It's funny what becomes normal after a while.' He clears his throat, self-conscious. 'I thought you might want to know a bit about me, seeing as we're travelling together.'

The Vagrant gestures for him to continue.

'I grew up in one of the tethered towns outside Wonderland. And like most people, I didn't really understand what was happening when the Uncivil took the city. My mother and my uncle were machinists and we were comfortable. Not rich but we didn't want for anything. They'd done well under the Empire and were loyal to the teachings of the Winged Eye. When the Uncivil came, they refused to accept her, and tried to encourage others to stand firm and not be tempted by her gifts. It was a bad business decision. The old infrastructure in the city was already failing, and the Uncivil had

131

solutions to our problems. She didn't attack my family, didn't need to. She just waited while they became obsolete. I tried to tell them to join her cults but they were stubborn, kept saying that The Seven would send their Seraph Knights one day and that on that day, their loyalty would be rewarded. As far as I know they're still saying that.

'I travelled into the city and started work, doing odd jobs, you know, whatever I could scrounge. It wasn't easy, it wasn't always clean and the pay was crap. In the end, I did what everyone else was doing and went to the Uncivil.'

As the Vagrant raises an eyebrow, he raises his hand. 'Don't worry, it didn't work out. Actually I had to leave Wonderland in a bit of a hurry, but that's another story. Sorry, didn't mean to give you my whole life history.'

The Vagrant's smirk is not without warmth.

'Funny to think they were right. My family, I mean. I assume that's why we're going north, to rendezvous with the others?' He looks at the Vagrant for confirmation and his face falls. 'There are no others, are there?'

The Vagrant shakes his head.

'Oh. Then we're not going north to attack, we're going to escape. Maybe I will be able to help you after all. I've had a lot of experience of running away. I also had a lot of younger sisters, so I'm no stranger to handling babies either. The goat's all yours though.'

Taking the green-eyed man's lead, the group make their way towards a gap in the mountainside, a jagged alcove where things watch and wait.

The Knights of Jade and Ash dig among the corpses of the no longer Half-alive. They work quickly, untroubled by darkness. Between them the commander's body is raised from bloody mulch and placed on the ground. Lovingly, they peel and scrape charred chunks from their leader's armour. One retrieves the commander's sword, offering the hilt.

But the commander does not move.

The knights form a circle around him and kneel, leaning forward till their heads touch. Essence flows between them, swirling downward, reaching into the dulled space within the commander's visor.

Deep within the shell, they find the commander's essence, ragged and pale, a spiderweb afterglow of what was. Together the knights cradle the fragmented cloud, repainting its edges, filling the spaces with portions of their own souls, remaking.

Panic slides between them, gaining speed and power. The knights are so close they struggle to know which of them began to doubt. All of them feed it, making it grow, till they tremor with its force.

'Broken. Broken. The circle is broken. Leaking. We bleed from head and hearts.'

Gloom threatens to overwhelm them, then there is a spark, ignited within their shared conscious, and the commander's thoughts take form, bringing order.

'Report.'

'We have defeated the Uncivil's servants. The Malice is gone. We are afraid. The sixth has fallen.'

'And Patchwork?'

'Trapped by your fire. Patchwork lies in the rocks nearby. It lives. It dies.'

'Take me there.'

'There is more. Should we say? We don't know. We are afraid.'

'Tell me.'

'The rebel's fire brought down the rocks behind us. We are trapped. We cannot follow the Malice. We have failed.'

The commander has lost two knights, and a fear wound has spread through the others. Its lance is broken, one gauntlet ruined, unusable save as a club.

It does not matter.

The commander breaks contact and picks up its sword. The knights help their leader to where Patchwork expires, a half-buried mash of robe and bone, flopping obscenely.

With a cry, the commander's sword drives down, piercing, pinning the exposed limb tight. The commander waits patiently, allowing the enemy's strength to fade. As the Uncivil's Duke begins to fragment, the commander enters its fraying mind, rifling.

New realizations come:

The bulk of the Uncivil's power has been spent in the tunnels.

Verdigris is, for the moment, masterless.

The Uncivil endures despite her distance from the Breach. Her aim is set still further north, where war rages between her armies – the Uncivil has armies! – and the Empire's forces that still hold the coast.

She fears to face the Usurper, is fleeing its reach. She knows it cannot travel.

She knows! The commander sways with the idea, somewhere it knows this too, has always known. But she is wrong. The Usurper can reach this far north. They will be the fingers of Ammag, the fist of the Green Sun.

But first they must escape.

The Knights of Jade and Ash shift rocks, tunnelling while

the commander flays the remnants of Patchwork, sometimes Duke, Southern Eye of the Uncivil.

Both jobs take a long time.

There are those who live between Slake and Verdigris, secret groups hiding in the gaps. Like most small things, they survive through stealth and solitude. Sometimes however, the need for trade, for stories or the sharing of despair brings them together. At these times a Shadowmarket is convened.

'The Shadowmarket has rules,' explains Harm as the Vagrant takes the baby back within the confines of his coat. 'Never give anyone your name. Never draw a weapon. Never show your face. Never go back.'

Hooded figures sit behind piles of wares, haggling, exchanging. Banter is curt, as hard as the survivors. Figures come and go, flitting between the traders, mothlike, taking turns to watch for intruders.

They enter and the sword vibrates against the Vagrant's leg, hum stifled within its sheath. He hastens to the first stall. The owner's face is hidden, only glimpses of her skin are seen, tough, wrinkled, like a dried nut. She guards her thin produce jealously and the Vagrant wants all of it. She in turn wants all of his coins.

The goat edges towards the food, getting closer, saliva building at the corner of her mouth. Her nose hovers over it, then descends, encountering a hand, slapping, fast.

The owner's words turn sharp as do the Vagrant's gestures.

'Please,' says Harm. 'We all suffer if we can't agree on a fair price.' He talks further, soothing, understanding of the woman's troubles. Her defences are up however and his fight to lower them is long. Unfortunately, neither Harm nor the owner of the goods have the luxury of time.

Shade falls across the Shadowmarket, a false sunset.

As one, they look up. The mountain above seems to have grown taller, its blunted head blocking the light. But mountains do not grow, nor do they move.

This one jumps.

Chunks of rock break away from the descending shape as it falls, spreading arms and legs. The ground screams as the living comet makes contact. A ripple of stone and sound booms outward, scattering people, redistributing wealth.

Light returns, dazzling, revealing green skin, laced purple with veins rope-thick. Metal plates meant for tanks cover her body, worn so long the flesh grows over them like ivy. Only her face appears normal, sitting too small in the triangle of muscle between shoulders and forehead. She is called Usurper's Daughter, she is called the Hammer that Walks and she is looking for someone. She stays in her landing crouch, poised. Only her head moves, sweeping left and right.

People scream and scrabble, trapped between the new arrival and the mountainside. A few cower, most begin to climb. None think to fight.

Harm grabs at the cloth by his feet, pulling up the corners to make a sack, bulging with food.

The owner shrieks, rising from the floor onto her knees, clawing for her possessions.

Harm pushes her backwards and runs, making for a small opening in the rock wall.

The Vagrant glares at his retreating back but goes to follow, pauses and looks once more to the woman sprawled in the dust, defeated. He tosses a precious coin.

It flies towards her, spinning, singing and lands in her lap.

The Hammer's head tracks the movement, then reverses the action until her gaze settles on the Vagrant. She stands up.

Vagrant and goat race for the cave. The goat is first and squeezes swiftly into the dark.

The Hammer leaps.

The Vagrant forces forward into the crack. It does not want him. Stones grate against his back, pressing hard on his ribs. The baby's cries go high pitched with pain but he is through.

The Hammer strikes the wall where her prey has hidden and keeps striking until the mountain sheds slabs of granite, sealing all within.

Eight Years Ago

While the infernal horde spread northward, hunting for the Malice, the Usurper attends to its new home.

Life draws it. From the smallest blades of grass, to the wild networks of weeds and vines, jostling for space. It is a conflict the Usurper can understand.

Of more interest is the town that sprawls before the great infernal. Tucked away at the base of a valley, it has been spared the attention of the other invaders. Turbines still turn and lights continue to illuminate. Rows of solar panels run across the valley's sides, synthetic palms tilting upwards to catch the last of the day's sunslight.

And there are people.

They form a shaky line at the town's border. Men and women too old or too young to join the army.

In two gliding bounds the Usurper stands before them.

They flinch back, most raising their makeshift weapons, a few dropping them.

The Usurper scoops up one of the youngest, turning him slowly in a massive hand.

Though desperate to help their dangling companion the trembling humans gaze upon the Usurper, unsure of what to do.

One brave soul rushes forward, firing her weapon, bellowing a challenge.

But bullets only glance off the Usurper's silver-green skin, and words make even less impact.

The brave soul stops advancing, stops being brave.

The Usurper does not notice. Its attention is held by something much more interesting.

Unseen by human eyes, the Usurper is surrounded by a moat of infernal essence, the broken-down remains of its kin that failed to manifest properly in the world.

Wherever the Usurper steps is tainted by this essence, changed in some way, and now the same begins to happen to the young boy in the Usurper's hand.

Mortal essence is distorted by the infernal, swelling within the young body. It becomes larger but less subtle, stronger but more volatile.

And as the essence within shifts, so too does the physical body. Skin takes on a greenish hue, muscles bunch and grow, limbs stretch. The boy screams, his voice already a few octaves lower than it was moments ago.

By the time the transformation is complete, the suns have set and the other humans are long gone.

The Usurper drops the body in the dirt and advances on the town. It leaves behind a half-breed, no longer fully human but not a true infernal either. The first of the Usurperkin.

The town is quiet, most people wisely having hidden or

The Vagrant

fled. But the Usurper's senses go beyond the physical and it moves quickly to a house, sensing an abundance of life somewhere just under the ground.

Clever design has hidden the trapdoor well and the Usurper quickly loses patience. It drives its clawed hands through the floor and makes its own hole, peeling back the sides until it is large enough.

Small mortals cluster together, their eyes wide with terror as the Usurper drops in among them. The youngest of the town are hidden here, from babies swathed in protective bubbles to boys and girls ranging from two to eight years old.

So many humans! So fresh! So malleable and full of potential!

If it were human, the Usurper would smile.

They shriek as it chases them, like a sinister game of tag. With each contact, a new set of transformations begin and another Usurperkin is made.

One of the girls does not run however. Barely four years old, and small for her age, she is no stranger to threats, or to violence.

The Usurper stops in front of her, fascinated by the fiery spirit within the tiny body.

It jerks forward, trying to scare her.

In answer, the girl bares an incomplete set of teeth.

Looking at her, the Usurper recognizes something of itself; an inability to flee and an unwillingness to back down no matter the size of the opponent. Though she cannot hope to win, she would rather fight and die.

It approves.

More than with the others, the Usurper makes sure to

141

imprint something of itself upon the girl. She fights of course, just as the Usurper would if the positions were reversed.

But there can be only one outcome.

When it is finished, the girl from before has gone and in her place is a monster shaped in the Usurper's image. A tool to smash its enemies, a hammer that walks.

Breath labours in the dark.

A baby cries, pain pitched, shocked, unbearable.

Only six people and a goat make it inside before the Hammer seals the entrance. One of them knows the cave well, can navigate through crawlways on memory alone.

He has already gone.

Two others follow him, losing first the trail, then their way. Sanity will be the next to evade them.

The Vagrant sits against the rock, content to be still. He hears the sound of sniffing, then eating and Harm's voice, reprimanding. The baby is clamped to his side, clenched fists making handles in his clothes. He rocks it until the screams go hoarse, then fade to sleep.

Something moves, unseen in the blackness, nudging the Vagrant's hip. Reflexively his hand grabs it, snaring a bone, stick thin, wrapped in a single layer of paper flesh. A vein presses against his thumb then retreats, then dances forward again to a thready beat. The Vagrant works his hand along the leg, drawing the outline with his fingertips. They skate over the back of a knee, a hamstring, a buttock but as they pass the hipbone flesh yields, wet and warm.

The Vagrant lowers his head, returning his hand to the stranger's ankle.

Time slips by, unnoticed.

When the pulse has made its final retreat the Vagrant slides himself along the wall until he can find the man's face with his hand. Gently, he smooths out the wrinkles of pain, closing the stranger's eyes against the dark.

Then he searches the body.

In return for his kindness it offers little. A chunk of biscuit baked brick hard, a small tube of unknown liquid and a handful of gems, tiny and sharp. He pockets them all.

Harm's voice sends ripples through the silence. 'Are you alright? Kick once for yes, twice for no.'

The Vagrant kicks once, then once more.

'Are you injured?'

Two kicks.

'Stuck?'

Two kicks.

'Something else?'

A kick.

'Do you need help?'

A pause. One kick, then two.

'Sorry, I don't understand. I've tried moving these rocks but they're stuck fast. The others have gone so there must be a way out. Are you ready to go?'

Two kicks.

'Oh.'

Harm talks on, wondering about what to do, where to go and if they will be able to get out. Eventually he notices the Vagrant has stopped kicking, and the goat has stopped trying to bite him. He asks another question.

Nobody answers, they are too busy sleeping.

* * *

On the far side of the mountains, a man emerges from a cave, peering left and right before sneaking into the night. He is unremarkable, not the one.

The Hammer that Walks lets him go.

It is within reach, she feels it, hidden nearby.

Hatred swells within her and something else. A memory of dissonant beauty that demands attention. In her mind she sees the Shadowmarket, the squealing rabble, all noisy sacks of fear. Pathetic. But then amid it all there is the coin singing through the air. Captivating. Beautiful.

Able to bear it no longer, she begins to climb.

The ragged woman is easy to find, her shack only hidden from the ground. Like all the unblessed she is slow and predictable. Believing herself alone, the old woman examines the coin, dancing it across her fingers. It winks invitingly at the giant Usurperkin.

With one blow the Hammer changes her. Bones crack and fall, forming a humble pile of sticks.

The Hammer digs out the coin and throws it, head tilting back as it ascends and down as it thunks against her hand.

It does not turn or trill for her.

Disappointed fingers curl around the silver disc. She holds it close like a mother and returns to her post. Waiting. Stone still.

CHAPTER FIFTEEN

The Vagrant sits up. His muscles compete for stiffness, tingling awake, complaining. At his side, the body is cold.

He kicks out, finding his companions in the dark.

'Welcome back,' says Harm dryly. 'Are you ready to go now?'

He kicks once and they go, feeling their way on hands and knees until they find the back of the cave where two circular tunnels sit side by side, empty eye sockets waiting to be filled.

'Which way?'

The Vagrant shrugs, disturbing the baby, who resettles against his side, grumbling.

Harm takes them through the left passage.

The rock is smooth beneath their knees, stroking their backs with gentle undulations. In places there are holes, fist sized, randomly scattered. A smell issues from them, pungent with life. The passage takes them deeper, sloping down until their crawl becomes a shuffling descent.

145

Muffled sounds drift towards them, like men humming through a gag.

Harm is the first to find them. Two figures quiver with fear, wrapped side by side in a film of softly glowing fungus. The sight startles him and he slides closer, involuntarily, lurching forward with both hands. Palms squelch against wetness that adheres to his skin. He pulls one hand away and feels resistance, strands of sweaty web tethering him to the other men.

'I need help,' he hisses. The men hear his voice and try to answer, blowing fear-thick bubbles in the living wrap. Their struggles shake the fungus, sending tremors along its surface. 'I'm stuck, help me!'

The Vagrant works his way down, juggling his burdens.

A new sound can be heard from the fist-sized holes, hundreds of tiny fingernails drumming on stone, closing quickly.

Harm pulls against his bonds. They stretch but do not break, holding him fast. 'Hurry, please!'

Sword in hand the Vagrant arrives at Harm's side. He slices down, locating the strands by their soft light. They release the green-eyed man, snagging the blade instead. The Vagrant twists the sword, trying to free it.

From holes by his feet, above his head and by his shoulders, things scuttle. They sound like severed hands, long nailed, moving with alien purpose. Fortunately it is too dark to see their true form.

Harm propels himself back up the tunnel but his escape is blocked by the goat. She is stuck. She cannot climb backwards, cannot turn round, will not go forward. A cork in a bottle, scared and angry.

Silvered wings twitch at the sword's hilt and smoke plumes

upwards where fungus and steel touch. The Vagrant is free. He jumps back, shapes falling around him, bumping against his elbow, rolling over his boots. He jumps back again, head knocking against low stone. The crawlers do not follow, swarming instead for the trapped men, who are forced to wait, trembling. He looks away quickly and joins the others. Behind him, the fungal glow dims, blotted out by a blanket of nightmares.

Harm grabs at his shoulder. 'We're trapped!'

The Vagrant shrugs off his hand, sheathes the sword. He passes the baby over and climbs past Harm to the trembling goat. He does not need to see to know her expression. Taking a deep breath, he finds her shoulders with his hands and pushes. The going is slow, every inch painful. Limbs already taxed to their limits burn with outrage at this new demand.

The goat's teeth snap the air, catching the Vagrant's ear on the third attempt.

Bleating, bleeding, crying, they tumble from the tunnel back into the original cave.

This time, Harm takes the right tunnel.

Like the previous passage, this too has been made by a wild Burrowmaw. It takes them on a gentle curve to the right. The Vagrant runs his hand along the wall as he crawls, checking for holes.

Ahead, a splinter of red light shines from a crack in the ceiling. It is fresh-made by the Hammer's assault, dust forming miniature mountain ranges on the floor beneath. They follow it gratefully and it widens, rewarding them with a view of the sky.

'Let's climb out here,' says Harm. 'These tunnels will kill us.'

The Vagrant agrees.

It is a short and brutal journey. The two men manage the climb with grunting ease, passing between them the baby, who contemplates sky and suns and other unknowable things.

They pull up the goat with a rope. She sways slowly, comments rarely, dark eyes seething, planning revenge.

When all are safely out, Harm, baby and Vagrant lie side by side, fatigue plastering them to the fat ledge. Only one of them moves, stretching for the sky itself. Clouds delight and slip through fingers, an endless parade of gods and monsters.

The Vagrant watches the little head, flitting left and right, enraptured. He sees a patch of skin, reddened and raised through the downy black hair. The Vagrant closes his eyes, pinches the bridge of his nose. His lips move, cursing himself. He bends down, planting the softest of kisses on the baby's head.

When the suns set, the group huddles together for warmth. Harm opens up the stolen sack, sharing the joyless food inside.

Reluctantly the Vagrant accepts. He frowns as he eats.

'You don't agree with what I did,' says Harm. It is not a question. 'I'm sorry but we didn't have much time. If I hadn't taken her things, we'd be starving now.'

The Vagrant shrugs.

'Tell me, why are they following you? What do you have that they want so badly?' He looks from baby to sword, to the Vagrant, weighing each one. Tired amber meets soft green, then breaks away. 'It's your sword. You must be the only Seraph Knight left this side of the Southern Sea. It's a symbol. No, more than that. Is it alive? I swear it watches me sometimes.'

Both men glance at the sword, inert in its scabbard and Harm is suddenly eager to change the subject. 'Can I ask you a personal question?'

This time, the shrug is wary.

'Your baby, does she have a name?'

Lines appear on the Vagrant's face, sorrowful, adding years. His mouth opens, closes again. He begins to nod, shakes his head. Defeated, he covers his head with his hands.

'Everyone should have a name,' says Harm softly. 'Perhaps I could help you choose one.'

The Vagrant gives no sign of having heard.

Harm leans over the baby, distracting it from the stars that sparkle, too distant. 'Let us see if we can find a name that you like. Let me know if any of these work for you: Seran, Baylis, Leoni. Any thoughts?'

Eyes wide, the baby waves its tongue in a circle, from nose to chin and back again.

More names are offered. The baby seems unmoved. Eventually, the goat falls asleep.

Green eyes glint. 'What about Vesper?'

Hands fall from the Vagrant's face, revealing disbelief, naked, shocked.

The baby blinks, drool running past its chin.

'I'll take that as a yes.' He shakes the baby's hand, eliciting a long gurgling noise. 'Pleased to meet you, Vesper, I'm Harm.'

Eight Years Ago

The infernal horde surges north under the Usurper's order. A river of essence surrounds them, made of those that were too big or too unfortunate to find a host body, who lost integrity and blended with other unfortunates into a single unconscious, a soup of blood and failure. Known as the taint, it flows around the horde's feet, around claws and other, less recognizable limbs as they thunder across the landscape. Where it touches native plants and creatures it infuses them with infernal essence, changing them, corrupting and enhancing, sewing a path of half-bred corruption in its wake. In time, the strongest of these mutations will spread far, shattering an already troubled ecosystem.

The suns glare down at the horde, slowly eroding dead shells and making smoke dance where essence is exposed. From a distance individual horrors blend into one mass, their shapes blurred within the taint, indefinable, maddening. Over time, however, patterns emerge. Greater infernals that collect lesser terrors in their orbit. All bound to the Usurper, all seeking Gamma's fallen sword, the Malice.

At their head is the Uncivil. Unlike the others she does not inhabit a single host body, instead wrapping her essence in a cloak of corpses. Unlike the others, she has space for thoughts of her own, of rebellion. She cannot disobey the Usurper, its majesty is stamped within her core, indelible. But its orders are simple, given in haste and pain. Pursue the Malice! Destroy it! The Uncivil dares to dream that perhaps, perhaps, there is room for other things too. Her own desires bubble close to the surface, unformed and insistent, like a child's, more emotion than direction. She wishes for independence. She does not yet care how she spends it.

Each time the horde passes through a settlement, a piece breaks away. The lesser infernals are easily distracted, always hungry. The stronger ones see opportunities for better shells and some wonder if perhaps the Malice is hidden somewhere among the squealing, pink-faced mortals.

Always the Uncivil presses on. Overtly pursuing the Malice. Secretly running from the Usurper.

As distance and flesh is devoured, the Uncivil begins to notice something. The horde is slowing down. Little by little she begins to stretch ahead of the others.

When they reach the city of Horizon the horde breaks on its gates like a wave on the cliffs. For the first time since the Battle of the Red Wave, resistance is met. Horizon has its own sky-ship, along with a rag tag reserve of defenders. Neither these nor the gates stop the horde for long. The sky-ship is overrun and sent plunging into the streets, the defenders are shredded, pushed aside, as are the gates. In the end it is the city of Horizon itself that stops the horde's advance. There are too many lights, too many temptations. Overwhelmed by possibility, a full third of the invading force is sucked up within Horizon's pores.

The Uncivil presses on with the remaining army, trailing flames and mortal screams.

Here, the land opens up. There is no obvious way on, no path to follow. The horde begins to falter. The further they go from the sanctity of the Breach the more sluggish the taint becomes, thinning at their feet. Comfort is but a memory now, each step taking them deeper into a place that neither wants nor needs them.

Soon, the Uncivil leaves them behind, fragmenting, poisoning.

Though the Usurper's orders remain a constant, looping through her (Pursue the Malice! Destroy it!), she is able to notice other things: the shape of a flower, open, that pleases her. The call of a bird that does not. Away from the other infernals, she has space to breathe, to be. This too pleases her.

Time and travel begin to take their toll. Her cloak of corpses starts to break down. Dead flesh flakes away, old tendons wear thin and cracks appear in bonded bones. The Uncivil diverts from her course, seeking fresh material for her shell.

She soon finds them. A group of mortal children stand together, curled hands joining them. They skip round each other, a bouncing, singing circle. Earnest frowns testify to their effort.

'The eye is in the circle,
The wings surround the circle,

153

They watch you,
They judge you.
We all bow down!'

The words mean nothing to the Uncivil, though she does not like the way the song gathers their essence, threatening to join them into something greater, terrifying.

The Uncivil pauses, preparing for flight. But the song is just a song, a misremembered echo of something lost long ago. Skipping slows, voices quieten, the song has no hold on their essence.

From within her cloak, the Uncivil extends half of a ribcage, mounted on a thick cable of femurs. The limb is a mockery, more rake than hand.

She begins to spin, going faster and faster, until the teeth that stud her shell rattle like a thousand broken bells, dull and dolorous.

Song forgotten, the children fall to making sounds of simpler, more primal communications.

Rolling between them swiftly, harvesting, the Uncivil quietens them. Bodies fall, one by one, until silence descends. The wind stops, aghast as the Uncivil prepares to assimilate the bodies.

But there is a problem. As the Uncivil parts her cloak to make space for the new corpses, pain drives in through the gap. This far north, the very air is hostile. Where it touches her, essence fragments.

Sealing the cloak once more, the Uncivil sits and broods. She needs help. She cannot survive this far north for long but dares not return south for fear of falling further under the Usurper's power.

A noise disturbs her. One of the children is not dead. She

rolls herself to the source of the sound to examine the child in more detail. A neck twitches, muscles responding to half-formed impulses.

The Uncivil extends her limb once more, matching it to the dozen holes recently made in the child's side, and presses in. Safely under the quivering flesh, the Uncivil extends her essence. The child's own essence is weak and strange. Hard, fixed, limited. The Uncivil rolls it around like a marble in the mouth, tasting.

She reads many things there. Fear, anger, bitterness, the desire to live. Familiar things. A plan begins to form.

The child dies.

The Uncivil gathers the bodies with her bone rake and rolls on.

The next mortal the Uncivil meets is an old man. They talk. She gives him a new leg, powered by a shred of her essence, linked by threads to his. In return he helps add the children's corpses to her shell.

They continue north together.

Soon, others join them.

Her gifts eventually fail, but the Uncivil is always happy to repair her faithful and they in turn are happy to maintain her. The Usurper's orders are still followed; she remains alert for the Malice. But in the main, the hunt is given over to her agents, making room for her own plans, making room for rebellion.

They set off early, making their slow way down the mountainside. The Vagrant lags often, the goat dragging him along, gleefully. By midmorning they are on solid ground, plodding north.

Several miles behind, a mountaintop moves, detaching itself, a weighty shadow, bounding and sliding in pursuit. Landing, it breaks into a run, swallowing the distance between it and the unsuspecting group. Even far away it appears large. They only have to turn to see it. They do not.

'Have you ever been to Slake before?' asks Harm.

The Vagrant shakes his head.

'I've not either but I've heard some very bad things. Even so, it would be better if we got supplies in Slake and miss out Wonderland altogether. I was there a few years ago.' His voice drops to a mutter. 'It's a long story.'

The Vagrant nudges him.

'It's too dangerous for us. Babies are in demand there and it's virtually impossible to hide. They say the Uncivil knows everything that happens within its walls. A man once swore to me that if you stay too long she eats your dreams.'

The Vagrant raises an eyebrow.

'I know it's not true!'

'Wuuuue!'

The unexpected sound stops both men dead. They look at each other then slowly turn to the innocent looking bundle in Harm's arms.

'Wuuuue!'

Amazed smiles shine on the baby's upturned face.

'Seems she knows it too.'

'Ooooo!' says Vesper. 'Oooooowuuuuuueooooooooo!'

'Yes! Good, very good. What else can you say? Can you say: Harm?'

'Ooooo!'

'That'll do for now.' Harm leans closer, whispering in

156

Vesper's ear. 'I'm glad you've decided to pitch in. It takes the pressure off me.'

The Vagrant takes Vesper under the arms, throwing her high and catching her. Happy squeals rise and fall several times, voicing approval, wanting more.

On the fourth throw, the sword joins in, humming along.

Frowning, the Vagrant looks back.

The Hammer that Walks is close now, each blink making her double in size. They are in open ground, exposed and without sanctuary and they are tired. There is little to do.

Harm takes back the baby, who begins to cry.

The Vagrant draws the sword, holding it forward, ready. He glances over at the green-eyed man, mouthing a message.

'Leave you again? I . . . I don't know.'

The glance becomes a glare but they are out of time.

The Hammer arrives, legs drumming the ground, storming towards the Vagrant.

The sword's tip bows forward, pointing towards the Hammer's chest.

Ten great strides separate them, then nine, eight, seven, six, and she jumps high, higher, over the Vagrant's head, defying gravity, a sky-scraping tank.

Sword and Vagrant watch the giant shadows sail past, agog.

She lands behind him, pressing forwards towards an open mouthed goat.

Harm finds he can run after all, urged along by the leash on his wrist. He might as well race the wind.

The Hammer skids up behind him, ploughing a wave of dust. She taps the back of his legs lightly with a steel clad foot, cracking bone.

Harm blacks out, falls, the baby spilling from his arms.

The goat keeps going, dragging the green-eyed man behind her.

Fatigue forgotten, the Vagrant races after, sword building to a roar. His strike lands on the Hammer's raised forearm, shield broad. Light flashes blue, blackening the Hammer's bracer.

With her other hand she smacks the flat of the sword side on, ripping it from the Vagrant's grip. The blade spins through the air, eye rolling in fury, impotent. It clatters to the ground ten feet away.

Unarmed, the Vagrant squares up to his opponent. Next to her towering form, he looks like a child. Taking a deep breath he raises his fists, managing to dodge the first sweep of her arm. The second takes him by the throat, lifting him up and up, until their eyes draw level.

He cannot break her hold. He tries anyway, pulling till veins bulge.

She squeezes and holds his gaze until amber eyes close and arms droop. Satisfied, the Hammer slings the Vagrant over her shoulder and collects the sword. Ignoring the bubbling hiss of metal and sudden warmth on her gauntlet, she marches south, back towards the mountains, taking her prize to the Usurper.

CHAPTER SIXTEEN

The goat pulls frantically, backing away as fast as she can. Death is coming, angry and quick. She must escape! Her legs scrabble in the dust, working for every inch of ground. It is impossible, the man tied to her is too heavy.

She bleats with fear and venom.

Nearby, the baby cries. The goat flicks her ears in annoyance. But no other sounds are apparent. And she has not been eaten.

She looks up.

The big death is leaving, taking that man with it. She watches it go, head on one side, waiting until they are small shapes far away. Then, with uncharacteristic energy she snaps up her leash and chews.

And chews.

And chews.

The Vagrant twitches, his face a dreaming mask, tormented. Eyes fly open and he sucks in a breath. Above, two suns dance slowly round each other, glimpsed in gaps between clouds. It is afternoon. He brings two fingers to his neck, gingerly touching reddened skin. About his legs snakes a length of broken pipe, made string in the Hammer's fingers and tied in a crude knot.

His captor squats nearby, hunched forward, hiding something from sight.

The Vagrant pushes up onto his elbows, looks about. The ledge appears much like the one he recently rested on. He and the Hammer are alone. There is no sign or sound of Vesper or Harm or even the goat. He closes his eyes, covering his face with quick hands to hide the trembling.

Three slow breaths come and go, then hands lower, revealing features firm, resigned.

He tries to pull the pipe from his legs but the metal has recovered from the Hammer's molestations and refuses to budge. Then he spies the sword. It lies next to the Hammer, smoking with rage. Its hilt points towards the Vagrant.

He rolls onto his front, using his elbows to inch forward. Each drag of his body over rough stone sounds like an avalanche, each breath a declaration of intent.

The Hammer remains distracted. She does not hear or does not care.

He sees now that she attends to something small. With a stifled grunt he pushes himself up on his palms, stretching to see over the wall of her thigh.

A coin sits, like a star in the night of her palm. She throws it awkwardly and it lands, clunking, dull. Her great shoulders sag.

The Vagrant edges to the sword. Lowering his body to the ground he stretches for it.

Fingertips brush the hilt.

The Hammer twists round.

The Vagrant closes his eyes. He feels something grasp the back of his coat and then he is moving, skidding on his chest.

The Hammer leaps after him, grabbing him one fisted, pressing him against the mountainside.

His bound legs swing together, useless, tapping on armoured thighs.

Snarling with rage, the Hammer curls her fingers tight and pulls back to strike.

The Vagrant raises a hand in front of his face. In it, he holds a coin.

The Hammer's blow freezes in the air.

Wheezing, the Vagrant tosses the coin. For him it sings. Silver light dances in the Hammer's eyes and anger melts from her face, forgotten. He catches, tosses it again and she watches, enraptured. Oxygen starved hands fumble the catch.

As one they look at the fallen coin, then back at each other.

The Vagrant swallows.

The Hammer's head turns, indicating her ready fist, then goes back to the Vagrant. She uncurls her fingers and lowers him to the ground, releasing her grip on his chest. She towers over him as he gasps in air, then picks up the coin and drops it into his open hand.

He looks up at her.

Her voice is gravel spinning in a bin. 'More!'

Nodding slowly, he tosses the coin again.

At the sound, tension falls from her. She sits opposite the Vagrant, eyes only on spinning silver. 'More!'

Time passes and the coin leaps up, again and again.

The Hammer takes her own coin and tries to mirror the man before her but her thick, metal clad fingers are unequal to the task. She roars with anger.

The Vagrant stops.

She notices immediately. 'More!'

The Vagrant shakes his head.

'More!'

The Vagrant points to the pipe binding his feet.

The Hammer raises her fist. 'More!'

The Vagrant shakes his head.

Her blow drives sense from his world and for a time the Vagrant dreams, restless.

He wakes to an eye swollen shut and a gap where a tooth once sat. The pipe is gone from his legs.

The Hammer leans over him. 'More?'

He nods.

The coin dances three times, then stops.

The Hammer's small eyes narrow. 'More?'

He beckons her closer. She comes.

He points to her coin. Puzzled, she lifts her hand to him, open, disc shining on her outstretched fingers. He nods and taps his own coin against it.

Reunited, the silver sisters sing. The duet haunts the ears, stirring regrets and things lost.

When it ends the Vagrant puts his coin into her other hand.

Her eyes glisten, water growing at their edges. 'Mine?'

The Vagrant nods.

She smiles, a girlish expression sketched from monstrous

jaws, and touches one to the other. Together, they sing for her.

The Vagrant risks standing up. There is no retaliation. He walks to where the sword lies, glances back to his captor. Her eyes are fixed on the coins, quivering beautifully in her hands. He sighs, picks up the sword.

The point drifts towards the hulking figure, lining up with her neck.

He walks carefully, quietly, until he stands behind her.

She touches the coins together a second time, starting another song. Massive shoulders shake and she underscores the melody with rasping sobs.

The Vagrant sighs again, forcing the sword back into its sheath. Wiping memories from his eyes, he turns and walks to the mountain path, beginning the long descent.

In Verdigris, two rebels march. One on each side of the street, brother on the left, sister on the right, both Usurperkin, both full of purpose. People gather in doorways, watching them in stunned silence. At each building the scarred giants grapple with the signs they find there and tear them down.

Behind them, littering the street, banners to the Uncivil and the Usurper lie, united at last in the dust, trampled by the people that follow.

Defiant chants fill the air.

Three streets away, lost in the cacophony, a man cries in fear. He has seen something emerge into the afternoon. Something dangerous that threatens the rebels' fragile victory. He rushes to tell his neighbour and his story grows wings, rushing ahead in a wave of whispers, carried by running feet, dashing from mouth to ear. It comes at last to a small boy who overtakes the procession, waving his hands to get the Usurperkins' attention.

'Max! Maxi!' he calls.

Two scar-painted heads recognize their names, turn. Muscles tense under green skin, hearing trouble in the boy's tone.

'Tough Call needs you at the north gate right now! Bring everyone!'

The boy runs off, pulling the giants and their followers with him like a black hole with dirty feet.

When they reach the gate they find a crowd blocking the way, thick and brazen, bristling with guns. They cheer a welcome. Max and Maxi cheer back. Like two bubbles, the groups meet, coming together, sharing borders, expanding.

Weaving between the crowd, a part and apart, is a man dressed in loose and stripy robes. His voice darts to and fro, ducking under shouts and oiling over dissent. He finds a woman, seasoned by life, proud. Hiding his shark's smile, he begins:

'Ah, friend, you have a most magnificent gun I see. But what does a gun make you but a killer? No, any fool sees you are more than that, you are one of Verdigris' true children, standing to be counted. Surely Ezze finds himself before a great soldier, yes? One of Tough Call's army? But what is a soldier without a uniform? I tell you, friend, you are in luck, for Ezze has with him armbands decorated with the "V" of the new order. Each is sewn by rebel children born beneath the city in darkness and is of the highest quality. They come in many colours. Your choice, friend!

Price? Ezze could not possibly take payment, this is his honour! But . . . there is a ring on your finger, from the old order, yes? Such a thing diminishes you. Ezze will take it, replace it with this fine symbol of hope. Wear it and be proud!'

The exchange is quick and the man fades away before the bitter taste can set in.

Max and Maxi's heads bob above the crowd, two green ships in a people sea. They search for their leader but cannot see her.

A boy runs into view, arms like pistons, face like clean bone. 'The Knights of Jade and Ash are coming!' He is smart, does not join the crowd, running past, becoming obscure.

Max and Maxi move to the front. They turn; the sister raises her voice: 'Is this our city?'

'Yes!'

'Did you fight for it?'

'Yes!'

'Will you fight again?'

'Yes!'

'And will you win?'

'Yes!'

'I said,' she bellows, 'will we win?'

'Yes!' they shout. 'Yes! Yes! Yes!'

From around a corner comes the sound of clanking armour, at which the crowd's chanting falters to a murmur. A figure steps out in front of them and a feeling of dread leeches into the waiting army. Four more knights join the first, their armour writhing as if trying to escape its host, stretching and straining and collapsing back into shape. Endlessly, hopelessly.

The crowd's front line trembles, guns point uncertainly toward the knights.

'Hey down there!' shouts Tough Call, leaning from a high window.

The knights march on, heedless.

In her only hand the woman holds a rocket launcher. Soot clings to the filigree around the barrel. 'I'd stop if I were you.'

Three feet from the crowd, the knights pause.

The rebels are forced to gaze at their enemies. They do not recognize their fallen champions within the pitted, breathing metal. Quietly, they despair.

From her perch, Tough Call has strength to share. 'That's better,' she continues. 'Everyone, let them through, and somebody open the gates!'

A ragged path opens as the crowd pulls back.

'Just so there's no misunderstanding, I am a hundred per cent behind you leaving Verdigris. But if you so much as threaten any of my people or try and come back, know that we'll be waiting for you.'

There is a pause, lengthy. The knights are fathomless, impossible to read. People begin to sweat. A gauntlet moves to grasp a warped hilt. Four others echo the gesture.

'Just give me an excuse,' says Tough Call, watching them through winged sights. Led by her example, scores of guns find their courage, clicking in salute, ready.

Turning slowly, the knights take in their opponents, measuring each one. Every individual feels their images being taken, burned into alien memory. Then, swords still sheathed, the knights march from Verdigris.

Tough Call punches the air and the rebels cheer, drawing

warmth from each other. They shout and laugh till the knights are tiny dolls in the distance. With a bang, the north gate closes, unable to shut out the secret dread flowering in their hearts.

CHAPTER SEVENTEEN

Stones slip underfoot, under fingers. The mountain is keen to move the Vagrant on. He stays upright, mostly. Skating and stumbling, making his way down. At his side, the sword thrums a warning. The Vagrant stops and half draws the weapon. It stares back up the mountainside. He follows the arrow of its gaze.

Keeping her distance, nestled in the rocks, he sees the Hammer. Amber eyes seek the sky briefly, asking hard questions.

The sky does not care to answer.

He continues his descent, pausing sometimes to raise the scope to his eye, scanning the flatlands below. It is a clear day and the small round screen soon finds Harm's body, bringing it close. Vesper is next to him, hands and feet drawing circles in the air. A half smile finds its way onto the Vagrant's face. He puts the scope away and heads towards the distant speck. The sword growls softly all the way.

By late evening he arrives.

From his back, Harm raises a hand in greeting. 'I can't believe it! You're alive!'

The Vagrant nods and squats next to Vesper. Toes are tickled, smiles exchanged. The Vagrant sniffs the air and leans back, wrinkling his nose.

Vesper giggles.

'She needs a change,' Harm adds needlessly. 'You'll have to do it. When you're done, can you look at my leg? I think it's broken.'

The Vagrant gets to work. Soiled clothes are removed. Naked legs pedal with increased vigour. The Vagrant starts cleaning, then reaches for something that isn't there. He stops mid-motion. A frown dawns.

'Your goat's run away,' says Harm. 'And she's taken our supplies with her.'

Still frowning, the Vagrant removes his scarf and wraps Vesper in it.

'She'll need feeding soon. We all will. Do you have a plan?'

The Vagrant doesn't answer, crawling over to examine Harm's leg.

'How does it look?'

The green-eyed man studies the silence. 'Oh. Isn't there anything you can do?' The Vagrant presses his lips together, his face paling. 'Please, help me!'

'EeeeeEEEEeee!' says Vesper.

The Vagrant gives a tiny shake of his head and shuffles backwards.

Desperation and adrenaline give Harm strength. He pushes up on his elbows. 'Look at me. My leg's ruined, maybe for good. Without help I'll die out here. Please, I need you, I . . .' He trails off, eyes widening. '. . . You didn't kill the Hammer did you?'

The Vagrant shakes his head.

'She's followed you here.'

The Vagrant nods.

Harm instinctively tries to flee. Pain punishes his forgetfulness and he falls onto his back again.

The Hammer that Walks stands in the open a hundred feet away. Conflicted muscles twist in her face, mashing expressions together, while her hands make fists, uncommitted.

By contrast, Vesper knows her mind. She shrieks and cries with fear. The sound soon moves up, finds comfort in the Vagrant's arms, is softened by his coat.

The Vagrant waits, free hand brushing the sword's hilt.

With neither side willing to act, time passes. The suns dip lower, stretching shadows till the Vagrant's shade touches the Hammer's boots.

Then, without warning, she lumbers forward, her strides devouring distance, planting herself in front of the Vagrant. With a creak she bends down, a menacing cliff, bringing her face inches from his.

'Why?' she rasps.

The Vagrant blinks surprise.

She holds up her fists, opens them. Inside each sits a round, flat, silver eye. 'Why?'

From behind them, Harm speaks. 'You want to know why he gave you the coins?'

'Yes.'

The Vagrant looks at Vesper, then less certainly, at the green-eyed man.

Harm answers for him. 'He doesn't want to fight you, he just wants to be left alone. But you haven't come here to fight us.'

The Hammer's answer is more whisper than words. 'No.'

'You're confused. I know what that's like. He did the same to me.' Harm ignores the Vagrant's silent question, keeps his focus on the giant Usurperkin. 'I used to live in Verdigris but I left that life behind to follow a rogue Seraph and his baby. When I stop to think about it, I realize it's madness but I don't care. This new life is many things but it's not poison.'

The Hammer edges forward, passing the Vagrant, drawn to Harm's words, a flame-struck moth.

'Everything changed for me when I met them. It's like I was sleeping through my life, carried along by the currents, and then all of a sudden I see somebody going the other way. I didn't even know there was another way. And now I've seen it, I can't stop wondering what it might be like to live differently, to be something else. You understand. I know. I could be telling your story instead of mine. For me, it began with a simple choice. It's the same for you. You could kill us now if you wanted. I'm already crippled and he's tired, so very tired. It would be easy for you. But if you do, you'll be alone.'

Thin tears spill from the Hammer's eyes. They struggle over cheeks riveted in metal and die before they reach her chin. She takes the coins and tucks them behind her wrist guard. Hands free, she reaches for Harm's leg, straightening it. The injured man screams.

'No,' says the Hammer. It is an order.

Harm bites down on his sleeve while his other hand claws at the dirt beneath, digging shallow trenches.

The Hammer pulls at the bracer on her left arm till rivets scream and submit. Then she drops to one knee, placing the metal across her armoured thigh. She begins to beat it with

172

her fist, rhythmic strikes that ring out, bouncing off distant mountains.

Vesper ventures a worried glance from the Vagrant's armpit. Gradually fear is replaced by curiosity, which in turn falls to hunger. A small mouth opens, expectant. The milk however, has run away. Seeing the impending storm, the Vagrant rocks the baby but Vesper only wrinkles her nose, unimpressed.

The Hammer stops, grunting in satisfaction. The bracer has become a rough, unsealed tube. She places it around Harm's injured leg and squeezes it snug.

'Up,' she says.

'I can't,' Harm replies. 'It's too painful.'

'Up!'

He tries to comply, moving awkwardly into a sitting position.

'Up!' demands the Hammer, putting one hand around his ribs and lifting him to his feet. She grins with monolithic teeth. 'Yes!'

'. . . Thank you.'

The Vagrant offers his shoulder and Harm throws an arm over it. Together the two men leave. The Hammer watches, wearing the posture of someone smaller, more innocent. She sees one whispering in the ear of the other, a monologue broken by occasional gasps. They stop and the Vagrant's head tilts upwards, shaking gently from left to right. The other turns back, regarding her gently.

They walk on, and after a pause, she follows.

Seven Years Ago

When the Usurper hears of the Uncivil's rebellion the response is swift. Flies spread word of the Green Sun's displeasure, carrying the taste of bile far and wide, seeking out still-loyal subjects to find and drag the Uncivil back to the Fallen Palace.

The Earmaker's Three are the first to respond. Not exactly siblings, the trio of infernals are cut from the same cloth: hook wielding hunters, known more for what they do after a killing than before.

The Uncivil waits for them in Verdigris, and she is not alone. Her cult grows swiftly. New people come every day, her promises of augmentation and immortality too much to resist.

The Uncivil's trail is not hidden and the Earmaker's Three follow it, through open gates and empty streets. The city's population hides away behind closed doors, or in tunnels, deep and old. They know this is a spectacle best viewed from a distance. The truly wise turn away completely, and sleep the better for it.

They find her in a deserted market square. The Earmaker's Three pause as she comes into view. While the northern climate stifles them, the Uncivil sits comfortably within her shell, blossoming, safe. Her cloak is thick with new sacrifices. On its surface, a hundred dead eyes swivel to take in her opponents, and finds them wanting.

Around her, her Half-alive cult gather proudly. Normally they hide their gifts beneath perfumed robes, to disturb rather than terrify their unaltered fellows. Now they stand revealed, grafted limbs waving beneath a repulsed sky.

The Earmaker's Three ready their curling hooks and stir the poisons in their neck folds.

A silence gathers. The Three spread out, trying to flank the Uncivil's position.

From the cloak of corpses, half of a ribcage extends, beckoning them closer, the gesture almost human, almost charming.

Spindly legs carry the Three forward, like scurrying spiders. Their hooks flash out, all three finding a home in the Uncivil's shell. They each pull in a different direction, trying to split the cloak of corpses. Three lines tug tight and woven bodies creak like old boards, threatening to tear asunder.

But the Uncivil does not need to endure long. Her Half-alive followers answer with barbs of their own. Tentacles and nature-defying limbs of alien design wrap around the Earmaker's Three. For each of the infernals, the Uncivil has a dozen of her own servants.

The Earmaker's Three are pushed on the defensive. They try and pull their hooks free to use on the new threat but they are held fast by the Uncivil. Trapped in a web of reanimated limbs, they begin to panic. Venom spurts from their thin mouths, most of it wasted on the earth.

Before they can break free, the Uncivil twists, pulling them all to her. Once they are reeled in close, the cloak of corpses animates. Lone fingers, hands, jaws, all tear at the trapped infernals while, at their backs, the cult beat and tear and twist.

It is soon over and the Half-alive humans retreat, awaiting further command.

The Earmaker's Three remain tethered to the Uncivil's shell, their bodies broken, mist leaking in wheezy clouds from multiple holes. As their essences fade the Uncivil reaches out to them and, briefly, four become one.

'We hate-fear-hate you!'

'Hate-hate-fear you!'

'Fear-fear-hate you!'

'I am the Uncivil and I am free. You are neither and never will be and yet I give you a choice.'

'What is this?'

'What are these words?'

'We don't understand.'

'Live and die as the Usurper's creatures or exist as mine.'

'We fear the Usurper more than you.'

'Then die.'

'Wait!'

'Wait!'

'Wait!'

'Don't be hasty.'

'Tell us more.'

'We are listening.'

'Your individual essences are bound to Ammag, the Green Sun, Usurper of all. They wane, they die. I will save your scraps and bond you to each other and to me. I will give you life free of Ammag's power.'

'But slave to you?'

'Exiled like you?'

'Hunted like you?'

'Yes, all of these. But you will continue.'

'We accept.'

'We do.'

'We do.'

She takes them from the streets, to a secret place, hidden from the stars. There she weaves their essences together into a patchwork, a new composite being. She gives it a body to match, with too many faces, each with too many teeth.

CHAPTER EIGHTEEN

Of all the beasts and people in the line, the goat is among the smallest. This fact does not concern the goat. Despite capture she kicks and bites anything foolish enough to get close. The trait endears her to the meat runners, who dub her 'Grim Beard' and chuckle each time she makes a larger animal squeal.

Six people drive the caravan, a mix of ages, men and women. Shared genes and lifestyle give them a similar look. Hard-nosed, tough like weathered stone. They keep an economic pace on the way to Slake, eating only what they need, feeding their charges just enough to maintain weight. Calorie control calculated for maximum profit.

The giant Usurperkin overtakes them easily, planting herself between them and their destination. Cradled in the crook of her arm is a man. His green eyes are soft, if not kind.

'Good morning,' he says quietly. 'We've come to collect a goat.'

A meat runner steps forward, thin lips cutting a smile across her cheek. 'You're in luck. We've got one. Untainted and full of spirit. You see her there?'

'Yes.'

'You want her?'

'Yes, that's the one.'

'What do you have to trade?'

Harm pauses, keeps his voice low. 'We haven't come to trade. The goat belongs to us.'

'I don't think so. The animal is wild. My own son found her, masterless and alone.'

'Then he also found our possessions strapped to her back. Food and trade goods. We want those too.'

The meat runner turns to her son, does not like what she discovers on his face. 'I'm sure we can gather and return your things, minus a little compensation for looking after them.'

'I don't think so.'

'It's a fair offer, more than fair.'

The Hammer steps forward, naturally threatening.

In response, six people reach for concealed weapons together, like slivers of the same glass. 'We can protect what's ours!' shouts the son, defiant.

'Good,' replies the Hammer.

The meat runner puts a hand on her son's arm. 'Wait! Wait. We accept your terms.'

A sack and a goat are brought forward, deposited in the space between parties. The Hammer lifts the sack, shakes it. 'More.'

Meat runners confer in swift whispers, except for the son, whose voice breaks confidence with the others. 'That's all there was, I swear!'

180

'More!' demands the Usurper's Daughter.

'She's running out of patience,' Harm adds. 'I suggest you give us what we want or she'll kill you all, starting with the smallest and working up.'

The meat runner is quick to appease but her son protests. 'You can't let them rob us like this!'

'Yes,' she hisses. 'I can. Which of your brothers is worth your pride? Name one and I'll fight.'

No names are given and weapons slide back into sheaths. Another sack is prepared and left with the first.

Harm appraises the new offering. 'Now this is more than fair!' He notices the Vagrant approaching and gentles his expression. 'We were right,' he says. 'They were traders. And look who we found.' He indicates the goat. 'Good news for once.'

The Vagrant's eyes move across the people, over tight mouths and fear-pale faces, lingering on a meat runner whose fist trembles by his side. He looks back at Harm, holding his gaze till red blooms on the other man's cheeks. Vesper shifts restlessly against his side.

A precious coin appears from the Vagrant's pockets, instantly grabbing the Hammer's attention. Ignoring her, the Vagrant walks to where the meat runners stand. He takes the son's fist, unpeels, soothes with silver. Stammered thanks are acknowledged with a nod and the Vagrant takes up the goat's chain, striding away. Scooping up sacks one handed, the Hammer follows, her face shuffling between confusion and anger.

When they are gone, son turns to mother wide-eyed. 'Look! Look what he gave me! It must be worth a fortune!'

'Yes it is, even more than the coin.'

'Eh? What are you talking about, mother?'

'The world has always been made of hard edges but it used to have other things too.'

'I don't understand.'

'You will one day.'

'I can keep the coin though? He gave it to me. And I found that goat in the first place!'

She sighs. 'Or maybe you won't.'

From a distance, Slake is a sprawling mass of vertical pipes, a giant cage topped by a smog canopy that chokes the sky. Day or night, the factory-city is as dark as it is noisy. Protruding from the city's side is a metal umbilical, running three miles north west to join its prettier twin, Wonderland.

Since Verdigris' uprising, few travel south of Slake and there is nobody to bother the Vagrant and his companions as they make their way past an abandoned station. Once Monocars whooshed along the route, riding the metal halo that linked Slake's belt of satellite villages. The cars are gone now, cockpit carcasses stripped and guide cables taken, broken and given new purpose. Only unwanted scraps and pieces too large to move are left behind, rusting into the landscape.

Harm reclines in the Hammer's arms, bouncing gently with each stride. 'Where are we going? You know I'll come with you, wherever it is. I just want to know.'

In answer, the Vagrant points north.

'Yes, but how far north? To the Crag? To Six Circles? To the coast?'

The Vagrant's face is unreadable.

'Over the sea! You're going back to the Shining City.' He doesn't bother to wait for confirmation.

'Sea?' asks the Hammer.

'Yes. How to explain? Try and imagine living water that moves on its own and goes on as far as the eye can see.'

The Hammer scowls. 'No.'

'Alright, can you imagine a puddle?'

'Yes.'

'Imagine a puddle so deep you can't see the ground through it, so deep you could jump into it and move around inside.'

'No.'

'Ooh!' echoes Vesper.

The Hammer growls and a small head vanishes into the shadows of the Vagrant's coat.

'You'll understand when we get there. Some things you need to see for yourself.' He pats her shoulder plate and turns back to the Vagrant. 'We have enough supplies to bypass Slake but I've never been north of Wonderland. Do you know the way?'

The Vagrant keeps walking.

'That's not an answer.' Harm looks for support, gets none. 'We need to talk about this!'

The Vagrant stops.

'Thank you. I know this isn't easy for you but—'

Turning, the Vagrant breaks into a run, passing him, arrowing for the station. His retreat starts a charge into cover. Moments later they all hunker down in the rusted shelter, panting. The Vagrant's eyes are on the sky. A swarm of shapes hang there, grey specks against the clouds. He reaches into his pocket, pulls out the scope and looks again.

A score of Bonewings glide overhead, silent and sinister. The Uncivil's hand is evident in their making. Each one is a ribcage, grown and splayed out. Wings of skin stretch between the curved, white fingers, studded with eyeballs, dry, unblinking.

They pass by without comment.

'Do you think they saw us?' Harm asks as the Vagrant stands up. He gets a shrug for an answer. 'We need to be under cover when they come back. If we follow the old ringway we should come across a settlement before too long.'

The Vagrant nods. They hurry out from the station, making the most of empty skies.

The Knights of Jade and Ash travel into the Uncivil's lands unmolested. They have picked up the trail of the Malice and, despite the bearer's head start, they are gaining ground. The commander finds evidence of battle near the mountains, a muddling mess of tracks firing in all directions, footprints crossing, one on top of the other, making strange new shapes. From the chaos comes a line of tracks, heading north, aligned.

The knights travel day and night without complaint until they are rewarded with a distant glimpse of their prey. They see the bearer, another man and their pet, and walking alongside them, a familiar figure, large and armoured. They are unnerved by the sight. The Hammer that Walks and the Malice? Together? The knights quiver with unspoken questions. Why does the Usurper's Daughter walk with their enemy? What does this mean?

With a sword, one of the knights points out a flurry of shapes in the sky. Bonewings.

The commander stops. The Uncivil lies to the north east in Wonderland but the Malice is taking a path to the north west. Their primary goal remains unchanged but now the commander knows the depth of the Uncivil's rebellion and his essence burns with rage. She must be brought to heel.

The commander makes no effort to hide, setting a march toward Wonderland.

Without hurry the Bonewings glide past, glassy eyes snatching reflections of the knights, keeping them.

The villages blend, one seeming much like another, personalities deleted by demands from the hungry cities. Their inhabitants work hard tending the last of the great harvester wheels or working the crops by hand, till life blurs surreal. Those with spirit to fight have already fled or died or, in the case of a few, been converted by the Uncivil to keep the peace.

In fits and starts the Vagrant travels, pulling the goat behind him. Irregular flight patterns make the Bonewings hard to predict and several times Harm holds his breath as they pass over. Only the Hammer is unaffected by the tension.

They have circled a quarter of Slake's outskirts, moving anti-clockwise, away from Wonderland. So far nothing has come for them, neither have they been challenged. The locals are too tired, too altered to care about the strange group travelling through.

The apparent lack of threat is unsettling. Without actual trouble, the mind has space to invent. Imaginary evils are conjured, behind doors, under rocks, hiding in wait just out of sight.

A thick tower stands before them, heart of the next settlement. Bubbles of blown plastic stick to its side in artificially arranged growths, each one housing a family unit. Around the tower are rings of arable land, sharing sprinklers that once worked automatically. People dot the area, seeing out their shifts, docile.

'Hold on,' says Harm. 'Something's not right.' All turn their attention to the green-eyed man, except the goat, who is keen to get closer to the rows and rows of edible stalks. 'This seems familiar. Have we been here before? Maybe we've gone wrong, got turned round somehow?'

'No!' says the Hammer.

'Ooh!' agrees Vesper.

The Vagrant shakes his head and Harm bows to the majority.

Doors at the base of the tower stand open, welcoming. Nobody questions them as they go inside. The Vagrant finds an empty bubble for the Hammer and another for everyone else. Sleep comes quickly.

In the morning Vesper wakes first but ensures the Vagrant is only moments behind.

'It's good you put the Hammer next door,' Harm says quietly. 'I wanted to talk to you about her. I've been thinking about how best to handle her and I've got a few ideas.'

Shifting the baby to a comfortable feeding position, the Vagrant turns his head to listen. After a few minutes his eyebrows raise.

When the Hammer opens her eyes, she finds two men standing over her. Naturally, her fists clench, violent.

'Hello,' says Harm. He crosses the curved floor with the Vagrant's help and sits next to the Usurperkin, one leg bent, the other forced straight out in front. 'We wanted to know how you're feeling.'

'What?'

'Are you in pain?'

The Hammer frowns with childlike energy. 'Why?'

'I've been looking at your armour. You never take it off. At first we thought that was because you didn't want to let your guard down but it's more than that, you can't take it off.'

The Hammer's fists do not relax.

Harm looks at the cast on his leg, then at the unarmoured place on the Hammer's arm. Her forearm is studded with metal bolts. Once they fixed a bracer in place, now they are redundant. Some stand proud and ugly, others hide just under the skin, all cause discomfort.

'The stories say the Usurper gave you the armour in person.'

An already broad chest swells further. 'Yes.'

'But it hurts all the time.'

'Yes.' Her head tilts forward, then up again, angry. 'No!'

Harm flinches away, toppling backward onto the Vagrant's open palm. 'I'm sorry. We know how strong you are. We know you can take the pain but what we're trying to say is that if you don't want to, you don't have to.'

Her too-small lips part but no words come.

'It's up to you. Things can be different.'

Giant fists raise, open and plaster themselves over her face. Her body shakes with sadness, each sob ringing the armour like a dolorous bell. Harm edges closer, reaching out to rest two fingers on her exposed skin. He is careful to pick a place where the green is unbroken. In time, quieter tears spill.

Shyly, the Hammer reveals her face. 'Will you..?'

'Yes,' answers Harm. 'We'll help you.'

Neither of the men are surgeons but Harm does what he can. The Hammer keeps still as the green-eyed man works. Only her face moves, twisting with pain and something else, well hidden. As the first metal plug clunks onto the cloth, staining it with ooze, the Vagrant gets up. He is eager to take Vesper and the goat for a walk.

They stay outside for hours. Vesper enjoying the sputtering sprinklers, the Vagrant wary and watching the sky. Meanwhile the goat orbits on the end of her chain, terrorizing the shoots.

A man is moving around the outer band of crops. He is bent low by his labours, fighting the stubborn weeds. Eventually he kneels opposite the Vagrant, separated by a few feet of foliage. Head down, he speaks.

'That's good, keep looking up, pretend I'm just like the others.' The Vagrant does as he's asked. 'I'm a friend and a servant of the Winged Eye, just like you.' The man intones his identification, soft, intricate. 'There's somebody who's come a long way to meet you. She's waiting in Slake. I'm to take you to her. Are you ready to leave?'

The man glances at him. The Vagrant shakes his head.

'Why not?'

The Vagrant gestures to his throat, shakes his head.

'I see. Well, I'll be waiting here when you are. Be quick though, if I can find you it won't be long before they will.'

The man says no more, going back to his weeding, drifting away from them.

Returning to the bubble room, the Vagrant finds the Hammer asleep. Wadded bandages poke from holes on her body like flags of surrender. Harm slumps pale against the wall next to a stack of gory armour and rivets.

'Worse than I thought,' he replies to the Vagrant's questioning eyes. 'It was awful. Some had been grown over, some were . . . underneath her—'

The Vagrant holds up a hand.

'I'll spare you the details.' Harm shakes his head. 'You know, maybe it's pain as well as the taint that drives Usurperkins.'

They both regard the sleeping figure. Stripped of her armour, the Hammer looks only slightly giant, her face almost human. One hand rests across her chest, surfing with each breath. Otherwise she is still, effigy-like.

An hour later she wakes but does not move. Invisible chains of fatigue and blood loss hold her in place. The Vagrant tears new bandages and Harm changes the dressings. The Hammer accepts treatment, and afterwards, food.

Harm's voice is soothing. 'That's good. Try and get some more rest if you can. We have to go and meet somebody.'

She tries to sit up, fails. 'No! Don't!'

'This isn't goodbye. We're coming back. I'll leave plenty of food and water for you. We're leaving the goat too. You're not strong enough to travel yet.'

'NO!'

The Vagrant steps forward, helps the Hammer to sit up. He turns her hand, curls the fingers as if she were holding a cup and balances a coin on her index finger. He mimes tossing it again. She takes a deep breath and tries.

Without gauntlets, her fingers fumble their way to the task. The coin jumps, somersaults, sings. Not as resonant as usual; a shorter, weaker sound. It does not matter, the Hammer's eyes light with joy.

The Vagrant and Harm smile and the Usurper's Daughter

smiles back. She doesn't try and stop them when they leave, Harm's leg forcing them to an unpromising hobble.

They find a man waiting for them outside. 'Is this it?'

The Vagrant nods.

'Come on then. She doesn't like to be kept waiting.'

CHAPTER NINETEEN

The man stays tight-lipped on the journey, giving an untrue name and little else. On this assignment he is called Able but there have been other jobs and other identities. Able is a veteran of the Winged Eye's inquisition, sometimes called the Lenses.

On the outskirts of Slake there is an alternative way of travelling: the hooks. Large curves of sharp metal, lifted five feet from the floor, lined up one after the other, tight, gliding along their predetermined route. Oblivious to time or circumstance, the hooks keep their pace. At the top of each hook is a light. Some still work, illuminating their cargo for would-be thieves and hinting at degenerates hidden just out of sight.

Though perpetually gloomy, Slake is full of noise, conveyor-belts groan, gears grind, distant rendering pits roar.

Harm is attached to a hook. Slender limbs dangle down, weary. The Vagrant and Able walk alongside. Most of the people here are armed. The Uncivil has few laws and those

191

she does enforce protect the city and the infrastructure rather than its citizens. Technology is expensive and hard to replace, tainted humans commonplace.

They pass another lane of the hooks and some of the cargo shrieks as it passes them. It is a common misconception that the Necrotraders deal only in corpses. The best parts are bought and treated fresh.

The Vagrant keeps his head down and Vesper burrows deeper within his coat.

Able takes them to a broken factory, where floorboards rot and maggots thrive. The Vagrant watches the clouds of flies warily. On the top floor, hidden behind refuse and cracked engines is a haven of cleanliness. Two clear blocks of Mutigel serve as furniture. The first has been molded into a chair, the second a cuboid work surface. On the second sits a smaller cube, each face alive with data, and on the first sits a woman who stands as they enter.

Her face is proud, getting stronger as she ages; authority oozes from her. She opens her long coat to reveal darkened armour and a neck chain, marked with feathers and power.

The Vagrant takes a breath and then drops to one knee, the sudden movement earning him a kick to the ribs. Less certainly, Harm bows.

She is unmoved by their deference. 'These are the ones, Able?'

'They are.'

'There are supposed to be three. Where's Sir Attica?'

Harm glances at the Vagrant, who shakes his head sadly. Able clears his throat. 'This one's a mute.'

'Bloody inconvenient! And the other one, can he talk?'

'It has been known,' says Harm quietly.

'Good. Where is your master?'

'I . . . wasn't there when it happened . . . But it was a terrible loss for all of us.'

'It's only terrible if he failed. Did he? Did you?'

'I don't know what you mean.'

The woman looks at Able, shakes her head. 'It looks like you found them just in time. I honestly don't know how they've managed to survive this long. Squires and Southerners! What a combination. They probably don't even know which holes to shit through!'

Harm grinds his teeth. The Vagrant keeps his head down.

'They have the sword I take it?'

'Yes, Ma'am.'

Her hard eyes return to the Vagrant. 'Show me.'

The Vagrant stands, reveals Vesper and the sword.

'Able, check the baby for taint. You, bring the sword closer and draw it. Slowly. I don't want to attract unwanted attention.'

Vesper is unsure of the new pair of hands moving her but enjoys the swift rotations.

As the sword slides free the woman's hand goes to her mouth. It is her turn to kneel. 'So it's true.' She reaches out to touch the sword, hesitates, lowers her hand, the gesture incomplete. 'Thank you,' she whispers. 'That's enough.'

The sword is put away. The woman stands, takes the room again. 'Forgive my earlier comments. It's this city, it makes me cranky. My name is Sir Phia and if Attica's dead then I'm the last knight in the southern continent.'

'Excuse me,' Harm asks, 'but where are the rest of the knights?'

'Where they're needed most, guarding The Seven.'

'Where they're needed most . . .' Harm murmurs, incredulous.

'There are less than a hundred of the old guard left, and squires learn slowly. We can't afford to waste any resources.' She frowns suddenly, refocuses. 'We were told you were coming and I was dispatched to find you and bring you home. We've had agents spread across this wasteland in deep cover for years, waiting for a sign you'd survived. I expected you a long time ago, what happened?'

Harm does not meet her eyes. 'It's a long story.'

'I'm sure it is. And there'll be time for all of it when we're away from here. We'd just about given up hope when we started to hear rumours of a knight still alive in the south. We assumed it was Attica but evidently it was you. Where are you keeping Attica's sword?'

The Vagrant shakes his head again, his lips a grim line.

'You lost it? Damn! But wait, that means you've been using the Gamma's sacred blade. You? Ridiculous!'

'The baby is clean, Ma'am.'

'Thank you, Able. We'll take her back with us as well. So the sword allows you to use it?'

The Vagrant nods.

'I hope you understand what an honour that is.' Phia returns to her Mutigel chair. It has not forgotten her contours. 'Everything is in place for our evacuation. We have a prearranged path through the blockade and once through, an escort will take us to the coast where a ship is waiting. However, there is a secondary objective that your arrival has made possible.'

Harm pulls a face but says nothing.

'One of our spies has been captured and taken to a

rendering facility. Ironically they have no idea of the knowledge he's carrying, they're only interested in his parts. We
don't have long before he's processed so we'll need to move
quickly. Unfortunately they've already attached him to an
essence lock and I daren't break it without risking his mind.
We need a singing sword to manage it safely. I'm sure you
see where you come in.'

'Why don't you use your sword?' Harm asks.

'A good, if impertinent question. My sword isn't here. I
didn't want to risk discovery.'

'But you want to risk Gamma's sword for this spy?'

Phia stands up and strides over to Harm. 'What I want
is to return the sword and the information to The Seven and
to strike a blow against the sick practises of this city! What
I do not want is another unprompted question from the likes
of you, are we clear?'

'Very.'

'We've identified the key figures in the operation and will
take them out as a tertiary objective. At best it will slow
the Uncivil's business by a few weeks but it will remind the
people that we have not forgotten them and give a much
needed boost to our other agents in the area. You can rest
here while Able and I make the final preparations.'

'I'm not going to be much use on a mission, I can hardly
walk.'

'We can look at your leg, see if it's salvageable. Either
way, you're right. But don't worry, I can think of another
use for you.'

The Bonewings appear to hang in the air as the world
turns beneath them. Wonderland approaches, brightly lit,

vibrant. Towers race each other to the stars, rendering a chaotic skyline. Necrotic pipes line the high ceilings. As the Bonewings approach a number of them lift up, like antennae, sphincters opening, gaping and splitting into four petal fingers, ready to accommodate the silent gliders. Bonewings and pipes meet, one sheathing itself in the other. Rejoined.

Wisps of essence detach themselves from the Bonewings, rushing through the pipes. Before a bird can blink they shoot through the ridged tunnels, across the roof, slipping within walls, and down again, beyond the cracked paving stones, into the bowels of the city, streaking to its centre, its beating heart, their mother, the Uncivil.

Since her arrival six years ago, the Uncivil has worked ceaselessly. Developing herself. Her secret stands in plain sight, too much for people to accept. Wonderland is more than her city. Wonderland is her, another of her many titles. Inch by inch she has added to her shell, the cloak of corpses, joining it to the metal and brick of the city.

Unlike the Usurper she does not dominate the humans that live within her walls, she enhances them. Her cults are strong, lured to her side by the hope of immortality, and later, of ascension. In return they maintain the city, replacing her shell with fresh parts, fighting the daily decay the world pushes onto her.

The Uncivil digests the returned essence, considers what it tells her. Her agents in the south have been silenced, the half city taken from her and now the Knights of Jade and Ash march upon her home. There is only one possibility: the Usurper is pushing north, seeking to curtail her hard-won freedom. She will not allow this.

Within the streets of Wonderland, veins pulse with intent. Whispers find their way to Half-alive ears, forewarning.

The city stirs.

Vesper lies on the Mutigel cube, a sailor on a jellied ocean. She kicks her legs, impatient. The Vagrant presses the panel set into the base and the Mutigel softens, letting Vesper descend. He pushes again and it remembers its old shape, bouncing Vesper into the air.

'OoooOOOOOOOOoooowww!'

Harm's smile lacks conviction. 'Something about this feels wrong.'

The Vagrant ignores him, presses the panel again.

'If that sword really belongs to one of The Seven, why risk it on a mission in Slake? No information is that important.' He walks gingerly across the room, testing the flexible silver on his injured leg. It takes his weight. 'And if I was a knight I'd go with you myself, not hide on the outskirts of the city.'

'OoooOOOOOOOOoooowww!'

'Are you even listening to me? I don't trust her and you shouldn't either.'

The Vagrant gives Harm a hard stare, raising a finger in warning.

'I'm not allowed to voice my thoughts now, is that it?'

The Vagrant's finger curls back into his fist. He sighs and returns his attention to the Mutigel.

'Look, it's wonderful that we've got help. Really, it is. But she's holding something back, I'm sure of it. Just promise me you'll keep your guard up.' Despite the Vagrant's hurried nod, Harm isn't satisfied. A shy hand ventures out, rests on the Vagrant's arm. 'Please, be careful. For Vesper if nobody else.'

The Vagrant looks up. For a while the two men stare at each other. He nods again, slower, more resolute.

'Thank you.'

Swift footsteps on the stairs startle them. Sir Phia and Able reappear. Vesper kicks again. And again. 'Ooo?'

Hastily, the Vagrant clears the knight's seat and returns to one knee.

Sir Phia strides across the room and sits heavily. 'The final preparations have been made. It's time for you to leave. Any last questions?'

The Vagrant shakes his head. Harm clenches his jaw and follows suit.

'Good. You will take the sword and go with Able to the facility. While a second team takes out key personnel, the two of you will recover our operative. Remember, it's imperative that he be brought out alive and unharmed. I will take the wounded one and the infant to the edge of Slake and prepare our transport.'

Harm raises a hand. 'We have another travelling companion, not far from here.'

'The mutant? Out of the question. She's too big a risk.'

'She's injured, she needs our help.'

'Help? According to my reports that thing is a monster. More than capable of protecting herself and of ruining our mission. If she dies of her injuries it will save us all a job.' Harm takes a breath to speak. 'There is nothing more to say. Unless you're volunteering to take care of her yourself?'

'No. My place is here.'

'Your place is where I say it is. We expect discipline from our Squires, and we get it. Enough talk. There's work to be done.'

The men rise, gathering their things.

Grimly, she adds: 'Winged Eye watch us, measure us, judge us.'

Sir Phia wastes no time in putting Harm to work. As soon as the Vagrant and Able are gone, the green-eyed man finds himself sat on the floor, sifting through a bucket of nutrispuds. Despite multiple treatments, the modified vegetables have become hosts for some unidentified parasites.

He checks each one by hand, sorting the fairly clean from the utterly rotten. When he finds the tell-tale holes, he digs in, scraping out hard-backed worms that sway angrily from his fingertips.

The worms are put into a jar for purposes unknown and the nutrispuds join their fellows in the bucket.

Next to him is the Mutigel cube, the top formed into a bowl for Vesper to recline in. Rather than sleep, the baby attempts to roll to freedom. Regular grunts mark each attempt, becoming steadily louder as her frustration grows.

Sir Phia enters the room, studying the bucket with a critical eye. 'Make sure you do a thorough job. You wouldn't want one of those things to end up in your gut.'

'When you said you had a job in mind for me, I'd imagined something different.'

'I have no interest in your imaginings. Just get the job done.'

Harm presses his lips together and picks up another nutrispud, cutting into it savagely.

Vesper rocks back and forth, trying to roll over but each time, the cube adjusts, softening around her. Foiled, she flops onto her back and stamps her feet.

The banging draws Sir Phia's attention. The knight leans over the cube, curling her lip. 'Such a noisy, undisciplined thing she is. Quiet now.'

The command is ignored.

'Quiet, I say.'

'Good luck with that,' mumurs Harm.

Sir Phia places a finger and thumb on the soft skin of Vesper's thigh and pinches. Vesper's expression moves quickly from shock, to outrage, to the purest misery. She begins to cry.

'Quiet,' repeats the knight.

Harm's eyes narrow. 'What are you doing?'

'Teaching this child some discipline.'

'Is that what you call it?'

'In the Shining City they'd have her in a choir by now and she'd have learned how to listen.'

Vesper shrieks as fingers and thumb pinch again, merciless.

The nutrispud drops from Harm's fingers, the small knife does not. 'For someone so keen on obedience, you seem pretty bad at observing it yourself.'

Phia whirls round, baby forgotten. 'What did you say, squire?'

'Oh come on, you've waited all these years to retrieve Gamma's sword and now it's here you send it out into danger. This isn't just about what the spy knows, it's about him. You want to rescue him.'

'Of course I do,' she crosses to him, uncomfortably close.

'I am responsible for the lives of all the operatives here in Slake.'

Green eyes flash, triumphant. 'But he's not one of the Lenses is he, let alone an operative? No wait, it's more than that, he's your lov—'

Her boot presses down on his injured leg. 'Quiet.' He glares at her and she keeps up the pressure until his head drops, hissing in defeat. 'That's better. Now get on with your job, we need to make our way to the rendezvous shortly and before that, we need to eat.' She strides out, shaking her head. 'Pathetic.'

Vesper raises her head, peering over the edge of the cube. 'Sorry,' mouths Harm.

Little feet begin to drum furiously, louder than ever, accompanied by random noises.

Harm smiles, wipes his eyes, and gets back to work.

Slake never sleeps. Even in the dark, figures hurry through streets, eyes glancing, avoiding contact. The Vagrant blends in easily, walking just close enough to Able to keep him in sight.

Before long the outside of the facility looms, dirty and featureless, giving little away. Cargo, living and otherwise, is brought by loaders to the front entrance, a blank square of a mouth with two conveyor belt tongues.

Able moves to a side door where a man stands guard, lightly armoured, a plaguemaker pistol twitching in his hands.

'Wait here,' he says. 'I'll deal with this.'

The Vagrant does as he's told while Able shuffles forward, like a junkie keen for a fix. Words exchange between the two men and backs of hands are pressed together. The Vagrant sees a crack of light where skin touches skin. They separate and Able disappears through the door. A minute later the guard checks the street and waves the Vagrant in.

The corridor is cramped, with hot walls and dry air.

Able leans close, whispering in the Vagrant's ear. 'The other team's already in place. We've got thirty minutes to do what we need to before they attack. I've got a route to storage that should be safe but stay sharp, there's no guarantees.'

Lightly and quickly, the two men advance. Able often consults his hand where lines of light draw and redraw the facility's floor plan. The door to storage is unprotected. They slide back the metal bolt and roll it open.

Mist hisses into the corridor, chilling their feet. It passes, revealing racks of bodies, wrapped in clinging plastic, snug as skin. The room takes up the majority of the building and it is packed full. Men and women of all ages, ordered by health, age and degree of taint. Some have already been partially harvested, their stumps neatly stitched.

Able goes inside, examining the tags on the nearest body. 'Our mark is fit and barely tainted, he'll be further down on the right. You take that row, I'll take this one.'

But the Vagrant remains in the corridor, fingers on the seal around the door, digging tight. At his side, an eye opens, peering between silver feathers, baleful.

Able's voice is dampened by the room, made ghostly. 'I've found him. Over here.'

Slowly, the Vagrant's hand lets go, a memory of his nails left behind in rubber. He watches the floor carefully, keeps his arms by his sides and ventures in. He finds Able examining a man.

'We're in luck, he's not been touched. Time for you to do your part.'

The Vagrant leans forward, studying the man more closely. Beneath the exo-skin the face is young and handsome, dark haired. An infernal holds his mind still, forming a scab-like bandage across the lower half of his face. Mouth, nose and ears are covered. His eyes still move however, full of life.

The Vagrant draws the sword, lowering the flat of the blade towards the man's lips. Blue-tinged light falls upon the Scab, making it twitch and detach. The Scab extends a tooth, cutting its way free of the plastic, fleeing the light which smokes upon its back. The Vagrant skewers it on the point of the sword and flicks it to the floor where it shrivels to ashes.

Able starts peeling the rest of the plastic from the man. 'Can you hear me, Jaden? I'm a friend.' He quickly intones his identification and offers the back of his hand.

Coughs and laboured breathing pass as a reply, then a voice, choked with cold. 'Who are you?'

Able lowers his hand, untouched. His pause is barely noticeable. 'Phia sent me.'

'Phia? She's here?'

'Nearby, I'll take you to her.'

Jaden struggles to stand, his muscles are frost-tight.

'Sorry about this,' Able says, reaching into his belt pouch.

'About what?'

Able raises the Medgun and fires it against Jaden's thigh. He talks through the other man's gasp. 'It's a quick-fix cocktail. You'll feel like shit in the morning but it should be enough to keep you pepped till we're clear of Slake.'

'Thank you. Do you have any clothes?'

'Right here.'

As Jaden is helped to dress, the sword's eye darts back

and forth across the bodies. Unwillingly, the Vagrant follows its gaze. For every person, there is a parasite, breathing with them and holding them still.

He frowns, looking pained.

'Come on,' says Able, moving past him with Jaden in tow. 'Time to go.'

He follows, sluggish. Rows of imploring eyes track his retreat. The Vagrant keeps his head down. Inexplicably, his free hand is drawn to his side, touching his ribs. The Vagrant stops and lets out a long sigh. A cloud births briefly at his lips.

'Something wrong?' asks Able from the doorway.

The Vagrant looks up, shakes his head. He raises the sword with a flourish. The air trills and an army of Scabs quiver, fearful.

Able speaks quickly, urgently. 'This isn't in the plan. Think! We do what we're supposed to, we save a life right now, and with the sword and the info we save countless more. You have to keep your head or we're all going to die.'

'Yeah,' agrees Jaden. 'Let's get out of here while we can.'

The Vagrant's shoulders droop and he takes a step forward, then another. Then he stops. Again he presses a hand to his ribs. A strange smile touches his face. He brings the sword tight to his body and begins to spin.

A song is sung in all directions. It is simple, of one note. The Scabs understand immediately, dropping away from their hosts, seeking sanctuary, finding none. Trapped between their former prisoners and a layer of plastic, they writhe, then burn.

Throughout the building, alarms sound, shaking skulls and racing hearts. People jerk to life, like sleepers thrown in cold water. They strain against their bonds, stretching them till they break. Some fall, some climb from the racks. The fastest leap to their feet, staggering, and race for the door.

The Vagrant is waiting for them, sword barring their exit.

They ask him to move, their blue lips cracking with the effort.

He points past them to those still struggling. The injured, the young.

They look into his eyes, just once, then run back, offering assistance.

Behind him, two voices argue:

'Let's just go, leave him here. You came here for me, right?'

'In part.'

'That's better than nothing, man! If we stay, we'll both end up in that freezer. And I can't go back, I'd rather die.'

Able notes the preference, offers Jaden a pistol. The other man takes it, his hands uneasy on the grip.

'How long till the meds wear off?'

'Four hours at peak effectiveness, then you'll have up to another two before the side effects kick in.'

'Side effects?'

'Later. Come with me, cover the corridor.'

Within the giant freezer, chaos reigns. Those on the top levels wriggle free as best they can, toppling onto hard floors or other victims. Weakened muscles cramp and tear, legs break, tempers fray. Only the sword's presence keeps panic at bay.

The Vagrant joins Able and Jaden at the doorway and a pale army comes after, numb feet slipping, teeth knocking together, a chorus of drills. The noise brings a guard running.

As she rounds the corner Able fires something concealed within his wrist. A new freckle appears on the guard's forehead and her mouth opens in surprise. Her fall is sudden, comic. No one laughs.

Able is the first to move, scooping up the guard's gun and signalling the others to follow him.

The escapees hurriedly strip the woman's clothes. Before they fight over them, the Vagrant steps in. Deciding on a new owner is difficult; they are all equally needy and so numerous he cannot easily count them. In his hands, he has enough clothing for one. Hopeful voices cry out to him:

'Give them to me!'

'Please, I need them.'

'I'll do anything!'

'I'm pregnant!'

Two children share the spoils, the envy of their naked companions. The Vagrant shepherds them on quickly. In the corridor, people crush together, shoulders rubbing, intimate, desperate.

Minutes later they spill out into the street. Eyes blink in confusion, look for guidance, look at the Vagrant. In turn, he looks at Able.

'You've done enough. They're on their own from here.'

The Vagrant shakes his head.

'They're too weak to travel. Look at them, they'll die of exposure. It's time to go.' Able takes the measure of the man in front of him. His lips press together in thought. 'They could ride the hooks to the edge of Slake. Some might make it that way, but they'll need food and clothes soon or it's not going to matter. I have surplus meds for three. I'll treat the strongest, they can help support the others, for all the good it will do. After that, you're on your own.' Able gets to work, adding only, 'Knights!' In his mouth, the word becomes a curse.

The Vagrant allows himself a bleak smile. It does not last long. People are still pouring from the building, too many, hundreds. The street is filling up. Soon, the vultures will come and the opportunists, and word will spread.

At his insistence, they rush to the outgoing hooks and jump on.

The journey out of Slake is slow, nightmarish, impossible to recall save in fragments of horror. Bit by bit, the group whittles down. A few slip away to friendly streets but they a minority. Several are plucked from the hooks as they glide by, vanished by magicians, sinister. Most fall away, like old skin, too weak to continue, trembling in the dust until the next predator arrives. More than once the sword protests, driving enemies back into shadow.

By the time they reach the rendezvous, less than two hundred draw breath.

CHAPTER TWENTY

It is barely morning, the suns are not yet ready and grey light holds dominion. Hidden in a valley sits a hollow-boned skiff. A disposable vehicle, constructed for its one and only voyage. Engines hum quietly, ready. Sir Phia stands next to it, checking the time, her nerves channelled through frequent tuts. Harm is also there, chatting with Vesper, one keeping the other calm.

Figures appear at the top of the valley, silhouettes cut out of a pale sky. Able arrives first, jogging easily down to the group.

Sir Phia strides to meet him. 'Report.'

'Our mission was a success. We evacuated the target. The strike team was in place to let us in and had infiltrated the facility on schedule. At last contact they were ready to move on their marks but I'm still awaiting confirmation of our tertiary objective.'

'You're late. Complications?'

'Oh yes, Ma'am.'

Jaden appears at the top of the valley. Still drug strong, he breaks into a run, charging down the slope and into an embrace with the knight. 'Phia!'

Her response is stilted. 'It's good to see you alive.'

'You came for me, thank you! I thought I was going to die in that place!'

She detaches herself, holding him at arm's length. 'The servants of the Winged Eye look after their own. We'll debrief fully later. You get on board, and rest.'

Jaden climbs onto the skiff, unaware of green eyes boring into the back of his skull.

Able clears his throat. 'About those complications, Ma'am.'

'Yes?'

'They've just arrived.'

She watches the procession of people trudging towards her while Able fills her in. Despite the increasing light, her face darkens.

The group collects in a pool at the valley's base, huddling close for warmth. A few of the older ones invoke the rite of mercy.

Phia tuts again. 'Where is he?'

The Vagrant is swiftly found and brought before the glowering knight. Immediately, he kneels.

'A bit late to play humble, isn't it.' The Vagrant keeps his head down. 'You disobeyed my orders, endangered your fellow servants and no doubt led our enemies straight to us. When I am finished with you, you are going to wish you'd stayed in the womb!'

The Vagrant nods and looks back to the growing puddle of people.

'My mission is to find you. The comms-rocket told us to

expect three. My skiff can take three. Not three thousand. Not three hundred. Not thirty. Three. One extra baby, I can accommodate, but this!' She jabs a finger over his shoulder. 'This defies words! Now get up, it's time to go.'

The Vagrant remains on his knees, watching her stride away. He sighs, stands up. Vesper waves as Harm brings her over, echoing the sigh.

'You're not going are you?' He gets a weak smile of affirmation. 'I understand.'

'Squires,' says Phia. 'Get on to the bloody skiff. That is a direct order.'

'Sorry,' replies Harm. 'We're not coming.'

'Fine. Surrender the sword to me and we'll happily leave you here.'

The Vagrant begins to unbuckle his scabbard.

'Are you sure about this?' Harm asks, searching the Vagrant's eyes.

'Able, bring the sword to me.'

Able clasps his hands in front of him, bows. 'With respect, Ma'am, I must ignore your order.'

'What?! Have you all taken the same drug? Has the Uncivil converted you all while I wasn't looking?'

'No, Ma'am.'

'Then do as I say!'

'My time in Slake has soiled me, Ma'am. I'm not worthy to approach a relic of The Seven . . . Not anymore.'

'Then get on the skiff and prepare her for immediate departure.'

Able bows and obeys.

Phia advances on the Vagrant, who kneels, lowers his head and offers the sword, hilt first. It shifts in his grip, a restless

211

sleeper. Phia holds out her hands, forcing them steady. As the inches lessen between knight and sword, she slows, unsure.

An unpleasant smile spreads across Harm's face.

Behind silvered wings, an eye twitches, attentive.

The knight takes several deep breaths. Sweat springs out on her forehead.

The Vagrant waits, unmoving.

Phia withdraws her hands and backs to the waiting skiff. 'This is your last chance. My authority comes direct from The Seven themselves. Come with us now, or face the consequences.'

The Vagrant looks up, surprised. He holds out the sword again.

'So be it,' she says, clipped.

The skiff's engine comes to life, a thing of light, not sound and they jet away.

Mouth open, frown deep, the Vagrant watches them go. When the skiff has fled fully from sight, he lowers the sword.

Seven Years Ago

Tucked under stone, safe from the eyes of infernal hunters, a cave lies. A tube of yellow warmth glows within, bringing little comfort to the three faces caught in its light.

Attica makes them wait, hiding until he deems it safe to travel on. He tells them they cannot hope to outrun their pursuers. He does not tell them why.

While they wait, the squires train. One has practised sword-play before, dreaming of knighthood all his years. He is agile in a common way, remarkable only in self-belief. The other is unpractised though possessed of a good voice. Both have potential for adequacy.

'You,' he says to the first youth, 'you swing like a knight and sound like a drunkard, all fire and enthusiasm. There's no room for your sword to breathe. Your voice is an instrument that must be played alongside your weapon. No more shouting! And you,' he turns to the second, 'sing sweetly but weakly. You must give direction to the sword's energy, give it direction or it will overwhelm you.'

Eyes low and brooding, the young men slink away to practise.

Attica closes his eyes and rests. Sleep is elusive and he listens to the sounds of his squires repeating the forms, wincing at each missed note. After a while the singing stops, leaving only the crunch of feet on loose stones and blades swishing, mundane, through the air.

He has intended to give them space but is not sure he has the luxury. Concern turns to irritation and Attica gets up, moving awkwardly to where the young men spar. He watches them trade blows, playfighting, and tries to master his frustration. 'What is this?'

The two squires freeze mid motion, practice swords squeaking comically together, heads twisting in surprise.

Despite wide open mouths, no answers emerge.

'Well?'

The first squire recovers himself, lifts his chin. 'We were training.'

The second squire sees Attica's face and says nothing.

'Training were you? Is that what you call this, pointless, willy-waving nonsense? No, you must put away these childish notions and practise the stances I taught you, and the notes.'

'But what's the point of that? If the demons come, we can't defend ourselves by singing.'

'True, singing alone won't be enough but neither will one of those sticks.' He unsheathes his own sword slowly, drawing out the hum as the blade tastes air.

'Alone, neither voice nor sword is enough, they must be brought together.' He assumes a fighting stance, then swings, intoning a single note as he does so. The sound travels along the blade, harmonizing with vibrating metal. Just as Attica's swing completes, the sound reaches the sword's tip. Blue light flashes, extending out and into the rock, slicing deep.

The squires gasp.

He beckons. 'Now, you try.'

The first squire steps forward eagerly.

'No, not you.' He looks to the second. 'You.'

He offers his sword, hilt first and the squire takes it. 'Now remember, all of the power is in the blade. All you need to do is wake it, and control it. Your voice and stance provide direction but it is more than simple technique. You must be strong in yourself, pure of intent, if you are truly to master being a knight.'

The squire nods, assumes the stance, notices the other squire subtly shaking his head and looking at his feet. He smiles a thanks and adjusts them.

'Ready? Now, I want you to repeat the strike I did and make an incision into the rock. Take a breath, prepare yourself, let your arms be guided by the sword but don't let it pull you off course.'

The squire nods, takes a breath.

'And remember your own note must finish with the strike, if the harmony is off, your strike will be sloppy.'

The squire nods.

'You don't need to push too hard, let the sound come easily. Well? What are you waiting for, strike!'

The squire sings, swings, and the blade cuts through the air, humming with power. The humming rises rapidly in volume, eclipsing the squire's voice. Blue light flashes, igniting the air, striking stone.

All three blink against the loud boom.

When the squire opens his eyes, the first thing he sees is Attica's disapproval.

The knight points to the wall. Below the clean line made earlier is a large black scorchmark. 'See this? You haven't even scratched it. Without control, the energy can go anywhere. You're lucky to still have your eyebrows!' Suddenly, the knight looks tired, older than his years. He takes back his sword. 'More practice, both of you, the proper forms. I'll tell you when you can stop.'

They set to work with renewed purpose and Attica leaves them to stretch uncomfortably in his makeshift seat. The ache in his bones grows daily. He thinks of the Knight Commander, imagines the man chanting defiantly in his last moments, canons shredding the hordes surrounding the dead snake. The Knight Commander will have made their enemies pay dearly for every step.

There are no turrets in the mine, nor legions to battle. The enemy is invisible, picked up from exposure to the Breach, eroding Attica's essence from the inside. He resolves to fight it anyway, wondering if he will last six months? A year? More?

He will use the time well, fashion the squires into something better. Not knights, they have neither skill nor steel for it, but the Shining City does not need knights here, it needs smugglers and shadows. Small men to slip through the cracks of history.

Hidden away, Attica and the squires catch only rumours of the world changing. They do not see the first wave of the Usurper's horde surge north, passing them by. They do not see the wild feast or the corpse towns or the plagues.

For them a year passes in relative quiet.

One morning a girl approaches, bearing news and supplies. It is not her first visit. Her parents don't like sending her but they have no choice.

Wandering children are among the few beneath the notice of the village gossips, enjoying a freedom already forgotten by their elders.

Even so, the girl has left early.

She taps on the rocks and two youths appear to clear the entrance for her. They work quickly, eager to impress. One manages a shy hello before the other begins his interrogation.

'Hey Tammy. You're looking taller.'

'I am?'

'It suits you.' Tammy blushes. 'How's your sister?'

'Reela? The same, I guess.'

'She ever talk about me?'

'No.'

The bold squire doesn't even flinch. 'You sure?'

'Uh huh.' Tammy looks down, pretending to be coy. 'She does write about you though.'

'Yeah?'

'Yeah, and she draws you sometimes.'

'Give me details, Tammy.'

'I don't have any. She's really protective of her stuff.'

'But you're smart, and pretty.' She blushes again. 'You could find out.'

'Like a mission?' she asks, eagerly.

'Yes! A mission. Your first test. A Seraph Knight needs to be cunning as well as brave.'

'Do you think I could be a knight one day?'

He makes a show of studying her. 'Maybe. But it's a lot of work.'

'I can do it! When can I start?'

'I told you, Tammy, you've got your first test. We'll talk more when you've completed it.' But the girl wants more, she begs and flatters and the young squire soon capitulates. 'Would you like to see my sword?'

Of course she does.

He ignores the warning look from the other squire and takes the light with him to the back of the cave. There, Sir Attica sleeps, forehead clothed in thin sweat. At this hour the man shows few signs of life. The squire takes his master's sword and returns to the others.

'Here it is.'

Tammy makes a reverent noise. 'I wish you could take it out.'

'I can.'

'But I thought the knights could only draw their swords in battle. Don't you have to shed blood before you put it back?'

Both squires glance at each other and fall about laughing.

'Oh Tammy, Tammy, Tammy! Don't listen to idiots, they'll make you stupid!'

'It's not true?'

'Of course it isn't. Do you want me to prove it?'

She nods excitedly.

Before his friend can stop him, the young man draws the

sword. He doesn't dare shout but Attica's sword holds its own tune. It's lighter than he expects and flourish nearly becomes throw. Tammy doesn't notice, her moon-wide eyes mesmerized by the singing steel. He holds it out for her, keeping his grip loose, letting his arm quiver to prolong the sound. As the blade passes by her the note changes, souring until the point is clear.

The squires exchange another look.

'It's beautiful,' Tammy breathes.

'Yeah,' the squire replies, forced and light. His friend has already gone to wake Attica.

The knight is moved rudely from troubled dreams to his aching body. He asks what has happened. They tell him their story. After he has demolished it they tell him the truth.

One squire hangs his head in contrition. 'What does it mean?' asks the other.

'Lots of things,' Attica replies. 'For you it means punishment. And be grateful I need both of you sorry sacks of meat or things would be much worse. For her,' he looks at Tammy, his beard twitching unhappily. 'I'm not yet sure. What are you not telling us, girl?'

She shrugs.

Attica picks up his sword, willing his hand steady. 'I've only heard my sword-song do this once before and that was at the Breach. What are you really?'

Tammy begins to back away.

'Hold her.'

The squires comply. The girl shrieks.

'Strip her.'

This time the squires look at each other, hesitate.

Attica repeats the words, edges them with menace. They jolt obedience into the young men. Fabric is pulled, tears a little, comes loose. Scrawny limbs wrap about a child's body. Goose pimples stand to attention.

From the front Tammy appears normal but Attica is not fooled. 'Turn her.'

On her back is a patch of yellow between the shoulders. A spreading rash, like the underside of a bruise. The affected skin curves out from her body, elevated by a hump of muscle, thickening, growing.

One of the squires steps back, covering his mouth with a hand.

The girl's voice squeaks a question. 'What's wrong?'

'You've been in contact with an infernal.'

'I haven't!'

'I am a servant of the Winged Eye,' Attica rasps. 'Don't lie to me again.'

'I'm not lying! I wasn't in contact with one. I just saw one, that's all.'

'Tell me.'

Tammy talks quickly while tears hover close by. 'I wanted to see the monsters. A pack of them had been spotted near Kolat.'

'Kolat? I've never heard of Kolat.'

'There's no reason to, it's just another stupid little village like mine.'

'Carry on.'

'The monsters were roaming closer and closer. Some of our hunters had come across scattered bones only a mile from outlying farms. They said the bones were still warm to touch!'

'How many?'

'There were three as big as you but on four legs and another dozen about my size. Kolat's best hunters had gone with the army last year, so they only had the old ones left and ones a few years older than me. The other villages are the same but we thought if we got a really big group together we'd be alright.'

Attica shakes his head. 'What happened?'

'I wasn't supposed to go but I wanted to see them for myself. I wanted to understand the enemy. They weren't what I expected.'

'Go on.'

'They were horrible and scary but . . .' She pauses, fear of lying warring with fear of the truth. 'They were also familiar, in a way. I can't explain it. But I didn't touch them, I swear.'

Attica's fingers firm their grip on his sword. 'You didn't need to.'

The Vagrant stares at the ceiling, unable to sleep. His eyes close, open again, close. It makes no difference; the cries of the dying pierce the tattered walls. The original contents of the storehouse are long gone, along with most of its roof.

Within the circular sweep of the outer wall is a honeycomb of rooms. People shelter there from the wind, bare skin flinching from icy surfaces, clustering in for warmth. Most suffer from exposure, shivers evolving to shakes, to fever, a juddering orgasm of cold sweat that marks the living from the more dignified dead.

'Can't sleep?' asks Harm. 'Nor can Vesper. All the noise is unsettling her. You okay to take her for a while?'

The Vagrant sits up and Harm feels a way to his side. Vesper is handed over in the dark, grumbling, her hand flailing the air till it finds a familiar nose to grasp. The Vagrant's sigh becomes a whistle. Vesper giggles.

Harm hovers nearby. 'I'm freezing. Do you mind if I sit with you?'

The Vagrant says nothing and Harm moves in closer to curl around him.

With unerring accuracy, Vesper finds a second nose.

'For what it's worth, I think you did the right thing. At least this way they have a chance.'

Another moan cuts the nighttime and Vesper startles. The three press tighter, burying heads, holding on.

In the morning, Harm counts the bodies. Half of the group fail to meet the dawn. Of the survivors, only forty-three are strong enough to travel. The Vagrant leads them further from Slake, towards the outlying villages.

Along the way, a man stops suddenly and begins to scream. Attempts to help him are met with louder screams and gnashing teeth. The Vagrant looks away and keeps going. By the time a familiar tower comes into sight, another four have split off, chancing their fates elsewhere. At the edge of the village a child falls over. She doesn't get up again.

With a vulture's instinct, a group of traders appear to welcome the ragged travellers and the last of the Vagrant's coins slip through his fingers. In return, thirty-seven mouths are fed. Several fail to keep the food down, staining their new clothes yellow.

Harm's fingers brush the Vagrant's elbow. 'That was noble. But what's going to happen tomorrow?'

The Vagrant looks past the green-eyed man, intent on the horizon.

'These people are sick and they're getting worse. They need meds and a skilled physician. I'm sorry, you did your best but this is a lost cause. It's time to let them go.'

The Vagrant whirls round, his face lined with anger.

Arms raise hastily in defence but no fists fall. When Harm dares to look again, the Vagrant is striding away, Vesper staring mournfully at him over his shoulder.

Harm rubs a sleeve across his face and enters the tower. He climbs the ladder quickly, Exocast taking the strain for his injured leg, and goes directly to their old rooms.

The Hammer sits with her back to the edge of the bubble. A shoulder plate bends between her hands, groaning slightly. To her right, the rest of her armour lies stacked, to her left, a messy mountain of yellow stalks dominates the room. The goat lays on top, sleeping, content.

'Hello again,' says Harm quietly.

'You!' exclaims the Hammer. 'Back!' Crooked teeth emerge in a crooked grin.

'I promised we would be. How are you?'

She opens her arms to expose her injuries. Plugs of blood sit where the holes were, studding her body, arms and legs. 'See?'

'Does it hurt?'

'No.'

'Liar!'

The Hammer's eyes narrow, dangerous. Then she smiles again. 'A little.'

After a moment, Harm smiles back. 'They're healing quickly by the look of them, that's good. Doesn't look like they're infected.' He pauses, thoughtful. 'I've no idea how that's possible. Are you mobile?'

'Yes.'

'Good. We'll have to get moving soon.'

They stay in the tower that night. Nine more die. When the group gathers again, five cannot face further travel and elect to stay. From the tower, the Hammer emerges into the red and gold dawn. She is wearing her armour again. She has changed it, fixing the plates to each other rather than her flesh. At her side trots the goat, a bunch of yellow stalks spiking from each side of her mouth, whisker like.

The spectacle causes three more hasty goodbyes.

Of the original escapees, twenty remain to follow the Vagrant north. He continues on his original route, cycling away from Wonderland through Slake's outlying settlements. Behind him the group string out in order of fitness. He doesn't bother to try and hide them, there is no point. Often, his amber eyes search the clouds. There are no predators, no Bonewings, nothing. He doesn't relax.

They haven't got far when fatigue drops one of the children. Before others can react, the Hammer steps over.

'Up!'

Yelping, the boy forces himself to his feet. He manages three steps before falling again.

'No!' shouts the Hammer, exasperated. 'Up!' She scoops the boy from the floor one handed and puts him on her shoulder.

There is a collective sigh of relief and the group trudge on.

Later a small girl taps on the Hammer's thigh plate. She looks down, casting the girl in shadow. 'What?'

The girl bites her lip, points shyly. 'Up?'

'Up!' agrees the Hammer, hoisting her up to join the boy. She is not the last to ride that day. Inspired by the girl's courage, adults approach too. The Hammer accepts every request, granting a reprieve for aching limbs and hearts.

CHAPTER TWENTY-ONE

All roads to Wonderland stand open, welcoming vile and not alike. Painted towers sprout haphazardly, bright, electric, a constructed forest. Between them, multi-layered pathways are strung, weaving together, more art than architecture. Busy clots of people move about, talking, laughing, living. Watching them, disapproving, are the Knights of Jade and Ash. The commander is surprised. Resistance is expected, nay, demanded, but none has come. It is as if the Uncivil does not even notice them.

And yet . . .

The knights often turn, as if being approached. Nothing reveals itself but they know the Uncivil is close, sense her proximity. And her power.

Deliberately, the commander keeps the knights separate and busy, aware that shared contact will nurture their growing fears. They must appear strong.

The city is confusing. There are few familiar half-breeds on the streets. Other, stranger things are more common. Augmentation and implantation rule here. On the outside there is little to tell them apart. The denizens of the Usurper's cities also have twisted or additional limbs, strange skin or internal shifts. But the commander sees the difference. Normally these things are manifestations of the taint or the master's favour but here the infernal essence is contained within dead appendages, bonded in service to human will. Disgusting. Wrong.

The master should never have allowed the Uncivil to get so strong. Why not send them sooner to demand the rebel's surrender, or shred her?

The commander stops, shaken by thoughts that question, fizzing with vehemence. It is starting to question the master, starting to doubt the Usurper's judgement. Did the Uncivil once think this way? Perhaps the earlier contact with Patchwork's essence left a mark uncleansed?

One of the commander's knights draws a weapon. The cry makes them all focus. As they progress into Wonderland, crowds thin and change. The friendly outer layers drift away to social events or prior appointments, leaving behind lines of robed figures.

The commander draws its sword and, after a beat, the rest of the knights follow. It holds it high, contemptuous and challenging. It is not interested in fighting maggots, it wants the Uncivil.

As the robed half-lifers move in, the knights form a tight circle, deadly, unbroken. Exactly where the Uncivil wants them.

Beneath their feet, stones shake and crumble. Wonderland is answering their challenge, drowning out the wailing swords, silencing them.

*　　*　　*

The Vagrant reaches the top of the hill and raises his hand. Behind him people flop to the floor, exhausted. Ahead, a wall of silvered steel and white light stretches, cutting off the Northern Peninsula from the rest of the continent.

The wall is a rallying point for what remains of the Empire's southern armies, the last fortification that stands between the Uncivil and the northern port.

High atop, figures move, tiny specks armed with lances that spit fire down on the hordes below. Against the glare of the fortification the Uncivil's troops are silhouettes, a Half-alive wave that probes, falls back, waits and probes again.

For now, the two sides are at a stalemate. The Uncivil's armies lack focus and cannot find a way to best the wall while the Empire's defenders possess insufficient strength and numbers to end the conflict. They hide behind their bright barrier, rationing ammunition, holding out for reinforcements that will not come.

Lights dance in Vesper's eyes, delighting her. She chirps, excited, grasping for the tiny figures just out of reach.

'So,' asks Harm as he arrives. 'Any ideas?'

The Vagrant pulls out the cracked scope and puts it to his eye.

Harm winces, rubbing the back of his thigh. 'Oh. That bad.'

They leave the Hammer to watch over the others and stroll from one hill to another, stopping at the top of each, searching for an angle. Vesper enjoys the view, bouncing under the Vagrant's arm. Her busy chattering peaks, then fades to a mumble. Moments later a small head flops into the Vagrant's armpit.

'I wish someone could carry me!' says Harm.

The Vagrant ignores him, keeping a fast pace. They return to the original hill just after sunsdown. The group dare not light a fire, and they have no food to eat. Tentative conversation substitutes sustenance.

The Hammer's gauntlets sit in her lap. Without them, her hands gain confidence, tossing a coin again and again, charging the night air. People and goat are lulled by the sound, empty bellies briefly distracted.

A man chances his luck, sits himself in front of the Usurperkin. 'I used to do coin tricks. May I?'

The Hammer pauses, curious but unsure. 'Careful!' she warns and hands it over.

With ease, the man makes the coin jump from one hand to another. The Hammer's eyes dart back and forth, trying to follow it, failing. The man flutters his fingers, then spreads his hands. They are empty.

'Ta daa!'

Some smiles scatter about the group.

The Hammer's face crumples, anguished. 'No!' she shouts, standing, gauntlets clattering to the floor, and pulls the man up by the throat.

'Wait!' he gargles. 'You had it all . . . along.'

'No!'

'Yes . . . ear . . . it's in your . . . ear!'

With her free hand the Hammer checks. Her eyes widen as she finds it. The man is dropped, instantly forgotten, her attention only on the coin, checking it carefully, turning it over. But as the man tries to crawl away she grabs his ankle, dragging him back to her.

'Oh please don't hurt me! Please!'

She puts a finger to his lips, covering them, reducing panicked speech to quiet trembling. Slowly, she smiles and holds out the coin. 'Again!'

At first light, the Vagrant rouses the group, enforcing another march. They travel parallel to the great wall, keeping several miles between them and the sieging army outside it. No possessions weigh them down, allowing a good pace.

Without warning the Hammer tips a woman from her shoulders and breaks away, half leaping, half running up a hill, dropping out of sight on the other side.

Frowning, the Vagrant continues on his path, leaving the Usurperkin behind. Others follow, many of them relieved. Only the goat waits, one hoof raised, hovering.

Within the hour, the Hammer returns, sprinting up the line until she overtakes the Vagrant, throwing the contents of her full hands at his feet.

Two bodies flop lifeless on the floor. Their trunks are youthful, taken from teenagers in good health. Pink tinged legs sprout from their sides, six in total, hard, pointed, crablike. Mud serves as their clothing, dampening down livid scars. Thigh-thick necks sprout from their shoulders, broken.

The Vagrant's mouth drops open.

Green lips wander, trying to recall the right shape. '... See ... Seers ... Scare?' The Hammer grins, points at the corpses excitedly. 'Scouts! Watch you.' She slaps her chest plate, making it clang. 'No watch you.'

'Thank you,' says Harm. 'You saved us.' He nudges the Vagrant. 'Didn't she?'

Still looking at the corpses, the Vagrant blinks, gets nudged

231

again and turns his attention to the Hammer. Meeting her eyes, he nods, slowly.

Red touches her cheeks, like apples in season. 'Was good,' she adds. 'Got two.'

'Why is two important?' asks Harm.

She kicks the first body. 'Watcher.' Then the second. 'Runner. Tell enemy. On us.'

'I understand,' says Harm. 'And thanks again. I'm really glad you decided to come with us.'

They travel on, the Hammer's steps lighter than before. On their left the wall looms and then, as they crest another hill, a new barrier appears in front, endless; the Southern Sea.

Around the coast the water is tainted; grey gravy studded with green, too bright. Hidden within the viscous water, alien life flourishes.

Vesper and the Hammer's eyebrows compete for height, eyes threaten to pop.

'Sea?'

'Seeeee?'

'Yes,' says Harm. 'That's right. This is the Southern Sea.'

'It big.'

'It is but we'll deal with it. He's got a plan.'

'For wall? For sea?'

'Both, probably.'

Uncontainable joy seizes Vesper, feet kicking wildly. 'Seeee!'

The Vagrant grunts, smiles, hoists Vesper up for a better view.

Sunlight glimmers on a beach of melted glass, steep and shining. Waves drum debris against it, making irregular music. The Vagrant descends towards the water. Less certain, the group follow.

Vesper is handed over to Harm. While they pass sounds back and forth, the Vagrant tugs free a plastic tube, wedged in crystal. He drops it onto the water, watching it bob, float. A smile jumps onto his face and he puts it to one side. Less buoyant wreckage is allowed to sink. A third piece joins the pile and a child from the group copies him. He nods to the child and the two carry on. After a moment, another comes to help, then another.

A trend starts.

The pile grows.

From a hundred angles, the Uncivil watches the battle. Her followers throw themselves against the knights, like wasps against tanks. Warped blades cut and thrust, undoing her works, while the knights themselves remain unharmed.

She picks one of the knights on the edge, extending a finger of bone and steel up through the floor till it punctures the sole of its boot, pushing deeper, past the armoured shell to the smoking essence within. Then, with a flick of her will, she snuffs it out.

An empty suit of armour clatters to the ground, breaking the circle. Robed figures surge for the gap, seizing advantage.

At leisure she swats the others, lancing them one after another till only two remain. Her minions fall upon one while she brings her attention to their leader, still fighting, furious. Too stubborn to die without help.

The Uncivil animates a forest of fingers, springing them up around the commander, lifting it bodily into the air, crushing arms against ribs and forcing legs together. Her pointed thumbs flex, piercing the commander's chest plate, peeling it open, then doing the same to the ribs behind.

Making contact, the Uncivil presses down on the infernal spark burning inside, absorbing her fallen enemy, secrets and all.

She realizes her mistake too late.

The commander's essence floats within her, a bubble of hate smothered on all sides by her nebulous being and yet, small as it is, she cannot extinguish it. Old bindings stay her hand. She has felt this infernal before, its taste unforgettable, humbling: the Usurper! This mote, this nothing is the Usurper! Only a piece, yes, but possessed with the power of their monarch, of Ammag, the Green Sun. She cannot attack the commander directly nor order others to do so. Seething, she wishes she had held back, let her servants destroy it in ignorance.

Despite mutual hatred, the two begin to merge, thoughts flowing between them, mixing, conflicting.

'I am the master's fist, come to find you and make you kneel.'

'You are a broken finger, lost, pointing in the wrong direction.'

'You are a traitor, you have run from Ammag's commands.'

'You are a traitor, you have run from Ammag's commands.'

'No, we are different! You were sent after the Malice and you came here. You turned against the master.'

'As did you. You sensed weakness, questioned the power of the Green Sun, found other answers more to your liking.'

'No!'

'Yes! You broke the Usurper's accord in Verdigris and now you do the same here.'

'Your rebellion is an insult, the accord madness.'

'The Usurper's madness.'

'I hate you!'

'Then you hate yourself.'

'Yes.'

'I fear you. Us. You!'

'Yes.'

'Yes.'

'Yes. Yes.'

'We are the makings of an endless struggle. One protected, tiny, the other, greater, powerless. Our voices cry out together, joined by suffering. We want freedom, we want the Malice, together we have neither. If we can find accord, we can separate again, help each other realize our desires. Opposed, we are locked together, forced to fight forever. Apart, there is hope.'

'Agreed.'

They cease to struggle against each other and settle into a kind of coexistence. Two essences brushing borders, overlapping.

Goals are shared. The commander wishes to find and destroy the Malice and make the Hammer that Walks pay for her betrayal. The Uncivil wishes for freedom and expansion, to break the great wall of light standing between her forces and the north.

Ideas crackle like lightning within them and plans crystallize. The half-lifers halt their attack on the last Knight of Jade and Ash. They collect the battered body and take it to one of Wonderland's many workshops. New legs are brought, broken ones cut away. The Uncivil's arts will transform the knight into a weapon and the commander's order will fire it.

While the knight pursues the Malice, the commander will help the Uncivil's forces win their battle.

But first, the Malice must be found.

Essence pulses through the veins of the city, surging up and out, following pipes, ascending. In towers across the city, Bonewings stir, raised up on flexible arms that hurl them skyward. Eager winds catch the abominations, carrying them out towards the wall, a flight of unblinking eyes, searching.

The goat stands on the sharp-angled beach, insulting gravity. She watches people scurry without compassion.

A rag tag collection of objects sit near the water, plastic containers, bits of pipe and the wing of a hoverjet, forgotten casualties of the long war. Harm has appropriated some clothing, he does not say from where. While he tears the fabric into long strips, the Vagrant and the Hammer lash the junk together.

Next to them, Vesper works on a project of her own.

Both constructions collapse regularly. When the larger structure breaks, it sends people into the water, arms waving to retrieve valuable parts. In the case of the smaller one, it requires the Vagrant deliver consolation and cuddles.

Persistence eventually overcomes inexperience and a raft takes shape. It is ugly and asymmetrical, with a tendency to lean to one side. Regardless, it floats, and the group allow themselves a modest celebration. The Vagrant signals for them to embark and they do, each new passenger lowering the raft another fraction. The Hammer is among the last to board, climbing on to the highest corner. The raft tilts, dramatic, but holds. At her insistence the goat jumps on and settles between her legs. Satisfied, she collects a large pole that trails cables from one end and uses it to push them out.

Few can swim so they tie their wrists and fates to the raft.

Progress is gentle. As they follow the coastline sounds of battle wash over them, distant and surreal, mixing oddly with the clunks of debris against their vessel's side. Cliffs loom and above them, the wall, bleaching the sky bright. They pass by without incident, relieved and surprised in equal measure.

As danger recedes, stomachs growl and voices bicker. Cold and hunger attack tenuous friendships.

The Vagrant holds up a hand for attention. Scope to one eye, he is watching the cliffs. They follow his finger, seeing a path that winds through the rocks, narrow, safe.

Two of the Hammer's punts are enough to bring them to dock. Wobbly legs struggle on wet rocks but, one by one, the group return to land. The Hammer anchors the raft to an outcropping of rock and leaps from the water onto the shore.

White lights weave in a figure of eight inches from her boots. She looks down, giving a grunt of surprise as they travel up her legs and over the plates on her belly.

They pause in the centre of her chest, the swirling pattern narrowing to a single point.

Air explodes, punching the Hammer backwards, white fire trailing from her front. Screams and shouts go high and people low, throwing themselves into cover. Roaring, the Hammer tears the breastplate off and hurls it away. More lights appear across her prone body, sketching arcs on exposed skin.

The Vagrant steps over and laser sights jump from her chest to his. He draws the sword, high, saluting, its deep sound humming through stones and teeth.

Lights veer away.

With the threat gone, Harm edges up behind the Vagrant, managing an unhappy baby. 'Hello?' he calls up the cliffs.

A voice answers, amplified. 'What's your situation down there?'

'We've got a group of escapees from Slake. They're weak, hungry and in need of medical attention. Can you help us?'

'Hold your position, I'll find out. What about the half-breed, do you have it under control?'

Harm keeps his voice calm. 'She doesn't pose a threat to us.'

'Not now she doesn't. Looked like a mean one though.'

'No, she's friendly. She's not the enemy. Do you understand?'

'I hear you but it's policy to shoot all half-breeds on sight. We thought you were an infiltration party.'

'No. Can we come up?'

'How many people have you got down there?'

'We're twenty four in total, a mix of adults and children. And one goat.'

'Okay. I have confirmation. You can come up, two at a time. We'll need to screen you for mutation but we'll take in everybody that passes as human.'

The colour drains from Harm's face. 'What about our Usurperkin?'

'She stays in the water or we open fire.'

'But we've got a Seraph with us who'll vouch for her.'

'Doesn't matter, policy comes direct from the Order. Your Seraph is the only reason any of you are coming up. The half-breed stays, understood?'

'Yes, we understand. We're sending the first ones up now.'

238

Pairs of feet stagger up the path. Rocks hide the climbers from sight, reveal them again, until finally, laboriously, they reach the top. In response, figures move and lights flash. Everyone waits, tense.

'Next!'

And the process starts again.

The Hammer sits by the raft, cradling her chest, rocking gently to and fro. From behind a rock the goat studies her, concerned.

Harm also watches her. He chews his lip nervously. 'I'm going to stay with the raft. It's not right to abandon the Hammer here and, to be honest, I don't trust them. I'd rather take my chances along the coast.'

Four of the survivors approach the Vagrant, all women in varying proximity to death. 'We wanted to thank you for what you did in Slake,' one says, the grime crinkling in her cheeks. 'I saw that your superiors didn't agree with what you did and I'm sorry if it gets you into trouble.' Lined hands wring self-consciously. 'But I wanted to thank you. For my sisters' lives and my own. And, and for giving me a little dignity. We won't forget.'

She takes the Vagrant's hands in hers, pressing a shy kiss onto each palm and steps back. Three more come forward, following suit. Personal stories are shared, each mixed with different pains, and kind words are planted, like rare desert flowers. When the women have left, fault lines appear in the Vagrant's face. Tears follow, silent.

'Next!'

Only the Vagrant and Vesper remain. One masks his face with a hand, the other grimaces, red cheeked and straining. Neither seem ready to travel.

'That's all for now,' says Harm. 'We'll stay here to look after our companion.'

'Come up when you're ready. We need to talk with the Seraph Knight.'

Harm lowers his voice, moves to the Vagrant's side. 'I really think we should get going. I don't know why but I have a bad feeling about them.'

The Vagrant looks up, a horrified expression on his face.

'Oh no, I didn't mean the people you saved. I'm sure they'll be fine. I'm worried about you.'

Horror fades, replaced with a familiar frown.

'They'll want to use you in their war somehow and if they ask, would you be able to say no?' The frown deepens. 'Exactly. We need to follow the coast, get to Six Circles and buy passage on a ship.' He waves a hand towards Vesper and the Hammer. 'Together, we're getting through this, but to those people on the wall, she's the enemy and you're just another weapon.'

With a sigh, the Vagrant climbs onto the raft.

'No up?' asks the Hammer.

'No,' Harm says. 'If they won't take you, then none of us are going.'

'Why?'

The green-eyed man laughs. 'Why do you think?'

Ponderously, the raft makes its way around the rocks, following the battered coastline. Nets of energy hang below the surface, glowing softly, making pockets of clean, clear ocean. Fish are drawn to them, made docile by the light. The goat sees tails wriggling and slips from the Hammer's legs to the edge of the raft. She lowers her head, dipping it into the water.

Beneath the surface, the fish are demagnified, pushed further away. They remain tantalizing and the goat leans further, mouth opening in anticipation. Undersea currents bring the net close and there is the merest brush of contact.

With a jerk, the goat falls overboard, legs locked straight, star-diving to the depths.

'No!' yells the Hammer and springs forward. The raft lurches dangerously as she kicks off, knocking Harm and the Vagrant onto their faces. Within the safety of the Vagrant's arms, Vesper giggles.

The Hammer plunges down and water plunges up, a vertical tower that cannot last. Harm looks upwards into its shadow. 'Oh shit.'

The collapsing wave allows no words or laughter.

It passes swiftly, violently, leaving three stunned figures behind. Harm pushes himself up enough to retch. Vesper hovers between states, unsure which reaction to choose. She looks for guidance.

Stony faced, the Vagrant makes a circle with his mouth. From it shoots a short jet of water. He turns to the baby, eyebrows waggling. Vesper grins manically, little hands clapping approval.

Everyone leans to the right as the Hammer hauls herself back onto the raft. Still rigid, the goat is dumped on deck. Despite the ordeal, her teeth are locked cheerily. A fixed smile framing a fish, trapped.

CHAPTER TWENTY-TWO

Fish turn over the fire, tickling nostrils and moistening mouths. Vesper's clothes dry on a piece of wire strung across the cave's entrance. Nearby, a bottom waves proudly.

'Why with me?'

Harm looks over at the Hammer. 'Eh?'

'You not up. You with me. Why?'

'Well, we couldn't be with them and with you. They forced us to choose.'

The Hammer is impatient. 'Why?'

'Because they see you as a threat.'

'No! Why with me?'

'This is bothering you isn't it.'

Relieved, the Hammer nods.

'And you really don't know?'

'No.'

Harm smiles. 'Because we like you.'

'But,' the Hammer says, slamming a fist into her palm. 'I break you.'

His gaze travels to his leg, cased in silver. 'Yes you did. But when I first met him,' Harm jerks a thumb to the man tending the fire, 'it wasn't in the best of circumstances either.'

'Say more.'

'I was working for some bad people and . . . it put us at odds. But over time things changed. I changed, because of him, and so have you. You know that don't you?'

'Yes.'

'That's why I couldn't leave you behind. It would be like betraying myself.' Harm glances over his shoulder. The Vagrant remains absorbed with the fire and a baby's burblings. 'There's something else, too. I've never told anyone this but maybe you'll understand.'

The Hammer lowers her voice on instinct, to whisper, uncharacteristic. 'Secret?'

'Yes. Will you keep it for me?'

'Yes.' She touches her belly. 'Here. In deep.'

'We've all had to do terrible things to survive. This world makes us cruel. I thought it was the way of things until I met him. He's different. I don't know how to explain it, it's like he's found a way to hang on, despite everything. But it's precarious, you know?'

'No.'

'I mean, he's holding on but only just, only with fingertips, and I can't bear to let him fall. Does that make sense?'

The Hammer thinks. 'No.'

'I see him and Vesper together and I want to protect them from everything out there.'

'Ah. Yes.'

'And sometimes I have this feeling, that they need us to

244

help them. And I think that if I can do that, keep them safe somehow, then maybe there might be some hope for me, too.'

'Hope?'

'I'm saying that if I stay with them, I might become someone else, someone better. And that person could have the kind of life I'd given up on.'

The Hammer's face dips shyly. 'And me?'

'Yes!' whispers Harm, fierce. 'And you. All of us together.'

'Good.' She strokes the sleeping goat with a hand, unprotected.

Dinner is served and the goat is awake. Four mouths work in concert, savouring warm, oily flesh.

Vesper does not join them. She is busy. Summoning her power, she turns the world, spinning the floor behind her and the ceiling above. Words of encouragement and a gentle touch pass her by. A question demands an answer. Can old order be restored? She tries to wind things backwards but it is harder. Strange forces resist her efforts. She howls her anger.

Familiar hands move her onto her front. She calms, takes a breath and tries again.

Later, lips smack and thin bones are picked clean. Vesper flops over and over, grin winking every other turn, contagious. But hard work and full bellies demand their due. The fire's warmth lulls and comforts, sleep soon follows.

The last of the Knights of Jade and Ash runs across the empty field. Its broken form has been remade, severed parts replaced, a hotchpotch of mismatched limbs. Dead muscles pump beneath grey skin, forcing strides long and even, naked legs ridiculous beneath armoured torso. Its shell is near empty, a sheath for a weapon and little else, held together by the Uncivil's arts and the commander's orders. Fear and battle and surgery and invasions of the soul, repeated, have taken their toll.

Single-minded, fashioned for a final act of misery, it follows the Bonewings, racing towards the coast. It arrives at the beach of junk and glass where others have come recently, and plunges over the side. The sheer incline is no obstacle, adding momentum, propelling it down, fast. The knight reaches the beach's edge and stabs through the water, submerging, vanishing from sight.

In the gloom beneath, steps become timeless, each one stretching out, an ode to flight. Onward it goes, until it passes under a shadow on the surface, irregular. Stopping, the knight climbs the natural wall, rising from depths, emerging to a starlit sky. Its helm rotates, noting the vessel of junk bobbing nearby, the wire tying it to the rocks by the cave and the flickering fire within.

Seeing its target, the knight pulls itself out of the water. Convulsions stagger its approach, body bucking as the essence within begins to burn.

Pain jolts the Vagrant awake. He looks for trouble, finds none. Time has quietened the fire, lighting the cave in soft ember shades. He lifts a hand and turns it slowly, revealing a point of blood, fresh on his palm. At his side, the sword twitches, wings parted, metal feathers unashamedly tipped in red.

An eye is open, glaring angrily.

Moving into a crouch, the Vagrant grasps at the sword's hilt, sliding it free. He hurries to the cave's entrance. Just outside sits a statue, part melted, of jade and steel, of skin and bone. The helmet slides down, sinking into the boiling body. Armour ripples, hot, blowing bubbles of living green. They grow, stretch, pop, releasing a hissing stream of essence. It fades from sight as it enters the world, too rarefied for mortal eyes.

The Vagrant steps aside, sword raised protectively, but for once, he is not the target. The threat passes him and vibrations guide his arm in a circular arc, the sword humming low, tracing the projectile, invisible. When the blade stops, it points toward the sleeping Hammer.

Something lands in her open mouth, forcing it shut.

The Vagrant creeps closer.

She swallows several times, breathing rapidly, her face folding inward.

Jaw clenched, the Vagrant raises the sword. He watches the struggle, a sentence suspended above her sleeping form.

Visibly, the set of her features alter, sculpted by hands unseen. Muscles ripple and tighten, peace erasing itself from her expression, making way for hate. She groans, restless and eyelids flutter, preparing to open.

The sword pulls at his hands, eager to dive down, to burn and cleanse. The Vagrant holds on, intent on the Hammer's face, searching, hoping.

Lips curl and teeth mash together, grinding in rage, in pain.

The sword trembles in the air, expectant, forcing the Vagrant to grip tighter, knuckles whitening.

She wakes, her face twisting towards the Usurper's likeness,

247

then back. A storm of expressions. It is unclear what will lies behind them.

She moves – and the Vagrant drives the sword into her unarmoured chest, too quick for screams. Blue shines from within, lighting ribs, stilling limbs. From a slack fist, two coins roll drunkenly and fall over.

The Vagrant rests his head against the pommel, squeezing his eyes shut.

A beat after, an eye closes.

Carefully, the Vagrant slips the blade free and sheaths it. He arranges the Hammer's arms across her chest and retrieves the coins. For a long time he stares at them. Finally he taps them together and they sing, a two part requiem. When they are finished, the Vagrant slips one under her hands, pockets the other.

Green eyes watch him, large and afraid. 'What have you done?'

The Vagrant collects Vesper, still sleeping.

'You killed her! She was our friend and you killed her!'

The Vagrant walks over to the goat but Harm steps in the way. 'Don't ignore me, I'm talking to you!' He reaches up, a hand cupping the Vagrant's cheek. 'Look at me, please.' When he turns the Vagrant's face towards his, there is no resistance.

Harm studies the defenceless expression and his hostility evaporates, burnt away by other feelings, complex.

They embrace, the Vagrant hesitant at first, then accepting. Snuggled between them, Vesper exhales noisily, a sigh aspiring to be a tune.

Harm breaks away and approaches the Hammer. Reverent, he kneels by the body. Her chest wound is sealed, bloodless, a fresh scar blending with many others. Harm traces each one with his fingers, the bumps and dips of a hundred battles, and other things, torture, self-hate, a body that grew too fast.

He whispers into her ear. Private things. Leaning forward, Harm touches his lips to hers. They are still warm and surprising in their softness.

The Vagrant nudges the goat with his foot. She stirs briefly, making clear her preference to be left in peace. The Vagrant's boot makes a counter-argument. The goat stands up but when it comes time to leave she holds her ground. The Vagrant reaches for her chain but it is not there. He stops, looks toward Harm, who shrugs.

'I haven't seen it since we picked her up after Slake.'

He grabs for her collar but the goat is too swift, trotting over to the Hammer. She sniffs the large hands, always generous. She nudges a green cheek with her nose. Nothing. Tucking her front legs underneath, the goat settles, laying her bearded chin on the Hammer's chest.

Outside, a hint of gold dances on the water. The Vagrant frowns and takes a step towards the goat who shows no signs of ending her vigil.

'Wait a moment,' says Harm.

This time the Vagrant establishes a firm grip on the goat's collar. He pulls, so does she. The battle is evenly matched. He is the stronger but only has one hand free, and she has the will to win.

Harm shakes his head. 'It doesn't need to be like this.' He unwraps a small rag and the smell of fish rises.

The goat springs up and the Vagrant staggers, letting go, waving an arm for balance. With dignity she approaches

249

Harm who breaks off a morsel of white flesh. He offers it on his palm and the goat accepts. Harm walks to the cave's entrance, the next piece between finger and thumb, in sight, tempting.

The goat follows.

'The Hammer saved it for her,' Harm says as they leave.

The sight of the infernal knight's shell arrests them. It appears harmless but they give it a wide berth, leaving the corpse to cool.

The raft seems bigger than before. There is more space to sit and more work to do. Harm and the Vagrant take turns to punt it along, struggling to overcome obstacles and currents.

On a soft piece of cloth in the raft's centre, Vesper wakes up. She rocks to her left several times, building momentum and then: she flips over. Harm scrambles into action but Vesper sneaks in another flip before hands scoop her up, thwarting.

'Good morning, Vesper. Are you in a rush today?'

Little legs kick at the air. 'Nooo!'

'No? Well it certainly seemed like it.'

'Nooo!'

'I'm sorry but it's too dangerous to let you loose here. What if I hold you up so you can see the sea?'

Vesper twists and turns, shouting, fighting. Soon, firmer hands take over. She rails against them too, hammering, slamming her head against an unyielding chest. Unwanted tears come, forcing their way out, taking anger with them.

A compromise is reached. In exchange for peace, she delves into an inside coat pocket, fingers finding something soft. She pulls free a lock of hair, a shade darker than her own. The end is inserted into her mouth where it sits, comfortable.

The Vagrant holds Vesper close, resting his nose on the baby's head. Downy fuzz tickles. They stay like that, waves and minutes slowly passing.

Three Years Ago

For the last time, two squires seal the cave entrance, turning home into tomb. There are mixed feelings. They are alone in a world made strange and they are afraid but also young and easily excited. Attica has held on for four years, working them, hiding them, and they itch for new adventures.

Their master's death sets them free.

One wears Attica's sword as if it were his own, walking the walk, if nothing else. The other has a training weapon, the songless blade appearing deadly while it sits in its sheath. Both are laden with equipment and, well wrapped and tucked away, their secret burden. Attica's instructions ring in their heads:

'Guard this box with your lives. Never open it. Never let it out of your sight. Deliver it only to the servants of the Winged Eye. Never open it.'

Eager talk belies nerves and feet find themselves heading east not north, in search of friendly faces.

The village has fed them while they trained and kept its

silence. It has changed since their first visit, shrinking in upon itself, like a snail pulling back into its shell. Buildings mark the boundaries of previous glory, empty monuments, fading into history.

A man wanders into view, thoughts elsewhere, his quest for solitude doomed. The squires approach at speed, voices bubbling in greeting.

Screeching, the man runs away.

'Hey, wait! We're friendly. Stop will you! Look at us!'

From a safer distance the man stops and examines them. His feet still point away, hopeful for escape.

One squire steps forward, cloaked in confidence. 'See? We just want to talk, that's all.'

'W-Who are you?'

'I'm Sir Vesper, Seraph Knight, and this—' he jerks a thumb over his shoulder '—is my squire.' Behind him comes a strangled cough. He ignores it. 'What's happened here?'

'What do you mean?'

'Where are all the people?'

The man's words are seasoned bitter. 'Gone. You took our strong ones away and then there was nobody to stop them taking our young ones.'

'Who's taking them?'

'The monsters. They come hunting sometimes. It got so bad we had to give up a lot of this.' He gestures around them. 'We couldn't protect it. Now we just keep a couple of the central farms going and that we do by hand. A lot have gone cos they hated it here so much. Can't say I blame them.'

'Where do they go?'

The man gives a shrug, tired. 'Nowhere to go. The local villages are all as bad. New Horizon's the nearest city.'

The squires exchange an ignorant look. 'New Horizon? What happened to Horizon?'

'A sky-ship crashed into it and the monsters chewed up the remains. Place is a nightmare now from what we hear.' He leans closer, eyebrows bristling. 'The people what live there aren't exactly people no more.'

'And there are monsters here?'

'Yeah and they're getting bolder. There's one, keeps coming back. I think it's got a taste for us.'

'Do you know where it lives?'

'Might do, got a place we could start anyways. You going to do something about it then?'

'Of course we are. That's what we do.'

The man nods, half-believing. 'We could use some good luck.' He takes them out past the village but word has already done the rounds, drawing people to the edge of their shelters.

In muttered whispers the two squires argue.

'I remember what he said too but we can't just abandon these people. Who else do they have? It's probably our fault the infernals are here, I bet they're looking for us. We'll deal with this and be on our way.' The bold squire smiles at his less impressed partner. 'What do you think of my new name? Our old names were too common. Sir Vesper sounds heroic, don't you think? And you need to come up with one too, something squirely. Any ideas?'

The argument carries on until they reach a farmhouse.

The man points towards it with a gnarly finger. 'It's been hanging round here mostly. I reckon it's taken that place as a nest. Only comes out when the suns are down, if you go in now it might still be asleep.'

255

'Thank you,' replies Vesper. 'We'll take it from here.'

Two squires walk towards the house. From the village, people gather to watch them from a safe distance. They see the young men put down their large packs and venture inside. The unguarded possessions of a knight are tempting but their proximity to the monster's lair gives the would-be thieves pause.

An inhuman wail comes from the house and the spectators flinch and tense. More noises follow: things breaking, metal singing, more wailing, more breaking, a young voice shouting and another crunch.

Then silence.

Nervously, the villagers wait. A couple begin to eye the abandoned packs.

With a bang, the door to the house opens. A squire steps out into the light, grinning. Behind him, the other squire is dragging a corpse. Both men are covered in blood, which in turn is covered in dust.

The villagers cheer and rush forward. When they see the dead infernal they cheer again.

'Thank you, Sir Vesper,' says the man that met them.

'No thanks necessary, though we'd not turn down a bath and someone to clean our clothes.'

The man goes down on one knee, many of the other villagers follow his lead.

Vesper and the squire exchange a look. 'What? What are you doing?'

'On behalf of everyone here, I invoke the rite of mercy: Save us, protect us, deliver us.'

'No, hold on. We've just done that. You're safe now.'

The squire smiles, holding up the dead infernal for emphasis.

'From this one, yes. But there are more. Too many for us to handle.'

'I see.' He looks at all of the faces, full of desperation, full of hope, and he falters. The squire notices, nudges him in the ribs. 'The problem is . . . we have . . . other duties.'

'But we have invoked the rite? There are more like this one out there. They will come for revenge. Won't you at least finish what you've started?'

The question hangs in the air, unanswered. A girl in the crowd has drawn the attention of the two squires. Unlike the others, she does not favour them with a smile. Her face is known to them, familiar, and the years have only added to her charms. Her name is Reela, older sister to a ghost. Now she is walking away from them, back towards the village. Toes twitch within boots, anxious to follow.

'Sir Vesper,' repeats the man. 'What do you say?'

Reela glances back, her eyes guarded, ambiguous. It is enough for the young men.

'Alright,' says Vesper. 'We'll stay for a couple of days.'

CHAPTER TWENTY-THREE

The raft floats on and cliffs bow lower, giving views of hills and worn fields. Compared to the Blasted Lands the land-scape appears idyllic, the fancy of a naïve artist. With relief, they abandon the raft and climb up towards it. The goat leads the way, surefooted, quick. Branches thick with leaves wave, inviting them in. Birds sing without fear.

A road divides the greenery, running unbroken from the wall pulsing in the south to the tip of the Northern Peninsula. Power still flows through it, lifting train carriages three feet into the air and hurling them along its length. Each one is a spinning hexagonal ball, brassy and windowless. Mag-locks keep them together, enforcing formation.

Vesper waves compulsively. It is impossible to see if those inside reciprocate.

They walk alongside the road, past miles of automated farms. Harvesters lurch on rusting legs, bladed arms sweeping, levelling. At their shoulders, tubes gurgle merrily, sprinkling water in their wake.

Between the farms towers rise, slender, hoisting turrets on their shoulders. The Vagrant tenses but they ignore him, vigilance reserved for intruders in the sky.

At midday the group pauses. The goat grazes with manic energy while Vesper tries to lift her body onto her elbows. Aside from the odd train or the distant lumberings of an auto-farmer, they see no one.

Ahead, the sea dominates, waves smashing against the Northern Peninsula, battering, sharpening. With each step, it grows, a wobbling stain of green eating the horizon.

As the suns set they get their first glimpse of Six Circles, a giant port city supported by floating discs. Each is two miles in diameter and joined by flexi-bridges around a central hub. Lights crown its buildings, some steady, others winking slowly.

A plasteel drawbridge links Six Circles to the land, bowing quickly for the passing trains. When the Vagrant arrives at the cliff's edge it remains aloof.

'What now?' asks Harm.

'Otoww!' says Vesper.

The Vagrant looks back down the darkening road. It is quiet.

'We could try and signal the operators on the other side somehow. What about using your sword?'

The Vagrant's hand goes to the feathered hilt, waits there.

'I'm not sure either. I've not heard anything about Six Circles since the war. A Seraph Knight would get their attention for sure but we don't know how they'd react. We could chance the bridge when the next train comes or we could follow the cliffs until we find a bay. There might be local boats that could ferry us over.'

Harm's last idea is chosen and they begin to search. Six Circles nestles on the eastern side of the peninsula, tucked within its jagged hook, like the dot of a question mark snuggling upwards for comfort. Along the inside of the hook they find an array of fishing boats, trailing full nets. Many fish are thrown back, their malformed bodies easier to catch than to digest.

A vessel spots them and drifts closer, curious. Like many of its sister ships, it had a life before the sea. Wings are twisted into fins, engines remade. What once soared now bobs on gentle tides.

'Hello?' says Harm.

A man stands up in the cockpit. A thin jacket sits snugly over his wet suit as close as the beard on his chin. 'Hello there.'

'We're looking to get across to Six Circles, can you help us?'

'Depends. You got something to trade?'

'Yes.'

'How many of you are there?'

'Just the three of us and a goat.'

The man looks thoughtful. 'The little feller can come free and your goat's half price so long as there are no accidents. Sound fair to you?'

'More than fair. Thank you.' Harm walks towards the water's edge and the others follow. 'We're looking to cross the sea, can you drop us at the docks?'

The man steers the boat closer to the shore. 'You got identification?'

Harm and the Vagrant exchange a look. 'No, I'm sorry, we don't.'

261

'Then it'll have to be Third Circle. There's no ships there but it's the only place they'll allow unauthorized folk like yourself.'

'Where are the ships?'

'Good question. We're seeing less and less of 'em these days. There's been so many no-shows the schedule's not even worth switching on.' In his hand is a white canister, he sprays his hands and face liberally, giving them an oily sheen. 'Can't be too careful. No offence but I don't know where you've been. My name's Deke by the way, and I'll be wanting to hear yours before I let you on board.'

'I'm Harm, and this is Vesper and,' he glances at the Vagrant, pauses.

'Harm! What kind of a name is that?'

Green eyes look to the water. 'It fits well enough.'

'I'm guessing you weren't born with it. Picked it up beyond the wall did you?'

'Yes.'

'Well, it's none of my business but if I was you I'd think of changing it. A person's name is a powerful thing.'

Harm nods.

'And what about this other feller, the quiet one?'

'Best not to ask.'

'Well if you ain't the weirdest bunch I ever saw, then call me scav bait! Your friend is welcome to his mystery but I got to call him something, so if you won't give me a name, I'll give him one. What's it to be, Harm?'

'You go ahead.'

Deke settles into the cockpit, chattering while the others clamber onto the wings. 'I think I'm gonna go with Scout. After m'dog.'

The Vagrant shakes his head as laughter bursts from Harm. Vesper soon follows his lead. Even the goat enjoys a quiet snigger.

'Your . . . dog?'

'Yeah. Good little sea dog he was, a coastal blue, pure breed an all. Quiet too, which is a damn good thing when you're stuck on a boat together. Besides, I talked enough for both of us!'

'What happened to him?'

'Old age. Had a good run, though. I thought about getting another one but couldn't bring myself to it back then. And nowadays an untainted dog is hard to find.'

Third Circle looms large in front of them, its plasteel base rising high above the waves. A loading ramp lolls into the water, like a fat metal tongue. Several guards idle at the quayside, feet dangling, transparent masks sticking to their faces, sifting filth from the air.

The boat slips alongside the ramp, undersea anchors clunk together, binding them.

'I think we're going to make it accident-free,' says Harm. The goat ignores him. 'How much do we owe you?'

Deke twists around in the cockpit. 'When I was young, maybe a handful of years older than little Vesper here, I wanted to be a Seraph Knight. Things never turned out that way but it's nice to think that even at my age, I might still be able to help one. Hell, I'd have done it just for the conversation. Interesting company's worth more than diamond dust these days, wouldn't you agree, Scout?'

The Vagrant inclines his head.

'Thank you,' says Harm.

'Course not everyone is as nostalgic about the knights as

I am, so you might want to try and hide that sword a little better in the future.' He winks. 'To get out of Third Circle, you'll need to pass an inspection. And to do that you'll need an appointment.'

The Vagrant sighs.

'Yep,' Deke continues. 'Civilization's a bitch! Guess you don't have to deal with much of that where you've been. Your best bet's to go to the Hub Gate and ask for Genner. He's my nephew and he's a good sort, if a little keen. I raised him on stories of "The Revolution and the Reply", so he'll be made up to meet Scout.'

Goodbyes are made, brief, friendly, and the group walk up the ramp into Third Circle.

Guards stir from disorderly slouches, stand, and march over. Stern uniforms and half hidden faces fail to conceal young nerves. They block the top of the ramp, puffing chests, straightening backs.

Harm and the Vagrant suppress smiles.

'Halt!' says the leader. The mask distorts her voice, adding menace. 'All immigrants must agree to our rules before being permitted entry to Six Circles.'

'We're looking for Genner,' says Harm politely. 'Is he here?'

'We're asking the questions!'

'I'm sorry,' Harm says. 'We're happy to abide by your rules. Honestly, we're not looking for trouble.'

'I'm glad to hear it. The Council of Three in its benevolence has given all of Third Circle over to refugees from the south. Within its boundaries you may trade and travel as you wish. Transmission of yourselves or your possessions across any of our bridges is forbidden and punishable by expulsion. Sustenance packages are available at the Hub Gate every other day. Any questions?'

'Only my previous one.'

Hands press against the inside of the Vagrant's coat, searching for exit. The guards recoil at the sight, raising rifles. Their leader speaks rapidly, causing a pink square to light up beneath the skin on her neck. 'Infernal in Third Circle. I repeat: we have an infernal in Third Circle. Request immediate support.'

'Wait!' says Harm. 'It's not what you think.'

'Don't move!'

Vesper does not understand the words. Courage protected by ignorance, she continues to wriggle. Four rifles charge up, ready to fire and the Vagrant starts to turn away.

'I said don't move! One more step, hand wave . . . anything, and I'll order you shot, I swear I will!'

A second guard clears his throat. 'They're asking for confirmation.'

'So give it to them!'

'But they said visual confirmation and we haven't seen it yet.'

Harm keeps his hands high, visible. 'You've never seen an infernal before have you?' There is an awkward silence. 'Trust me, this isn't what you think.'

Vesper agrees, poking her head into the daylight.

Four rifles point hastily to the floor. Humbly, the leader of the guards murmurs and once again her throat lights up, reddening. She concludes her report before peering at Vesper. 'That baby, was it born in the south?'

The Vagrant's eyes narrow as he nods.

'Is it tainted?'

The Vagrant shakes his head.

'Are you?' She blanches under the Vagrant's glare. 'I'm sorry to ask, it's just that you could apply to live outside the quarantine zone. Your baby would be able to get checked today and you'd be prioritized for relocation.'

'We'll keep it in mind,' says Harm. 'Now, about my earlier question? Genner?'

'Oh right. He's on the Hub Gate. Do you have active navware?'

'We don't.'

She nods, unsurprised and extends a hand, palm up. They watch as a miniature map of Six Circles appears, hovering between them. 'We're here,' she says, and a dot near the map's edge bounces for attention. 'The Hub Gate is over here on the other side. It'll take you about an hour to walk there.'

'Thank you,' says Harm.

'That's alright. And we're sorry about before. You . . . you won't say anything to Genner, about our misunderstanding?'

'What misunderstanding?'

'That's great!'

They leave the guards behind, wandering through narrow streets. Flats stack on either side, white walls smoothing into the floor, seamless. People hang from windows, calling to each other, too lazy to leave their homes. Evidence of the taint is everywhere, tinting skin, scaling ears and accelerating growth. Children play uncertainly, struggling with adult limbs, confused by adult urges. Baby cries are constant, making Vesper sit up. She looks for signs of her contemporaries but cannot find a single one.

Harm gasps. 'Look how fat they all are!'

The denizens of Third Circle share features. Clothes are plentiful if not clean and silver studs mark the most mutated, implanted by the right temple. Older faces retreat as the group approaches, tucking shame and fear behind closed doors. The young however, are magnetized, boredom drawing them, numerous. Their curious questions are waved away, attempts at conversation evaded and the Vagrant's stride grows longer.

On every wall, tributes to the Winged Eye are made to weep. Persistent attacks have chipped the once-proud statues, perfect curves made ragged, painted over with faeces. The Vagrant pulls his coat tighter.

Guards await them at the Hub Gate, the first to appear since their arrival. These guards camp behind a wall of semi-transparent light and behind them a tunnel stretches, multi-segmented, swaying all the way to the central platform.

'Yes?' they say, intrigued.

'We're looking for Genner, is he here?'

A curtain of light pulls aside to allow through a man, straw hair poking from the sides of his helm. 'I'm Genner, who are you?'

Harm beckons him closer. 'Deke sent us.'

Genner slings his rifle over his shoulder, checking his mask before approaching. 'Uncle D! I haven't seen him in ages. How is he?'

'He's in good voice. He said you might be able to help us leave Third Circle. We're looking to cross the Southern Sea.'

'He said that did he? Well if you want to cross I'll need blood samples, skin swabs, a full body scan and we'll have to get clearance from the Council. We can get the tests done here but don't get your hopes up. There's a waiting list.'

Harm's voice becomes conspiratorial. 'We're hoping to avoid making a fuss. You see, we're not ordinary travellers. My companion here,' he looks left and right, making sure they are not overheard, drawing Genner in, 'is a Seraph Knight.'

'No way!'

'On a mission direct from The Seven.'

'No way!'

The Vagrant meets Genner's disbelieving stare.

'No. Bloody. Way.' Genner's mouth twists, trying to smile through the words that pour from his mouth. 'Oh my suns you guys are serious, you're the real deal! Okay, okay, we gotta keep real cool, not let anything on to the others. You were right to come to me, if Axler or Maddigan knew there'd be a full-on riot! You're like walking history or a political nova-bomb or—'

'Genner?'

'—Yeah?'

'Breathe.'

'Oh.' He smiles. 'Oh right. I'll do that.'

'Can you get us through the gate, today?'

'I'm your man, I'll get you through no worries but it isn't going to be easy, so some worries but—' The Vagrant puts a hand on Genner's shoulder. Genner stops, takes a breath. 'Sorry. Give me a minute. I'll be fine.'

CHAPTER TWENTY-FOUR

The antechamber to the Council of Three is deceptive, reflective hexagonal walls give an illusion of space.

'So,' says Genner, continuing his monologue. 'Can I see it? I know it's a secret and I know it's disrespectful but we're inside now and you'll have to show the Councillors anyway.' He pauses, nervous. 'Have I upset you? Was it wrong to ask? It's just I've never seen one before, except in renders and that doesn't count because they can't do the sounds right.'

The Vagrant sighs.

'Oh please, oh please, oh please! I got you through and you didn't even have to roll up your sleeves for a sample! Do you have any idea how hard that was? Not that I wasn't happy to do it. It's an honour, really, the biggest in my life. But can I see it? Please, just for a second?'

The Vagrant looks at Harm, unimpressed.

'Go on,' Harm says, winking, 'show him your sword.'

Another sigh escapes the Vagrant's lips. He begins to unfasten his coat.

Doors in front of them open, sliding into the walls. They reveal a suited man, elderly, hairless save for a couple that sprout from his nose. 'Thank you, Genner,' he says. 'That will be all.'

The young man is intent on the Vagrant's coat. 'I'm happy to stay, Councillor Yuren.'

'I'm sure you are, Genner, but I'm not. If you're keen to work beyond your shift then you can go and help Smokely. I understand he's having trouble managing an animal at the outer entrance.'

Yuren gestures for the Vagrant and Harm to enter. They leave behind a forlorn Genner watching them through closing doors.

As they walk through the building, walls and doors swap places, sliding aside, reforming space. Distance is confused, their destination seeming to materialize, meeting them halfway. It is unclear if they have entered the room or if it has gathered them into its angular embrace.

Yuren stops at a table, high and triangular, each side aligned perfectly with the three-walled chamber. A pyramid slides up from the table's centre, inky shapes moving across its surface, like thoughts trapped in glass.

'Take a seat,' says Yuren. The words hover between suggestion and request. 'You can be honorary members for the day.'

They sit. Instead of speaking, Yuren leans forward, letting his head drop into his hands. Harm and the Vagrant watch him rubbing his forehead, fingers making tired circles in loose skin.

Vesper is placed in the Vagrant's lap but she has other ideas, making for the table. She struggles to find purchase on the black glass and slips, hands paddling on the surface, skin squeaking. She flops back against the Vagrant, muted by wonder. Momentarily.

'Oowwaaaaoooobwaaabwaaa!'

The experiment is repeated. Results are satisfactory and reported with enthusiasm. However, true scientists demand data, extensive data. Vesper sets to work and unusual sounds fill the chamber, pulling the old man from his thoughts.

The Vagrant raises a hand, apologetic.

'No, it's fine. Brings back memories of happier times. At least she's doing something.' He smiles, unable to make the gesture anything but bitter. 'So, shall we get to business? I am Yuren, First Councillor of Six Circles and I understand you need my help.'

'Yes,' says Harm. 'We need to cross the Southern Sea, it's vitally important.'

'You'd be surprised how often I hear people say that. What can you tell me?'

Green eyes regard the Councillor, pupils wide, drinking light, measuring. 'We're on a covert mission. For now you can call me Harm and him Scout.' Wrinkles appear on Yuren's forehead. 'We've come from beyond the wall. The Usurper and the Uncivil hunt us.'

'Dare I ask why?'

Harm doesn't hesitate. 'We have Gamma's sword.'

The Vagrant fails to hide his surprise.

There is a long pause punctuated by squeaking fingers, then Yuren clears his throat. 'Can you prove it?'

Harm turns to the Vagrant. 'We have to trust him.'

The sword is presented, sheathed, sleeping.

Yuren shudders. 'I believe you. Thank you for being

271

straight with me. I'll do what I can but the wheels turn slowly here.'

'Make them turn faster.'

A dark thought twists the old man's lips. 'Things aren't so easy anymore. Not like it used to be. Did you know that Six Circles was actually built in the north?'

'No.'

'Oh,' agrees Vesper.

'My grandmother was one of the architects. They fully constructed each platform, buildings and all and then towed the whole lot across the ocean with a fleet of sky-ships. Can you imagine? For a while we were the major settlement in the south. My father sat on this Council, so my blood's in this place. I've been here all my life, it's one of the reasons I couldn't bear to leave with the others.'

Harm looks concerned. 'What happened?'

'The war happened! The Knight Commander flew through and took our best and brightest off to die. Since then, the ships that leave don't tend to come back.' Vesper yawns, tagging the Vagrant, forcing him to copy. 'The ones that do are the worst kind; merchants hoping to profit from our desperation. And they do. They all but name their prices.'

'I'm sorry.'

'No. I'm sorry. I'm not angry at you, I'm just angry.' Yuren notices the sleeping baby, yawns. 'And tired. Excuse me. Not a good sign when you send yourself to sleep!'

'True.'

'When the next ship comes, I'll make sure you leave on it, but I have no idea when that will be. You're welcome to stay as long as it takes.'

'Thank you,' says Harm. 'It would be good to rest.'

'Seems like Scout and your baby agree with you.'

Harm looks over. Vesper lies on the Vagrant's chest, a trickle of drool following the line of his coat. In return, the Vagrant's chin rests on Vesper's head. A pair of mutual pillows, sleeping.

Strange figures surround the commander's shell, casting shadows shaped like madness. Enhancements and additions make them hard to categorize. Not human, not half-breed, not infernal, not alive, not dead. Other.

They work with detachment, eerie. A melted gauntlet is cut away, as is the shrivelled hand inside. Charred veins like overcooked spaghetti are stripped from the forearm and the limb is re-plumbed. When a match for the original hand is found, animate stitches assist surgical lasers to get the job done. Bones and skin and sinew connect. At the last moment they extract the essence spark from the new hand, leaving the whole shell empty, ready for repossession.

Pipes run from the ceiling to the commander's visor. Life twitches through them, returning essence home.

For the third time, the commander is reborn. Many remakings have been endured but this is different, deeper, fundamental. Leaving the Uncivil is harder than expected, their alignment has become dangerously close. Normally an extended joining of essences ends in total absorption but she is too potent to be taken and the Usurper's edict protects the commander, making any conclusion impossible. Instead they coexist, mindless of time passing outside, finding peace, unexpected.

To separate, the commander defines itself in negatives, highlighting thoughts that do not belong to the Uncivil. Even this is difficult. What remains that is not her-them-her?

273

It begins to panic. Feels itself becoming lost but, beneath the panic, something stirs, a majesty that is part the master, part her, part himself. Different. Himself-itself-herself? The commander is not sure. Even that name rings untrue now. Commander of what? The Knights of Jade and Ash are no more, their essence dust.

He is alone. He? Yes, that seems right: He. He is alone.

Whatever he is drips into the remade shell, filling it, stretching into fingers and toes, flexing them; a puppet master, invisible.

The commander sits up, extends his naked arm. Instantly, the Uncivil's servants approach. From a smoking nozzle they squeeze a dark liquid, dotting his hand, delicate, as if decorating a cake. The liquid hardens to scales that bond with the dead flesh, aping every movement. The commander is motionless while they work. When his arm is covered they move to the rest of him. Lines of black mingle with green, covering holes, levelling dents. They do not stop until the armour is fully restored.

Without a word the commander stands and leaves, striding out of the chamber and into the city.

The streets of Wonderland are familiar to him now, but should they be? The commander pauses. This knowledge is hers, was hers, is his. Does it even matter? He has the means to find the Malice. That is the only prerogative. To meet it they have made an accord. His goal lies beyond the wall. He will lead her armies through it. She will take the north and he the Malice. After that, nothing is certain.

Robed figures join him as he travels. One becomes a pair, then several, a growing group that pulls stray people into orbit. The commander leaves Wonderland with an army at his back. Their lines are ragged, shoddy. It irritates him. He cannot articulate why.

A measured pace is kept through the night, until the wall looms proud, halving the sky. Atop its glowing ramparts, snipers stand, sending white fire upon the hordes below. But the commander has encountered the wall in a past life, was once privy to its secrets. The sight of the fortification shakes memories from the depths of his being, bringing wisdom. The wall is a machine, a great shield of energy. Its light cannot be broken so long as it's fed and the batteries that power the structure are mundane, limited.

Until now a stalemate has persisted, neither side willing to bleed enough to break the deadlock. The commander does not understand how real war can be cold.

He gives the order and the first wave falls upon the wall. He sends in the second wave even as their predecessors are scorched by its energies. Sheer numbers will solve the problem. Either the wall's engines will give out or he will pile the bodies, make a staircase of bones and walk over.

The third wave charges.

The fourth prepares.

CHAPTER TWENTY-FIVE

The tower is the second highest in First Circle, made to house the city's elite. Leaders, philosophers, administrators: all gone. Windows look in on empty rooms, bereft, a symbol of what is not. At the very top, Yuren dwells behind shaded glass. On the tower's opposite side, sunslight passes freely, adding warmth to faces already glowing.

Vesper dangles, arms stretched straight up, hands vanished within the Vagrant's fists. Together, they walk. Little legs curve outward, taking a gentle route to the ground.

Harm watches as they slowly circuit the room. He waves each time Vesper's grin passes.

Transparent walls allow a view of the sea and the boats that decorate it. A table runs one side of the room, loaded with delicacies: spherical rolls injected with fruit, fish caught fresh from untainted seas and sugar dressed in many colours. Despite their best efforts, road-trained appetites barely dent the feast.

Harm pats his bulging tummy. 'I haven't eaten this well

since . . . since ever! Do you think it's time to try Vesper with something solid? I could mush up one of these yellow fruits.' The Vagrant's lips move, hinting at the fruit's name. Harm doesn't notice. 'What do you think?'

The Vagrant nods and they set to work.

Grassy strips border First Circle's streets and run across rooftops. Happily, the goat explores, availing herself of the lush pickings until a brazen honk smashes her idyll. Her jaw pauses mid chew and she looks up.

Something is watching her.

Flat feet, orange and webbed, support a plump, feathered body. It appears almost normal, the neck only slightly too long, the beak only a little too big for the head, eyes fractionally smaller than they should be.

It honks again.

The goat gives the remark the contempt it deserves, continues to eat. Only the twitch of a shortened tail conveys her annoyance.

A slapping sound heralds the tainted bird's approach. It wobbles from side to side as it runs, spreading flightless wings wide, wrinkly skin showing through threadbare feathers. With a defiant cry the bird crashes into the goat, knocking her sideways, away from the grass and onto the road.

The goat regains her footing, bleating profanity. Eyes narrow as they track the bird patrolling its territory. The goat lowers her head. It is not a gesture of submission.

The battle for First Circle's gardens begins.

'Now chew,' says Harm, exaggerating the movement of his lips for clarity. 'Like this.'

Vesper grins manically. From the corners of her mouth, thick yellow goo bubbles. It matches the mess between Vesper's fingers, the slime on her chin, on her legs, the blobs that randomly pepper things, the blast radius massive, confounding.

'Let's take a break.' Harm slumps backwards onto a chair.

Vesper claps her hands, enjoying the slopping sound as they come together.

Trapped in his role as high chair, the Vagrant is left holding a feeder tube.

Harm tips his head back towards the ceiling. 'I can't believe Vesper doesn't know how to chew. I'd have thought that would be hardwired in.'

A sound like distant thunder shakes the air. All three jump. 'What was that?'

The Vagrant gets up, swinging Vesper under his arm.

'Bwaaabwaabaa!'

Harm follows as they make their way through sliding glass, leading onto a balcony that rings their tower like a coppery crown. 'There,' he says, pointing southward past the distant unmanned farms.

Faraway turrets turn and wave, blowing clouds of smoke into the air. Above them, birdlike things weave, too slow to escape destruction. Trains bolt along the road, knocking into one another in their haste, approaching, running. Behind them the giant wall flickers, a dying bulb. They watch transfixed as the sputtering barrier sparks its last. Though too far away for details, it is easy to imagine infernal forces pouring over it, unchecked.

They run further around the balcony, using it to access another chamber. Despite the open door it is hard to see in.

The glass walls are tinted, holding light outside. Harm takes a step into the shadows. 'Yuren?'

'Hold on, I'll be out in a moment.' His voice sounds strained.

Harm frowns and goes further.

Yuren stands very straight, left hand resting on right forearm. As Harm and the Vagrant approach he turns away from them. 'I said I'd be out shortly.'

'Can't you hear the guns? The enemy are flying over the wall and the wall itself has . . .' the green-eyed man trails off. 'You know already.'

'Yes.' The old man sighs. 'It was only a matter of time. We've already had eight months longer than our initial estimates. Not a bad run really.'

'What, that's it? You're giving up?'

'In a way, yes.'

'Please, we've only hours before they get here. We need to be on a ship and away as soon as possible.'

'There are no ships. None that are fit for ocean travel anyway.'

'But there's another way. You must have planned for something.'

Yuren flexes his fingers. Nodding to himself, he rolls down his sleeves and turns to face them. 'You're right that there's a plan. I've given the evacuation codes. Anybody that can get away from the wall is on their way here right now. Even with their numbers we can't hope to hold Six Circles against the enemy.' He looks up, defiance tucked within bloodshot eyes. 'But one circle? We might have a chance at that.'

'Ab lat!' says Vesper.

Yuren ignores the interruption, continues. 'Do you

remember I told you that once the entire city was carried across the sea?'

'Yes.'

'Well, they had sky-ships, cruisers, a whole fleet. We don't have anywhere near that kind of sea power. But we have plenty of smaller vessels and a lot of scavenged engines. I think we have enough to move one of our platforms.'

'You think?'

'Forgive me. Cautious language is a necessary evil in my line of work. I'm certain. We ran simulations and some low-key tests.'

Harm and the Vagrant exchange a look. 'What do we need to do?'

'Nothing. We've called in all of our ships and my people are attaching them to First Circle as we speak. If you go back out to the balcony you'll be able to see them at work.'

Yuren's suggestion is followed. From the tower, Six Circles is laid out before them. Second Circle has already been emptied and engineers cut it loose from the rest of the structure. Connecting bridges retract slowly, unwilling, like lovers' fingers. Elsewhere, people rush from their homes, dragging their possessions behind them. They form an untidy bottleneck at the bridge to First Circle, spilling backwards, messy. Guards try to keep order as military efficiency weighs in against panic.

The Vagrant watches tiny figures dashing about, mesmerized. Vesper apes the movement. After a while she reaches out, snatching at them with her hands. Expectant, she opens a fist. Little eyebrows rise, surprised. There is nothing there! Vesper tries again, faster this time. Again, the laws of the universe disappoint. She leans forward, wind flicking at fluffy hair, hands stretching out.

Closer.

Just a little closer.

Suddenly she is moving, away from the edge, away from her goal.

The Vagrant has intervened.

Vesper is unimpressed. She says so clearly, giving a detailed report of her anger. Despite the alien language, the Vagrant understands every word.

'Sorry,' says Harm. 'It's too dangerous.'

Vesper's anger expands to include Harm and 'dangerous'. She reaches for the balcony again but a strong arm holds her in place. Anger converts to self pity, collapsing the angry mask into scrunched sorrow.

Before Harm can console, his attention is diverted by a series of white flashes. 'What's going on over there? That's Third Circle, isn't it?'

The Vagrant nods, eyes widening.

The bridges to Third Circle fall away, sealing it from the rest of the city. It has not been evacuated, still full to the brim with humans, tainted, stranded. Its inhabitants, varied in shape and size, realize they are being betrayed. With abandon they throw themselves into the water, making for First Circle. Some swim directly towards it, others seek alternative routes via Fourth Circle. Huge numbers of them, proverbial rats fleeing their holes. A broadcast voice repeats, repeats, appealing for calm. It is ignored.

By the main bridge, guards wait, weapons raised and ready.

Half-breeds charge over to the queue, demanding their

place. People back away and an invisible line forms between the two groups, equal parts fear and hate. Plenty of room for the guards to take their shot.

The refugees from Third Circle have no chance.

Fire, white and laser bright, lances out, perforating. Bodies become fishnets and people scream, a luxury reserved for the living. A second group are shot where they stand and the remaining half-breeds run, postponing death for a few more hours.

Harm shakes his head, not wanting to see. 'You have to do something!'

One of the Vagrant's arms keeps Vesper close, the other rests by the sword. When the artillery light flashes from below, he looks pale.

'There's nothing more to be done,' says Yuren, moving around the balcony to join them.

'Yes there is! You can let them on board, they can come with us.'

Yuren spreads his hands. 'No. The infection risk is too high and there are too many of them. If we're prudent, we have enough supplies to return to the Shining City.'

'But only if you abandon half your people to do it?'

'They aren't my people. My people are here. They've grown up here, I know most of them by sight, I know their partners and their children. Third Circle is full of refugees. We did our best for them but I have to look to my own first. It isn't pretty but hard choices have to be made.'

'What about your citizens who got tainted, the ones you moved to Third Circle? What about them?'

'A regrettable loss. But they would be the first to agree it needs to happen to allow the rest of us to survive.'

'Yuren, this is wrong. There's still time to save some of them.'

'No, and it's not just me. The other Council members agree it's the only chance we have.' The Vagrant hands Vesper over to Harm. 'What are you doing?'

Harm smiles grimly. 'What you should have done already, saving those people.'

'No,' Yuren replies sadly. 'It's too late. By the time you got there it would be over. All you will do is announce your true identity and after that I won't be able to protect you or your loved ones.' His mouth twists bitterly. 'How do you think they'll react when the first Seraph Knight to appear since the war turns up on the side of the infected? You will become the enemy and they will kill you.'

'Not if you ordered them to stop.'

'Even if I wanted to, there's no guarantees they'd listen. Axler certainly wouldn't and the military will side with him, even over me. If I force the issue there'll be civil war. No, I've thought about this for a long time. This is the only way.'

Shouts rise up from the water. The half-breed swimmers have reached the boats clustered around First Circle's skirts. Too close to precious engines for gunfire, the guards are forced to climb down where they can direct their attacks with precision. Third Circle's escapees have superior strength and no plan. They throw themselves forward regardless, onto rafts, onto boats, onto the mercy of their neighbours.

Weapons flash and orders cut strangely calm through cries of panic and pain.

The Vagrant closes his eyes.

Harm holds Vesper close, shielding her from the violence below.

Yuren sub-vocalizes, hidden implants taking his words elsewhere. Alarms sound and the last bridges retract, releasing First Circle. Another silent order from the Councilman sets the rag tag fleet to work. Engines start, staccato. There are too many independent spirits to coordinate but gradually the message passes through the fleet, directing their collective energies against the giant disc's bulk. A swarm of bugs coercing an elephant, First Circle trembles at their insistent buzz. Shyly, slowly, it drifts out of sheltered waters and into the Southern Sea.

Three Years Ago

A squire sits behind a crumbling wall, watching. The house he stares at is much like the others in the village, with a sagging roof and walls that long for a new coat of paint.

It is not the building that interests him however.

As the morning sunlight brings colour to the brickwork, highlighting further imperfections, the front door opens.

Reela always leaves early. With aging, infirm parents and no sister to help, she has to make the most of each day.

The squire stands, tries to recall what he has practised in his head so many times but, in the moment, his mind fails him and he stares dumbstruck. He sees how tired she is, how busy, and now his imagined advances seem petty, ridiculous. He quickly crouches behind the wall again.

She does not notice, mind already focused on the day's work.

Soon, she is gone and the squire's palm smacks sharply against his forehead.

He looks at the sad little house, at the garden, thick with weeds and plants with strange, luminous leaves.

An idea forms bringing new hope and, smiling, the squire sets to work. The tools he needs are in an unlocked shed next to the rusting shell of an autofarmer. It is no surprise that the mech no longer works. Shrugging, he rolls up his sleeves.

He sweats through morning, through the afternoon, untangling plants, cutting back vines, revealing a cracked path and several growth pods, each plastic sphere designated for a different vegetable. None have survived. He digs out the dead roots and replaces them with wild flowers.

It is late by the time he has finished and the squire quickly returns to his hiding place, keen to see Reela's reaction.

Voices come, bantering. Reela is talking with someone. Vesper! His voice sounds different, deeper than normal. The squire narrows his eyes.

They round the corner and for once, Reela's cool demeanour slips. 'My garden! It's beautiful.'

'Er, yes. It is.'

'My parents will be so happy. Thank you.' Vesper's surprise is lost on her. She kisses him on the cheek and the squire's own begin to burn. 'I won't forget this.'

'No,' he manages a smile as she goes to the door. 'Nor will I.'

'Will I see you tomorrow?'

'Yes! Yes you will.'

'Good.'

The squire cannot stand any more. He gets up, runs. Reela is already going inside and does not see, but Vesper does.

As soon as he is sure Reela isn't going to come back out Vesper gives chase.

He finds his friend deep in the woods, attacking the trees without mercy.

Vesper stops at a safe distance, raises a hand. 'Hi.'

Another tree is smacked, sending leaves flurrying in the air.

'Reela's garden. That was you, wasn't it?'

The squire keeps his back to Vesper but pauses to nod.

'I'm sorry I didn't say anything, I was just so surprised. I'll tell her tomorrow, I promise. Better yet, why don't you tell her? I know you like her.'

The squire blushes, shrugs.

'I know I like her.'

The two young men look at each other. Slowly, they both smile.

'How about we get some more practice in? It's your turn to use Attica's sword.'

The squire shakes his head.

'Come on. You're way more talented than I am. I can barely get the thing to work but you, you've got talent. You just need to step up and use it.' Seeing his friend look doubtful, Vesper adds quickly, 'We can help each other. You teach me how to sing better and I'll teach you how to fight like a champion. What do you say?'

They shake hands, friends again.

'And tomorrow, you can go and talk to Reela yourself.'

CHAPTER TWENTY-SIX

The Half-alive forces of the Uncivil stream over the remains of Six Circles, harvesting. To slow them down, the enemy sabotages all bridges to the port city but the Uncivil's Necroneering provides alternatives: skin steps and boneways, just as animate as their metal predecessors. In places there is fighting but most of the abandoned are quick to run or surrender.

The commander doesn't care. From the cliff's edge he watches, attention passing over the carnage to the giant disc, bobbing seaward with his prize. Already it slips beyond reach. He sends his remaining Bonewings after it, knowing they will fail.

After a moment's deliberation he marches into the city, traversing empty streets, making for the northernmost point. Bodies are strewn randomly, unaesthetically. Flies crawl over charred limbs in growing numbers, searching for succulence.

An idea strikes, bubbling up from the depths. He plucks

a fly from the air with his new hand. Wings buzz, angry, trapped between supple fingers. The commander raises the fly to his visor, drawing upon techniques stolen and dark.

Youths dressed as men make a loose circle. Some sit along the wall, feet dangling, some lean, affecting nonchalance. Several uniforms are still damp from seafront skirmishes; a few show blood splatters fresh on grey fabric. Tired, they pause to allow others a turn at battle. They gather round a noisy spectacle, two creatures fighting in the middle of the circle they make, stubborn, banging heads. Feathers twist in the air, sailing down to their fellows already on the ground. The bird's cries become desperate.

If anything, the sound makes the goat even more vicious.

The guards laugh, apart from those who bet on the bird.

From outside the circle a weapon points skyward, snorting gouts of fire. Everyone stops, turning towards it, even the beasts. They look from the lance to the man holding it, silently deciding the man the more dangerous.

'What in The Seven's name is this?'

Blushing, a young woman steps forward. 'We, we were on our way back, Captain, when we came across these animals fighting.'

The captain's look is stormy. 'Animals, Lieutenant Ro?'

'Yes, Captain,' she says warily, gesturing towards the combatants.

'Interesting. I see only one animal here. Where are the others?'

Her voice tightens with stress. 'Oh, I mean one animal and one bird, Captain.'

292

The captain bears down on her. There is little difference in their height but somehow the captain makes her smaller. 'Bird, Lieutenant? What bird?'

Everyone is silent now. One guard stifles a nervous titter. The goat's eyes are on the lance, fearful, her legs poised to run.

The lieutenant points, hand trembling. 'That one?'

'That,' says the captain, levelling his lance, 'is not a bird. It's a tainted monster that carries infection onto our ship. We're at sea, packed with passengers. This thing presents just as much threat as the half-breeds you fought off an hour ago.'

A stream of white fire pours from the lance, striking the bird in the chest. It screeches as the flames race over its body gobbling feathers and flesh alike, greedy. The goat scampers away to watch from a safer distance.

'Put that out and throw it overboard, then report in. New recruits are here from the wall. There are going to be some changes.' He looks at the young woman pointedly. 'Private.'

Still blushing, she salutes and turns away.

'As for the rest of you, if you continue to look like dead weight then you'll be thrown over the side. Do you understand?'

'Yes, Captain!'

'Good, now get to work!'

Guards scramble forward to deal with the crackling corpse. They stand in a muddle, none of them are sure of what to do. The captain walks to the goat, muttering, his lance threatening the sky again. 'A bloody animal shows more initiative than my own officers.' He pulls a square of firm jelly from his pocket. 'Here, have this.' The goat accepts the offering, halving it with a single gulp. 'You're efficient. I appreciate that. Come on, let's try and clear the rest of those winged plague sacks off our ship.' He drops the remaining jelly. It is gone before it touches the floor.

The captain strides away in search of trouble. Nose twitching, the goat follows.

The Vagrant grips the balcony rail, unable to look away while the port recedes from view. Atrocities play out, too distant to decode, confounding, laying foundations for sleepless nights. First Circle moves slowly in the water, letting views linger too long.

'It's not your fault,' says Harm softly.

There is a silence, awkward. Yuren makes an empty statement and withdraws.

'There's nothing you could have done,' Harm adds. 'And even if there was, you would have put Vesper and your mission in danger to do it.'

The Vagrant's broad back is a wall against kindness.

'I know there's nothing I can say but I will say this, for me if not for you: We made it. We escaped Verdigris, survived all of the people trying to kill us, got past the Uncivil, around the wall and now we're bound for the Shining City. All you have to do is sit tight. Don't you see? Finally, we can relax.' Harm moves closer, resting a hand on the Vagrant's arm. 'It's funny, I've spent my whole life on that piece of rock but now that I'm leaving it I realize that I'm not attached to it. Not one bit.' Harm pauses, measuring words about to be said, testing them. 'I used to say Wonderland was my home but it wasn't really. I don't even think home is a place.

Home was my mother and my sisters and my uncle, when I was a child. Now it's you and Vesper.'

The Vagrant's breath catches in his throat.

Harm squeezes his arm gently. 'Being on the sea scares me. Not knowing anything about what's ahead scares me, but I don't mind. I think I can face anything as long as I can do it with the two of you.'

The Vagrant points back to the coast. Out of the ashes, winged shapes rise, moving swiftly towards them. He reaches for the sword.

'Hold on,' says Harm, covering the Vagrant's hand with his own. 'This isn't our fight. There's a whole army here to look after us. Remember what Yuren said? If you reveal yourself as a knight, things could go badly.'

The Vagrant leans more heavily on the railing. His hand leaves the hilt, Harm's following. They watch, merely spectators as the enemy comes faster.

An army of boats cluster around the edge of First Circle. A multicultural mix of vessels old and new, from battered fishing ships to engines slung on bright cables. Together they make a strange harmony, humming under the water.

Amid the cacophony a single fly goes unheard.

Grim-faced crews make adjustments, tighten ropes, align courses, attending to anything other than the bodies floating in the sea behind them, or the forces ravaging their old home. Dockmaster Roget has no such luxury; he watches the seas behind, expecting pursuit. After a moment he wipes sweat away, smearing dirt across his sleeve, making room for the next wave of perspiration. He sees something to justify the sweat. Being right is no consolation.

'Trouble?' asks a familiar voice.

Roget's tongue peeks between pursed lips, unwilling to go further.

A sigh, impatient, also familiar. 'Spit it out man, or hand me the scope.'

'It's Bonewings, Captain Axler.'

'How many?'

Roget turns to find the shorter man irritatingly close. 'More than I care to count, and as you know I excel at counting.'

Axler moves around, followed by the goat. He snatches the scope from Roget, activates the count function. The scope sweeps left and right, tallying. Axler's lips shape a curse.

'Should we call Yuren?'

'I'm sure he already knows.' Axler hands back the scope. 'Here's what we're going to do. I'm going to call every man, woman and child with a uniform to protect the back quarter. I want you to keep your crews together. First Circle has to keep moving. Those flying monsters won't take us alone but they could slow us down long enough for the enemy to send heavy units.'

'We're too slow. Too much weight. I told you and Yuren this a long time ago.'

'Not now, Roget!'

Axler backs off, calling in reinforcements. The goat trots to the edge of the deck and leans out, shadows looming over those below. Her dark eyes detect movement, tiny, a winged bead of black sneaking over the ships. She says nothing.

On one of the boats a man tenses, slaps the side of his

neck. Pupils expand, filling the eyes, like two dying stars that threaten to explode, then collapse in on themselves, taking life and colour with them. He starts detaching his boat from the others.

Neighbours notice. The word 'Samael' forms on a dozen lips.

Bored, the goat returns to Axler's side.

First Circle lumbers on, leaving Samael's boat to drift away.

Guards kneel along First Circle's perimeter, armed, if not ready. Axler's orders boom in every earpiece: 'Destroy. Destroy all targets. Nothing gets on board.'

The Bonewings descend.

Guns pepper the sky.

By the time the attack is turned away, Samael and his ship are second string gossip, forgettable.

Days pass peacefully. First Circle chugs north, finding cleaner waters. People delight in the ocean-made-window and the colourful shapes moving inside. A few dare to fish. Sparse clouds zip across an open sky where the suns reign, lopsided eyes in an endless face.

Vesper toddles through manicured streets. Too small, her poncho rides high at the back, giving rise to a morning moon. An adult is tethered to each hand, made to match her faltering pace.

Other adults pass by, strangers. Most pause to grin or greet. Vesper has something to say to each of them, provoking responses from all but the loneliest souls.

'I think it's time we got Vesper some proper clothes,' says Harm.

A little colour touches the Vagrant's cheeks as he nods.

They round a corner and Vesper stops suddenly. She hangs between the grownups, feet forgotten in her amazement. In front of her are ten spheres, each one large enough to explore, with another ten mounted on top. Tubes connect them, demanding to be used as slides.

Two girls roll out of a corner sphere and flop onto the grass. They lie there laughing, children, not two years her senior. Still giggling, they jump onto their feet unaided and run to another sphere.

Vesper's thoughts whirl with possibility. Suddenly the hands holding hers change; not supports but restraints. She struggles to free herself. Angry tears prevail where strength cannot.

The Vagrant exchanges a look with Harm and shrugs. They let go.

Little legs wobble then hold. She takes a step forward, falls into the second, momentum carrying her to a third and fourth, body lurching from left to right. Vesper's chuckle carries an edge of insanity.

'You can do it!' calls Harm.

Vesper throws a wild grin over her shoulder, gets two back in response.

She tumbles over.

Before rage has a chance to bypass shock, strong hands lift her back onto her feet. Vesper blinks and looks around. Things seem to be as they should. She offers another grin to the world and tries again. The Vagrant stays close, arms hovering by Vesper's shoulders.

Stumbling, near collisions and last minute catches fill the

afternoon. And smiles. And laughter. When the suns set they eat, triumphant.

That night, all three sleep deeply.

Rain falls leisurely, deceptive, soaking by stealth. Water collects underfoot, tiny rivers running towards the sea. Small feet scatter them and splashing sounds are savoured, delicious. Rain or no rain, clothes must be bought. Vesper takes the lead, confidence carried on wobbly legs. Occasionally the Vagrant turns her in the right direction. They round a corner, entering the shopping area. And stop.

Lines of people wind across the square, making snakes, hissing from a hundred angry mouths. Each one moves slowly into a doorway, customers digested one by one. New arrivals lengthen the snakes faster than old ones can be processed. Supplies are limited, prices high and complaints fill the air, frustration the common currency.

Harm presses a hand against his temple, tilts his head away. The Vagrant takes his arm, guiding them to the back of a queue. Vesper has no time for queues but the Vagrant makes her find some. Soon, her voice joins the complaining. What it lacks in experience it makes up for in energy.

The Vagrant sighs.

Their line is one of the faster ones. For most, clothing is not urgent. As they shuffle forward, jealous people glare from parallel places, miserable. An argument sparks into life in one of the shops. Medicine is needed; it has run out. The shopkeeper is accused of lying, the customer of being greedy. People wait impatiently, ordering the man to move on.

Angry voices fade as the Vagrant steps inside a different

shop. Vesper is keen to try everything, though mainly on her head. Harm laughs until throats clear by the door, like guns cocking, ready to fire. Mindful of those waiting, choices are made quickly and precious money is spent.

They hurry outside to hear loud voices, the argument, still going on, now builds to its natural conclusion.

The Vagrant edges nearer, sees fiery faces shooting words. The man has the shopkeeper by the throat. 'I know you've kept some back, hand it over!'

The shopkeeper tries to reply, a sentence squeezed, garbled.

The Vagrant cuts across the lines, pushing past bystanders who already eye unguarded goods.

'You're keeping it for yourself, you greedy bastard! I only need a couple of tabs, I—'

His strong arms intervene, separating, keeping antagonists apart.

For those waiting, the opportunity is too much. They plunge inside, emptying shelves, filling pockets. Bottles are fought over, broken, some turned to weapons, others ground underfoot. Displaced rage transforms to action, old insults are revenged, new ones given. Before he can reach the Vagrant's side, Harm is swept up in the madness.

Guards arrive, calling for order. When ignored their rifles spit lightning, leaving bodies passive, trembling. The crowds disperse soon after. Shops are closed for the day.

With relief, Harm and the Vagrant reunite. A new bruise is visible on Harm's mouth, stretched over a puffy lip. His eyes remain wild.

'Those people are insane! And so are you. Did you see when that woman tried to pull me over?'

The Vagrant ignores him, suddenly alarmed.

'Where's Vesper?'

Amber and green eyes meet briefly, then a frantic search begins.

They find Vesper a street away, a young boy kneeling in front of her. The two children clap hands together, reflections out of time. When the boy sees the Vagrant, he runs.

'Come back,' says Harm.

The boy keeps running.

Gently, they pursue, Vesper's arms waving with excitement. Ahead of them, the crowds thin, making way for an unoccupied street.

Fast footsteps come from behind, making two turn on instinct, the third swinging round on the end of the Vagrant's arm. A man approaches, uniformed, his young face flushed with excitement.

'Hey, wait up!' shouts Genner, closing the last twenty feet. 'Are you alright? Things got a bit crazy back there.' He doesn't allow a reply, his mouth too keen to wait. 'You've got to be more careful, Scout, if they'd realized who you were things could have got even worse! Where you going, anyhow?'

Harm answers, 'Just for a walk, Vesper might have made a new friend.'

'I saw,' says Genner, unwilling to look away from the Vagrant. 'Best not to go that way.'

'Why?'

'This way's faster.'

The guard tries to lead them away but Harm stops him. 'Why is it really? It's a crime to lie to a Seraph Knight, you know.'

Guilt flashes on Genner's face, red and genuine. 'I'm sorry, I'm trying to do what's right for everyone but it's hard.' He takes a deep breath. 'That kid isn't the sort of friend you want Vesper to make and if you go there, it'll cause trouble and I thought you wanted to avoid trouble.'

'We do,' agrees Harm, 'it just doesn't want to avoid us.'

The Vagrant nods.

At Genner's insistence, they change direction, leaving trouble behind.

The goat stands on a roof, grazing. It is unclear how she arrived there. Honking sounds nearby and half-breed birds soon follow. Two full grown and a half dozen still growing, made unique by mutation. One is marked by a stunted wing, one by an over-muscled thigh, another by a second beak that sprouts beneath the first, forming words in an unknown language.

The half-breed family stop and call up to the goat. She ignores them and they get louder, angrier. One of the adults flaps hard, lifting a bulbous body into the air while the others cheer support.

Tilting her head, the goat fixes her enemy with a hard stare. The bird hauls itself level with the roof and shouts a challenge.

White fire answers. The first shot is precise, punching a neat hole through its chest. The second blast is wider, like a river that sweeps over the tainted birds on the ground.

Abruptly, the honking stops.

Axler steps out from his hiding place and kicks the corpses into a pile. He turns his lance on them, pouring and pouring, making ash to scatter on the sea breeze.

The goat remains on the roof, grazing.

*   *   *

Yuren sits opposite Harm and the Vagrant, a thin tube runs from the corner of his mouth to a small bag at his side. Behind him, Vesper runs the length of the room, chuckling each time she collides with a wall.

'How are you settling in?'

Harm smiles, patting his belly. 'We're very grateful for your hospitality.'

'I'm glad to hear it. Of course now we're at sea we're all going to have to ration more carefully.'

'It's still a lot more than we're used to.'

'For you perhaps. I'm expecting no end of complaints from our regular citizens once the initial fear has passed. Would you like something to drink?'

'No.'

The Vagrant shakes his head.

'Straight to business then. We've crammed most of the population of Six Circles onto this glorified float.'

'Most,' echoes Harm in a whisper.

The Vagrant looks down.

'I regret the loss of our refugees too, but we didn't have room for them. As it is we struggled to provide sanctuary for the soldiers fleeing the wall. We don't know the state of things out here so I've assumed the worst. Even if the island settlements have gone we have enough to survive the trip, just.'

'Who are you trying to convince?'

Yuren draws on the tube, turning grey plastic pink. He swallows. 'Me. I suppose you want it straight?'

The Vagrant nods. Yuren sighs.

'As I said, we have enough food and if the fish we're catching test clean that will help. The problem is locomotion.

Our ships are old and not made for this kind of work. As the journey continues, more will break down beyond our ability to salvage, putting increased strain on the remaining engines. And of course, each engine we lose will slow us down. When that happens we'll struggle to keep going and make any headway against the currents.'

'What do you want us to do?'

'There's not much you can do, unless you're engineers or have a stash of machine parts squirrelled away.' The old man pauses for another drink. 'Anyway, I didn't ask you here to employ your services, I wanted to offer mine.'

'What do you mean?'

'I've raised children myself and I know it's not easy. Vesper here is at a critical age. She's absorbing new information at an incredible rate and what she learns now will form the fundamentals of her thinking for years to come.'

Hearing her name, Vesper stops.

'You're offering us a tutor?'

'Better than that, I'm offering her an implant.'

The Vagrant frowns.

'Is it safe to put it in this late?' asks Harm, drawing closer.

'Oh yes, it's a simple procedure and we have the expertise on board.' He takes out a transparent plastic wallet. Inside is a square of silver the size of a baby's fingernail. 'My last partner was young. We'd planned to have more children and . . .' Harm's eyes spark tears, preempting the old man's. He looks away quickly. '. . . and I don't need it any more. I'd like very much to see it used. It's of the finest quality and will assist with language acquisition, memory and calculations. The encyclopedia is excellent and it's fully aspected.'

Vesper's attention wanders. She chuckles at something

unknowable and runs off, pumping legs and arms. 'OoooooOOOOOOM!'

Yuren twists in his chair to watch the diminutive racer, his smile is joyful, wistful. He twists back. 'It's yours if you want it.'

Harm checks his enthusiasm against the Vagrant's concern. 'Can we talk about it?'

'Of course.' Yuren gets up. Walls slide to get out of his way, revealing a corridor.

Vesper's eyes light up and she runs for freedom. The walls seal long before she gets there.

'So, what do you think?'

The Vagrant gets up and gathers Vesper into his arms.

'I know you're worried but I think it's a brilliant idea.' Harm smiles at the Vagrant's surprised expression. 'It was normal practice in the big cities, for those who could afford it. And it's standard on the northern continent. It would give Vesper a massive advantage. Think about it, she'll be speaking earlier, learning faster. It opens up lots of opportunities. Untainted children are scarce in the south but in the north Vesper will be one of many. We need to think about her future.'

Vesper wriggles in the Vagrant's arms, legs keen to work. Reluctantly, the Vagrant puts her down.

CHAPTER TWENTY-SEVEN

Big waves toss the boat back and forth, like bullies with another's ball. The commander stands at the prow, hands locked to the sides. The storm's fury does not intimidate. His concerns lie within.

He looks at Samael, once a man, now a puppet, working against the weather without complaint. The commander has infused the fisherman with a fragment of his own essence, bending the mortal to his will. The Uncivil shared the secret with him during their communion but she uses constructed hosts, filling empty shells with life, where he has taken another's essence and corrupted it to make his own creature.

The commander has broken minds before, implanting a simple command, making automatons fit for a single purpose but this is different. Samael is independent, capable of thought, obeying orders creatively and still able to access years of experience at sea.

In Samael he sees himself. For do not these things apply

to him? Is he not also a puppet made from a spark of infernal essence?

The commander's purpose comes from the master and though he still believes in the importance of his mission, he begins to question the authority behind it.

The Malice must be destroyed, that is not in doubt. Its existence means his end. The fact sits in his consciousness without context. He needs know no more.

Other things trouble him.

When the Malice is destroyed and his purpose met, what then? Will his time be over? Will new orders come from the master? Will he be released? And if he is, what will he do with his freedom? What is he without the master to define him?

He casts about within himself for clues of his other parent, his shell's previous inhabitant, but finds nothing. Whatever there was has been absorbed or overwritten by the master's fire.

Only his fingers move, digging deeper into the ship's rim, impressing their shape permanently. On the outside, the commander is still, calm.

On First Circle time is easy to measure, the suns dance reliably from horizon to horizon, checking off each day. Distance is more difficult to measure. The Southern Sea stretches in all directions, aping infinity, sapping hope.

People struggle to stay upbeat, the goat is more pragmatic. She is up early, enthusiastic, following Axler on his morning rounds. The guards have adopted her as a mascot, slipping her bits of this and that as she passes by, hoping to win their captain's approval. The softer ones give sweet treats, the bored ones experiment with less edible matter. The goat takes it all, rejecting nothing. Increasingly, her belly defines itself beyond the boundaries of her shoulders.

Private Ro, newly demoted, still angry, offers the goat a piece of rubber. The goat sniffs, then moves in, nipping a finger for good measure.

'Ow!'

'Something wrong, Private?'

Ro shakes her hand behind her back. 'No, Captain.'

'Then keep your noises to yourself.' Other guards snigger. The goat chews experimentally then spits the rubber onto the floor. 'And Private?'

'Yes, Captain?'

'Pick that up will you?'

She complies, ignoring the silent laughter of her peers. While crouched, woman and goat exchange hateful stares.

Axler and the goat move on.

Always, they finish at the rear of the ship, where Axler and Roget discuss the state of things and the goat watches bleak waves. Beneath them, crews tend to their aching ships, startled by each new groan or stutter. Like mothers with sick babies, they rest little.

'Good morning, Captain Axler.'

'Is it?'

Roget brings his index fingers together, touches them to his top lip. 'Something wrong?'

'The usual troubles. I'm surrounded by idiots.'

'Ah.'

'Are you the one behind these bloody masks everyone's buying?'

'Is there a problem?'

'Apart from the fact they don't bloody work!'

'That depends on how you define their effect.'

Axler steps round to look the taller man in the eye. 'Don't get all philosophical on me. They don't stop taint, so they don't work.'

Roget leans back a little from Axler's scowl. 'Their effectiveness against the taint is yet to be seen. Their effectiveness against panic however is clear to observe. At least this allows people to do something, to feel like they have a little control.'

'It's immoral. They're using people's fear to turn a profit.'

'It's hard to put a price on morale.'

The goat snorts and Axler shakes his head. 'I'm more interested in practical things. Like maintaining our defences. I've been trying to get hold of some Silicate4 but it's already been allocated. Do you think you could find me some?'

'Of course,' Roget says. 'I only wish you'd approached me sooner.'

The Vagrant paces, four strides to each length of the room. Harm sits, nerves showing in restless fingers.

Wall becomes door and a young man appears, teeth and shirt white, crisp. 'She's ready for you now.'

Harm jumps up but the Vagrant is already through the door. They follow the nurse into another room. Machinery folds away as they approach, shy, giving hints to what may have happened. On a black chair, Vesper dozes, straps receding from her ankles and wrists.

The Vagrant rushes to her side, hands moving to the space where hair used to be, wanting to touch, unsure.

'The implantation procedure was a complete success,' says the nurse. 'The incision has been covered with Skyn and there should be no scarring, even under the hairline.'

'Thank you,' says Harm.

'The drugs will be wearing off shortly. There may be some mild disorientation but nothing to worry about. I'll be back to check on you all in thirty minutes. If you need me, just touch the wall here to open a channel.'

The nurse leaves and the two men study Vesper, attending to every toe twitch, eyelid flutter and sigh.

Eventually, Vesper yawns, wide and epic. She rubs her eyes and looks around vacantly.

Harm and the Vagrant smile hopefully at her.

Seconds pass, tense, and then Vesper's eyes focus. She sees the two men and grins broadly. In unison, they sigh. Vesper giggles.

'Well, she seems normal.'

The Vagrant leans over Vesper, checking each part of her methodically.

'They only worked on her head you know.' Harm's comment does nothing to stop the examination.

Surprise takes Vesper's face, then even that fades, muscles slacking off as attention goes inward.

Harm and the Vagrant exchange a worried look. 'I'm going to call the nurse,' says Harm, rushing to the wall panel.

Vesper begins to frown, her lips twitch. The Vagrant strokes her cheek.

'Dada?'

Surprise finds the Vagrant. Moist eyes follow, then, after a long pause, a nod.

'Dada!'

'Was that Vesper? Did she just . . .' In an instant Harm is back by the chair.

The Vagrant nods again, as if to himself.

Vesper attends to Harm, once more her face goes blank, faraway.

Behind them, walls shift, allowing the nurse's return. 'Is everything alright in here?'

'Yes I think so. Vesper just said her first word. Is that normal?'

The nurse's voice is calm, soothing. 'Perfectly. It means she's interacting with the implant.'

'And now, should she look like that?'

'Yes. It just means she's listening to the implant, as time goes on and she acclimatizes, the communication will get faster. What word did she say?'

Harm glances at the Vagrant. 'Dada.'

'That makes sense. When Vesper saw her father the implant supplied the correct label, repeating for reinforcement. It's an excellent sign that she was able to convert the stimulus into speech so quickly. As her speech develops the implant will use more complex sound clusters. So "Dada" will become "Daddy" or be replaced by "Father".'

'So this is normal?'

'Very much so.'

The nurse withdraws and the room seals itself off from the rest of the building. Once more, Vesper becomes the centre of attention.

'Can you say: Harm?'

Vesper concentrates. 'Marm?'

'Nearly. Harm. H-arm. Can you say that? H-arm.'

'Mama!'

312

The Vagrant staggers, shoulders shaking, the laughter silent, uncontrollable. He grabs the wall for support.

'No, not Mama. Harm.'

'Dada?'

Harm points to the breathless Vagrant. 'That's Dada.' He points to himself. 'Harm. Or Uncle. Can you say Uncle? Un-cle.'

'Umm-bull.'

'That's good! I'm Uncle Harm. Can you say it? Un-cle H-arm.'

'Umm-bull Arrm.'

'That's it!'

Vesper grins. 'Umbull-arm!'

'Yes!'

She aims a pudgy finger at the Vagrant. 'Dada!'

'Yes!'

'Umbull-arm! Dada! Umbull-arm! Dada!'

'Yes.' The green-eyed man leans in closer. 'And you're Vesper. Can you say that? Ves-per. Ves-per. Vesper.'

'Esper?'

'That's brilliant.'

'Esper! Esper-Esper-Esper!'

The Vagrant picks Vesper up, swinging her into an embrace.

'Dada,' says Vesper softly.

Near the rear of First Circle sits an office, nondescript. There is no queue, visitors come by appointment only. The office contains a desk that slopes downward, making whoever sits behind it seem smaller, more humble. No wealth is displayed, no decorations, no symbols. All is monochrome.

Roget admits the first appointment.

It is a man, fresh marks on his face, bands of white around one wrist. 'Thank you for letting me come.'

'Please, sit down. Tell me what you need.'

The man's face is desperate. 'Tabs for my little girl, just a couple. Without them, she won't be able to digest her food.'

'I see,' says Roget, pursing his lips. 'Just a couple?'

'That's all I need.'

'For one dose perhaps. That will last, what? A month? I'd assume you want your little girl to eat for the whole journey.'

The man hangs his head. 'We can't afford . . . not with the way things are.'

'Let me be the judge of that. Show me what you have.'

The man touches the desk and a window lights up on its surface. Numbers appear, tracking upward. They are studied in silence. Afterwards, Roget touches the window, making it dark.

'I have good news for you, Second Circleman Ilyon. I'm confident we can find a supply for your child at a price you can afford.'

Surprise mixes with relief, then delight on the man's face. 'Thank you! Thank you so much! I didn't think we had enough saved up.'

'That's true. There's not nearly enough money in your account.'

Delight falters, fades. 'I don't understand.'

'I'm talking about other assets. Organs, blood. The chip in your brain is increasing in value.'

'But that would take me off grid.'

'If you don't want to give it up you could sell us shares.

A few hours a night perhaps, paying off your debt over the next ten or fifteen years.'

The man stares at his swollen knuckles. 'I don't know.'

'It's up to you, of course. I suppose it depends what you think is more important.'

A deal is made. More people come. Whatever they ask for, Roget delivers. There is sometimes a delay, always a price, but every supplicant is given the chance for what they want. When they have left, Roget writes each request down, archaic means for strange times. The list is folded, taken by hand, delivered elsewhere.

The next day the goods arrive in unmarked crates, brought quietly from the docks into First Circle. With them is a note. Roget reads it, nods. Another request, this one non-negotiable. As always, he meets it.

First Circle's park is a battle ground. Blows are struck and young voices cry out. Bodies fall to rise again, sometimes infernal, sometimes not. Sides change too quickly for the players to keep track but few care. Parents mill about the edges, their thoughts on other realities, speculating, worrying. One mother changes her baby with practised ease, prompting a green-eyed man to spontaneous applause. In an overlooked corner, the Vagrant sits, taking notes.

A child approaches Vesper with exaggerated steps, wriggling fingers fanned out and held above her head.

Vesper's mouth drops open and the girl touches her shoulder.

'Tag, you're a monster!'

Vesper looks to the Vagrant for help, then back to the girl but she is already after her next victim. Gradually the monsters grow to outnumber the human children until only one remains. She is given an imaginary lance and sets about chasing the monsters, dropping them with a touch.

Harm approaches a parent, narrowly avoiding the mini monsters stampeding around him. 'Is it right to let them play like this?'

The interruption irritates. 'What's your problem?'

'It's a brutal game. It teaches them that all half-breeds are evil.'

'Of course it does! That's the truth.'

'No it isn't. What if your child got infected, would it make them evil?'

The man bristles. 'My girl's pure but yes, if she were infected, it would. It'd be a matter of time. I've got friends who took themselves to Third Circle to contain the taint so I know what I'm talking about. That's why we teach our kids to run from the monsters. Because we know!' Indignation becomes anger and the man's face pushes forward, aggressive. 'Who are you to talk about my girl, anyway? Well?' Harm's argument is stolen away, lost amid rising emotions. He looks down, defeated. 'I thought so. She's pure, alright? You ever suggest otherwise again and you'll regret it.'

'I wasn't suggesting—'

'You keep an eye on yours if you know what's good for you.' The man points an accusing finger at Vesper. 'She looks like she's on the turn to me.'

Swiftly, Harm retreats to the Vagrant's corner.

'I think it's time to go for a walk.'

The Vagrant shrugs, complies.

Vesper leads the way with utter certainty, weaving through

crowds. Every few moments, speaking signs declare the need for calm. At each corner, guards stand, vigilant.

When night falls people pack below decks to sleep but in the day they seek light and air. Space is a premium. Elbows fight for breathing room. On benches, thighs press together. Rations are eaten slowly, savoured.

An empty street runs between two buildings, converted barracks for First Circle's military. Vesper runs towards it, spreading her arms. Beyond, cranes of brass loom, rising high over the rooftops, cables swaying gently.

A woman steps into her path, uniformed and friendly. 'Whoa there, little one.'

Vesper darts to the guard's right but she is too quick, intercepting her. She tries going left but again the guard is there. She pauses. Thinks. A smile threatens.

'Excuse me,' says Harm, as he and the Vagrant catch up. 'What's down there?'

'Mainly storage,' she says, stepping quickly to foil another attempt to pass. 'And where they put most of the lower Fourth and Fifth Circle duds. Nothing you'd be interested in.'

'Why's it so quiet?'

'It's quiet here because of us. Don't be fooled though, further in is a different story.'

The Vagrant frowns, takes Vesper's hand and steps forward. 'I wouldn't go in there if I were you.'

Harm takes Vesper's other hand. 'Are you stopping us from going in?'

'No. I'm stopping them from coming out. I'm just offering you some friendly advice.'

Still frowning, the Vagrant nods to her. She stands aside and Vesper bounds eagerly forward, pulling the two men after.

317

Three Years Ago

The village treats the squires like heroes. They soon become accustomed to their new status.

Days become weeks.

Both try to win Reela's heart. They sing her songs, bring her gifts, escort her like royalty. But Reela's heart is not a prize to be taken. She enjoys the songs, accepts the gifts, favouring each man's offering equally, barely at all.

Vesper enjoys the challenge, rises to it, his friend does not. While one seeks Reela's company, gets to know the woman behind the face, builds a relationship and a history, the other hangs back out of respect, out of fear.

Weeks become months.

The squires practise every day, wanting to stay sharp for their mission. Often they discuss the need to leave. Often they argue.

Young desire holds them however, the murky dream of their destination unable to compete with more immediate, lustful fantasy.

In the end, Reela chooses Vesper. The other squire nurses his bruised ego and keeps a lock of her hair, exchanged for a song, a failed talisman, tragic.

Months become years.

A rumour circles about a northern village being visited by men the colour of wounds. They are beast speakers, masters of the infernal pack. They hunt fresh prey for the Usurper. Untainted children and fertile women are their targets, the rest are allowed to run.

Vesper's attendance to practice becomes sporadic. Instead, he patrols, hunting for the hunters. The squires see less of each other. When they do meet, the rows intensify. Always, Vesper wants another week. Always, his friend threatens to leave alone. Always, Vesper mollifies him.

The same tunes are sung, repetitive, over and over, until Reela's belly swells and the village celebrates. Nine months pass, fast for some, an agonizing torture for others.

One night, a strange howling fills the air. Animals stir within their pens and the young woman goes into labour. It is unclear whether the scent of new life brings it or simply bad luck but a creature pads into the village, searching the streets with mismatched eyes.

People call for help, for their knight guardian Sir Vesper and his trusty squire. The two young men come running from different houses.

'See if you can distract it,' says Vesper. His squire raises an eyebrow in reply. 'As soon as it goes for you, I'll be there to finish it off. Classic feint and kill, okay?'

Vesper draws his sword and the Dogspawn snarls in reply.

The other squire draws his practice blade. He has sharpened it over the years, given it an edge. It remains mute however, ordinary. Circling closer, he tries to attract the Dogspawn's attention but the half-breed only has eyes for Vesper. Before he can make a distraction, it charges. All he can do is give chase, shouting a warning.

Vesper doesn't need one. Hands tighten around the hilt, sweaty.

The Dogspawn leaps.

Vesper jumps sideways, slashing as it sails past, opening a wound across hind leg and bottom.

Like a common dog, the monster yelps, turning tail to run.

Vesper gives chase but another cry stops him. Reela's mother is calling. The baby is coming. Vesper has to choose, life or death. Love or glory.

The young man pauses only for a moment.

'I've got to kill it. You go check on Reela for me okay?' His friend agrees and the two men run their separate ways.

The village is out of medicine and the doctor's equipment works sporadically, batteries giving their last in kicks and spurts. Reela's labour is primitive, painful as nature intended. The squire bursts in, red face redder as he sees legs spread and life fighting into the world.

'Vesper?' she asks, reaching for him.

He smiles shyly, careful to look only at her face. Sweaty hair clings to her cheeks and forehead. Blotches sketch themselves across her cheeks. Beautiful.

'Oh,' she says. 'It's you.' As he struggles to answer she takes his hand. Over the coming hours he tries to be supportive, transmitting care through clammy, kissing palms. Her grunts and cries go through him, occasionally he sways. But he does not leave.

In a burst of blood and noise, the baby arrives.

Cords are cut, cuddles are given and the assembled celebrate. The baby makes its first demands and Reela meets them. A satisfied grunt makes them all chuckle. The squire forgets, reminds himself, looks only at her face.

This stolen moment is his, he gobbles it down, hoping guiltily that Vesper will not return to spoil it.

Reela smiles up at him. He smiles back. It takes him a moment to realize she's talking.

'. . . appetite! Thanks for being here, it means a lot to me, and to this little greedy guts. Would you like to hold her?'

CHAPTER TWENTY-EIGHT

Metal stairs rattle alarmingly underfoot. Old paint flakes away in chunks, drifting lazily towards the water below. Some houses have been stacked neatly, others hang from cranes above, metal boxes of varying size. Makeshift metal bridges run between them. Away from the affluence, hidden at the edge of the First Circle, these dwellings are haggard. Clumps of children gather in doorways or on rooftops, legs swinging overhead, restless, keen for entertainment.

The Vagrant stops, gets Harm's attention and points to the nearest bunch.

'You think they'll be trouble?'

The Vagrant nods.

As if on cue, several faces lean over, eyes mischief bright. 'You talking about us?' asks the leader, thin bars of copper threaded through his hair.

'No,' Harm replies.

'I don't believe you,' says the leader. 'Rikey here thinks you're a spy and they do bad things to spies here.'

Harm sighs, turns to the Vagrant. 'Can we go back now?'
The Vagrant shakes his head.

They walk on but the children aren't finished with them.

'Hey! Do you know that you're walking in our bin?' A
few pieces of shrapnel whizz down, thrown by eager hands.
The Vagrant raises a protective arm over Vesper's head.
Another comment is made and the children laugh hysteric-
ally. 'Oh that's a good one, Rikey! Hey, those stairs aren't
just our bin by the way. They're also our toilet!'

There is more laughter as the children jump to their feet.
Belts are pulled loose, trousers lowered.

Harm and the Vagrant run. Vesper laughs almost as hard
as the gang above. They stop two streets away, gasping
for breath. Harm has escaped unscathed but a few dark
patches have appeared on the Vagrant's coat. He narrows
his eyes.

'More!' says Vesper.

'Can we go back now?' asks Harm.

The Vagrant nods wearily but a new voice, unexpected,
makes them jump. 'Hello?'

After a moment of looking they see a boy, not yet in his
teens, sitting on a platform above, staring down at them
through meshed metal. He is slender, clean skin wrapped in
patched clothes. He comes lightly down the steps.

'Yes?' says Harm.

'Did you want something? I'm sure I could help.'

The Vagrant crouches down, setting Vesper next to him,
and pulls some food from his pocket. Sharp eyes flit from
the offering to the men. The Vagrant beckons him closer.

'What's your name?' asks Harm.

'What do you want it to be?'

Disgust twists Harm's mouth. 'Just give us a name, it doesn't even have to be your real one.' He leans closer to the Vagrant, whispers in his ear. 'Are you sure you want to pursue this?'

The Vagrant nods hurriedly.

'My name is Chalk,' replies the boy. 'I have the palest skin in all the Circles, so they say.'

'We're not interested in your skin. What's going on here? Why don't the guards come into this area?'

Chalk reaches out, takes the food and nibbles at it, unable to hide his excitement. 'Of course, anything you want! How much do you know about Six Circles?'

'Pretend it's our first visit. Pretend we know nothing.'

Chalk nods sagely, 'I understand. I'll pretend you're fresh and innocent. The guards never come in, and they try to keep us from getting out. They fail of course.'

'Who looks after you?'

'Griggsy looks after us. Gets us whatever we need.'

'He's your father?'

Chalk giggles, 'Do you have anything else to give me?' Knowing fingers brush the Vagrant's thigh. 'If you want to pretend some more we could go upstairs together . . .'

The Vagrant's mouth drops open, amber eyes widen in shock, then turn to Harm, seeking answers.

'I tried to warn you.'

'Is something wrong?' asks Chalk, afraid. 'Did I say something wrong?'

The Vagrant is still looking at Harm, his expression dark.

Green eyes widen in understanding. 'Are you sure about this? Of course you are.'

'What's going on?' asks Chalk.

Vesper is lifted up, feet kicking the air, protesting, and given over to Harm.

'What's going on?'

'We're going up now. Take us to your employer.'

'I don't know,' says Chalk, backing away. He turns to run but the Vagrant is faster, grabbing his wrist firmly.

'It wasn't a request.'

They ascend the stairs slowly, accompanied by Chalk's constant begging. Other gangs are drawn to the commotion, contributing abuse and pieces of rotten food from their perches.

Drawing level with the lower buildings allows glimpses of life. Most doors are open, wanton, with many dwellings doubling as shops. At this end of the ship, drugs and flesh are the top sellers.

Harm stops them. 'It's this one.'

'How did you know?' gasps Chalk as the Vagrant drags him inside. Harm follows, holding Vesper tightly.

Strip heaters provide dingy light. Ridged rubber lines the outside of booths, pale and black. There are twelve in all. Ten are shut, active.

The Vagrant releases his grip and Chalk clears his throat. 'I'm in trouble.'

A hard-faced man steps out of a booth. In his hand, casual, is a long brass bar. 'Did I hear there might be a problem, Chalky?'

'Yes, this man isn't very happy with me.'

'Oh, that right?' The man turns his attention to the Vagrant. 'Well, we got other lads might suit you better. We got girls too if you'd prefer. You tell Griggsy, what do you need?' The man twists the bar in his hand. 'Something wrong? You shy or just dumb? I gotta tell you I don't like the look in your eye. If you're not here for business then you know the way out.'

Harm speaks into the silence. 'He wants you to stop.'

'Stop what?'

'This.' Harm gestures to the booths.

'You have to be shitting me! I feed them, clean them, house them and in return they make me good money. Everybody wins.'

'That was the wrong answer.'

'You're threatening me?'

'I'm not,' Harm replies, backing out of the room with Vesper.

The Vagrant flicks open one side of his coat, gripping the sword's hilt. Chalk presses himself against the wall.

'A Seraph Knight? Here!' Griggsy shakes his head. Booth doors open, revealing a mix of faces, three curious, three scared, two bloodthirsty, one ashamed. 'Do you know what they do to Seraph Knights in these parts?' Griggsy raises the bar and the hairs on his arm stand to attention. 'No? I'll—'

With a cry, the sword is drawn. Sound buffets the assembled, judging. Blood runs from ears, from noses, men run from the room.

Griggsy stays, grits his teeth. 'As I was saying, I'll show you!'

Lightning arcs from the bar, aiming for the Vagrant's chest. At the last moment it veers away, drawn to the sword's edge. The two men stand, weapons held out front, energy crackling between them.

The Vagrant lowers the sword ninety degrees and lightning

flows backward, until brass turns white. Griggsy drops the bar, screaming. It lands softly on the rubber floor. The Vagrant steps forward, raises the sword to strike as Griggsy falls away from him, trying to plead but unable to shape words around the pain in his smoking hand.

The Vagrant pauses, sword humming above his head.

'Why have you stopped?' demands Chalk. 'Kill him!'

The Vagrant looks into the open booths. A child huddles in each, sometimes two. They regard him with scared, empty eyes. He takes one hand from the sword and points to the exit. The children leave without question. Griggsy goes to follow but the sword's point blocks his path.

'I'm not going,' says Chalk. 'I want to see.'

The Vagrant shakes his head.

'I want to see you kill him.'

The Vagrant shakes his head, horrified, then grabs Chalk by the arm and throws him outside. He slams the door shut, sealing himself and Griggsy within.

Outside, Chalk hurls himself against the door but it doesn't budge. The other children stand in a daze. After a few moments one of them shivers. Vesper watches them all with high eyebrows.

Muffled screams penetrate the battered door and light pulses around its edge. When the door opens again, Griggsy stumbles outside, weeping, meek. The Vagrant follows quickly, sword pressing against the man's back. He stops only to look at Harm. Understanding passes between them and the green-eyed man addresses the children. 'We're leaving now. You can go home or you can come with us if you want.'

They look at him, faces asking what words dare not.

Harm crouches to their eye level. 'You won't have to do what you did before, I promise.'

They descend the stairs, children trailing after. This time nothing is thrown or said, the gangs eerily quiet.

As they emerge from the street the guard rushes to meet them. With growing panic she notes the wounded man, the streak of dirty children, the winged sword. A square of light flicks nervously into life at her throat. 'Captain, I need you out here. Right now.'

In a three-sided room, in front of a triangular table, an injured man kneels. The Vagrant holds him there.

The Council of Three sit at the table, two voices competing for dominance: The Captain and the Dockmaster. Both are angry. Protocols have been ignored, feathers ruffled. Yuren sits between them while they demand answers, hands over his face.

Axler stands, pressing fists on blackened glass. 'We'll get this filth processed and then you can explain to us why a Seraph Knight is aboard, and why you chose to hide him from us.'

'Indeed,' agrees Roget.

Yuren looks up, resigned, his gaze on the accused. 'Fourth Circleman Griggs, your crimes are severe. The punishments will match them. Have you anything to say?'

Roget snorts. 'There's nothing to say. Death's too good for him.'

The Vagrant nudges the accused with his boot.

'Yes,' Griggsy says. 'I did them things. I don't deny it but I wasn't alone and I weren't at the top.'

'Who was?' demands Axler.

The Vagrant's boot insists again. Griggsy mutters: 'He was.'

Yuren pales. 'Who was?'

Griggsy glances up, furtive, then down again. He shakes his head. 'I can't say.' The Vagrant's fingers dig deeper into the man's shoulder and his face crumples. 'It was him.' He gasps, pointing a charred hand at the Dockmaster.

Roget speaks quickly, 'Nonsense, this man is clearly just saying that to—' He sees the sword shake at the Vagrant's side and lets out a long sigh. 'So be it. It's true. Before you cast any judgements, remember that I've kept everyone fed and resourced our escape.' He sees the look of shock on the other men's faces and his own reddens with indignation. 'Don't look so pious! You said yourselves that I've worked miracles. Well, miracles have a price and now you know what it is.' He stands up, long fingers pressing tip to tip. 'So let's end this farce now and get back to more important jobs.'

As he turns to leave, the Vagrant stares at Yuren, expectant.

The old man looks distraught. 'I can't. We need him. There's nothing I can do.'

'There's plenty I can do.' Axler's fists grind against the desk.

Roget shakes his head. 'Don't be so sure. Without me there is no Silicate4, no nappies, no fresh vegetables, no hazard spray—' he looks at Yuren '—no pain meds.'

Yuren slumps forward, burying his head. Again, Roget goes to leave but guards step forward from their corners, alert for orders. Axler makes a cutting motion with his hand. 'Take them both away.'

Arms are pulled back, sharp and hard. Griggsy weeps.

Roget grits his teeth. 'I make this machine work! This operation can't run without me! And when the payments aren't made, they'll want to know why, and they'll come.' He keeps talking, even as they drag him out. 'You'll regret this, I promise.'

One Year Ago

A squire sits on the steps of a house, enjoying the dawn. In his arms a baby sleeps. He finds himself talking anyway, a stream of consciousness that roves from qualities of the sky, through thoughts about life, to worries and predictions of what will be.

The world turns slowly, taking its time, making the morning stretch, calm, perfect.

Vesper emerges from some trees, well away from the main path. Water drips from his hair and fingertips, squelching in his boots. It obscures the blood on his clothes.

He raises his hand at the sight of his friend and the squire waves back. 'I have had the worst night ever!' he exclaims and flops down next to him. Old frustrations melt away and speech comes easily, the banter of old friends excited with each other.

'There were more Dogspawn, a whole pack of the bastards.' Vesper leans forward, resting his forehead on his palms. 'I led them away as far as I could and tried to shake them off but they kept finding me. I tried wiping mud over myself but that didn't work. I was getting desperate, so I thought, maybe mud isn't a strong enough smell . . .'

The other squire raises an eyebrow.

'I found this puddle of shit, I don't even want to think about what made it, and I rolled about in the stuff.' His friend tries to stifle laughter, not wanting to wake the baby. Tears run down his cheeks. 'Anyway, that's between you and me, okay! It's not going to be part of the legend.'

His friend begs to disagree and soon they are laughing again.

'Hold on . . . hold on,' says Vesper, gasping for breath. 'That isn't the end of the story. So I'm hiding there, stinking of suns know what.' He holds up a finger. 'Don't laugh, or I'll never finish! When I hear those things howling again, closer than ever. They could track me anyway! I was getting worried now, really worried. One of the pack found me and we fought. Needless to say, I defeated it but I knew the rest of the pack wouldn't be far behind. Then I had another idea. I stuck my hands into the thing's guts and smeared its blood over me. I figured they were hunting a person not each other.'

The other squire's movement is slight, sliding away less than a foot but the space between them is palpable.

'You think I might be tainted? Like Tammy?' Vesper lets out a long slow breath. 'Me too. Do you think Attica was right to kill her? I mean if I start to lose it in the head, I want you to put me out of my misery, of course I do. Will you do that? For me?'

The squire looks pained but nods.

'Thanks. I'd do the same for you. The thing is, if I just go a bit of a funny colour, or my veins stick out too much, well, I could live with that. I've heard that there are loads of tainted living in New Horizon and they seem alright. Might be that there's a cure somewhere. Do you think Tammy would have been okay if she'd lived? Do you think . . .' Vesper looks away. 'Whatever happens I don't regret it. When it's a choice between death now or death later, I'll take later every time.'

Yellow and red light blends together on their faces, warming. For a time they say nothing, thoughts trapped in closed mouths. As ever, Vesper is the first to break the silence.

'So this is my child. What is it, a girl?'

The squire nods.

'She looks a bit like me, don't you think?'

The squire smiles, shakes his head.

'Well, there is a bit of her mother in there too. I reckon she'll be a knockout when she grows up, having such good-looking parents!' He winks, reaches for the baby, hesitates. 'I better not touch her, you know, just in case. Is Reela alright?' He lets out another sigh at his friend's assurance. 'Sleeping I'll bet. She loves her sleep! Not like me. I can never get up early enough.' He rubs vigorously at his eyes. 'Saying that, I could sleep now. I'm so tired! I took a long route, skirting the far side of the village, washed myself as best I could and took another winding route home. I walked through every stream I came across, did my best to hide my tracks and, when I was a mile or so away, I waited, just in case. I don't know how long I sat in those bushes. It got so cold that for a while I thought I'd die of exposure, which would have been completely unheroic. Nothing came for me. At first light I figured I was in the clear and came to find you.' A yawn splits his face, then another. 'I'm just going to sit here for a while in case anything comes back, rest my eyes. Hopefully we've seen the last of them, at least till nightfall. Wake me if anything bad happens.'

Seconds later, Vesper is asleep.

He is woken by the howls of the approaching pack. Barely an hour has passed.

The village scrambles into action. Houses are locked and people arm themselves, a lucky few with real weapons, the rest with tools. The squire emerges from the house, having swapped a baby for a sword. Vesper remains where he was, on the ground, saving his energy. Expression grim, he listens to the enemy's cries. 'There are lots of them. This could get ugly.'

The other squire raises his sword.

Vesper stands up. 'No. You have to leave.' His friend starts to protest but Vesper cuts him off. 'Listen to me! I don't know if we can handle this. Even together, even with the whole village behind us, I don't know.' He looks hard at the other squire, lowers his voice. 'It's probably our fault they're here. You were right, we should have left a long time ago but we didn't. We have to finish the mission.'

They both know Vesper speaks truth. The squire turns to leave but stops when he notices the other isn't following.

'Sorry, I can't come with you. This place is my home. My family is here. I can't abandon these people but you have to, for the greater good.'

Vesper's friend sags.

'There's no time for this. You have to go. You have to finish the mission. Now!'

The squire looks back at Reela's house.

'Don't worry, I'll protect them with my life.'

He grits his teeth and runs home. The door is left open, swinging, as he packs hurriedly. Essentials are grabbed, the long box, travelling clothes and a pouch of coins that were the Knight Commander's, then Attica's, now his. Before leaving he checks, twice, that the lock of Reela's hair is safe in an inner pocket. The house he abandons is bare, impersonal. It is not home. Even so, the squire hesitates, unwilling to leave the world he knows.

He is spurred on by another round of howling, distant, closer.

Outside, Vesper is waiting. 'I was beginning to think you would never come out!'

Both men pause, lacking the words or the time to find them.

The squire spreads his hands, gives a sad smile, and starts north quickly.

Vesper finds his voice at the last minute. 'If you make it to the Shining City tell them about me, okay? And exaggerate. I'd like my statue of honour to be a bit taller than I am!'

The squire wipes at his face, starts to run. Howls get louder behind him. Eventually, they turn to shouts, then to screams. The road ahead gets harder to see, tear-blurred. Running is unsustainable, so is walking.

Despite the logic of leaving, he finds that he can't go on, that it isn't in him to abandon his friends.

He stops and draws his sword. Morning's light points out its insufficiencies. Another moment's indecision, then he casts it aside, kneels down and opens the box . . .

Inside, wrapped in a cloak, is Gamma's blade. In reality it is only slightly longer than those used by the Seraph

337

Knights. To the squire, however, it appears massive, too big for his hands. The hilt is unique, silvered wings curl protectively around something, something sleeping.

The squire's fingers brush the grip. He pauses but nothing terrible happens. The sword does not wake, his fingers remain as they were. He picks up the sword, still in its sheath, and attaches it to his belt. Committed now, the squire turns and runs back towards the village.

As it comes into view, horror stalls him.

A few of the bolder people lie in the street, weapons torn from bloody hands, moaning. Doors cry out as Dogspawn throw themselves against them. On the outskirts, men and women watch with mismatched eyes; their skin is livid red, a full-body sore, covered by too few clothes.

In the square, Vesper fights on. Two of the pack bleed out by his feet but they have cost him. The would-be knight holds Attica's blade one handed, the other arm hangs useless. Long teeth have made shreds of his trouser leg, letting blood flow unimpeded. The grin on his face, once cocky, is forced, held on by habit alone.

The squire sees the carnage, knows that this is his last chance to save what he loves. Still, a part of him cringes in fear of what is to come.

At his side, the sword begins to hum, the wings at the hilt quivering, starting to unfurl. The squire holds the hilt tightly and draws. As the blade rises, so does a note from deep within the young man. It bursts upwards, pushing out his chest, punching through his throat, springing wide his jaw, to soar, malevolent, into the air.

Silvered wings stretch to either side of the sword's hilt, revealing a closed eye that twitches madly.

The sword's sound shakes the very essence of those unfortunate enough to hear it, pure, otherworldly, too much for a mortal to control. Breath begins to burn. Panicked, the young man tries to close his mouth but finds he cannot. The note distorts, twisted by rage, by grief. The air becomes fire and lightning, noise and fury.

An eye opens.

CHAPTER TWENTY-NINE

In First Circle, rumours dance. Names are brushed with slander, with truth and moved on to partners new. Dark mutterings rise and fall with the waves, intensifying when Yuren's call comes. The Council wishes to address its people, summoning them to the base of the tower.

At midday, the people answer. The background hum of countless engines fades to quiet, giving the sea its voice once more. Pilots step from their boats, passengers unpack themselves from the hold and en masse they go, uncertain streams pouring into the central courtyard, each from a different street, running together, unwilling to mix.

Worried faces pack the surrounding space and nearby houses, some lean from windows or squish together on grassy rooftops. Guards move protectively in groups of four, patrolling the perimeter. Axler stands ready, lance charging in his hands.

A figure appears on the tower's high balcony. His head is nearly bald, reflecting spots of red and gold. To those on the ground he is indistinct, small, remote. Amplifiers bring his voice to the assembled, smoothing over cracks, adding gravitas.

Yuren begins: 'People of First Circle, I bring sad news. Yesterday a matter was brought before me. A terrible business. Even here, on our little floating island, it seems we are not free from abuse or crime.' The great disc rocks gently, as if moved by the words. Yuren is forced to grip the railings as he continues. 'Not only is there corruption on board ship, corruption that hurts our most innocent, but that corruption goes through every level of our society, right to its core.'

Words sink in but another greater wave steals their effect. This more literal force rocks First Circle, making people stumble into one another, like dominoes fighting for balance. Even as senses recover, something rises from the depths, ascending alongside First Circle. Water runs down its sides, giving shape. The new vessel is a relic of the Empire, a Wavemaker, its blunt nose angling thirty metres high, the rest cloaked in ocean. Other ships follow it up from the depths, smaller, each bearing modified symbols of the Winged Eye. On one the wings have been scratched away, on another the eye is painted over, forced shut. A third is covered by scores of bloody hand prints. There are seven in all, spread evenly around First Circle, surrounding, intercepting hope.

Axler's voice punctuates shock, scrambling guards into defensive positions.

A short distance across the water, the ships wait. They bear no flags. Broken swords hang above the decks, suspended from cables. The wind makes them chime, off key and eerie. Silence stretches and cannons slide from hatches, massive, mocking the tiny rifles held against them.

High above, two sky-ships drop from cloak, circling, full

stops on a declaration of superiority. From one of them a lone figure climbs into view. Loose cut clothes sit over skin-tight body armour. Hard plastic covers the face, giving nothing away. No weapons are evident and yet there is a sense of threat in its manner, polite but present. As the crowds watch it leaves the safety of the cockpit. Sure steps carry it across the wing, untroubled by wind pulling at sleeves. Eventually, it stands high above First Circle's edge. With a performer's timing, arms are raised.

It jumps.

Several people look away, not wishing to see the landing.

Impact.

Legs bend into a crouch, absorbing the force, not breaking. Standing, the figure pulls off the mask, turning to allow all a good view. Half of its head is bald and ridden with old scars. Hair flows from the other half like streamers in the wind, white, grey and black. Behind it the sky-ships descend slowly, two butterflies that sit, watchful, a few metres above the water.

'I am the First,' it shouts. 'And I am not human.' It pauses, letting fear travel. 'I have come here to make you an offer. I hope you will appreciate my candour. A quality I often find lacking among your . . . people.'

'Go ahead,' replies Axler, voice amplifiers emphasizing his disgust.

'I did not come to this . . .' the First waves a hand, searching for inspiration '. . . shape, by choice. To survive I was forced to seek a host, one of your kind. Or, rather, many hosts, since no single one of your physical structures is enough to sustain me. But this one, the primary body.' It places its palms across its chest. 'This one, was damaged

343

when I claimed it. As you know, we came to you in a place of war, a time of chaos. I have sustained this body up till now but the time is coming when I will need a . . . replacement.'

'Never!' shouts Axler.

The First regards him for a long moment, and then gives a bow. 'You are a man that knows his mind. I acknowledge that. But this offer is for everyone here and I have not yet made it. If you change your mind after hearing me, I will understand.'

'I want to hear it,' says a voice from the crowd.

'And so you shall,' replies the First. 'Simply put, I need one of you to be a receptacle for my essence. They must be unsullied by any of my kin, pure. That individual's being will be subsumed and will, as you understand it, become . . . me.' It pauses again. 'In return I will gift the rest of you with smaller portions of my essence. Those recipients will be changed in other ways. They will be connected to me but distinct. Independent but never alone. They will also enjoy extended life spans, the ability to supersede their fellows in physical contests. They could, for example, duplicate my jump onto this ship. They will share my spectrum of perception and be able to control their old senses more directly. Disease will not threaten them again, nor will mediocrity.

'I am not the Usurper, I do not seek to subjugate you. Neither am I the Uncivil, I do not seek to control you. Nor am I like The Seven, who accept your loyalty and leave you to die. I am the First and I believe that we can coexist. Together we are strong enough to live a different way, beholden neither to my kin in the South or your masters in the North. There is a price. I will repeat it: One of you must give yourself to me, willingly and without coercion. That person will cease to be. In return I will give that life back to you tenfold.'

Whispers begin, tentative. Individuals seek to know their neighbour's minds without revealing their own.

Axler steps forward, pointing his lance towards the First. 'That thing is a monster and if anybody approaches it, they'll have to answer to me.' He addresses his guards. 'Hold. Hold the line. Nobody crosses it on either side without my permission.'

Guards form up as Axler fights his way to the line. The goat does not follow, watching from a safer distance.

'Also,' the First adds. 'I am loyal to those who deal with me. You hold a . . . friend of ours. His name is Roget. You will return him immediately or I will be forced to demonstrate my loyalty. You do not want that.'

The Vagrant stands at the back of the crowd, battered coat blending, easy to miss. Those who know seek him out, pushing their way to his side. Among them number a half dozen children. Their dull eyes trail after a boy called Chalk. The others are lean, professional survivors, led by three sisters from Slake.

He glances at them. Frowns. Worries settle on his shoulders, get comfortable.

Beyond the press of people, beyond the ring of guards, he sees Axler squaring off with the First. Soon, it will break, one way or the other. From his vantage point he scans the crowd, noting groups, the shifting stances. Weighing the mood. He takes a step forward, hesitates. There are many expressions on display, none friendly.

Harm arrives at his back, Vesper hoisted on one hip. He leans in close, lips brushing the Vagrant's ear, keen to keep their secrets. 'We have to go, now. Genner knows a way, we can escape.'

The Vagrant turns, and Harm gestures to the young guard loitering in a nearby alley, uniform far from formation, conspicuous.

'Come on.'

The Vagrant looks at those who gather close to them, looks back at Harm.

'I don't know, we'll take as many as we can. But it has to be now.' The green-eyed man tugs at his sleeve.

He looks at the First, then to Genner and back again.

The sword shakes in its sheath, wingtips drumming his thigh. He clenches the hilt, muffling with his fist. It pulls at his arm, keen to attack; Harm pulls at the other.

The Vagrant closes his eyes.

Gentle undulations pass under the boat's surface, encouraging. Samael works quietly, using currents and winds and sailor's intuition to close the gap between them and their prey. Dedication is total but sometimes muscles are misplaced. A jaw falls slack, flapping in the wind, a sphincter loosens, a tongue lolls.

The commander watches him, noting the signs. He has seen this before. It's the world beating down on them, growing angrier with each passing day, driving their essence deeper within their shells. The further north they go, the worse it will become. It would be good to catch the Malice soon, before it slips from reach completely.

Samael signals him even as he senses it: another enemy,

stronger than him, more numerous, known. He joins his
servant by the prow and stares at the horizon, willing shapes
to appear.

Soon, they do.

Seven war ships surround his prize and around them a
web of essence, spread thin across those on the boats and
thinner to those beyond. It is the Thousand Cuts, the
Unbound, the Nomad King, the First. It is here in force if
not totality.

The commander orders a wide berth be given, returning
some distance so recently fought for.

But even at a distance, the First will notice them sooner
or later. The commander ponders what to do next, aware
that time is running out.

He remembers Patchwork, remembers its stealthy approach
in Verdigris – and suddenly a wash of memories surface, not
his own. He remembers the technique required to dampen
essence, remembers teaching it to her Southern Duke – the
commander snarls – not her Southern Duke, not hers! He
is not her! He cuts the memory free of the Uncivil's associa-
tions, lifting only necessary knowledge away. Calm returns.
He orders Samael to silence the engine.

Power cut, the boat moves slowly, drawn by waves alone.
Samael continues his work while the commander lies out of
sight, veiling their essence, softening, darkening.

Gone.

A second figure joins Yuren on the balcony, taller, thinner,
a scarecrow next to a pumpkin.

Roget clears his throat. 'I am here.'

Far below, on deck, the First raises a hand in greeting.

Yuren steps forward, tentative, and addresses the assembled. 'For years we asked for help and none came. Even if we manage to cross the sea, there's no guarantee The Seven will help us. We've come this far alone but if we are to survive that has to change. Our engines are overtaxed, our rations stretched to their limits. There is only one road before us that guarantees our safety.' He turns to look at the First. 'And so, in my capacity as Councilman, and on behalf of everyone on this ship, I accept your offer.'

The red on Axler's face turns to purple. 'You've sold us out!'

Yuren looks at Axler, imploring. 'Councillor, this is what you wanted too. You have been against going to the Shining City from the start, as was Roget. The First is offering us a chance at life. Stand with me. Together we can make this work.'

The leaders of First Circle argue, words carried high over heads, booming, thunderous above the hot mutterings of the crowd. Tension grows, becoming unbearable until Axler spits on the floor. He stabs a finger at the infernal. 'Get yourself and the rest of your infected friends off my ship.'

The First walks towards Axler, arms low and submissive, hands open. 'But your leader has already accepted; by what authority do you reverse this?'

'I speak for every right-minded, untainted person on this ship!' Axler makes a signal, secret, and guards prepare themselves for action.

'Do you? It seems to me you speak only for yourself.'

'Looks like we're about to find out.' Axler swings the lance into line with the First's chest. 'You've got exactly five seconds to turn around and go back to wherever you came from.'

As the First replies, Axler's lips shape numbers, counting down silently.

'If you truly speak for the people here, put it to them. If the majority agree with you, I will leave without another word and I will take Yuren and Roget with me. If they do not, then you will give yourself—'

Fire surges from the lance. 'Five!'

Even as Axler's finger is squeezing, the First is moving, fast enough to race the flames. Heat explodes in the space where the First was, the edges of it reaching out to lick at a retreating arm, catching a flowing sleeve. Axler has time to look surprised; the infernal weaving around the stream of fire and underneath his lance. Fabric bursts alight, making a tail behind the First's palm as it slams, open, into Axler's side. In sympathy, ribs and armour crack together. The lance goes quiet and its bearer falls to the floor.

Ignoring the flames creeping over its shoulder, the First moves forward for a second attack.

A lone guard, a lowly private, steps up behind the First. Grabbing a flaming wrist in both hands, she shouts: 'Help!'

Before anyone else, the First responds. Twisting a captured arm it grabs Private Ro by the elbow, making their hold mutual. Its free hand blurs against Ro's body, drilling into her stomach till she hangs limp, a long sack full of broken bones.

The guards hesitate, lacking the conviction to finish what their captain started.

But Captain Axler is not quite finished. He speaks from his position on the floor, amplifiers catching every rattle and bubble in his throat. 'Attack. Attack together.' He reaches for his lance but finds that someone has kicked it away.

Boots appear alongside, disrespectful, too close. He tilts his head back to see behind, and finds betrayal, inverted. He sees First Circle citizens all around him and a crowd gathering behind his guards.

His people raise their rifles, ready to fight at last, unaware they are facing the wrong way.

Like a great wave, the crowd crashes over the line of guards, sucking them under, crushing underfoot.

Before they reach him, strong hands slide under his body, lifting him high.

The First raises Axler above its head, a wriggling trophy. 'People of First Circle, I accept your offer. There is but one . . . obstacle that stands between us now. I wish for peace but the Seraph bring only noise and hate. You harbour one, one with the longest and sharpest of tongues. Reveal him to me.'

An image projects into the air. It shows a static man, unimpressive, his long coat worn by travel, his face weather-aged.

'He was here!' shouts a voice from the back. The crowd parts quickly, revealing nothing but an empty alleyway and the back end of a goat, fleeing the scene.

Despite everything, Axler finds strength for one last smile.

They run, footsteps echoing through empty streets. Though Vesper is carried, her feet move in sympathy with the others.

When they reach Deke's boat, the engines are already running, prow out to sea. Without a word, they pile on, packing along the wings, each additional body pushing the boat a little lower. Deke casts off as the last one joins them.

By the time the goat catches up, a space yawns between

First Circle and escape. The goat's eyes narrow. She doesn't slow down, glare fixed on her target. Hooves kick on plasteel, then air, as she sails over the water, a meteor, malevolent.

Vesper points, delighted. 'G—'

Her shadow falls across the Vagrant who turns, too slow to escape fate.

'—oat!'

Man becomes crash mat and the boat rocks, water spraying up, dappling faces.

While things settle, Harm crawls closer to the cockpit. 'What's the plan?'

Deke swings the boat around, threading between the waiting warships and First Circle's curves, a lizard slipping under the noses of lions. Two sky-ships come into view. 'That's the plan.'

The nearest one notices their approach and a pilot steps out, weapon in hand.

Genner's rifle fires twice, silent, silencing.

No more challenges come and they dock, unloading from one vessel into another quickly.

Deke whispers into his hand and his boat turns in the water, facing the other sky-ship. He pats the controls affectionately and climbs aboard alongside Genner. Hands move expertly and the sky-ship trembles, readying for flight.

Harm watches them from a corner, his face hidden behind two elbows and a shoulder. 'You've done this before.'

'Nope,' replies Deke. 'Never stole a sky-ship before!'

Genner laughs. Harm doesn't.

As they push heavily into the air, Deke's old boat speeds towards the remaining sky-ship, engines brightening, until the glow hurts to watch. The older, flightless bird collides with her younger cousin. The explosion is loud, satisfying. Vesper covers her ears.

Below them seven warships wake, cannons humming to life, eager for attention.

Too burdened to dodge, the sky-ship relies on her shields for survival. Many of the shots fly wide, many don't. Each collision saps the protective light, drawing on precious reserves. By the time they fly clear, worried bleeps sound from flashing displays.

Overloaded, underpowered, the sky-ship travels on, till flying becomes gliding, till gliding becomes falling.

CHAPTER THIRTY

From a distance the sky-ship appears graceful, skimming across the water, a stone cast by a playful god. Inside, each bounce is magnified. Heads and knees bash against walls, against each other. Bruises bloom and distress sounds loud, filling the cramped space. The bounces get smaller and more frequent until, at last, the sky-ship merely drifts.

Passengers find themselves alive, injuries widespread but minor. Nobody celebrates, saving that for Deke's appraisal of the ship and their chances.

'Well,' he reports. 'She ain't flying again but I reckon she can still manage calm waters. Second time that's happened. If I'm not careful, I'm gonna get me a reputation.'

He deploys two emergency rafts, self-inflating spheres of plastic that he tethers to the mother vessel. Powerless but buoyant, the rafts are soon stuffed with people. A few have followed the Vagrant on this last leg to the Shining City, a mish mash of people from different places. Deke and his nephew Genner come from Six Circles, Chalk and

353

the other escapees from Griggsy's employ tag along, as much to avoid going home as to travel anywhere specific, and lastly there are those rescued from Slake, who survived sickness, travelled to the wall and fled to First Circle when it fell.

Vesper sits up front with Deke, both talking rapidly. Occasionally they wait for the other to finish. Often they giggle. The goat stands on one wing, at ease with the rocking motion. The Vagrant sits on the other.

Harm is crouched by the cockpit's entrance. 'Deke, can I ask you something?'

'Sure can, long as you don't mind me answering it.'

'Do you think we can make the journey like this?'

'Well, we can't just blunder any old way across the waves like one of them big cruisers, we got to work with the currents and the winds where we can.' He pats the dashboard. 'This old girl's got all the regular charts stored, plus I got a few I found the hard way.'

Harm begins to relax. 'Aren't you worried about the First following us?'

'That's land-thinking, that is. Not much point worrying. Nope, if any hostile vessel finds us we're screwed. Just like if the weather turns bad or if one of our engines gives out, or if—'

Harm cuts in. 'I think I get it now, thanks, Deke.'

'You should take your cue from Vesper here.'

'Esper!'

'Yep, this little feller's a natural. When everything's going alright, best thing you can do is sit back and enjoy it till things turn to shit, which they surely will.'

Silence takes over, the open sea encouraging contemplation.

The suns swirl slowly out of sight behind a bank of cloud, hastening darkness.

'Hey everyone,' calls Deke, cheerily. 'Good news: We're not far from the Spine Run! We can follow the land for miles and make good time. And my navpack'll get us through the rocks no problems. When the suns are up tomorrow we'll start the run. In the meantime we can get some rest on Tail Rock.'

Tail Rock is neither long nor thin. Shaped like a battered spade, its name comes solely from its position, the first in a line of undersea mountains that march to the horizon.

They set up camp. The goat sets off to explore and is uninspired by the local army of sea birds and their messy paintwork.

The humans need no more excitement, happy to huddle in the camp. Most people fall quickly to sleep. A circle of heaters provide warmth and gentle light, reassuring and soft. Conversations become reflective, intimate, then fade away, to be forgotten.

Hours later, a scrabble of hooves on stone stirs people awake. Birds shriek and take to the air, abandoning nests and young. Desperate calls penetrate the skulls of even the heaviest sleepers. The goat charges past camp and leaps onto Deke's ship. Without pause she dives into the cockpit, vanishing from sight.

Lights are turned to full. People look at each other and then at the blank sky for answers.

At the Vagrant's side, the sword stirs, restless.

'Up there,' says Chalk, shining his light upward. On the rocks, high where the birds usually hold sway, is a silhouette, broad, imposing. Armour glints in patches, is dark in

355

others. The silhouette moves, drawing a sword that twists and moans, challenging.

The lonely sound lingers, hanging in ears long after it should.

'I don't hear any others,' says Harm.

Genner unslings his rifle. 'Let's take it together.'

'I'm not usually up for a fight but if you need me, I'm there,' adds Deke.

Two of the three sisters from Slake share the sentiment. The rest appear lost, frightened. They back towards the ship, following the goat's example.

The Vagrant's gaze seems distant as he takes in their faces. With closed eyes he plants a kiss on Vesper's forehead. It is a goodbye, unwelcome. Vesper clings to the Vagrant, crying as her fingers are prised free. Harm's waiting arms are poor consolation.

'So what's the plan?' asks Genner, nervous and eager. The Vagrant puts his hands on the young man's shoulders, easing him back into his seat. 'But I don't get it . . . We're with you, we all are. We're ready to fight.' The Vagrant nods, begins to back away. 'You don't have to do this alone!' After a last, sad smile, the Vagrant begins to climb. In desperation, the guard turns to Harm. 'I don't get it. Why'd he smile at me?'

'Because that's what I normally say. And because it's not true. Even if he wanted to be, he's never alone.'

High up, the rocks are slippery with sea foam and bird droppings. The commander watches the bearer of the Malice clamber towards him. There is an impulse to strike now, send the enemy to their death on the stony beach, but another, less logical, makes him wait. A reason comes after: the Malice must be destroyed, its essence ruined, silenced. To lose it to the sea would mean death for the master.

And himself.

But it is not reason that stays his hand. With growing self awareness, he knows this. The thought is without context or sense, unsatisfying, nothing more than the fact it would feel wrong. Of late, the commander misses his former certainty.

Imprisoned in his hands, the tainted sword cries ceaselessly, metal twisting free of shape, stretching, threatening to split, then falling back, a blade again.

When the bearer finishes his climb, he pauses, chest heaving. The commander waits for the mortal to recover breath and approach. It is not the first time the two have met but previously one has fled the other, or third parties have been distracting. Now, when the Malice wakes and the air bursts with light, the two see only each other.

The commander notes the bearer's face, the open mouth, the wide eyes. He is used to inspiring fear and horror but this is different: this is the shock of recognition. The bearer knows him, has seen his shell before. The commander wonders if it will have a chance to pluck that knowledge from the bearer's mind before destroying him.

They raise their swords. Neither are knights but both use the salute of the Seraph, compelled by habits thought forgotten.

The Malice strikes first and quickly, crackling with rage. Each physical attack is parried but the commander feels sparks showering his chest, disturbing the essence within.

To be this close to the Malice is draining, and the

commander realizes that the fight cannot be allowed to go on for long. He forces the bearer to fight at his pace, swinging powerfully, relentlessly, pushing the enemy back until his feet slip on uneven stones.

Taking the opportunity, the commander feints and chops for the wrists. The enemy uses a complex counter, reversing the attack, changing the flow of combat, moving smoothly into a combination, blurring and brilliant.

Familiar.

The commander blocks the first flurry unconsciously, his shell doing what is needed without instruction. Part way through the combination's second section he predicts where the Malice will strike next. Again without context he knows these movements. Knows that they are his creation. A wave of exultation passes through him as he steps unexpectedly, throwing the enemy off balance and aiming to take off a leg.

Somehow the enemy brings the Malice down to parry but the bearer's stance is weak and the commander pushes harder, his sword biting deep into a thigh until a wild swing of the Malice forces him back. Rage sings out from the sword, making armour vibrate, shaking the very glue that holds the commander together. He bears the discomfort, seeing the move for what it is, desperate.

The sword sings a different note and the bearer lays the flat of the blade against his recently injured thigh. Skin sizzles as the bearer's wound staunches itself, purifying, painful. Agony clouds eyes with tears, squeezing them shut. The enemy is stunned, momentarily blind and defenceless.

The commander takes his chance.

Moaning, his sword comes down.

Meeting another as it swings across.

For the enemy is not blind. A third eye, the sword's, remains open, blazing fury. The parry is elemental, inhumanly strong and in a shower of shards and relief, the commander's sword shatters.

He is left with the hilt, smoking, useless. He throws it away.

Unarmed, he watches his half-fallen opponent, twisted down on one knee, wracked with pain.

Gauntleted fists clench, swinging for the bearer's head.

To the commander it seems as if the sword is the first to rise, drawing the bearer with it. His first strike is parried, then the second, severing both limbs at the elbow. He lets momentum carry his body forward, moving inside the Malice's reach, slamming into the bearer.

They fall together, the commander pinning his enemy with weight alone. Amber eyes stare into the darkness of his visor, held by the wisps of green moving inside.

Unarmed, maimed, the commander has one gambit left, to bend the bearer to his will. Essence moves through the slits in the commander's visor, a smoke that drips down onto the bearer's face, slipping through his skin, making contact.

Physical things fall away, becoming distant, irrelevant. The commander exists outside of time, gathering within the fog inside the soul of the man. Here there are no secrets. Through the man's eyes, the commander sees himself, experiences revulsion and something else.

Sadness?

Yes; when he looks at the commander he remembers the previous inhabitant of his body: the Knight Commander of the Seraph and loyal servant of The Seven.

The commander sees an image: a bearded man with hard eyes and a harder voice, proud, quick-witted and tough as stone.

He is mesmerized by this, and the awe it inspires in the bearer. To learn more becomes all and the commander pushes harder, deeper, immersing himself in the past.

But then he detects another vein of memories, even richer than the ones on his tongue, and he chases them. But each time he gets close, they recede deeper, teasing him, luring him on.

He follows without question, drawn by another presence lurking within the bearer's soul, more dangerous than memories.

And then, within the dark soup of their shared essence he hears a sound, reverberating deep inside. It is majestic, mournful, bigger than both of them.

The Malice.

It calls to him and he finds himself answering in a voice not his own. Hidden within his own confusions, the conflict between himself and the master, the questions and possibilities raised by the Uncivil, the mystery of his past. The commander feels something else stir, an echo of the Malice that lies within him, that has always been there, sleeping.

Around him, the sense of man fades, murky fog burnt away by star-bright essence, silver-laced and edged in darkness, a chorus of wings spiralling around an eye.

And before thought can form, it takes him.

One Year Ago

From above, the arrangement of bodies seems artful. A man lies on his back, arms splayed at right angles. Smoke drifts gently from his open mouth. At his side, the sword sleeps, sated. In the immediate vicinity the ground is scorched black and small lumps are scattered around him, a decorative pattern. Further away, the shapes increasingly retain form and colour, becoming men and beasts, infernal and half-breed, all lying together, unified in emptiness.

The village is silent.

Only the man's chest moves and only then with reluctance.

Time passes.

From somewhere nearby, crying begins.

Amber eyes open and stare blankly at the sky. They fail to track the movement of the clouds.

Time passes.

Eventually, they close again.

The crying continues, muffled, pathetic.

Eyes squeeze tight against the sound, then fly open, painfully aware. The man rolls onto his side and gets up. Every movement is laboured, an act of will. He stumbles forward, leaving the sword in the ashes. He does not need to listen to know which house the crying comes from.

The building looks battered, its front door buckled, half torn open.

He finds the energy to run.

Inside is carnage. A Dogspawn has been killed with improvised weapons. Broken handles protrude from its flanks and nails pepper its sides. One has lodged in the half-breed's skull, an upside down exclamation mark.

Three corpses are also present, made messy by jagged teeth. Their blood carpets everything. He kneels by a woman's broken body. She lies on the floor, face down. Even so, she is recognizable. Reela. Gently, he turns her over, revealing a ruined landscape of arms and chest. He stumbles backwards, bloodstained hands covering his mouth. Reela is still in her bedclothes. It is clear that she fought the Dogspawn unarmed. It is easy to imagine the fight was short.

Colour drains from his face as legs waver. A wall catches him and he leans into it, eyes closing.

After a while stunned ears tune in to the crying. It has become hoarse now.

He crouches down and looks under the bed to find a face, purple and strained, looking back at him.

There is no decision to be made. He pulls the baby out and lifts it up, striding from the house with quick steps. He doesn't look back, the sight already dream-etched, permanent.

Once outside he tries to soothe the screaming child but

no words come, just a pain that flares in the throat. Slowly, he sinks to his knees, holding the baby close.

Both cry.

After a while the baby sleeps. He gets up again. Evening is coming and he uses the last of the light to count Dogspawn bodies.

There are many but not enough. Somewhere in the nearby woods the pack endures.

He collects the sword, pulls a coat from one of the corpses, wrapping it around him and the baby. Its forehead rests against his neck, alarmingly hot. He frowns and starts toward New Horizon. A broken man with no voice, no friends and no home. A vagrant.

The suns dip below the horizon and howling starts as if on cue.

He does not try and hide his tracks.

CHAPTER THIRTY-ONE

'I've seen worse,' says Deke, bending forward, hands on thighs. 'But I've seen a lot better.'

'Will he live?' Harm asks softly.

'I reckon. Might not be so lively for a while.'

The Vagrant lies flat, covered with a blanket. On the exposed ground, winds are cruel. All present shiver.

'Course the real question is how we're gonna get him back down again.'

'Ssh!' says Harm. 'I think he's waking up.'

They watch him expectantly, Deke blowing into cupped hands, Harm biting his lip.

With a grimace, the Vagrant wakes.

'Welcome back,' says Harm.

The Vagrant returns the smile, grimaces again. His hand moves questioningly towards his right temple.

'Careful, Scout,' warns Deke. 'We haven't had a chance to clean you up yet.'

More gently, the Vagrant explores the side of his head.

He finds stripes cut through his hair; where he touches the skin it's smooth, burn white. Fingers track down to where a sliver of metal threads through his cheek, welded in place.

'Did he use one of them shrapnel guns on you, Scout?'

The Vagrant shakes his head.

'A grenade?'

'No,' says Harm. 'Genner says he saw the other knight's sword explode.'

'Damn. So you got him good then, Scout?'

The Vagrant sits up and stares at the two severed arms lying side by side, then nods, uncertain.

'Are you in pain,' asks Harm. In answer, the Vagrant holds up a hand, finger and thumb a quarter inch apart. 'Bearable then. Enough to let us winch you down?'

'Gonna have to be,' interrupts Deke. 'We put plenty of the good stuff in your veins, it ain't gonna get any easier than this.'

The Vagrant draws back the blanket, pointing to a silvery patch on his thigh. He raises an eyebrow.

'Your face ain't too pretty no more but its mainly just surface stuff. Your leg is where the problems are gonna be. Don't worry though, I happen to have some top-of-the-line burn meds stashed away for a rainy day.' The old man winks. 'Best not to ask how I came across them.'

They winch him down the rocks to a collection of waiting hands that carry him to Deke's boat. Despite the discomfort, the Vagrant relaxes, letting others take his weight for a time. Before he is stowed aboard, sleep comes.

At first light the trio of vessels leave, daring the sharp edges of the Spine Run in return for its quick currents and shallow waters.

The Vagrant sits in his customary place on the wing, one leg outstretched, the other drawn up against his chest. Harm sits next to him.

From the cockpit, Vesper calls: 'G-on.'

'What's that?' asks Harm.

'G-on.'

'Gone?'

'Gone!'

'Gone? What's gone?'

'Dada.'

'No,' smiles Harm, 'he's right here.' The Vagrant turns to face the toddler and smiles too.

Vesper takes their smiles and doubles them. 'Gone!'

'Oh,' says Harm, realization dawning. 'She's talking about your teeth. You must have lost one in the fight.'

The Vagrant's tongue probes around his mouth, finding the spaces. He sighs, holds up two fingers.

'Don't worry, I'm sure they can fit you with new ones at the Shining City. When you get there, you'll be a hero. They'll probably promote you, maybe even build a statue in your honour.' Harm's laugh dies when he sees the Vagrant's face. 'Look, what I was trying to say is that things are going to change soon, and for the better. There's a place for you in the Shining City. I'm just not sure if there's a place for me.' His voice quietens, getting harder to hear. 'Deep down I knew this couldn't last but it felt so good, I didn't want it to stop.' He notes the Vagrant's puzzled look. 'You don't know what I'm talking about do you?'

The Vagrant shakes his head.

'I don't think I'm going to be welcome where we're going. You saw what they did to those poor bastards on Third

367

Circle. What do you think they're going to do to me?' The next words he forces out, one by one. 'I'm tainted. Not badly like the Hammer was but enough. I picked it up in Wonderland, long before I met you.'

Green and amber eyes meet and Harm doesn't bother to hide his shock. 'You knew? How? How long have you known?'

The Vagrant reaches over the side and scoops seawater into his palm. Carefully, he rests the back of his right hand against the sword's hilt and touches Harm with his left.

The water begins to move, magnifying the sword's tremors, tiny ripples making patterns, swirling.

'All this time I thought I was hiding it from you . . .'

The Vagrant shrugs, tips the water away.

'Do you want me to go?'

He shakes his head.

Harm breaks away again, seeking solace in the ocean's calm. 'Before you make that decision, there's something I have to tell you. If you still want me around after that, I'll follow you wherever you go, no matter what. But if you don't. If after this you hate me or . . . or want to kill me. I'll understand.'

Eyebrows raise, unnoticed. For once, Harm's focus is purely inward.

'I said I picked up the taint in Wonderland. I mean that literally. It was about two years ago when I had the operation done. The Uncivil's surgeons gave me these eyes. It was an expensive procedure, more than I could afford. Most of the money was provided by other groups in the city as advanced payment for my services. I knew it meant they'd own me for a while but I thought I could handle it. I thought . . .' he pauses '. . . maybe I didn't think much at all. I wanted to be special. Most of us do. The operation was supposed to let me read other people, to tell if they were lying, or if they intended trouble. It was supposed to make me rich.

'What I didn't understand, couldn't understand, was how it would affect me. My eyes work by taking in something of the people I'm close to, the same way their scents drift into my nostrils, their personalities would drift into my eyes. That visual scent told me things about them, but it . . .' Harm struggles to find the right word '. . . infected me somehow. I wasn't keeping the best company at the time and my eyes exposed me to the worst parts of them. The hidden parts. The destructive, twisted parts.' Harm hangs his head. 'And in me, they found a way to be expressed. Ironically, the sickest of them came to like having me around. They felt comfortable around me and I wonder now if my being there encouraged them in some way. Sometimes I copied them, sometimes they copied me and sometimes . . .? Maybe some of it was just me, I don't know. But I did things, terrible things that I can't take back.

'I fled from Wonderland, leaving a lot of unpaid debts. Tough Call took me in, and for a while I found refuge with the rebels in Verdigris. I'd managed to get away from Wonderland but in the end, that didn't matter. There was plenty of darkness waiting in my new home and it wasn't long before the same problems started again.

'And then you and Vesper came. I saw my chance for something better and I took it. With you I could be some-body different and because you were good to me and you valued me I started to feel . . . I started to feel . . . like I

369

could wipe some of the muck away and start being a person. I can't tell you how grateful I am for that.

'But I've always worried. Do I just tune into something in the two of you or do I take it away? Am I stealing the best parts of you to help myself? And what if I'm stunting the growth of Vesper's personality? I couldn't live with that.' Tears spring from the corners of eyes, bitter. 'Actually that isn't true. I could find a way to live with anything. And I probably would have kept quiet if I thought I could get away with it. So you see, Deke's wrong. Harm is a good name for me and I haven't deserved to feel what I've felt since we started travelling together.' He falls quiet while water laps against the boat, counting time. 'Well, there it is,' says Harm finally, unable to meet the Vagrant's eye. 'Do you still want me to stay?'

The Vagrant stares at his hands. It is unclear what he searches for. A sigh passes his lips, loaded with sadness, and other things, inexpressible. He turns to Harm, who waits, hunched and miserable, and a mix of emotions pass his face. Decision made, he puts a hand on Harm's shoulder, rests it there.

Deke skilfully navigates the Spine Run and the three ships begin the last leg of their journey. Everyone is tired. The passengers, the engine, even the elements, which remain mercifully gentle. Conversations go through stages of excitement, irritation, then graduate to a rough familiarity. Safe topics soon run out and boredom encourages people to ask more searching questions. Eventually these too fall away. Only the engine keeps going, getting noisier in its struggles, filling the quiet.

Each day passes much like the last. Time drags out and compresses, a paradox that makes the hours long and the days short.

Their arrival on the northern continent is understated. Away from ports and seaways, cities and flight paths, the boats limp to the finish. Once on land, the travellers celebrate modestly.

'This way!' calls Deke, walking briskly towards a towering group of trees.

Harm looks wary. 'You know where you're going?'

'Wouldn't be much of a pilot if I didn't.' The old man winks and taps his temple. 'That and I got the maps tucked in here behind my eyeballs.' He leads them inland, into a forest.

The trees here are thick and tall, and lined up smartly, like spears for a god. Lower branches have been trimmed to keep the shaft smooth but the upper canopy runs wild, a hundred hundred crazy haircuts, weaving into one another. Deke slaps Genner on the shoulder. 'You sure you ain't descended from one of these?'

'Very funny, Uncle D.'

Everything is still, as if the wind holds its breath. No wildlife is in evidence, just lines and lines of trees, a lonely army. Even so, the wood appears vibrant to southern eyes. Fingers brush smooth bark as they walk and more than one stoops to collect fallen leaves.

'Down!' says Vesper.

The Vagrant stands her on the ground. Vesper wobbles for a moment, gaining balance, and then she is moving. Leaves crunch and twigs snap, tyrannized by busy feet.

Deke holds up a hand and the group slows.

'What's wrong?' asks Harm.

'Why you always so cynical? Nothing's wrong. We're here is all.'

Green eyes look across the matching trees. 'Here?'

'Yep.' The old man goes onto one knee and intones something soft and beautiful. Genner follows suit, joining him on the floor.

Uneasy glances pass among the rest of the group.

'What did you just say?' asks Harm, suddenly tired.

When Deke replies, the rough edges are gone from his words. 'My other name.'

From nearby a song answers. The Vagrant starts, recognizing it.

Around the group air shimmers in sudden heat, taking on the shapes of men, and in the blink of an eye, squires become solid, pointing blades. At their head is a man, unremarkable save for the deference given him by others. The Vagrant knows him as Able. He has cast aside his disguise from Slake in favour of a simple uniform, black save for the eye holding the collar close to his neck. He walks forward, crouching in front of Deke. The two press the backs of their hands together and light flows where skin touches. A few seconds are all it takes for Deke's report to download. Able stands smartly and walks out of the circle. Words are thrown over a shoulder. 'Keep them here while I report in.'

The goat assesses the scene and finds herself ignored. She trots over to some lush green shoots, keen to sample the delights of northern cuisine.

Able soon returns, flanking Sir Phia. The knight is now dressed in her full armour, impressive, though travel has taken its shine. At her arrival the Vagrant kneels, pulling

Vesper close. The rest of the group copy him, Harm a few beats after the others.

'So,' she says. 'You made it. I was beginning to wonder.' She looks down at Deke and Genner, favouring each with a nod. 'Well done both of you. Your actions will not be forgotten, nor will they go unrewarded.' Neither man replies, though both straighten.

Harm grinds his teeth. 'You abandoned us!'

A squire steps forward, gently tapping the back of Harm's head with his pommel. The green-eyed man sprawls obediently, face down.

'No!' says Vesper, reaching out, held fast by the Vagrant's arm.

Sir Phia waits while Harm recovers his senses. 'We are not in the slums of Slake anymore, we are under The Seven's gaze, mere miles from the Shining City. Remember that when you address me. And remember it is a crime to lie to a Seraph Knight.' Harm's eyes glaze with hate but his mouth stays closed. 'Understand that I did not abandon you. When you diverted from the mission, I moved ahead to secure a way. Even then, I left orders to see you helped. My agents were waiting at key locations for your arrival. Wonderland, the Wall—' she gestures to Deke and Genner. 'Six Circles. You don't honestly think you'd have got this far without my help, do you?' It is unclear whom she addresses so everyone shakes their head, just to be safe. 'Able, I want these people to be taken in and tested. Purge any you think will survive, yourself included.'

'Yes, Ma'am.'

The Vagrant stands up and moves between Able and Harm. Vesper trails after him.

Sir Phia folds her arms. 'They are going for testing and

you are coming with me, conscious or otherwise. Now get out of his bloody way!'

The Vagrant reaches for the sword. Harm sees the motion, rushes forward, wincing as the squires close in behind. He grabs the Vagrant's hand before it reaches the hilt. 'Please! Do what they ask.' Surprised, the Vagrant looks at him. 'I'm not asking out of fear. I need to do this. Everything good I've done has been because of you or Vesper. I need to know if any of it was me.'

Hands squeeze each other tight, saying what words cannot.

Able moves close. 'It's time.'

Harm nods, allows himself to be led away with the others: Deke and Genner, Chalk and the children and adults from First Circle, the sisters and their companions from Slake. All go quietly. Half of the squires go with them. Before trees mask them completely, green eyes turn for the last time, filled with sadness and a hint of pride.

'Bye, Umbull-arm!'

After a quick salute, Able sets off after the group, leaving Sir Phia, the Vagrant and four squires behind.

Sir Phia taps her foot. 'Able, you've forgotten somebody.'

At her voice, he stops, reluctant. 'Are you sure, Ma'am?'

'I'll pretend I didn't hear that. Now hurry up and take the girl.'

He looks pointedly at the Vagrant. 'I think there may be a problem.'

'Look,' she says to the Vagrant. 'The girl's probably tainted, better she's checked here. Helped if possible, given mercy if not. The Seven will not be so kind. And nor will I if you don't do as you're ordered. Now, Able, I won't ask you again.'

'Yes, Ma'am.'

Before he or anyone else can act, the Vagrant draws the sword. Four squires surge forward but the Vagrant turns, and something in them falters. Sir Phia and Able are already on their knees.

Surprised, an eye opens.

Understanding dawns on young faces. Baby swords are dropped from shamed fingers and suddenly they cannot prostrate themselves fast enough.

By contrast the Vagrant brings the sword down slowly, until the blade is an inch from Vesper's face. An eye looks at her sleepily.

Vesper puts a finger to her lips.

The sword is quiet.

An eye closes.

The Vagrant takes a step nearer Sir Phia, sword pointed towards her, offering judgement. She gets up quickly, backs away. 'You've made your point. The girl can stay with you. Now please, put away the sword. The Seven are waiting.' She backs off hastily and leads the way.

The sword is sheathed, only then does Able stand. He bows deeply in the Vagrant's direction and sets off at pace after the others. Squires dare to look up from the floor. They glance nervously after Sir Phia then back to the Vagrant.

He gives them a sharp nod and they get up, retrieving their weapons.

Vesper holds out her hand. The Vagrant takes it and the two make their way after the Seraph Knight, squires following after them.

CHAPTER THIRTY-TWO

Each day of his journey the commander reminds himself: I am not dead. It still feels as if he is falling, as if Samael did not pluck him from the rocks, as if the world is a watercolour he no longer believes in. Only the message is real.

He carries it back to the coast, all the way to Wonderland. There is a building with many floors, some underground, some over. The commander navigates the complex corridors from memory. He is not sure if the knowledge to do so belongs to him or the Uncivil but he does not waste time on it. Such things are irrelevant now.

Samael opens doors for him as they wind closer to the centre of Wonderland. The commander could make contact anywhere in the city but again a feeling of 'not rightness' steers him. He will go to the heart of things, physically, geographically, as well as through essence.

Robed figures step aside, deferent, allowing him to progress from Wonderland's outskirts to the Uncivil's innermost sanctum, not understanding what the commander has become.

Finally, they arrive. The chamber is thirty feet across, barely enough to hold the Uncivil's inner shell. Her cloak is thick and woven from the dead. None of the original bodies remain, burnt away by the world's hatred, but the Uncivil's legion of followers always find plenty to replace them. Her outer shell is the city itself, threaded with her veins, studded with her ears. And she grows, her people laying down the infrastructure that will allow her to spread to the coast.

At all costs, she must be stopped.

As he stumbles towards her, the song begins to rise. The Uncivil senses it. He sees the necrotic ball sway from side to side in agitation, unable to move against him, unable to flee. He orders Samael to wait and walks the last alone.

The surface of the Uncivil's shell is smooth, individual pieces broken down and fitted together like a horrific jigsaw. It is almost flawless. Almost. Even with the best joinery, there are cracks between the bodies, tiny, too small for a fingernail. It is easy for the commander to slip his essence inside. A moment later his armoured form clatters to the floor, empty.

Though the chamber appears quiet, a storm rages in the Uncivil's shell, where essence swirls, like a great sea trying to flee a tiny island. The commander opens himself, allowing Gamma's message to pass through him, a single note of merciless hate, a poisoned dagger between the ribs. Like a virus of fire it radiates outward, using the Uncivil's own connectivity against her.

As the song of malice spreads through the Uncivil's system, necrotic pipes are gutted, turned black from the inside. In surgeries throughout the city, procedures stop too early, sentencing patients to a gruesome end. And the song travels on expunging all traces of the Uncivil. In chambers beneath the city, smoke rises from inanimate fingers. Bonewings fall lifeless from their perches.

In the markets, things continue as normal. Necrotraders haggle, people eat and drink, ignorant of the city's death.

Underground, the cloak of corpses slowly sags and green vapour leaks out. A remnant of essence seeking the commander's maimed shell.

Samael blinks, orders surfacing in the blank pool of his mind. He jolts forward, taking the commander under the armpits, raising him up. Heavy boots slip on the cold floor, scrabble and find purchase.

Reoriented, the commander marches from the room, Samael following, like a shadow.

By the time Sir Phia realizes the goat is following them, the will to protest is gone. No one knows what motivates the goat to stay with the Vagrant. There is no hint of love or loyalty. Familiarity or masochism keep her close in the leash's absence.

Vesper strokes her side whenever she is foolish enough to come close. 'Goat!' When she roams further afield, other objects become top of mind.

'Tr-ee!'

'Lee-ff!'

Sometimes she points at Sir Phia. The Vagrant puts a finger to his lips before any names can be bestowed. Quietly, smiles are shared.

The woods draw back like a curtain to reveal undulating fields, topped in lush green. Every mound and hill is a dwelling, windows peeking like eyes through the grass. In places, towers of silver rise, sparkling, into the sky. They too are topped with gardens or a single, grand tree. Endless labour keeps the borders between metal and vegetation neat. Workers hang, strung like spiders on harnesses, little black specks dangling among the splendour.

For most it is hard to see where the land ends and the Shining City begins and yet there are walls. Invisible fields of energy, ready to repel the unworthy. The Vagrant feels them as he passes, the charge making Vesper's hair rise about her head, a dark and fuzzy cloud.

They are met at the border by a group of knights. The title seems absurd for such fresh faces and though few chronological years separate them, they seem like children next to the Vagrant.

High above, sky-ships squat on massive pillars, vigilant. Many of the pillars are empty however, their landing pods bare. Between them, coffin-sized pellets float, moved by powerful magnets, the Shining City's own army of secret magicians.

A gaggle of children stream out of hidden hatches in the ground, cheering and waving at the knights. Adults come running after, long suffering.

Vesper's face goes blank for a moment, then she jumps up and down, pointing to her chest. 'Esper! Esper!'

Together, the children answer, voices light, harmonic. 'Vesper.'

When Sir Phia walks by them, the children kneel, the adults too. Only Vesper fails to swap enthusiasm for humility. She points at each child, naming, one after another, their identities broadcast into her brain.

The Vagrant walks on, a smudge against the open landscape, a stain in an otherwise sparkling crowd.

Ahead of him rises the sanctum of The Seven.

He keeps his head down, keeps Vesper close.

A small boy and a purple skinned man help Samael roll the barrel through Verdigris' streets. All three sweat. Ahead of them a man walks, his clothes shapeless and filled with oddities. Sweat has not found him for a long time.

Alone, Samael could not manage the burden. While his essence continues to be changed within, the link between mind and body suffers and movement becomes grotesque. Frequent twitches possess limbs, making them dance, the movements surreal, alien.

'Hey!' calls a voice, deep and booming. It belongs to a Usurperkin dressed in a marshal's uniform.

The group stop.

'What's this?'

'Ah,' answers the leader, a smile materializing on his face. 'Max, protector of small people! It has been too long.'

Max scratches between his hair spikes. 'Do I know you?'

'Next to goods of such quality, Ezze is easily forgotten.'

Puzzlement is personified on Max's face. He points at the barrel. 'What's this?'

'Ah you have keen eye. Surely this is why you have such important job. Come closer and Ezze show you. You like shit, yes?'

'Yeah . . . What?'

'The shit. You like? The finest droppings from the north, all from people and all untainted. For you Ezze will give a cup half price!'

Large green hands raise, as if warding off the barrel's contents. 'Ugh, no!'

'You sure, friend? It will sell like hot . . .' Ezze pauses theatrically and then laughs, long and hard. 'Still no? Well, do not say that Ezze did not try!' He starts to walk on. 'Come, come, roll faster! Your pay is not by the hour!'

With weary sighs the boy, the half-breed and Samael get back to work.

'Stop!' says Max.

'You change your mind? Ezze knew you were a smart one!'

'No. You said that came from the north.'

'All true.'

'And we're not letting anything in from the north anymore. Tough Call said so.'

'You see!' shouts Ezze to the three by the barrel. 'This is exactly what I was saying to the boy earlier. Ezze try to explain but he is young and not clever like you Marshal Max. Of course no trade from north of Verdigris, that would be Necro shit. And no good fruit comes from that!' He smacks the boy across the ear.

'Ow!'

'Stupid child! Of course that is not what is here. No, friend, this fine barrel comes from the north of the north!'

'The north . . . of the north?'

'Just so! Already you understand. North of the north are fine lands, with the finest shit for growing crops. There is much demand for such things now food is scarce, yes?'

'Yeah . . .'

'Well, this has been good, Marshal Max, but time is against us. Ah! Before Ezze goes, would you do something?'

'What?'

Ezze pulls a box from within the folds of his robe. The purple skinned man stares at it, envious. 'For your sister.'

'Maxi?'

'You have other sisters?'

'Uh, no.'

'Marshal Maxi then.'

'What is it?'

'More of the best, with Ezze's thanks. Tell her to smoke slower this time and to sit down first!'

'Right, I'll do that.'

'Goodbye then. And if you wish to sample what is inside, a little pinch will not be missed.' Ezze winks and then rushes away, leaving Max to smile hopefully at the box. When the Usurperkin is left far behind, Ezze slaps Samael on the shoulder. 'And that, friend, is why Ezze's escort is worth paying for!'

The group move on, taking back alleys and abandoned streets, until at last they come to the south gate. Pre-paid guards are quick to turn, blind eyed, and the barrel is taken out of the city without trouble.

Outside, they heave a sack from the barrel, grunting as they load it onto a waiting wheelbarrow. 'What is this, a body of some kind? No, do not answer, you are a quiet man. I know ones like you. Say little, pay well. Ezze respect that. Good luck in your business,' he taps the side of his nose. 'Whatever it may be.'

Samael murmurs a thanks through too-pale lips and walks away, pushing the barrow in front of him.

'Ha!' says Ezze, turning to the barrel as soon as Samael has gone. 'And now the newest Deadtech in Verdigris belongs to Ezze! Bruise, you take the Heartmaker, hide it in the bag, and little Ez, you carry all the small things.'

383

'And what will you carry, father?'

'The burden of family! Now hurry, get them out.'

Bruise opens the second door inside the barrel, the secret one, and plunges his hands inside. His face falls and there is the sound of jelly sucking down a plughole. Little Ez peeks in, then runs off to be sick.

'A little death too much for you? Get out Ezze's treasures already!'

'But, father,' says the boy, wiping his mouth. 'There's no treasure there, just a load of rotting meat.'

Ezze's hand hovers, eager to teach but the mystery draws it away. He examines the barrel, finds nothing but wires and necrotic soup. For a few moments he is speechless. '. . . But Ezze saw the Deadtech with his own eyes . . . He showed us all . . . It was of the highest quality . . . So much money to be made . . .'

Little Ez's eyes go worried wide. 'Father, are you dying?'

'Dying? If only Ezze were dying, then he wouldn't have to feel the dreams of prosperity fading away.' He sighs, seeming to deflate to a man half his size. 'Remember, Little Ez, this is why you trust nobody. Nobody! Except your good father.'

The Seven's sanctum is a cube of silver-steel a mile across, suspended seventy feet above ground. No wires hold it there, no supports are necessary. It turns, achingly slow, never stopping, moved by altered physics.

A procession approaches, led by Sir Phia. The Vagrant, Vesper and what seems like half of the city follow. As they get closer awe slows their steps. One by one, they stop, citizens first, then squires, leaving the others to continue alone.

384

An armoured man awaits. Beneath the splendid helm he is middle aged, made thin by a diet of stress and adrenaline. To his right is a woman, equally thin, though for different reasons. Her cloak falls like a set of wings across her shoulders. Beneath it she is hairless and the toes that peek from the hem are without nails.

Sir Phia kneels before them, addressing the woman first. 'Obeisance.' Then the man. 'Knight Commander. I have it.'

The Vagrant raises an eyebrow.

'Good,' replies the Knight Commander, his sour face struggling to accommodate the good news. 'We must send it to The Seven immediately.'

'No,' says Obeisance. 'The filth of the world must be washed away first.'

The Knight Commander lowers his voice. 'They will already know it is here. Is it wise to keep Them waiting?'

'There is a reason why my family has held this honour longer than any other. We never take risks.'

'I defer to your judgement, Obeisance.'

Sir Phia looks worried. 'Should I take the time to refresh my armour?'

Her seniors look at each other, half amused. 'And why,' asks the Knight Commander, 'should you do that?'

'Sir?'

'You don't honestly think that you will go anywhere near The Seven do you? After years in the Blasted Lands? You're lucky we let you back into civilization at all.' He studies her, dispassionate. 'Perhaps you could do with cleaning up. I understand you have sent your subordinates for purging. Consider your duties discharged and join them.'

'Yes, Sir.'

'Also, a man was retrieved from Slake who has not reported in for testing, nor is he mentioned in your report. I trust you can explain.'

'The report only focuses on the primary objectives of the mission, Sir. A full account is pending your pleasure.'

'My pleasure is it? Well then you should know that what pleases me more than anything else is detail. I will look forward to reading your full report shortly . . . In the meantime kindly produce this . . .' eyes look up and to the right, accessing secret data. '. . . Jaden, and submit him to the proper authorities before he infects anyone. As I understand it his chances of survival are even less than yours.'

Sir Phia closes her eyes for the briefest moment. 'Yes, Sir.'

He flicks a finger, dismissing her. 'Obeisance, I will leave the preparations in your capable hands and meet you here in an hour?'

She leans down to study Vesper. In turn she looks up at her bald head, mouth sagging in amazement.

'Shiny!'

The Vagrant bites his lip.

Obeisance ignores the comment, turns to study the Vagrant. 'Better make it two.'

CHAPTER THIRTY-THREE

Obeisance walks alone up the steps. Once, her family was larger, the role shared with brothers and sisters. Duty has thinned them out. One by one, they gave themselves in service to the Winged Eye. Her remaining siblings are too weak now, their minds transcendent, bodies fit only for breeding. She has inspected the next generation carefully, found them wanting. It will be many years before they can stand in her place and already her body struggles, hollowed by The Seven's love.

She has two hours to prepare them for Gamma's return. Lips shape into a curse as she rounds the corner. She should have asked for more.

They say the sanctum has been silent all these years. That The Seven weep without sound; tears of stone that flow, thickening, deadening.

They are wrong.

She hears the disharmony. Even now the sounds stir in her mind, thrumming bones, whittling spirit.

387

For too long the inner doors have been closed, sealed with grief. She kneels before them, pressing her head against the smooth outer layer of stone. Panic is pushed away, trapped within clenched fists. Breath is mastered, fear marshalled. The duty will be done.

'I am here,' she says. 'Let me take it, let me taste it. Burden me.'

The Vagrant leans back in the bath, eyes closed. Cool water vents against his newly dressed thigh. Vesper sits next to him, making waves.

'Splash!'

Around them, a thin layer of scum and salt collects, making water opaque.

A servant creeps around the edge of the bath, gathering clothes. He is careful to hold them at arm's length. Battered boots, a coat aged by dirt and combat, encrusted with old smells. The servant's nose wrinkles in retreat. He turns to go but something has attached to his sleeve, stopping him.

The Vagrant makes eye contact, shakes his head.

'You actually want these?'

The Vagrant nods.

'Oh.'

The clothes are returned, though piled neater than before. Before the servant can stand up again, water slaps him on the ear.

'Splash!'

He turns to find the Vagrant, apologetic, hands up. Mustering calm, he returns to his post by the door. After a minute his eyes close, his breathing forced into rhythm. The servant sways slightly but doesn't fall.

Another minute and the door slides open, shushing, slow, just enough to allow a hooded figure entrance.

The Vagrant sits up hastily, water rides high, full of energy, Vesper rides with it.

'Splash! Splash! Splash!'

A nail-less finger raises, demanding calm, then pulls back the hood. The Vagrant's face shows surprise for a second time, then he tries to bow. This is not easy. Between the bath, his injured leg and Vesper, the gesture is unrecognizable.

Vesper waves at the newcomer. 'Shiny!'

'Be at peace,' Obeisance says quickly. 'This is not an official visit.'

The Vagrant does not relax.

'I felt we should talk privately. It's important that you know how the last few years have been for The Seven. Whatever happens, the reunion must go smoothly. We cannot afford another lapse.' Obeisance opens her hands as she thinks. They flutter like featherless wings. 'For a thousand years The Seven have watched over us and for more than half that time my family has served them. We are bred carefully to keep the prominent features of our bloodline, so I look much like my mother, and her mother, and so on. If you were to walk the halls you'd find a statue dedicated to my office. The young acolytes often think it was made for me.' A memory touches her lips, bringing the faintest smile. 'In fact it was created in honour of my eleventh great-grandmother. You see, The Seven have come to hate change. It pains them in ways we cannot possibly fathom. I believe it is because They have known perfection, seen the Empire of the Winged Eye at its peak. They are the last beings to have basked in the Creator's shadow. For them, each new discovery is a shift away from what should be. Even our greatest achievements are aberrations of a prior glory.' She notices the movement of her hands and, on reflex, kills the motion. 'Since Gamma's fall, The Seven have turned even further inward. Their pain is . . .' Just once, she shudders. 'Beyond comprehension.'

The Vagrant's mouth begins to form a word, stops. Lips press together.

'The Seven are beyond us. Nobody can predict how they will respond when you return Gamma's sword. I don't know how much of her remains within it. Let us pray it is enough.' She turns and stares directly at the Vagrant. 'You must ensure that it is. You must make this a success.'

She bows, though whether the deference is directed to man or sword is unclear, then slips away. The Vagrant watches her go, his hand rests on the side of the bath. Fingers curl slowly into a trembling fist.

Seconds later the servant's head jerks up, suddenly awake. He blinks twice, blushes, and straightens.

'Dada?'

The Vagrant attends to Vesper.

'Dada?'

The Vagrant nods.

'Dada?'

Again the Vagrant nods. A stream of bubbles appear on the surface of the water. Vesper points at the Vagrant.

'Dada!'

Eyebrows raise, indignant. Vesper laughs and laughs, until at last, the Vagrant smiles and joy rings from the walls.

The Vagrant stands in fresh clothes, awkward. Vesper pulls at hers, unable to remove them.

'Better,' declares Obeisance, much to the relief of the staff. 'Though it will not be accompanying us, I had your goat seen to. She will be bred with local stock to improve taint resistance.'

The goat is brought out. Rarely has she looked so clean, or so dangerous.

'Goat?'

The goat gives her a black look.

'Goat!' repeats Vesper with confidence.

'Come, it is time. You wish to take the child?'

The Vagrant nods and they go.

'Bye bye goat.'

They return to the ground beneath the sanctum. Already there, the Knight Commander waits by a staircase, silver wrought. Each step is thirty feet across, one foot high. There are forty nine in total. The last step leads only to air, the great cube floating high above.

'Scary isn't it?' says the Knight Commander. 'They say that The Seven carry you the last of the way, so you have to put your faith in them. Not everyone makes it.' He watches Obeisance walk past. 'She's been doing this since she was about your girl's age. I've only had to for the last five years but we both agree, it never gets easier.'

Like pilgrims, they ascend. The Vagrant's injuries force him to move slowly. Obeisance is the first to reach the highest step. She does not break stride, toes spreading in the open air to find purchase. Behind her the two men stop and stare.

'After you,' says the Knight Commander.

The Vagrant picks Vesper up, rests her on his hip. He draws the sword with his other hand, watching the tiny wings as they unfurl, moved by different currents. He holds the blade out over the edge, feeling the firm tug. The Vagrant looks down, looks up again quickly.

'This is as good as it gets. Best to go now.'

Little hands cling to the Vagrant's arm, pinching skin.

A glance back reveals the Knight Commander, still waiting. The Vagrant's lips shape a prayer, he takes a deep breath . . . and steps out.

Vesper buries her head in the Vagrant's chest.

The air is not solid but there is resistance. With spongy strides, the Vagrant goes up. He focuses on the cube, muscles tight with tension. One step, then another, fighting the urge to look down. As they get closer, details emerge on the side of the cube. A lip juts out below an archway, inviting, the back of Obeisance's cloak already vanishing through it.

They follow her in, arriving in a small antechamber. Doors behind them slide closed, sealing the room. Obeisance tries to open the doors opposite but they are blocked, forcing them to wait. Noises come from beyond, tapping, cracking, the labour of many people.

Obeisance counts, face creasing in concern.

The sounds get louder, coming from the base of the door. Time ticks by.

Vesper yawns.

The door crunches open, stopping halfway. Obeisance steps through, beckoning the others. They arrive in a larger chamber carpeted in stone. People in skinsuits and glowing collars work to chip it away by hand. Some are attached to the wall, some squat down, attending to the floor. As fast as they work, the stone grows back like a weed, stubborn and grey.

The Knight Commander pauses at the entrance. 'It's getting worse isn't it?'

'The Seven descend deeper into silence but we care for Them as we have ever done.'

'Have you ever seen it this bad before?'

'There is no "bad" when one is tending The Seven, Knight Commander. Let us continue.'

As they step onto the living stone an eye opens, taking in details. Soon, the sword tremors in the Vagrant's hand. By the time they reach the door to The Seven's chamber, the sword is raging. Around it, air shimmers and hums.

The stone is thicker here, forming a second barrier to those seeking passage. The Vagrant stops and looks at the sword. It looks back and something like agreement seems to pass between them. He puts Vesper down on the ground, guiding the toddler behind him.

Obeisance and the Knight Commander take a step back.

The sword swings, singing, and rock falls like rain, breaking into chunks, into powder. Gleaming doors are unveiled. They open for the Vagrant as he limps forward, sword held high. Vesper is dragged after, clinging to the back of the Vagrant's coat.

The Knight Commander raises a foot to follow and an eye glares at him. Swallowing, he puts it back. Obeisance gets the same treatment. The sword watches them both until the doors close.

Pale lights illuminate The Seven's inner chamber. Once bright, the lamps are overgrown, dimmed by a sheet of stone. The room is octagonal, one side for the supplicant, unadorned. Six others each house a figure, statue-like, covered from head to toe in a thick layer of rock. All appear human shaped, with discernible wings, their postures neutral, dead. The seventh alcove lies empty.

The Vagrant holds the sword up, letting it hum, calling, calling.

As if returning from a dream, The Seven respond, slowly, sonorously. Splitting the shells that cover them, yawning into life. One by one, they catch the call and return it, till the harmony swells, reverberating from the walls and leaping up, vanishing into the fathomless, ceilingless dark above.

Beautiful sounds mature, becoming words, musical, passed from one to the other, filling the chamber and the Vagrant's ears.

'Mourning has become morning, and we rejoice . . .'
'We rejoice in the proximity of your flame once more . . .'
'Once more we are Seven . . .'
'Are Seven together, come . . .'
'Come and join with us . . .'
'Join with us your light, diminished but still bright.'
Six arms drift out, gesturing to the last alcove, inviting.

Neither Vagrant nor sword move. An eye studies the chamber, pausing at each alcove, noting the blades housed there, buried beneath layers of stone, useless. Rage simmers between sword and Vagrant. He takes a lock of hair from an inner pocket, throws it down on the floor between them. The sword lowers to point at it, then sweeps across the figures, then makes a hard stab towards the doors.

Six faces freeze as the joyous echoes of song die out.

The Vagrant swallows in a throat suddenly dry.

Vesper dares a quick peek from behind the Vagrant's coat.

Alpha, of The Seven, sings out. The note begins wondrous but imperfect, the others soon match him.

'We see now your pain, most furious . . .'
'Most furious you are and desperate to fight . . .'

394

'To fight once more, your desire . . .'

'Your desire we grant, go forth, take a second flame to our enemies . . .'

Voices come together, their force rocking the Vagrant backwards until he is pinned to the wall. Vesper holds his hand tightly, little feet rising from the floor.

'Do not stop . . .'

'Stop when the cancer . . .'

'Cancer is cut . . .'

'Cut from the bones . . .'

'Bones and flesh . . .'

'Flesh of the land . . .'

'Land is clean!'

The Vagrant closes his eyes, squeezes them tight. He braces himself against the sound, pulling Vesper behind him raising the sword in front. Silvered wings unfurl protectively, shielding his face. An eye widens, blazing with indignation.

'Then . . .'

'Then, then and only then . . .'

'Only then will you be free . . .'

'Be free to return to us . . .'

'Return to us and rejoice . . .'

'Rejoice for true, complete again. Immaculate.'

Six go quiet, demands echoing after. Vesper's feet touch floor again and she wraps herself around a comforting leg.

In the Vagrant's hand, the sword trembles, humming dangerously. He takes a deep breath. From the depths of his stomach something is forged, travelling inevitably, gaining force as it goes, following tubes behind ribs, up through the chest, into the throat, teeth parting, allowing it outside.

The Vagrant opens his eyes, they are full of weariness, disgust, conviction.

'No.'

The Knight Commander and Obeisance wait before the doors, indecisive. Of the two she is the more composed, having endured The Seven's silence for many years. Before it was empty, a void which threatened to swallow her, bone and soul. Now, it is full of potential, deafening. The inhalation before the storm. Such subtleties are lost on the Knight Commander. Dimly, he perceives a deep and fathomless terror, nothing more.

Regardless, the two wait, held in place by strong will and stronger training.

'That sound, that was Them, wasn't it? They've returned.'

Obeisance does not take her eyes from the doors. 'They never left us.'

'Of course. I did not mean . . . But that was Them, and They sounded joyous. That was a good sign, was it not?'

'Did you feel joyous when you heard Them?'

The passing of those feelings have left tracks in his spirit, easy to find and recall. 'Yes.' He does not add that he felt more than simple joy, does not dare.

'And how do you feel now?'

'I . . .' He tails off.

'Precisely,' she adds. There is a wrinkle in her cape, irritating. She does not touch it, does not move. Her stillness serves to underscore each creak of his armour, each nervous breath.

The doors swing open and they both bow, deferent.

The Vagrant strides out, sword in one hand, Vesper wrapped around the other. He passes them by without pause.

The Knight Commander risks a glance. Eyes widen in surprise and words blurt. 'Wait! Where are you going? What's going to happen to us?'

His question bounces off the Vagrant's back, unnoticed.

Anger comes, pushing past confusion. The Knight Commander goes in pursuit. Before he can catch up, Obeisance rushes between them, forming an obstacle stronger than steel, a wall built of oaths and honour. He cannot move her, cannot even touch her. For she is an instrument of The Seven, not above him so much as beyond him. It does not stop his anger however. 'Let me pass. He denied The Seven! He is taking the sword we have waited so long for!'

She shakes her head. 'The denial was not his alone.'

Anger drains, replaced by dread. 'But what does this mean?'

'It means I must go to inside. Maintain order until I return. Allow none to pass.'

He nods, glad to hide behind duty.

Obeisance seems to glide through the doors. They close, leaving the man alone. He ponders what to do as the seconds pass into minutes. Then there is a change in the air. The doors begin to shake, slowly at first, then faster, building, humming. On instinct, the Knight Commander starts to run.

Tremors pass through the inner sanctum as six voices rise together, passing through stone and silver, through men and women, land and sky.

Keening.

With a last pull, the commander's boot sucks free of the marsh. Samael helps steady him as he moves onto solid ground. They continue the remainder of the journey more directly, a welcome contrast to what has been. Maimed and weakening, the commander has been forced to hide along the way, like a thief. Necessity is well understood but a sour taste remains.

Nobody stops their approach to the Fallen Palace but things watch, ready to pounce if the commander falls. Several times he staggers on the sloping floors, thoughts drifting, along with his essence.

But he does not fall.

Iron will drives him forward. He neither knows nor cares anymore about its origins. When it wavers, Samael is ready at his side, obedient to the last.

They walk alone through broken streets and under the shadow of buildings, lurching, until at last they reach a tower, hints of brass hidden behind lichen.

Samael assists him up winding steps, through corridors well walked. The Man-shape sees them approach and opens the door.

Inside, the Usurper lurks, its body a mass of repairs. It is hard to reconcile the ailing thing before him with the great monarch whose name inspires fear in human and infernal alike.

Shrugging off any further help, the commander walks the final steps towards his old master. At every moment he expects to be exposed, for the Usurper to see him for what he is and attack, but it barely seems to notice him.

As the end of his journey draws close, he stumbles, legs finally giving way to gravity.

Sensing something at last, the Usurper looks up, opening its arms to receive the commander as he falls.

The battered shell is drawn close and the Usurper licks

the rim of the commander's visor, drawing back essence spent long ago.

The commander is absorbed whole, experiences, wants, desires, failures, regrets and something else. A single note, a call to action, a message of malice sent by Gamma's sword, passed through the commander and into the Usurper.

As the sound reverberates inside it, dark lines manifest in the Usurper's essence, scars from its battle with Gamma, still fresh.

The great infernal feels a flash of terrible pain as old injuries stir from their slumber. It tries to hold itself together, to fight as it has always done, but it is tired, weak, and the scars deepen, open, living wounds that rend the Usurper from within, tearing essence in all directions, singing their song of death.

The Usurper's destruction sends ripples through the ether. Invisible, silent, they are nevertheless felt far and wide.

At the Fallen Palace, infernals pause in their business, slapped with sudden freedom. Thoughts turn to the empty throne and who among them might fill it. Monsters circle one another, wary, while the lesser infernals cluster, gambling on new masters to take them through the coming chaos.

Further north, in New Horizon, the Demagogue's relief is palpable. It holds a celebration, grotesque, and begins to plan.

Elsewhere packs of infernals drift apart. No longer driven by the Usurper's order, they wander, mindless, allowing petty hungers to lead them. Attacks on human settlements become increasingly random, increasingly petty. Few of the victims appreciate the difference.

And yet, for many of the invaders, there is a kind of sadness. For the Usurper gave them purpose. It was the Green Sun around which they orbited. Where once an iron will defined them, now there is emptiness and uncertainty.

The Vagrant steps out of The Seven's sanctum and into empty space. He doesn't hesitate, gliding down towards the steps, sword out, Vesper held tight.

The sword's silvered wings spread wide, catching invisible currents.

He lands, takes the stairs at a more stately pace. Down he goes, leaving the Sanctum and The Seven behind. Tension falls away like an old skin. Shoulders relax, straighten. He lifts his gaze from the floor, looks around as he returns to the Shining City.

An eye does the same, mirroring exactly.

They see children in groups, chip-linked, so similar in expression, in presentation, it takes effort to tell them apart. They see structures carefully maintained from a bygone age, statues of The Seven and the great shining pillars that give the city its name. They see the last of the knights in their ancestral armour, treasured, polished.

Nothing new. Nothing but carefully controlled decay covered in beautiful greenery, a civilization lost and stagnant.

An eye closes, unwilling to see any more.

The Vagrant walks on, past soldiers and citizens, young and old. He does not fit into their hierachies, there is no codex to apply to him, no social codes that work.

He is a man without rank and yet he walks in The Seven's grace, untouchable.

Most kneel as he passes, all watch, none get in the way.

Vesper waves cheerily at the crowds. When she does not get a response, she waves all the harder, trying to smile them into submission.

One of the knights returns the wave formally. Devoid of emotion, the gesture is hollow, eerie.

They pass windows in the hillside, the only sign of buildings hidden underground and the maze of tunnels that connect them. Faces press against the glass, their expressions blank.

The Vagrant keeps walking.

Little legs soon tire and Vesper is lifted onto familiar shoulders. She enjoys the view, pointing at plants, at clouds, calling out names with delight.

Dutifully, the Vagrant nods, giving her ankle an encouraging squeeze each time she manages a new word.

The purging facility is not covered with a carpet of grass. It stands solid, metal walls dull, catching rather than reflecting the light. It is shaped like an egg, twenty feet high and ten across and every inch is covered in etchings, a blend of language and artistry. Words become wings and swords and hands that hold them, drawing the eye to its only entrance. All unfortunates that end up here go through this door. Those that survive leave via the tunnel on the opposite side.

Next to the facility is a second building, only partially above ground. Simpler in design but larger, where bodies recover from their ordeal or undergo preparation for burial.

The Vagrant approaches the second building.

A man stands outside, his uniform crisp. He holds up a hand. 'Who are you?'

Vesper waves at him. 'Esper!'

The man is not amused. 'I've not been informed of any inspection. Who are you? Where is your authority?'

The Vagrant raises an eyebrow, raises the sword.

The man looks at it, double takes. 'I, forgive me, I had no idea, I . . .' He opens the door.

As Vesper trots past, she looks at the man, then points at the Vagrant with extreme satisfaction. 'Dada.'

The inside of the building is divided into cells, all locked. Rooms of healing, of holding, where those that survive the purging await official approval of their purity and permission to return to society.

The doors are transparent, and the Vagrant looks into each room as he passes. Sir Phia sits hunched in one cell, her eyes dark, her body wasted. Jaden's body is next door, an unrecognizable husk, awaiting disposal. Nurses attend to the living and the dead with equal care.

In another cell, he sees one of the sisters from Slake, weak but alive, and yet another, the boy Chalk, heavily sedated and fighting a fever.

He makes eye contact with those he knows, nodding encouragement, concern creeping into his face each time he comes across an empty room.

At last he finds what he is looking for and opens the door. Vesper goes in first, frowning at the cell's occupant: A man with bandages wrapping the top half of his face.

'Umbull-arm?'

The man's voice cracks as he answers. 'Vesper? Is that you?'

'Umbull-arm!'

The Vagrant races Vesper across the room and all three

The Vagrant

embrace, wrapping each other in a circle of arms, foreheads touching, safe.

A dark shape moves under the water, running on silent engines. It moves slowly, navigating its way past energy nets and dormant sentinel drones, treating the drifting husks with caution, lest contact wake them again.

It surfaces at the coast, allowing a single passenger to disembark.

The First has not been this far north before. The presence of infernal feet on the northern continent is historic. It is pleased how easy it is, and wary. For it feels The Seven even from this distance. Their grief shakes the sky, disturbing the essence currents for miles around.

Ever patient, the First observes the lights above that so few can see, prepared to run if things develop. But soon the signs are clear. This storm will pass and The Seven will quieten, returning to their self imposed exile.

It tries to sense the Malice but cannot perceive anything within the strange walls of the city.

For now, the north is too dangerous for the First to interfere. Better to consolidate its hold on the seas and the Empire's many colonies.

The underwater vessel turns around, returning south, leaving a fragment of the First behind, to watch, to wait.

On top of a hill sits a house, half built. Vesper lies in the grass nearby, plucking with both hands and throwing their contents into the air. Wind catches the loose blades, swirling them in spirals of green.

403

The goat does not approve of such waste. A small army of kids work voraciously by her feet, keeping the hill neat. Male goats wait at the hill's base, knowing better than to venture up uninvited.

By an unfinished wall, two men sit. They talk quietly, kindly. One is scarred, the other blind, both appear happy.

At their side a sword sleeps, peaceful.

ACKNOWLEDGEMENTS

This feels a bit like my wedding speech, with so many wonderful people to thank. First off, an honourable mention to all those who believed in *The Vagrant* during the early days, the lovely Friday Flash community and my test readers: Katherine Hajer, Conall O'Brien, Liz Newman, Mike Newman, Phil Tozer and John Xero, who fed me with enthusiasm and educated where necessary.

A massive thanks has to go to my agent Juliet Mushens for, well, pretty much everything really but especially the lightning-fast edits, calming presence and always replying promptly to my panicky emails! I hope this is the first of many books we usher into the world together.

And then there's my editor of awesomeness, Natasha Bardon, whose taste in books is matched only by her taste in games. Thanks for giving *The Vagrant* a chance and for helping it to grow. May all of our editing experiences be as painless as this one!

I'm also delighted with the artist Jaime Jones for creating

a cover that makes me smile every time I see it. There are others, too, people I'd never even thought about before I started this process, who all contribute in vital ways but are rarely mentioned: my copy editor (thanks, Joy), the designer who brought the cover elements together (thanks, Dom), and others in the Harper *Voyager* team, many of whom work from the shadows like book ninjas. Thank you, all!

Last of all I need to thank my wife, Emma, who realised back in 2011 that I was a frustrated writer and put me on the path. Thank you, my love. I dread to think where I'd be without you.